*"A magical mystery tour of Victorian England
. . . with a sexual encounter so explosive that
it nearly blows the top of your head off. . . .*
THE FRENCH LIEUTENANT'S WOMAN
*delights, teaches, bewitches. It has all the sur-
prise, the unpredictability of life. It is most
warmly recommended"*

—Saturday Review

---

*"*THE FRENCH LIEUTENANT'S WOMAN
*leaves one wondering which century was the
more sexually liberated. It is a shock. It signals
the sudden but predictable arrival of a remarkable novelist"*

—The New York Times

*"A dazzler . . . impossible to put down. A
Victorian novel no Victorian would have written, a dark and powerful love triangle through
which the author comments on a whole era"*

—Cosmopolitan

"A wonder of contemporary fiction. . . . The age of Victoria meets the age of aquarius. John Fowles confronts 19th Century sensualism with 20th Century existential freedom. The result is a novel of such riches that it meets the oldest, simplest, and least fashionable test of excellence. You never want it to end."

—Life *Magazine*

"The publication of THE FRENCH LIEU-TENANT'S WOMAN *is an event. It is one of the finest novels of the year. It seizes the reader from the first page and holds him tight to the end. . . . One finishes the book with a sense of being torn away. When the last page has been read, one sits quietly with the book and still doesn't want to put it down, caught in the grip of a master novelist"*

—Columbus Dispatch

"A love story told with passion and delicacy . . . A deeply satisfying, original and strongly talented work . . . Brilliant, ambitious and compelling."
—Literary Guild News

THE
FRENCH
LIEUTENANT'S
WOMAN

John Fowles

A SIGNET BOOK

SIGNET
Published by the Penguin Group
Penguin Books USA Inc., 375 Hudson Street,
New York, New York 10014, U.S.A.
Penguin Books Ltd, 27 Wrights Lane,
London W8 5TZ, England
Penguin Books Australia Ltd, Ringwood,
Victoria, Australia
Penguin Books Canada Ltd, 10 Alcorn Avenue,
Toronto, Ontario, Canada M4V 3B2
Penguin Books (N.Z.) Ltd, 182–190 Wairau Road,
Auckland 10, New Zealand

Penguin Books Ltd, Registered Offices:
Harmondsworth, Middlesex, England

This is an authorized reprint of a hardcover edition published by Little, Brown and Company, Inc. The hardcover edition was published simultaneously in Canada by Little, Brown & Company (Canada) Limited.

First Signet Printing, August, 1970
39 38 37 36 35 34 33

 REGISTERED TRADEMARK—MARCA REGISTRADA

Printed in the United States of America

Every emancipation is a restoration of the human world and of human relationships to man himself.

MARX, *Zur Judenfrage* (1844)

ACKNOWLEDGMENTS

I should like to thank the following for permission to quote: the Hardy Estate and Macmillan & Co. Ltd. for extracts from *The Collected Poems* of Thomas Hardy; the Oxford University Press for quotations from G. M. Young's *Victorian Essays* and *Portrait of an Age;* Mr. Martin Gardner and the Penguin Press for a slightly compressed quotation from *The Ambidextrous Universe;* and finally Mr. E. Royston Pike and Allen & Unwin Ltd., not only for permission to quote directly but also for three contemporary extracts and countless minor details I have "stolen" from his *Human Documents of the Victorian Golden Age* (published in the United States by Frederick A. Praeger, Inc., under the title *Golden Times: Human Documents of the Victorian Age*). I recommend this brilliant anthology most warmly to any reader who would like to know more of the reality behind my fiction.

J. F.

1

Stretching eyes west
Over the sea,
Wind foul or fair,
Always stood she
Prospect-impressed;
Solely out there
Did her gaze rest,
Never elsewhere
Seemed charm to be.

HARDY, "The Riddle"

An easterly is the most disagreeable wind in Lyme Bay—
Lyme Bay being that largest bite from the underside of
England's outstretched southwestern leg—and a person of
curiosity could at once have deduced several strong probabili-
ties about the pair who began to walk down the quay at
Lyme Regis, the small but ancient eponym of the inbite, one
incisively sharp and blustery morning in the late March of
1867.

The Cobb has invited what familiarity breeds for at least
seven hundred years, and the real Lymers will never see
much more to it than a long claw of old gray wall that flexes
itself against the sea. In fact, since it lies well apart from the
main town, a tiny Piraeus to a microscopic Athens, they seem
almost to turn their backs on it. Certainly it has cost them
enough in repairs through the centuries to justify a certain
resentment. But to a less tax-paying, or more discriminating,
eye it is quite simply the most beautiful sea rampart on the
south coast of England. And not only because it is, as the
guidebooks say, redolent of seven hundred years of English
history, because ships sailed to meet the Armada from it,
because Monmouth landed beside it ... but finally because it
is a superb fragment of folk art.

Primitive yet complex, elephantine but delicate; as full of
subtle curves and volumes as a Henry Moore or a Michelan-

9

gelo; and pure, clean, salt, a paragon of mass. I exaggerate? Perhaps, but I can be put to the test, for the Cobb has changed very little since the year of which I write; though the town of Lyme has, and the test is not fair if you look back towards land.

However, if you had turned northward and landward in 1867, as the man that day did, your prospect would have been harmonious. A picturesque congeries of some dozen or so houses and a small boatyard—in which, arklike on its stocks, sat the thorax of a lugger—huddled at where the Cobb runs back to land. Half a mile to the east lay, across sloping meadows, the thatched and slated roofs of Lyme itself; a town that had its heyday in the Middle Ages and has been declining ever since. To the west somber gray cliffs, known locally as Ware Cleeves, rose steeply from the shingled beach where Monmouth entered upon his idiocy. Above them and beyond, stepped massively inland, climbed further cliffs masked by dense woods. It is in this aspect that the Cobb seems most a last bulwark—against all that wild eroding coast to the west. There too I can be put to proof. No house lay visibly then or, beyond a brief misery of beach huts, lies today in that direction.

The local spy—and there was one—might thus have deduced that these two were strangers, people of some taste, and not to be denied their enjoyment of the Cobb by a mere harsh wind. On the other hand he might, focusing his telescope more closely, have suspected that a mutual solitude interested them rather more than maritime architecture; and he would most certainly have remarked that they were people of a very superior taste as regards their outward appearance.

The young lady was dressed in the height of fashion, for another wind was blowing in 1867: the beginning of a revolt against the crinoline and the large bonnet. The eye in the telescope might have glimpsed a magenta skirt of an almost daring narrowness—and shortness, since two white ankles could be seen beneath the rich green coat and above the black boots that delicately trod the revetment; and perched over the netted chignon, one of the impertinent little flat "pork-pie" hats with a delicate tuft of egret plumes at the side—a millinery style that the resident ladies of Lyme would not dare to wear for at least another year; while the taller man, impeccably in a light gray, with his top hat held in his free hand, had severely reduced his dundrearies, which the arbiters of the best English male fashion had declared a shade vulgar—that is, risible to the foreigner—a year or two previously. The colors of the young lady's clothes would

10

strike us today as distinctly strident; but the world was then in the first fine throes of the discovery of aniline dyes. And what the feminine, by way of compensation for so much else in her expected behavior, demanded of a color was brilliance, not discretion.

But where the telescopist would have been at sea himself was with the other figure on that somber, curving mole. It stood right at the seawardmost end, apparently leaning against an old cannon barrel upended as a bollard. Its clothes were black. The wind moved them, but the figure stood motionless, staring, staring out to sea, more like a living memorial to the drowned, a figure from myth, than any proper fragment of the petty provincial day.

2

In that year (1851) there were some 8,155,000 females of the age of ten upwards in the British population, as compared with 7,600,000 males. Already it will be clear that if the accepted destiny of the Victorian girl was to become a wife and mother, it was unlikely that there would be enough men to go round.

E. ROYSTON PIKE, *Human Documents of the Victorian Golden Age*

I'll spread sail of silver and I'll steer towards the sun,
I'll spread sail of silver and I'll steer towards the sun,
And my false love will weep, and my false love will
weep,
And my false love will weep for me after I'm gone.

WEST-COUNTRY FOLKSONG: "As Sylvie Was Walking"

"My dear Tina, we have paid our homage to Neptune. He will forgive us if we now turn our backs on him."

"You are not very *galant*."

"What does that signify, pray?"

"I should have thought you might have wished to prolong an opportunity to hold my arm without impropriety."

"How delicate we've become."

"We are not in London now."

"At the North Pole, if I'm not mistaken."

"I *wish* to walk to the end."

11

And so the man, with a dry look of despair, as if it might be his last, towards land, turned again, and the couple continued down the Cobb.

"And I wish to hear what passed between you and Papa last Thursday."

"Your aunt has already extracted every detail of that pleasant evening from me."

The girl stopped, and looked him in the eyes.

"Charles! Now Charles, you may be as dry a stick as you like with everyone else. But you must not be stick-y with me."

"Then how, dear girl, are we ever to be glued together in holy matrimony?"

"And you will keep your low humor for your club." She primly made him walk on. "I have had a letter."

"Ah. I feared you might. From Mama?"

"I know that something happened . . . over the port."

They walked on a few paces before he answered; for a moment Charles seemed inclined to be serious, but then changed his mind.

"I confess your worthy father and I had a small philosophical disagreement."

"That is very wicked of you."

"I meant it to be very honest of me."

"And what was the subject of your conversation?"

"Your father ventured the opinion that Mr. Darwin should be exhibited in a cage in the zoological gardens. In the monkey house. I tried to explain some of the scientific arguments behind the Darwinian position. I was unsuccessful. *Et voilà tout.*"

"How could you—when you know Papa's views!"

"I was most respectful."

"Which means you were most hateful."

"He did say that he would not let his daughter marry a man who considered his grandfather to be an ape. But I think on reflection he will recall that in my case it was a titled ape."

She looked at him then as they walked, and moved her head in a curious sliding sideways turn away; a characteristic gesture when she wanted to show concern—in this case, over what had been really the greatest obstacle in her view to their having become betrothed. Her father was a very rich man; but her grandfather had been a draper, and Charles's had been a baronet. He smiled and pressed the gloved hand that was hooked lightly to his left arm.

"Dearest, we have settled that between us. It is perfectly proper that you should be afraid of your father. But I am not marrying him. And you forget that I'm a scientist. I have

12

written a monograph, so I must be. And if you smile like that, I shall devote all my time to the fossils and none to you."

"I am not disposed to be jealous of the fossils." She left an artful pause. "Since you've been walking on them now for at least a minute—and haven't even deigned to remark them."

He glanced sharply down, and as abruptly kneeled. Portions of the Cobb are paved with fossil-bearing stone.

"By jove, look at this. *Certhidium portlandicum.* This stone must come from the oolite at Portland."

"In whose quarries I shall condemn you to work in perpetuity—if you don't get to your feet at once." He obeyed her with a smile. "Now, am I not kind to bring you here? And look." She led him to the side of the rampart, where a line of flat stones inserted sideways into the wall served as rough steps down on to a lower walk. "These are the very steps that Jane Austen made Louisa Musgrove fall down in *Persuasion.*"

"How romantic."

"Gentlemen were romantic . . . then."

"And are scientific now? Shall we make the perilous descent?"

"On the way back."

Once again they walked on. It was only then that he noticed, or at least realized the sex of, the figure at the end.

"Good heavens, I took that to be a fisherman. But isn't it a woman?"

Ernestina peered—her gray, her very pretty eyes, were shortsighted, and all she could see was a dark shape.

"Is she young?"

"It's too far to tell."

"But I can guess who it is. It must be poor Tragedy."

"Tragedy?"

"A nickname. One of her nicknames."

"And what are the others?"

"The fishermen have a gross name for her."

"My dear Tina, you can surely—"

"They call her the French Lieutenant's . . . Woman."

"Indeed. And is she so ostracized that she has to spend her days out here?"

"She is . . . a little mad. Let us turn. I don't like to go near her."

They stopped. He stared at the black figure.

"But I'm intrigued. Who is this French lieutenant?"

"A man she is said to have . . ."

"Fallen in love with?"

"Worse than that."

13

"And he abandoned her? There is a child?"

"No. I think no child. It is all gossip."

"But what is she doing there?"

"They say she waits for him to return."

"But . . . does no one care for her?"

"She is a servant of some kind to old Mrs. Poulteney. She is never to be seen when we visit. But she lives there. Please let us turn back. I did not see her."

But he smiled.

"If she springs on you I shall defend you and prove my poor gallantry. Come."

So they went closer to the figure by the cannon bollard. She had taken off her bonnet and held it in her hand; her hair was pulled tight back inside the collar of the black coat—which was bizarre, more like a man's riding coat than any woman's coat that had been in fashion those past forty years. She too was a stranger to the crinoline; but it was equally plain that that was out of oblivion, not knowledge of the latest London taste. Charles made some trite and loud remark, to warn her that she was no longer alone, but she did not turn. The couple moved to where they could see her face in profile; and how her stare was aimed like a rifle at the farthest horizon. There came a stronger gust of wind, one that obliged Charles to put his arm round Ernestina's waist to support her, and obliged the woman to cling more firmly to the bollard. Without quite knowing why, perhaps to show Ernestina how to say boo to a goose, he stepped forward as soon as the wind allowed.

"My good woman, we can't see you here without being alarmed for your safety. A stronger squall—"

She turned to look at him—or as it seemed to Charles, through him. It was not so much what was positively in that face which remained with him after that first meeting, but all that was not as he had expected; for theirs was an age when the favored feminine look was the demure, the obedient, the shy. Charles felt immediately as if he had trespassed; as if the Cobb belonged to that face, and not to the Ancient Borough of Lyme. It was not a pretty face, like Ernestina's. It was certainly not a beautiful face, by any period's standard or taste. But it was an unforgettable face, and a tragic face. Its sorrow welled out of it as purely, naturally and unstoppably as water out of a woodland spring. There was no artifice there, no hypocrisy, no hysteria, no mask; and above all, no sign of madness. The madness was in the empty sea, the empty horizon, the lack of reason for such sorrow; as if the spring was natural in itself, but unnatural in welling from a desert.

14

Again and again, afterwards, Charles thought of that look as a lance; and to think so is of course not merely to describe an object but the effect it has. He felt himself in that brief instant an unjust enemy; both pierced and deservedly diminished.

The woman said nothing. Her look back lasted two or three seconds at most; then she resumed her stare to the south. Ernestina plucked Charles's sleeve, and he turned away, with a shrug and a smile at her. When they were nearer land he said, "I wish you hadn't told me the sordid facts. That's the trouble with provincial life. Everyone knows everyone and there is no mystery. No romance."

She teased him then: the scientist, the despiser of novels.

3

But a still more important consideration is that the chief part of the organization of every living creature is due to inheritance; and consequently, though each being assuredly is well fitted for its place in nature, many structures have now no very close and direct relations to present habits of life.

DARWIN, *The Origin of Species* (1859)

Of all decades in our history, a wise man would choose the eighteen-fifties to be young in.

G. M. YOUNG, *Portrait of an Age*

Back in his rooms at the White Lion after lunch Charles stared at his face in the mirror. His thoughts were too vague to be described. But they comprehended mysterious elements; a sentiment of obscure defeat not in any way related to the incident on the Cobb, but to certain trivial things he had said at Aunt Tranter's lunch, to certain characteristic evasions he had made; to whether his interest in paleontology was a sufficient use for his natural abilities; to whether Ernestina would ever really understand him as well as he understood her; to a general sentiment of dislocated purpose originating perhaps in no more—as he finally concluded—than the threat of a long and now wet afternoon to pass. After all, it was only 1867. He was only thirty-two years old. And he had always asked life too many questions.

Though Charles liked to think of himself as a scientific young man and would probably not have been too surprised had news reached him out of the future of the airplane, the jet engine, television, radar: what *would* have astounded him was the changed attitude to time itself. The supposed great misery of our century is the lack of time; our sense of that, *not* a disinterested love of science, and certainly not wisdom, is why we devote such a huge proportion of the ingenuity and income of our societies to finding faster ways of doing things—as if the final aim of mankind was to grow closer not to a perfect humanity, but to a perfect lightning flash. But for Charles, and for almost all his contemporaries and social peers, the time signature over existence was firmly *adagio*. The problem was not fitting in all that one wanted to do, but spinning out what one did to occupy the vast colonnades of leisure available.

One of the commonest symptoms of wealth today is destructive neurosis; in his century it was tranquil boredom. It is true that the wave of revolutions in 1848, the memory of the now extinct Chartists, stood like a mountainous shadow behind the period; but to many—and to Charles—the most significant thing about those distant rumblings had been their failure to erupt. The 'sixties had been indisputably prosperous; an affluence had come to the artisanate and even to the laboring classes that made the possibility of revolution recede, at least in Great Britain, almost out of mind. Needless to say, Charles knew nothing of the beavered German Jew quietly working, as it so happened, that very afternoon in the British Museum library; and whose work in those somber walls was to bear such bright red fruit. Had you described that fruit, or the subsequent effects of its later indiscriminate consumption, Charles would almost certainly not have believed you—and even though, in only six months from this March of 1867, the first volume of *Kapital* was to appear in Hamburg.

There were, too, countless personal reasons why Charles was unfitted for the agreeable role of pessimist. His grandfather the baronet had fallen into the second of the two great categories of English country squires: claret-swilling fox hunters and scholarly collectors of everything under the sun. He had collected books principally; but in his latter years had devoted a deal of his money and much more of his family's patience to the excavation of the harmless hummocks of earth that pimpled his three thousand Wiltshire acres. Cromlechs and menhirs, flint implements and neolithic graves, he pursued them ruthlessly; and his elder son pursued the portable trophies just as ruthlessly out of the house when he came into his inheritance. But heaven had punished this son, or blessed him, by seeing that he never married. The old man's younger son, Charles's father, was left well provided for, both in land and money.

His had been a life with only one tragedy—the simultaneous death of his young wife and the stillborn child who would have been a sister to the one-year-old Charles. But he swallowed his grief. He lavished if not great affection, at least a series of tutors and drill sergeants on his son, whom on the whole he liked only slightly less than himself. He sold his portion of land, invested shrewdly in railway stock and unshrewdly at the gambling-tables (he went to Almack's rather than to the Almighty for consolation), in short lived more as if he had been born in 1702 than 1802, lived very largely for pleasure ... and died very largely of it in 1856. Charles was thus his only heir; heir not only to his father's diminished fortune—the baccarat had in the end had its revenge on the railway boom—but eventually to his uncle's very considerable one. It was true that in 1867 the uncle showed, in spite of a comprehensive reversion to the claret, no sign of dying.

Charles liked him, and his uncle liked Charles. But this was by no means always apparent in their relationship. Though he conceded enough to sport to shoot partridge and pheasant when called upon to do so, Charles adamantly refused to hunt the fox. He did not care that the prey was uneatable, but he abhorred the unspeakability of the hunters. There was worse: he had an unnatural fondness for walking instead of riding; and walking was not a gentleman's pastime except in the Swiss Alps. He had nothing very much against the horse in itself, but he had the born naturalist's hatred of not being able to observe at close range and at leisure. However, fortune had been with him. One autumn day, many years before, he had shot at a very strange bird that ran from the border of one of his uncle's wheatfields. When he discovered what he had shot, and its rarity, he was vaguely angry with himself, for this was one of the last Great Bustards shot on Salisbury Plain. But his uncle was delighted. The bird was stuffed, and forever after stared beadily, like an octoroon turkey, out of its glass case in the drawing room at Winsyatt.

His uncle bored the visiting gentry interminably with the story of how the deed had been done; and whenever he felt inclined to disinherit—a subject which in itself made him go purple, since the estate was in tail male—he would recover his avuncular kindness of heart by standing and staring at Charles's immortal bustard. For Charles had faults. He did not always write once a week; and he had a sinister fondness

17

for spending the afternoons at Winsyatt in the library, a room his uncle seldom if ever used.

He had had graver faults than these, however. At Cambridge, having duly crammed his classics and subscribed to the Thirty-nine Articles, he had (unlike most young men of his time) actually begun to learn something. But in his second year there he had drifted into a bad set and ended up, one foggy night in London, in carnal possession of a naked girl. He rushed from her plump Cockney arms into those of the Church, horrifying his father one day shortly afterwards by announcing that he wished to take Holy Orders. There was only one answer to a crisis of this magnitude: the wicked youth was dispatched to Paris. There his tarnished virginity was soon blackened out of recognition; but so, as his father had hoped, was his intended marriage with the Church. Charles saw what stood behind the seductive appeal of the Oxford Movement—Roman Catholicism *propria terra*. He declined to fritter his negative but comfortable English soul— one part irony to one part convention—on incense and papal infallibility. When he returned to London he fingered and skimmed his way through a dozen religious theories of the time, but emerged in the clear (*voyant trop pour nier, et trop peu pour s'assurer*) a healthy agnostic.* What little God he managed to derive from existence, he found in Nature, not the Bible; a hundred years earlier he would have been a deist, perhaps even a pantheist. In company he would go to morning service of a Sunday; but on his own, he rarely did.

He returned from his six months in the City of Sin in 1856. His father had died three months later. The big house in Belgravia was let, and Charles installed himself in a smaller establishment in Kensington, more suitable to a young bachelor. There he was looked after by a manservant, a cook and two maids, staff of almost eccentric modesty for one of his connections and wealth. But he was happy there, and besides, he spent a great deal of time traveling. He contributed one or two essays on his journeys in remoter places to the fashionable magazines; indeed an enterprising publisher asked him to write a book after the nine months he spent in Portugal, but there seemed to Charles something rather *infra dig.*—and something decidedly too much like hard work and sustained concentration—in authorship. He toyed with the idea, and dropped it. Indeed toying with ideas was his chief occupation during his third decade.

* Though he would not have termed himself so, for the very simple reason that the word was not coined (by Huxley) until 1870; by which time it had become much needed.

Yet he was not, adrift in the slow entire of Victorian time, essentially a frivolous young man. A chance meeting with someone who knew of his grandfather's mania made him realize that it was only in the family that the old man's endless days of supervising bewildered gangs of digging rustics were regarded as a joke. Others remembered Sir Charles Smithson as a pioneer of the archaeology of pre-Roman Britain; objects from his banished collection had been gratefully housed by the British Museum. And slowly Charles realized that he was in temperament nearer to his grandfather than to either of his grandfather's sons. During the last three years he had become increasingly interested in paleontology; that, he had decided, was his field. He began to frequent the *conversazioni* of the Geological Society. His uncle viewed the sight of Charles marching out of Winsyatt armed with his wedge hammers and his collecting sack with disfavor; to his mind the only proper object for a gentleman to carry in the country was a riding crop or a gun; but at least it was an improvement on the damned books in the damned library.

However, there was yet one more lack of interest in Charles that pleased his uncle even less. Yellow ribbons and daffodils, the insignia of the Liberal Party, were anathema at Winsyatt; the old man was the most azure of Tories—and had interest. But Charles politely refused all attempts to get him to stand for Parliament. He declared himself without political conviction. In secret he rather admired Gladstone; but at Winsyatt Gladstone was the arch-traitor, the unmentionable. Thus family respect and social laziness conveniently closed what would have been a natural career for him.

Laziness was, I am afraid, Charles's distinguishing trait. Like many of his contemporaries he sensed that the earlier self-responsibility of the century was turning into self-importance: that what drove the new Britain was increasingly a desire to seem respectable, in place of the desire to do good for good's sake. He knew he was overfastidious. But how could one write history with Macaulay so close behind? Fiction or poetry, in the midst of the greatest galaxy of talent in the history of English literature? How could one be a creative scientist, with Lyell and Darwin still alive? Be a statesman, with Disraeli and Gladstone polarizing all the available space?

You will see that Charles set his sights high. Intelligent idlers always have, in order to justify their idleness to their intelligence. He had, in short, all the Byronic ennui with neither of the Byronic outlets: genius and adultery.

But though death may be delayed, as mothers with mar-

19

riageable daughters have been known to foresee, it kindly always comes in the end. Even if Charles had not had the further prospects he did, he was an interesting young man. His travels abroad had regrettably rubbed away some of that patina of profound humorlessness (called by the Victorian earnestness, moral rectitude, probity, and a thousand other misleading names) that one really required of a proper English gentleman of the time. There was outwardly a certain cynicism about him, a sure symptom of an inherent moral decay; but he never entered society without being ogled by the mamas, clapped on the back by the papas and simpered at by the girls. Charles quite liked pretty girls and he was not averse to leading them, and their ambitious parents, on. Thus he had gained a reputation for aloofness and coldness, a not unmerited reward for the neat way—by the time he was thirty he was as good as a polecat at the business—he would sniff the bait and then turn his tail on the hidden teeth of the matrimonial traps that endangered his path.

His uncle often took him to task on the matter; but as Charles was quick to point out, he was using damp powder. The old man would grumble.

"I never found the right woman."

"Nonsense. You never looked for her."

"Indeed I did. When I was your age . . ."

"You lived for your hounds and the partridge season."

The old fellow would stare gloomily at his claret. He did not really regret having no wife; but he bitterly lacked not having children to buy ponies and guns for. He saw his way of life sinking without trace.

"I was blind. Blind."

"My dear uncle, I have excellent eyesight. Console yourself. I too have been looking for the right girl. And I have not found her."

4

What's DONE, is what remains! Ah, blessed they
Who leave completed tasks of love to stay
And answer mutely for them, being dead,
Life was not purposeless, though Life be fled.

MRS. NORTON, *The Lady of La Garaye* (1863)

Most British families of the middle and upper classes
lived above their own cesspool . . .

E. ROYSTON PIKE, *Human Documents
of the Victorian Golden Age*

The basement kitchen of Mrs. Poulteney's large Regency
house, which stood, an elegantly clear simile of her social
status, in a commanding position on one of the steep hills
behind Lyme Regis, would no doubt seem today almost intolerable for its functional inadequacies. Though the occupants in 1867 would have been quite clear as to who was the
tyrant in their lives, the more real monster, to an age like
ours, would beyond doubt have been the enormous kitchen
range that occupied all the inner wall of the large and ill-lit
room. It had three fires, all of which had to be stoked twice
a day, and riddled twice a day; and since the smooth domestic
running of the house depended on it, it could never be
allowed to go out. Never mind how much a summer's day
sweltered, never mind that every time there was a southwesterly gale the monster blew black clouds of choking
fumes—the remorseless furnaces had to be fed. And then the
color of those walls! They cried out for some light shade, for
white. Instead they were a bilious leaden green—one that
was, unknown to the occupants (and to be fair, to the tyrant
upstairs), rich in arsenic. Perhaps it was fortunate that the
room was damp and that the monster disseminated so much
smoke and grease. At least the deadly dust was laid.

The sergeant major of this Stygian domain was a Mrs.

21

Fairley, a thin, small person who always wore black, but less for her widowhood than by temperament. Perhaps her sharp melancholy had been induced by the sight of the endless torrent of lesser mortals who cascaded through her kitchen. Butlers, footmen, gardeners, grooms, upstairs maids, downstairs maids—they took just so much of Mrs. Poulteney's standards and ways and then they fled. This was very disgraceful and cowardly of them. But when you are expected to rise at six, to work from half past six to eleven, to work again from half past eleven to half past four, and then again from five to ten, *and* every day, thus a hundred-hour week, your reserves of grace and courage may not be very large.

A legendary summation of servant feelings had been delivered to Mrs. Poulteney by the last butler but four: "Madam, I should rather spend the rest of my life in the poorhouse than live another week under this roof." Some gravely doubted whether anyone could actually have dared to say these words to the awesome lady. But the sentiment behind them was understood when the man came down with his bags and claimed that he had.

Exactly how the ill-named Mrs. Fairley herself had stood her mistress so long was one of the local wonders. Most probably it was because she would, had life so fallen out, have been a Mrs. Poulteney on her own account. Her envy kept her there; and also her dark delight in the domestic catastrophes that descended so frequently on the house. In short, both women were incipient sadists; and it was to their advantage to tolerate each other.

Mrs. Poulteney had two obsessions: or two aspects of the same obsession. One was Dirt—though she made some sort of exception of the kitchen, since only the servants lived there—and the other was Immorality. In neither field did anything untoward escape her eagle eye.

She was like some plump vulture, endlessly circling in her endless leisure, and endowed in the first field with a miraculous sixth sense as regards dust, fingermarks, insufficiently starched linen, smells, stains, breakages and all the ills that houses are heir to. A gardener would be dismissed for being seen to come into the house with earth on his hands; a butler for having a spot of wine on his stock; a maid for having slut's wool under her bed.

But the most abominable thing of all was that even outside her house she acknowledged no bounds to her authority. Failure to be seen at church, both at matins and at evensong, on Sunday was tantamount to proof of the worst moral laxity. Heaven help the maid seen out walking, on one of her rare free afternoons—one a month was the reluctant allowance—with a young man. And heaven also help the young man so in love that he tried to approach Marlborough House secretly to keep an assignation: for the gardens were a positive forest of humane man-traps—"humane" in this context referring to the fact that the great waiting jaws were untoothed, though quite powerful enough to break a man's leg. These iron servants were the most cherished by Mrs. Poulteney. *Them,* she had never dismissed.

There would have been a place in the Gestapo for the lady; she had a way of interrogation that could reduce the sturdiest girls to tears in the first five minutes. In her fashion she was an epitome of all the most crassly arrogant traits of the ascendant British Empire. Her only notion of justice was that she must be right; and her only notion of government was an angry bombardment of the impertinent populace.

Yet among her own class, a very limited circle, she was renowned for her charity. And if you had disputed that reputation, your opponents would have produced an incontrovertible piece of evidence: had not dear, kind Mrs. Poulteney taken in the French Lieutenant's Woman? I need hardly add that at the time the dear, kind lady knew only the other, more Grecian, nickname.

This remarkable event had taken place in the spring of 1866, exactly a year before the time of which I write; and it had to do with the great secret of Mrs. Poulteney's life. It was a very simple secret. She believed in hell.

The vicar of Lyme at that time was a comparatively emancipated man theologically, but he also knew very well on which side his pastoral bread was buttered. He suited Lyme, a traditionally Low Church congregation, very well. He had the knack of a certain fervid eloquence in his sermons; and he kept his church free of crucifixes, images, ornaments and all other signs of the Romish cancer. When Mrs. Poulteney enounced to him her theories of the life to come, he did not argue, for incumbents of not notably fat livings do not argue with rich parishioners. Mrs. Poulteney's purse was as open to calls from him as it was throttled where her thirteen domestics' wages were concerned. In the winter (winter also of the fourth great cholera onslaught on Victorian Britain) of that previous year Mrs. Poulteney had been a little ill, and the vicar had been as frequent a visitor as the doctors who so repeatedly had to assure her that she was suffering from a trivial stomach upset and not the dreaded Oriental killer.

Mrs. Poulteney was not a stupid woman; indeed, she had

23

acuity in practical matters, and her future destination, like all matters pertaining to her comfort, was a highly practical consideration. If she visualized God, He had rather the face of the Duke of Wellington; but His character was more that of a shrewd lawyer, a breed for whom Mrs. Poulteney had much respect. As she lay in her bedroom she reflected on the terrible mathematical doubt that increasingly haunted her; whether the Lord calculated charity by what one had given or by what one could have afforded to give. Here she had better data than the vicar. She had given considerable sums to the church; but she knew they fell far short of the prescribed one-tenth to be parted with by serious candidates for paradise. Certainly she had regulated her will to ensure that the account would be handsomely balanced after her death; but God might not be present at the reading of that document. Furthermore it chanced, while she was ill, that Mrs. Fairley, who read to her from the Bible in the evenings, picked on the parable of the widow's mite. It had always seemed a grossly unfair parable to Mrs. Poulteney; it now lay in her heart far longer than the enteritis bacilli in her intestines. One day, when she was convalescent, she took advantage of one of the solicitous vicar's visits and cautiously examined her conscience. At first he was inclined to dismiss her spiritual worries.

"My dear madam, your feet are on the Rock. The Creator is all-seeing and all-wise. It is not for us to doubt His mercy—or His justice."

"But supposing He should ask me if my conscience is clear?"

The vicar smiled. "You will reply that it is troubled. And with His infinite compassion He will—"

"But supposing He did not?"

"My dear Mrs. Poulteney, if you speak like this I shall have to reprimand you. We are not to dispute *His* understanding."

There was a silence. With the vicar Mrs. Poulteney felt herself with two people. One was her social inferior, and an inferior who depended on her for many of the pleasures of his table, for a substantial fraction of the running costs of his church and also for the happy performance of his nonliturgical duties among the poor; and the other was the representative of God, before whom she had metaphorically to kneel. So her manner with him took often a bizarre and inconsequential course. It was *de haut en bas* one moment, *de bas en haut* the next; and sometimes she contrived both positions all in one sentence.

24

"If only poor Frederick had not died. He would have advised me."

"Doubtless. And his advice would have resembled mine. You may rest assured of that. I know he was a Christian. And what I say is sound Christian doctrine."

"It was a warning. A punishment."

The vicar gave her a solemn look. "Beware, my dear lady, beware. One does not trespass lightly on Our Maker's prerogative."

She shifted her ground. Not all the vicars in creation could have justified her husband's early death to her. It remained between her and God; a mystery like a black opal, that sometimes shone as a solemn omen and sometimes stood as a kind of sum already paid off against the amount of penance she might still owe.

"I have given. But I have not done good deeds."

"To give is a most excellent deed."

"I am not like Lady Cotton."

This abruptly secular descent did not surprise the vicar. He was well aware, from previous references, that Mrs. Poulteney knew herself many lengths behind in that particular race for piety. Lady Cotton, who lived some miles behind Lyme, was famous for her fanatically eleemosynary life. She visited, she presided over a missionary society, she had set up a home for fallen women—true, it was of such repentant severity that most of the beneficiaries of her Magdalen Society scrambled back down to the pit of iniquity as soon as they could—but Mrs. Poulteney was as ignorant of that as she was of Tragedy's more vulgar nickname.

The vicar coughed. "Lady Cotton is an example to us all." This was oil on the flames—as he was perhaps not unaware.

"I should visit."

"That would be excellent."

"It is that visiting always so distresses me." The vicar was unhelpful. "I know it is wicked of me."

"Come come."

"Yes. Very wicked."

A long silence followed, in which the vicar meditated on his dinner, still an hour away, and Mrs. Poulteney on her wickedness. She then came out, with an unaccustomed timidity, with a compromise solution to her dilemma.

"If you knew of some lady, some refined person who has come upon adverse circumstances . . ."

"I am not quite clear what you intend."

"I wish to take a companion. I have difficulty in writing now. And Mrs. Fairley reads so poorly. I should be happy to provide a home for such a person."

25

"Very well. If you so wish it. I will make inquiries."

Mrs. Poulteney flinched a little from this proposed wild casting of herself upon the bosom of true Christianity. "She must be of irreproachable moral character. I have my servants to consider."

"My dear lady, of course, of course." The vicar stood.

"And preferably without relations. The relations of one's dependents can become so very tiresome."

"Rest assured that I shall not present anyone unsuitable."

He pressed her hand and moved towards the door.

"And Mr. Forsythe, not too young a person."

He bowed and left the room. But halfway down the stairs to the ground floor, he stopped. He remembered. He reflected. And perhaps an emotion not absolutely unconnected with malice, a product of so many long hours of hypocrisy—or at least a not always complete frankness—at Mrs. Poulteney's bombazined side, at any rate an impulse made him turn and go back to her drawing room. He stood in the doorway.

"An eligible has occurred to me. Her name is Sarah Woodruff."

5

O me, what profits it to put
  An idle case? If Death were seen
  At first as Death, Love had not been,
Or been in narrowest working shut,

Mere fellowship of sluggish moods,
  Or in his coarsest Satyr-shape
  Had bruised the herb and crush'd the grape,
And bask'd and batten'd in the woods.

TENNYSON, *In Memoriam* (1850)

The young people were all wild to see Lyme.

JANE AUSTEN, *Persuasion*

Ernestina had exactly the right face for her age; that is, small-chinned, oval, delicate as a violet. You may see it still in the drawings of the great illustrators of the time—in Phiz's work, in John Leech's. Her gray eyes and the paleness of her skin only enhanced the delicacy of the rest. At first meetings she could cast down her eyes very prettily, as if she might

26

faint should any gentleman dare to address her. But there was a minute tilt at the corner of her eyelids, and a corresponding tilt at the corner of her lips—to extend the same comparison, as faint as the fragrance of February violets—that denied, very subtly but quite unmistakably, her apparent total obeisance to the great god Man. An orthodox Victorian would perhaps have mistrusted that imperceptible hint of a Becky Sharp; but to a man like Charles she proved irresistible. She was so very nearly one of the prim little moppets, the Georginas, Victorias, Albertinas, Matildas and the rest who sat in their closely guarded dozens at every ball; yet not quite.

When Charles departed from Aunt Tranter's house in Broad Street to stroll a hundred paces or so down to his hotel, there gravely—are not all declared lovers the world's fool?—to mount the stairs to his rooms and interrogate his good-looking face in the mirror, Ernestina excused herself and went to her room. She wanted to catch a last glimpse of her betrothed through the lace curtains; and she also wanted to be in the only room in her aunt's house that she could really tolerate.

Having duly admired the way he walked and especially the manner in which he raised his top hat to Aunt Tranter's maid, who happened to be out on an errand; *and* hated him for doing it, because the girl had pert little Dorset peasant eyes and a provokingly pink complexion, and Charles had been strictly forbidden ever to look again at any woman under the age of sixty—a condition Aunt Tranter mercifully escaped by just one year—Ernestina turned back into her room. It had been furnished for her and to her taste, which was emphatically French; as heavy then as the English, but a little more gilt and fanciful. The rest of Aunt Tranter's house was inexorably, massively, irrefutably in the style of a quarter-century before: that is, a museum of objects created in the first fine rejection of all things decadent, light and graceful, and to which the memory or morals of the odious Prinny, George IV, could be attached.

Nobody could dislike Aunt Tranter; even to contemplate being angry with that innocently smiling and talking—especially talking—face was absurd. She had the profound optimism of successful old maids; solitude either sours or teaches self-dependence. Aunt Tranter had begun by making the best of things for herself, and ended by making the best of them for the rest of the world as well.

However, Ernestina did her best to be angry with her; on the impossibility of having dinner at five; on the subject of the funereal furniture that choked the other rooms; on the subject of her aunt's oversolicitude for her fair name (she would not believe that the bridegroom and bride-to-be might wish to sit alone, and walk out alone); and above all on the subject of Ernestina's being in Lyme at all.

The poor girl had had to suffer the agony of every only child since time began—that is, a crushing and unrelenting canopy of parental worry. Since birth her slightest cough would bring doctors; since puberty her slightest whim summoned decorators and dressmakers; and always her slightest frown caused her mama and papa secret hours of self-recrimination. Now this was all very well when it came to new dresses and new wall hangings, but there was one matter upon which all her *bouderies* and complaints made no impression. And that was her health. Her mother and father were convinced she was consumptive. They had only to smell damp in a basement to move house, only to have two days' rain on a holiday to change districts. Half Harley Street had examined her, and found nothing; she had never had a serious illness in her life; she had none of the lethargy, the chronic weaknesses, of the condition. She could have—or could have if she had ever been allowed to—danced all night; and played, without the slightest ill effect, battledore all the next morning. But she was no more able to shift her doting parents' fixed idea than a baby to pull down a mountain. Had they but been able to see into the future! For Ernestina was to outlive all her generation. She was born in 1846. And she died on the day that Hitler invaded Poland.

An indispensable part of her quite unnecessary regimen was thus her annual stay with her mother's sister in Lyme. Usually she came to recover from the season; this year she was sent early to gather strength for the marriage. No doubt the Channel breezes did her some good, but she always descended in the carriage to Lyme with the gloom of a prisoner arriving in Siberia. The society of the place was as up-to-date as Aunt Tranter's lumbering mahogany furniture; and as for the entertainment, to a young lady familiar with the best that London can offer it was worse than nil. So her relation with Aunt Tranter was much more that of a high-spirited child, an English Juliet with her flat-footed nurse, than what one would expect of niece and aunt. Indeed, if Romeo had not mercifully appeared on the scene that previous winter, and promised to share her penal solitude, she would have mutinied; at least, she was almost sure she would have mutinied. Ernestina had certainly a much stronger will of her own than anyone about her had ever allowed for—and more than the age allowed for. But fortunately she had a very proper respect for convention; and she shared with

28

Charles—it had not been the least part of the first attraction between them—a sense of self-irony. Without this and a sense of humor she would have been a horrid spoiled child; and it was surely the fact that she did often so apostrophize herself ("You horrid spoiled child") that redeemed her.

In her room that afternoon she unbuttoned her dress and stood before her mirror in her chemise and petticoats. For a few moments she became lost in a highly narcissistic self-contemplation. Her neck and shoulders did her face justice; she was really very pretty, one of the prettiest girls she knew. And as if to prove it she raised her arms and unloosed her hair, a thing she knew to be vaguely sinful, yet necessary, like a hot bath or a warm bed on a winter's night. She imagined herself for a truly sinful moment as someone wicked—a dancer, an actress. And then, if you had been watching, you would have seen something very curious. For she suddenly stopped turning and admiring herself in profile; gave an abrupt look up at the ceiling. Her lips moved. And she hastily opened one of the wardrobes and drew on a *peignoir*.

For what had crossed her mind—a corner of her bed having chanced, as she pirouetted, to catch her eye in the mirror—was a sexual thought: an imagining, a kind of dimly glimpsed Laocoön embrace of naked limbs. It was not only her profound ignorance of the reality of copulation that frightened her; it was the aura of pain and brutality that the act seemed to require, and which seemed to deny all that gentleness of gesture and discreetness of permitted caress that so attracted her in Charles. She had once or twice seen animals couple; the violence haunted her mind.

Thus she had evolved a kind of private commandment—those inaudible words were simply "I must not"—whenever the physical female implications of her body, sexual, menstrual, parturitional, tried to force an entry into her consciousness. But though one may keep the wolves from one's door, they still howl out there in the darkness. Ernestina wanted a husband, wanted Charles to be that husband, wanted children; but the payment she vaguely divined she would have to make for them seemed excessive.

She sometimes wondered why God had permitted such a bestial version of Duty to spoil such an innocent longing. Most women of her period felt the same; so did most men; and it is no wonder that duty has become such a key concept in our understanding of the Victorian age—or for that matter, such a wet blanket in our own.*

* The stanzas from *In Memoriam* I have quoted at the beginning of this chapter are very relevant here. Surely the oddest of all the odd arguments in that celebrated anthology of after-life anxiety is stated in

Having quelled the wolves Ernestina went to her dressing table, unlocked a drawer and there pulled out her diary, in black morocco with a gold clasp. From another drawer she took a hidden key and unlocked the book. She turned immediately to the back page. There she had written out, on the day of her betrothal to Charles, the dates of all the months and days that lay between it and her marriage. Neat lines were drawn already through two months; some ninety numbers remained; and now Ernestina took the ivory-topped pencil from the top of the diary and struck through March 26th. It still had nine hours to run, but she habitually allowed herself this little cheat. Then she turned to the front of the book, or nearly to the front, because the book had been a Christmas present. Some fifteen pages in, pages of close handwriting, there came a blank, upon which she had pressed a sprig of jasmine. She stared at it a moment, then bent to smell it. Her loosened hair fell over the page, and she closed her eyes to see if once again she could summon up the most delicious, the day she had thought she would die of joy, had cried endlessly, the ineffable . . .

But she heard Aunt Tranter's feet on the stairs, hastily put the book away, and began to comb her lithe brown hair.

6

> Ah Maud, you milk-white fawn, you are all unmeet
> for a wife.
>
> TENNYSON, *Maud* (1855)

Mrs. Poulteney's face, that afternoon when the vicar made his return and announcement, expressed a notable ignorance. And with ladies of her kind, an unsuccessful appeal to knowledge is more often than not a successful appeal to disapproval. Her face was admirably suited to the latter sentiment; it had eyes that were not Tennyson's "homes of silent prayer" at all, and lower cheeks, almost dewlaps, that pinched the lips

---

this poem (xxxv). To claim that love can only be Satyr-shaped if there is no immortality of the soul is clearly a panic flight from Freud. Heaven for the Victorians was very largely heaven because the body was left behind—along with the Id.

together in condign rejection of all that threatened her two life principles: the one being (I will borrow Treitschke's sarcastic formulation) that "Civilization is Soap" and the other, "Respectability is what does not give me offense." She bore some resemblance to a white Pekinese; to be exact, to a stuffed Pekinese, since she carried concealed in her bosom a small bag of camphor as a prophylactic against cholera ... so that where she was, was always also a delicate emanation of mothballs.

"I do not know her."

The vicar felt snubbed; and wondered what would have happened had the Good Samaritan come upon Mrs. Poulteney instead of the poor traveler.

"I did not suppose you would. She is a Charmouth girl."

"A girl?"

"That is, I am not quite sure of her age, a woman, a lady of some thirty years of age. Perhaps more. I would not like to hazard a guess." The vicar was conscious that he was making a poor start for the absent defendant. "But a most distressing case. Most deserving of your charity."

"Has she an education?"

"Yes indeed. She was trained to be a governess. She was a governess."

"And what is she now?"

"I believe she is without employment."

"Why?"

"That is a long story."

"I should certainly wish to hear it before proceeding."

So the vicar sat down again, and told her what he knew, or some (for in his brave attempt to save Mrs. Poulteney's soul, he decided to endanger his own) of what he knew, of Sarah Woodruff.

"The girl's father was a tenant of Lord Meriton's, near Beaminster. A farmer merely, but a man of excellent principles and highly respected in that neighborhood. He most wisely provided the girl with a better education than one would expect."

"He is deceased?"

"Some several years ago. The girl became a governess to Captain John Talbot's family at Charmouth."

"Will he give a letter of reference?"

"My dear Mrs. Poulteney, we are discussing, if I understood our earlier conversation aright, an object of charity, not an object of employment." She bobbed, the nearest acknowledgment to an apology she had ever been known to muster. "No doubt such a letter can be obtained. She left his home at her own request. What happened was this. You will

31

recall the French barque—I think she hailed from Saint Malo—that was driven ashore under Stonebarrow in the dreadful gale of last December? And you will no doubt recall that three of the crew were saved and were taken in by the people of Charmouth? Two were simple sailors. One, I understand, was the lieutenant of the vessel. His leg had been crushed at the first impact, but he clung to a spar and was washed ashore. You must surely have read of this."

"Very probably. I do not like the French."

"Captain Talbot, as a naval officer himself, most kindly charged upon his household the care of the ... foreign officer. He spoke no English. And Miss Woodruff was called upon to interpret and look after his needs."

"She speaks French?" Mrs. Poulteney's alarm at this appalling disclosure was nearly enough to sink the vicar. But he ended by bowing and smiling urbanely.

"My dear madam, so do most governesses. It is not their fault if the world requires such attainments of them. But to return to the French gentleman. I regret to say that he did not deserve that appellation."

"Mr. Forsythe!"

She drew herself up, but not too severely, in case she might freeze the poor man into silence.

"I hasten to add that no misconduct took place at Captain Talbot's. Or indeed, so far as Miss Woodruff is concerned, at any subsequent place or time. I have Mr. Fursey-Harris's word for that. He knows the circumstances far better than I." The person referred to was the vicar of Charmouth. "But the Frenchman managed to engage Miss Woodruff's affections. When his leg was mended he took coach to Weymouth, there, or so it was generally supposed, to find a passage home. Two days after he had gone Miss Woodruff requested Mrs. Talbot, in the most urgent terms, to allow her to leave her post. I am told that Mrs. Talbot tried to extract the woman's reasons. But without success."

"And she let her leave without notice?"

The vicar adroitly seized his chance. "I agree—it was most foolish. She should have known better. Had Miss Woodruff been in wiser employ I have no doubt this sad business would not have taken place." He left a pause for Mrs. Poulteney to grasp the implied compliment. "I will make my story short. Miss Woodruff joined the Frenchman in Weymouth. Her conduct is highly to be reprobated, but I am informed that she lodged with a female cousin."

"That does not excuse her in my eyes."

"Assuredly not. But you must remember that she is not a

32

lady born. The lower classes are not so scrupulous about appearances as ourselves. Furthermore I have omitted to tell you that the Frenchman had plighted his troth. Miss Woodruff went to Weymouth in the belief that she was to marry."

"But was he not a Catholic?"

Mrs. Poulteney saw herself as a pure Patmos in a raging ocean of popery.

"I am afraid his conduct shows he was without any Christian faith. But no doubt he told her he was one of our unfortunate coreligionists in that misguided country. After some days he returned to France, promising Miss Woodruff that as soon as he had seen his family and provided himself with a new ship—another of his lies was that he was to be promoted captain on his return—he would come back here, to Lyme itself, marry her, and take her away with him. Since then she has waited. It is quite clear that the man was a heartless deceiver. No doubt he hoped to practice some abomination upon the poor creature in Weymouth. And when her strong Christian principles showed him the futility of his purposes, he took ship."

"And what has happened to her since? Surely Mrs. Talbot did not take her back?"

"Madam, Mrs. Talbot is a somewhat eccentric lady. She offered to do so. But I now come to the sad consequences of my story. Miss Woodruff is not insane. Far from it. She is perfectly able to perform any duties that may be given to her. But she suffers from grave attacks of melancholia. They are doubtless partly attributable to remorse. But also, I fear, to her fixed delusion that the lieutenant is an honorable man and will one day return to her. For that reason she may be frequently seen haunting the sea approaches to our town. Mr. Fursey-Harris himself has earnestly endeavored to show to the woman the hopelessness, not to say the impropriety, of her behavior. Not to put too fine a point upon it, madam, she is slightly crazed."

There was a silence then. The vicar resigned himself to a pagan god—that of chance. He sensed that Mrs. Poulteney was calculating. Her opinion of herself required her to appear shocked and alarmed at the idea of allowing such a creature into Marlborough House. But there was God to be accounted to.

"She has relatives?"

"I understand not."

"How has she supported herself since . . .?"

"Most pitifully. I understand she has been doing a little

needlework. I think Mrs. Tranter has employed her in such work. But she has been living principally on her savings from her previous situation."

"She has saved, then."

The vicar breathed again.

"If you take her in, madam, I think she will be truly saved." He played his trump card. "And perhaps—though it is not for me to judge your conscience—she may in her turn save."

Mrs. Poulteney suddenly had a dazzling and heavenly vision; it was of Lady Cotton, with her saintly nose out of joint. She frowned and stared at her deep-piled carpet.

"I should like Mr. Fursey-Harris to call."

And a week later, accompanied by the vicar of Lyme, he called, sipped madeira, and said—and omitted—as his ecclesiastical colleague had advised. Mrs. Talbot provided an interminable letter of reference, which did more harm than good, since it failed disgracefully to condemn sufficiently the governess's conduct. One phrase in particular angered Mrs. Poulteney. "Monsieur Varguennes was a person of considerable charm, and Captain Talbot wishes me to suggest to you that a sailor's life is not the best school of morals." Nor did it interest her that Miss Sarah was a "skilled and dutiful teacher" or that "My infants have deeply missed her." But Mrs. Talbot's patent laxity of standard and foolish sentimentality finally helped Sarah with Mrs. Poulteney; they set her a challenge.

So Sarah came for an interview, accompanied by the vicar. She secretly pleased Mrs. Poulteney from the start, by seeming so cast down, so annihilated by circumstance. It was true that she looked suspiciously what she indeed was— nearer twenty-five than "thirty or perhaps more." But there was her only too visible sorrow, which showed she was a sinner, and Mrs. Poulteney wanted nothing to do with anyone who did not look very clearly to be in that category. And there was her reserve, which Mrs. Poulteney took upon herself to interpret as a mute gratitude. Above all, with the memory of so many departed domestics behind her, the old lady abhorred impertinence and forwardness, terms synonymous in her experience with speaking before being spoken to and anticipating her demands, which deprived her of the pleasure of demanding why they had not been anticipated.

Then, at the vicar's suggestion, she dictated a letter. The handwriting was excellent, the spelling faultless. She set a more cunning test. She passed Sarah her Bible and made her read. Mrs. Poulteney had devoted some thought to the choice of passage; and had been sadly torn between Psalm 119 ("Blessed are the undefiled") and Psalm 140 ("Deliver me, O Lord, from the evil man"). She had finally chosen the former; and listened not only to the reading voice, but also for any fatal sign that the words of the psalmist were not being taken very much to the reader's heart.

Sarah's voice was firm, rather deep. It retained traces of a rural accent, but in those days a genteel accent was not the great social requisite it later became. There were men in the House of Lords, dukes even, who still kept traces of the accent of their province; and no one thought any the worse of them. Perhaps it was by contrast with Mrs. Fairley's uninspired stumbling that the voice first satisfied Mrs. Poulteney. But it charmed her; and so did the demeanor of the girl as she read "O that my ways were directed to keep Thy statutes!"

There remained a brief interrogation.

"Mr. Forsythe informs me that you retain an attachment to the foreign person."

"I do not wish to speak of it, ma'm."

Now if any maid had dared to say such a thing to Mrs. Poulteney, the *Dies Irae* would have followed. But this was spoken openly, without fear, yet respectfully; and for once Mrs. Poulteney let a golden opportunity for bullying pass.

"I will not have French books in my house."

"I possess none. Nor English, ma'm."

She possessed none, I may add, because they were all sold; not because she was an early forerunner of the egregious McLuhan.

"You have surely a Bible?"

The girl shook her head. The vicar intervened. "I will attend to that, my dear Mrs. Poulteney."

"I am told you are constant in your attendance at divine service."

"Yes, ma'm."

"Let it remain so. God consoles us in all adversity."

"I try to share your belief, ma'm."

Mrs. Poulteney put her most difficult question, one the vicar had in fact previously requested her not to ask.

"What if this . . . person returns; what then?"

But again Sarah did the best possible thing: she said nothing, and simply bowed her head and shook it. In her increasingly favorable mood Mrs. Poulteney allowed this to be an indication of speechless repentance.

So she entered upon her good deed.

It had not occurred to her, of course, to ask why Sarah, who had refused offers of work from less sternly Christian

souls than Mrs. Poulteney's, should wish to enter her house.
There were two very simple reasons. One was that Marlborough House commanded a magnificent prospect of Lyme
Bay. The other was even simpler. She had exactly sevenpence
in the world.

7

The extraordinary productiveness of modern industry
. . . allows of the unproductive employment of a larger
and larger part of the working class, and the consequent reproduction, on a constantly extending scale, of
the ancient domestic slaves under the name of a servant class, including men-servants, women-servants,
lackeys, etc.

MARX, *Capital* (1867)

The morning, when Sam drew the curtains, flooded in upon
Charles as Mrs. Poulteney—then still audibly asleep—would
have wished paradise to flood in upon her, after a suitably
solemn pause, when she died. A dozen times or so a year the
climate of the mild Dorset coast yields such days—not just
agreeably mild out-of-season days, but ravishing fragments
of Mediterranean warmth and luminosity. Nature goes a little
mad then. Spiders that should be hibernating run over the
baking November rocks; blackbirds sing in December, primroses rush out in January; and March mimics June.

Charles sat up, tore off his nightcap, made Sam throw
open the windows and, supporting himself on his hands,
stared at the sunlight that poured into the room. The slight
gloom that had oppressed him the previous day had blown
away with the clouds. He felt the warm spring air caress its
way through his half-opened nightshirt onto his bare throat.
Sam stood stropping his razor, and steam rose invitingly, with
a kind of Proustian richness of evocation—so many such
happy days, so much assurance of position, order, calm,
civilization, out of the copper jug he had brought with him.
In the cobbled street below, a rider clopped peacefully down
towards the sea. A slightly bolder breeze moved the shabby
red velvet curtains at the window; but in that light even they

36

looked beautiful. All was supremely well. The world would always be this, and this moment.

There was a patter of small hooves, a restless baa-ing and mewling. Charles rose and looked out of the window. Two old men in gaufer-stitched smocks stood talking opposite. One was a shepherd, leaning on his crook. Twelve ewes and rather more lambs stood nervously in mid-street. Such folk-costume relics of a much older England had become picturesque by 1867, though not rare; every village had its dozen or so smocked elders. Charles wished he could draw. Really, the country was charming. He turned to his man.

"Upon my word, Sam, on a day like this I could contemplate never setting eyes on London again."

"If you goes on a-standin' in the hair, sir, you won't, neither."

His master gave him a dry look. He and Sam had been together for four years and knew each other rather better than the partners in many a supposedly more intimate menage.

"Sam, you've been drinking again."

"No, sir."

"The new room is better?"

"Yes, sir."

"And the commons?"

"Very hacceptable, sir."

"*Quod est demonstrandum*. You have the hump on a morning that would make a miser sing. *Ergo,* you have been drinking."

Sam tested the blade of the cutthroat razor on the edge of his small thumb, with an expression on his face that suggested that at any moment he might change his mind and try it on his own throat; or perhaps even on his smiling master's.

"It's that there kitchen-girl's at Mrs. Tranter's, sir. I ain't 'alf going to . . ."

"Kindly put that instrument down. And explain yourself."

"I sees her. Dahn out there." He jerked his thumb at the window. "Right across the street she calls."

"And what did she call, pray?"

Sam's expression deepened to the impending outrage. " ' 'Ave yer got a bag o' soot?' " He paused bleakly. "Sir."

Charles grinned.

"I know the girl. That one in the gray dress? Who is so ugly to look at?" This was unkind of Charles, since he was speaking of the girl he had raised his hat to on the previous afternoon, as nubile a little creature as Lyme could boast.

"Not exackly hugly. Leastways in looks."

"A-ha. So. Cupid is being unfair to Cockneys."

Sam flashed an indignant look. "I woulden touch 'er with a bargepole! Bloomin' milkmaid."

"I trust you're using the adjective in its literal sense, Sam. You may have been, as you so frequently asseverate, born in a gin palace—"

"Next door to one, sir."

"In *close* proximity to a gin palace, but I will not have you using its language on a day like this."

"It's the 'oomiliation, Mr. Charles. Hall the hosslers 'eard." As "all the ostlers" comprehended exactly two persons, one of whom was stone deaf, Charles showed little sympathy. He smiled, then gestured to Sam to pour him his hot water.

"Now get me my breakfast, there's a good fellow. I'll shave myself this morning. And let me have a double dose of muffins."

"Yes, sir."

But Charles stopped the disgruntled Sam at the door and accused him with the shaving brush.

"These country girls are much too timid to call such rude things at distinguished London gentlemen—unless they've first been sorely provoked. I gravely suspect, Sam, that you've been fast." Sam stood with his mouth open. "And if you're not doubly fast with my break*fast* I shall *fast*en my boot onto the posterior portion of your miserable anatomy."

The door was shut then, and none too gently. Charles winked at himself in the mirror. And then suddenly put a decade on his face: all gravity, the solemn young paterfamilias; then smiled indulgently at his own faces and euphoria; poised, was plunged in affectionate contemplation of his features. He had indeed very regular ones—a wide forehead, a moustache as black as his hair, which was tousled from the removal of the nightcap and made him look younger than he was. His skin was suitably pale, though less so than that of many London gentlemen—for this was a time when a suntan was not at all a desirable social-sexual status symbol, but the reverse: an indication of low rank. Yes, upon examination, it was a faintly foolish face, at such a moment. A tiny wave of the previous day's ennui washed back over him. Too innocent a face, when it was stripped of its formal outdoor mask; too little achieved. There was really only the Doric nose, the cool gray eyes. Breeding and self-knowledge, he most legibly had.

He began to cover the ambiguous face in lather.

Sam was some ten years his junior; too young to be a good manservant and besides, absentminded, contentious, vain, fancying himself sharp; too fond of drolling and idling, leaning with a straw-haulm or sprig of parsley cocked in the corner of his mouth; of playing the horse fancier or of catching sparrows under a sieve when he was being bawled for upstairs.

Of course to us any Cockney servant called Sam evokes immediately the immortal Weller; and it was certainly from that background that this Sam had emerged. But thirty years had passed since *Pickwick Papers* first coruscated into the world. Sam's love of the equine was not really very deep. He was more like some modern working-class man who thinks a keen knowledge of cars a sign of his social progress. He even knew of Sam Weller, not from the book, but from a stage version of it; and knew the times had changed. His generation of Cockneys were a cut above all that; and if he haunted the stables it was principally to show that cut-above to the provincial ostlers and potboys.

The mid-century had seen a quite new form of dandy appear on the English scene; the old upper-class variety, the etiolated descendants of Beau Brummel, were known as "swells"; but the new young prosperous artisans and would-be superior domestics like Sam had gone into competition sartorially. They were called "snobs" by the swells themselves; Sam was a very fair example of a snob, in this localized sense of the word. He had a very sharp sense of clothes style—quite as sharp as a "mod" of the 1960s; and he spent most of his wages on keeping in fashion. And he showed another mark of this new class in his struggle to command the language.

By 1870 Sam Weller's famous inability to pronounce v except as w, the centuries-old mark of the common Londoner, was as much despised by the "snobs" as by the bourgeois novelists who continued for some time, and quite inaccurately, to put it into the dialogue of their Cockney characters. The snobs' struggle was much more with the aspirate; a fierce struggle, in our Sam's case, and more frequently lost than won. But his wrong a's and h's were not really comic; they were signs of a social revolution, and this was something Charles failed to recognize.

Perhaps that was because Sam supplied something so very necessary in his life—a daily opportunity for chatter, for a lapse into schoolboyhood, during which Charles could, so to speak, excrete his characteristic and deplorable fondness for labored puns and innuendoes: a humor based, with a singularly revolting purity, on educational privilege. Yet though Charles's attitude may seem to add insult to the already gross enough injury of economic exploitation, I must point out that

39

his relationship with Sam did show a kind of affection, a human bond, that was a good deal better than the frigid barrier so many of the new rich in an age drenched in new riches were by that time erecting between themselves and their domestics.

To be sure, Charles had many generations of servant-handlers behind him; the new rich of his time had none—indeed, were very often the children of servants. He could not have imagined a world without servants. The new rich could; and this made them much more harshly exacting of their relative status. Their servants they tried to turn into machines, while Charles knew very well that his was also partly a companion—his Sancho Panza, the low comedy that supported his spiritual worship of Ernestina-Dorothea. He kept Sam, in short, because he was frequently amused by him; not because there were not better "machines" to be found.

But the difference between Sam Weller and Sam Farrow (that is, between 1836 and 1867) was this: the first was happy with his role, the second suffered it. Weller would have answered the bag of soot, and with a verbal vengeance. Sam had stiffened, "rose his hibrows" and turned his back.

8

There rolls the deep where grew the tree,
  O earth, what changes hast thou seen!
  There where the long street roars, hath been
The stillness of the central sea.

The hills are shadows, and they flow
  From form to form, and nothing stands;
  They melt like mist, the solid lands,
Like clouds they shape themselves and go.

TENNYSON, In Memoriam (1850)

But if you wish at once to do nothing and be respectable nowadays, the best pretext is to be at work on
some profound study . . .
  LESLIE STEPHEN, *Sketches from Cambridge* (1865)

Sam's had not been the only dark face in Lyme that morning. Ernestina had woken in a mood that the brilliant promise of the day only aggravated. The ill was familiar; but it
was out of the question that she should inflict its consequences upon Charles. And so, when he called dutifully at ten
o'clock at Aunt Tranter's house, he found himself greeted
only by that lady: Ernestina had passed a slightly disturbed
night, and wished to rest. Might he not return that afternoon
to take tea, when no doubt she would be recovered?

Charles's solicitous inquiries—should the doctor not be
called?—being politely answered in the negative, he took his
leave. And having commanded Sam to buy what flowers he
could and to take them to the charming invalid's house, with
the permission and advice to proffer a blossom or two of his
own to the young lady so hostile to soot, for which light duty
he might take the day as his reward (not all Victorian
employers were directly responsible for communism),
Charles faced his own free hours.

His choice was easy; he would of course have gone wherever Ernestina's health had required him to, but it must be confessed that the fact that it was Lyme Regis had made his pre-marital obligations delightfully easy to support. Stonebarrow, Black Ven, Ware Cliffs—these names may mean very little to you. But Lyme is situated in the center of one of the rare outcrops of a stone known as blue lias. To the mere landscape enthusiast this stone is not attractive. An exceedingly gloomy gray in color, a petrified mud in texture, it is a good deal more forbidding than it is picturesque. It is also treacherous, since its strata are brittle and have a tendency to slide, with the consequence that this little stretch of twelve miles or so of blue lias coast has lost more land to the sea in the course of history than almost any other in England. But its highly fossiliferous nature and its mobility make it a Mecca for the British paleontologist. These last hundred years or more the commonest animal on its shores has been man—wielding a geologist's hammer.

Charles had already visited what was perhaps the most famous shop in the Lyme of those days—the Old Fossil Shop, founded by the remarkable Mary Anning, a woman without formal education but with a genius for discovering good—and on many occasions then unclassified—specimens. She was the first person to see the bones of *Ichthyosaurus platyodon;* and one of the meanest disgraces of British paleontology is that although many scientists of the day gratefully used her finds to establish their own reputation, not one native type bears the specific *anningii.* To this distinguished local memory Charles had paid his homage—and his cash, for various ammonites and *Isocrina* he coveted for the cabinets that walled his study in London. However, he had one disappointment, for he was at that time specializing in a branch of which the Old Fossil Shop had few examples for sale.

This was the echinoderm, or petrified sea urchin. They are sometimes called tests (from the Latin *testa,* a tile or earthen pot); by Americans, sand dollars. Tests vary in shape, though they are always perfectly symmetrical; and they share a pattern of delicately burred striations. Quite apart from their scientific value (a vertical series taken from Beachy Head in the early 1860s was one of the first practical confirmations of the theory of evolution) they are very beautiful little objects; and they have the added charm that they are always difficult to find. You may search for days and not come on one; and a morning in which you find two or three is indeed a morning to remember. Perhaps, as a man with time to fill, a born amateur, this is unconsciously what attracted Charles to them; he had scientific reasons, of course, and with fellow hobbyists he would say indignantly that the *Echinodermia* had been "shamefully neglected," a familiar justification for spending too much time in too small a field. But whatever his motives he had fixed his heart on tests.

Now tests do not come out of the blue lias, but out of the superimposed strata of flint; and the fossil-shop keeper had advised him that it was the area west of the town where he would do best to search, and not necessarily on the shore. Some half-hour after he had called on Aunt Tranter, Charles was once again at the Cobb.

The great mole was far from isolated that day. There were fishermen tarring, mending their nets, tinkering with crab and lobster pots. There were better-class people, early visitors, local residents, strolling beside the still swelling but now mild sea. Of the woman who stared, Charles noted, there was no sign. But he did not give her—or the Cobb—a second thought and set out, with a quick and elastic step very different from his usual languid town stroll, along the beach under Ware Cleeves for his destination.

He would have made you smile, for he was carefully equipped for his role. He wore stout nailed boots and canvas gaiters that rose to encase Norfolk breeches of heavy flannel. There was a tight and absurdly long coat to match; a canvas wideawake hat of an indeterminate beige; a massive ash-plant, which he had bought on his way to the Cobb; and a voluminous rucksack, from which you might have shaken out an already heavy array of hammers, wrappings, notebooks, pillboxes, adzes and heaven knows what else. Nothing is more incomprehensible to us than the methodicality of the Victorians; one sees it best (at its most ludicrous) in the advice so liberally handed out to travelers in the early editions of Baedeker. Where, one wonders, can any pleasure have been left? How, in the case of Charles, can he not have seen that light clothes would have been more comfortable? That a hat was not necessary? That stout nailed boots on a boulder-strewn beach are as suitable as ice skates?

Well, we laugh. But perhaps there is something admirable in this dissociation between what is most comfortable and what is most recommended. We meet here, once again, this bone of contention between the two centuries: is duty* to

---

* I had better here, as a reminder that mid-Victorian (unlike modern) agnosticism and atheism were related strictly to theological dogma, quote George Eliot's famous epigram: "God is inconceivable, immortality is unbelievable, but duty is peremptory and absolute." And all the more peremptory, one might add, in the presence of such a terrible dual lapse of faith.

drive us, or not? If we take this obsession with dressing the part, with being prepared for every eventuality, as mere stupidity, blindness to the empirical, we make, I think, a grave—or rather a frivolous—mistake about our ancestors; because it was men not unlike Charles, and as overdressed and overequipped as he was that day, who laid the foundations of all our modern science. Their folly in that direction was no more than a symptom of their seriousness in a much more important one. They sensed that current accounts of the world were inadequate; that they had allowed their windows on reality to become smeared by convention, religion, social stagnation; they knew, in short, that they had things to discover, and that the discovery was of the utmost importance to the future of man. We think (unless we live in a research laboratory) that we have nothing to discover, and the only things of the utmost importance to us concern the present of man. So much the better for us? Perhaps. But we are not the ones who will finally judge.

So I should not have been too inclined to laugh that day when Charles, as he hammered and bent and examined his way along the shore, tried for the tenth time to span too wide a gap between boulders and slipped ignominiously on his back. Not that Charles much minded slipping, for the day was beautiful, the liassic fossils were plentiful and he soon found himself completely alone.

The sea sparkled, curlews cried. A flock of oyster catchers, black and white and coral-red, flew on ahead of him, harbingers of his passage. Here there came seductive rock pools, and dreadful heresies drifted across the poor fellow's brain—would it not be more fun, no, no, more scientifically valuable, to take up marine biology? Perhaps to give up London, to live in Lyme ... but Ernestina would never allow that. There even came, I am happy to record, a thoroughly human moment in which Charles looked cautiously round, assured his complete solitude and then carefully removed his stout boots, gaiters and stockings. A schoolboy moment, and he tried to remember a line from Homer that would make it a classical moment, but was distracted by the necessity of catching a small crab that scuttled where the gigantic subaqueous shadow fell on its vigilant stalked eyes.

Just as you may despise Charles for his overburden of apparatus, you perhaps despise him for his lack of specialization. But you must remember that natural history had not then the pejorative sense it has today of a flight from reality—and only too often into sentiment. Charles was a quite competent ornithologist and botanist into the bargain. It might perhaps have been better had he shut his eyes to all

44

but the fossil sea urchins or devoted his life to the distribution of algae, if scientific progress is what we are talking about; but think of Darwin, of *The Voyage of the Beagle*. *The Origin of Species* is a triumph of generalization, not specialization; and even if you could prove to me that the latter would have been better for Charles the ungifted scientist, I should still maintain the former was better for Charles the human being. It is not that amateurs can afford to dabble everywhere; they ought to dabble everywhere, and damn the scientific prigs who try to shut them up in some narrow *oubliette*.

Charles called himself a Darwinist, and yet he had not really understood Darwin. But then, nor had Darwin himself. What that genius had upset was the Linnaean *Scala Naturae*, the ladder of nature, whose great keystone, as essential to it as the divinity of Christ to theology, was *nulla species nova:* a new species cannot enter the world. This principle explains the Linnaean obsession with classifying and naming, with fossilizing the existent. We can see it now as a foredoomed attempt to stabilize and fix what is in reality a continuous flux, and it seems highly appropriate that Linnaeus himself finally went mad; he knew he was in a labyrinth, but not that it was one whose walls and passages were eternally changing. Even Darwin never quite shook off the Swedish fetters, and Charles can hardly be blamed for the thoughts that went through his mind as he gazed up at the lias strata in the cliffs above him.

He knew that *nulla species nova* was rubbish; yet he saw in the strata an immensely reassuring orderliness in existence. He might perhaps have seen a very contemporary social symbolism in the way these gray-blue ledges were crumbling; but what he did see was a kind of edificiality of time, in which inexorable laws (therefore beneficently divine, for who could argue that order was not the highest human good?) very conveniently arranged themselves for the survival of the fittest and best, *exemplia gratia* Charles Smithson, this fine spring day, alone, eager and inquiring, understanding, accepting, noting and grateful. What was lacking, of course, was the corollary of the collapse of the ladder of nature: that if new species *can* come into being, old species very often have to make way for them. Personal extinction Charles was aware of—no Victorian could not be. But general extinction was as absent a concept from his mind that day as the smallest cloud from the sky above him; and even though, when he finally resumed his stockings and gaiters and boots, he soon held a very concrete example of it in his hand.

It was a very fine fragment of lias with ammonite impressions, exquisitely clear, microcosms of macrocosms, whirled galaxies that catherine-wheeled their way across ten inches of rock. Having duly inscribed a label with the date and place of finding, he once again hopscotched out of science—this time, into love. He determined to give it to Ernestina when he returned. It was pretty enough for her to like; and after all, very soon it would come back to him, with her. Even better, the increased weight on his back made it a labor, as well as a gift. Duty, agreeable conformity to the epoch's current, raised its stern head.

And so did the awareness that he had wandered more slowly than he meant. He unbuttoned his coat and took out his silver half hunter. Two o'clock! He looked sharply back then, and saw the waves lapping the foot of a point a mile away. He was in no danger of being cut off, since he could see a steep but safe path just ahead of him which led up the cliff to the dense woods above. But he could not return along the shore. His destination had indeed been this path, but he had meant to walk quickly to it, and then up to the levels where the flint strata emerged. As a punishment to himself for his dilatoriness he took the path much too fast, and had to sit a minute to recover, sweating copiously under the abominable flannel. But he heard a little stream nearby and quenched his thirst; wetted his handkerchief and patted his face; and then he began to look around him.

9

> . . . this heart, I know,
> To be long lov'd was never fram'd;
> But something in its depths doth glow
> Too strange, too restless, too untamed.
>
> MATTHEW ARNOLD, "A Farewell" (1853)

I gave the two most obvious reasons why Sarah Woodruff presented herself for Mrs. Poulteney's inspection. But she was the last person to list reasons, however instinctively, and there were many others—indeed there must have been, since she was not unaware of Mrs. Poulteney's reputation in the less elevated *milieux* of Lyme. For a day she had been undecided; then she had gone to see Mrs. Talbot to seek her advice. Now Mrs. Talbot was an extremely kindhearted but a not very perspicacious young woman; and though she would have liked to take Sarah back—indeed, had earlier firmly offered to do so—she was aware that Sarah was now incapable of that sustained and daylong attention to her charges that a governess's duties require. And yet she still wanted very much to help her.

She knew Sarah faced penury; and lay awake at nights imagining scenes from the more romantic literature of her adolescence, scenes in which starving heroines lay huddled on snow-covered doorsteps or fevered in some bare, leaking garret. But one image—an actual illustration from one of Mrs. Sherwood's edifying tales—summed up her worst fears. A pursued woman jumped from a cliff. Lightning flashed, revealing the cruel heads of her persecutors above; but worst of all was the shrieking horror on the doomed creature's pallid face and the way her cloak rippled upwards, vast, black, a falling raven's wing of terrible death.

So Mrs. Talbot concealed her doubts about Mrs. Poulteney and advised Sarah to take the post. The ex-governess kissed little Paul and Virginia goodbye, and walked back to Lyme a condemned woman. She trusted Mrs. Talbot's judgment; and no intelligent woman who trusts a stupid one, however kindhearted, can expect else.

Sarah *was* intelligent, but her real intelligence belonged to a rare kind; one that would certainly pass undetected in any of our modern tests of the faculty. It was not in the least analytical or problem-solving, and it is no doubt symptomatic that the one subject that had cost her agonies to master was mathematics. Nor did it manifest itself in the form of any particular vivacity or wit, even in her happier days. It was rather an uncanny—uncanny in one who had never been to London, never mixed in the world—ability to classify other people's worth: to understand them, in the fullest sense of that word.

She had some sort of psychological equivalent of the experienced horse dealer's skill—the ability to know almost at the first glance the good horse from the bad one; or as if, jumping a century, she was born with a computer in her heart. I say her heart, since the values she computed belong more there than in the mind. She could sense the pretensions of a hollow argument, a false scholarship, a biased logic when she came across them; but she also saw through people in subtler ways. Without being able to say how, any more than a computer can explain its own processes, she saw them as they were and not as they tried to seem. It would not be enough to say she was a fine moral judge of people. Her

47

comprehension was broader than that, and if mere morality had been her touchstone she would not have behaved as she did—the simple fact of the matter being that she had not lodged with a female cousin at Weymouth.

This instinctual profundity of insight was the first curse of her life; the second was her education. It was not a very great education, no better than could be got in a third-rate young ladies' seminary in Exeter, where she had learned during the day and paid for her learning during the evening—and sometimes well into the night—by darning and other menial tasks. She did not get on well with the other pupils. They looked down on her; and she looked up through them. Thus it had come about that she had read far more fiction, and far more poetry, those two sanctuaries of the lonely, than most of her kind. They served as a substitute for experience. Without realizing it she judged people as much by the standards of Walter Scott and Jane Austen as by any empirically arrived at; seeing those around her as fictional characters, and making poetic judgments on them. But alas, what she had thus taught herself had been very largely vitiated by what she had been taught. Given the veneer of a lady, she was made the perfect victim of a caste society. Her father had forced her out of her own class, but could not raise her to the next. To the young men of the one she had left she had become too select to marry; to those of the one she aspired to, she remained too banal.

This father, he the vicar of Lyme had described as "a man of excellent principles," was the very reverse, since he had a fine collection of all the wrong ones. It was not concern for his only daughter that made him send her to boarding school, but obsession with his own ancestry. Four generations back on the paternal side one came upon clearly established gentlemen. There was even a remote relationship with the Drake family, an irrelevant fact that had petrified gradually over the years into the assumption of a direct lineal descent from the great Sir Francis. The family had certainly once owned a manor of sorts in that cold green no-man's-land between Dartmoor and Exmoor. Sarah's father had three times seen it with his own eyes; and returned to the small farm he rented from the vast Meriton estate to brood, and plot, and dream.

Perhaps he was disappointed when his daughter came home from school at the age of eighteen—who knows what miracles he thought would rain on him?—and sat across the elm table from him and watched him when he boasted, watching with a quiet reserve that goaded him, goaded him like a piece of useless machinery (for he was born a Devon man and money means all to Devon men), goaded him

48

finally into madness. He gave up his tenancy and bought a farm of his own; but he bought it too cheap, and what he thought was a cunning good bargain turned out to be a shocking bad one. For several years he struggled to keep up both the mortgage and a ridiculous façade of gentility; then he went quite literally mad and was sent to Dorchester Asylum. He died there a year later. By that time Sarah had been earning her own living for a year—at first with a family in Dorchester, to be near her father. Then when he died, she had taken her post with the Talbots.

She was too striking a girl not to have had suitors, in spite of the lack of a dowry of any kind. But always then had her first and innate curse come into operation; she saw through the too confident pretendants. She saw their meannesses, their condescensions, their charities, their stupidities. Thus she appeared inescapably doomed to the one fate nature had so clearly spent many millions of years in evolving her to avoid: spinsterhood.

Let us imagine the impossible, that Mrs. Poulteney drew up a list of fors and againsts on the subject of Sarah, and on the very day that Charles was occupied in his highly scientific escapade from the onerous duties of his engagement. At least it is conceivable that she might have done it that afternoon, since Sarah, Miss Sarah at Marlborough House, was out.

And let us start happily, with the credit side of the account. The first item would undoubtedly have been the least expected at the time of committal a year before. It could be written so: "A happier domestic atmosphere." The astonishing fact was that not a single servant had been sent on his, or her (statistically it had in the past rather more often proved to be the latter) way.

It had begun, this bizarre change, one morning only a few weeks after Miss Sarah had taken up her duties, that is, her responsibility for Mrs. Poulteney's soul. The old lady had detected with her usual flair a gross dereliction of duty: the upstairs maid whose duty it was unfailingly each Tuesday to water the ferns in the second drawing room—Mrs. Poulteney kept one for herself and one for company—had omitted to do so. The ferns looked greenly forgiving; but Mrs. Poulteney was whitely the contrary. The culprit was summoned. She confessed that she had forgotten; Mrs. Poulteney might ponderously have overlooked that, but the girl had a list of two or three recent similar peccadilloes on her charge sheet. Her knell had rung; and Mrs. Poulteney began, with the grim sense of duty of a bulldog about to sink its teeth into a burglar's ankles, to ring it.

49

"I will tolerate much, but I will not tolerate this."

"I'll never do it again, mum."

"You will most certainly never do it again in my house."

"Oh, mum. Please, mum."

Mrs. Poulteney allowed herself to savor for a few earnest, perceptive moments the girl's tears.

"Mrs. Fairley will give you your wages."

Miss Sarah was present at this conversation, since Mrs. Poulteney had been dictating letters, mostly to bishops or at least in the tone of voice with which one addresses bishops, to her. She now asked a question; and the effect was remarkable. It was, to begin with, the first question she had asked in Mrs. Poulteney's presence that was not directly connected with her duties. Secondly, it tacitly contradicted the old lady's judgment. Thirdly, it was spoken not to Mrs. Poulteney, but to the girl.

"Are you quite well, Millie?"

Whether it was the effect of a sympathetic voice in that room, or the girl's condition, she startled Mrs. Poulteney by sinking to her knees, at the same time shaking her head and covering her face. Miss Sarah was swiftly beside her; and within the next minute had established that the girl was indeed not well, had fainted twice within the last week, had been too afraid to tell anyone . . .

When, some time later, Miss Sarah returned from the room in which the maids slept, and where Millie had now been put to bed, it was Mrs. Poulteney's turn to ask an astounding question.

"What am I to do?"

Miss Sarah had looked her in the eyes, and there was that in her look which made her subsequent words no more than a concession to convention.

"As you think best, ma'm."

So the rarest flower, forgiveness, was given a precarious footing in Marlborough House; and when the doctor came to look at the maid, and pronounced green sickness, Mrs. Poulteney discovered the perverse pleasures of seeming truly kind. There followed one or two other incidents, which, if not so dramatic, took the same course; but only one or two, since Sarah made it her business to do her own forestalling tours of inspection. Sarah had twigged Mrs. Poulteney, and she was soon as adept at handling her as a skilled cardinal, a weak pope; though for nobler ends.

The second, more expectable item on Mrs. Poulteney's hypothetical list would have been: "Her voice." If the mistress was defective in more mundane matters where her staff was concerned, she took exceedingly good care of their

50

spiritual welfare. There was the mandatory double visit to church on Sundays; and there was also a daily morning service—a hymn, a lesson, and prayers—over which the old lady pompously presided. Now it had always vexed her that not even her most terrible stares could reduce her servants to that state of utter meekness and repentance which she considered their God (let alone hers) must require. Their normal face was a mixture of fear at Mrs. Poulteney and dumb incomprehension—like abashed sheep rather than converted sinners. But Sarah changed all that.

Hers was certainly a very beautiful voice, controlled and clear, though always shaded with sorrow and often intense in feeling; but above all, it was a sincere voice. For the first time in her ungrateful little world Mrs. Poulteney saw her servants with genuinely attentive and sometimes positively religious faces.

That was good; but there was a second bout of worship to be got through. The servants were permitted to hold evening prayer in the kitchen, under Mrs. Fairley's indifferent eye and briskly wooden voice. Upstairs, Mrs. Poulteney had to be read to alone; and it was in these more intimate ceremonies that Sarah's voice was heard at its best and most effective. Once or twice she had done the incredible, by drawing from those pouched, invincible eyes a tear. Such an effect was in no way intended, but sprang from a profound difference between the two women. Mrs. Poulteney believed in a God that had never existed; and Sarah knew a God that did.

She did not create in her voice, like so many worthy priests and dignitaries asked to read the lesson, an unconscious alienation effect of the Brechtian kind ("This is your mayor reading a passage from the Bible") but the very contrary: she spoke directly of the suffering of Christ, of a man born in Nazareth, as if there was no time in history, almost, at times, when the light in the room was dark, and she seemed to forget Mrs. Poulteney's presence, as if she saw Christ on the Cross before her. One day she came to the passage *Lama, lama, sabachthane me;* and as she read the words she faltered and was silent. Mrs. Poulteney turned to look at her, and realized Sarah's face was streaming with tears. That moment redeemed an infinity of later difficulties; and perhaps, since the old lady rose and touched the girl's drooping shoulder, will one day redeem Mrs. Poulteney's now well-grilled soul.

I risk making Sarah sound like a bigot. But she had no theology; as she saw through people, she saw through the follies, the vulgar stained glass, the narrow literalness of the Victorian church. She saw that there was suffering; and she

51

prayed that it would end. I cannot say what she might have been in our age; in a much earlier one I believe she would have been either a saint or an emperor's mistress. Not because of religiosity on the one hand, or sexuality on the other, but because of that fused rare power that was her essence—understanding and emotion.

There were other items: an ability—formidable in itself and almost unique—not often to get on Mrs. Poulteney's nerves, a quiet assumption of various domestic responsibilities that did not encroach, a skill with her needle.

On Mrs. Poulteney's birthday Sarah presented her with an antimacassar—not that any chair Mrs. Poulteney sat in needed such protection, but by that time all chairs without such an adjunct seemed somehow naked—exquisitely embroidered with a border of ferns and lilies-of-the-valley. It pleased Mrs. Poulteney highly; and it slyly and permanently—perhaps after all Sarah really was something of a skilled cardinal— reminded the ogress, each time she took her throne, of her *protégée*'s forgivable side. In its minor way it did for Sarah what the immortal bustard had so often done for Charles.

Finally—and this had been the cruelest ordeal for the victim—Sarah had passed the tract test. Like many insulated Victorian dowagers, Mrs. Poulteney placed great reliance on the power of the tract. Never mind that not one in ten of the recipients could read them—indeed, quite a number could not read anything—never mind that not one in ten of those who could and did read them understood what the reverend writers were on about . . . but each time Sarah departed with a batch to deliver Mrs. Poulteney saw an equivalent number of saved souls chalked up to her account in heaven; and she also saw the French Lieutenant's Woman doing public penance, an added sweet. So did the rest of Lyme, or poorer Lyme; and were kinder than Mrs. Poulteney may have realized.

Sarah evolved a little formula: "From Mrs. Poulteney. Pray read and take to your heart." At the same time she looked the cottager in the eyes. Those who had knowing smiles soon lost them; and the loquacious found their words die in their mouths. I think they learned rather more from those eyes than from the close-typed pamphlets thrust into their hands.

But we must now pass to the debit side of the relationship. First and foremost would undoubtedly have been: "She goes out alone." The arrangement had initially been that Miss Sarah should have one afternoon a week free, which was considered by Mrs. Poulteney a more than generous acknowledgment of her superior status vis-à-vis the maids' and only then condoned by the need to disseminate tracts; but the vicar had advised it. All seemed well for two months. Then one morning Miss Sarah did not appear at the Marlborough House matins; and when the maid was sent to look for her, it was discovered that she had not risen. Mrs. Poulteney went to see her. Again Sarah was in tears, but on this occasion Mrs. Poulteney felt only irritation. However, she sent for the doctor. He remained closeted with Sarah a long time. When he came down to the impatient Mrs. Poulteney, he gave her a brief lecture on melancholia—he was an advanced man for his time and place—and ordered her to allow her sinner more fresh air and freedom.

"If you insist on the most urgent necessity for it."

"My dear madam, I do. And most emphatically. I will not be responsible otherwise."

"It is very inconvenient." But the doctor was brutally silent. "I will dispense with her for two afternoons."

Unlike the vicar, Doctor Grogan was not financially very dependent on Mrs. Poulteney; to be frank, there was not a death certificate in Lyme he would have less sadly signed than hers. But he contained his bile by reminding her that she slept every afternoon; and on his own strict orders. Thus it was that Sarah achieved a daily demi-liberty.

The next debit item was this: "May not always be present with visitors." Here Mrs. Poulteney found herself in a really intolerable dilemma. She most certainly wanted her charity to be seen, which meant that Sarah had to be seen. But that face had the most harmful effect on company. Its sadness reproached; its very rare interventions in conversation— invariably prompted by some previous question that had to be answered (the more intelligent frequent visitors soon learned to make their polite turns towards the companion-secretary clearly rhetorical in nature and intent)—had a disquietingly decisive character about them, not through any desire on Sarah's part to kill the subject but simply because of the innocent imposition of simplicity or common sense on some matter that thrived on the opposite qualities. To Mrs. Poulteney she seemed in this context only too much like one of the figures on a gibbet she dimly remembered from her youth.

Once again Sarah showed her diplomacy. With certain old-established visitors, she remained; with others she either withdrew in the first few minutes or discreetly left when they were announced and before they were ushered in. This latter reason was why Ernestina had never met her at Marlborough House. It at least allowed Mrs. Poulteney to expatiate on the cross she had to carry, though the cross's withdrawal or absence implied a certain failure in her skill in carrying it, which was most tiresome. Yet Sarah herself could hardly be faulted.

But I have left the worst matter to the end. It was this: "Still shows signs of attachment to her seducer."

Mrs. Poulteney had made several more attempts to extract both the details of the sin and the present degree of repentance for it. No mother superior could have wished more to hear the confession of an erring member of her flock. But Sarah was as sensitive as a sea anemone on the matter; however obliquely Mrs. Poulteney approached the subject, the sinner guessed what was coming; and her answers to direct questions were always the same in content, if not in actual words, as the one she had given at her first interrogation.

Now Mrs. Poulteney seldom went out, and never on foot, and in her barouche only to the houses of her equals, so that she had to rely on other eyes for news of Sarah's activities outside her house. Fortunately for her such a pair of eyes existed; even better, the mind behind those eyes was directed by malice and resentment, and was therefore happy to bring frequent reports to the thwarted mistress. This spy, of course, was none other than Mrs. Fairley. Though she had found no pleasure in reading, it offended her that she had been demoted; and although Miss Sarah was scrupulously polite to her and took care not to seem to be usurping the housekeeper's functions, there was inevitably some conflict. It did not please Mrs. Fairley that she had a little less work, since that meant also a little less influence. Sarah's saving of Millie—and other more discreet interventions—made her popular and respected downstairs; and perhaps Mrs. Fairley's deepest rage was that she could not speak ill of the secretary-companion to her underlings. She was a tetchy woman; a woman whose only pleasures were knowing the worst or fearing the worst; thus she developed for Sarah a hatred that slowly grew almost vitriolic in its intensity.

She was too shrewd a weasel not to hide this from Mrs. Poulteney. Indeed she made a pretense of being very sorry for "poor Miss Woodruff" and her reports were plentifully seasoned with "I fear" and "I am afraid." But she had excellent opportunities to do her spying, for not only was she frequently in the town herself in connection with her duties, but she had also a wide network of relations and acquaintances at her command. To these latter she hinted that Mrs. Poulteney was concerned—of course for the best and most Christian of reasons—to be informed of Miss Woodruff's behavior outside the tall stone walls of the gardens of Marlborough House. The result, Lyme Regis being then as now as riddled with gossip as a drum of Blue Vinny with maggots, was that Sarah's every movement and expression—darkly exaggerated and abundantly glossed—in her free hours was soon known to Mrs. Fairley.

The pattern of her exterior movements—when she was spared the tracts—was very simple; she always went for the same afternoon walk, down steep Pound Street into steep Broad Street and thence to the Cobb Gate, which is a square terrace overlooking the sea and has nothing to do with the Cobb. There she would stand at the wall and look out to sea, but generally not for long—no longer than the careful appraisal a ship's captain gives when he comes out on the bridge—before turning either down Cockmoil or going in the other direction, westwards, along the half-mile path that runs round a gentle bay to the Cobb proper. If she went down Cockmoil she would most often turn into the parish church, and pray for a few minutes (a fact that Mrs. Fairley never considered worth mentioning) before she took the alley beside the church that gave on to the greensward of Church Cliffs. The turf there climbed towards the broken walls of Black Ven. Up this grassland she might be seen walking, with frequent turns towards the sea, to where the path joined the old road to Charmouth, now long eroded into the Ven, whence she would return to Lyme. This walk she would do when the Cobb seemed crowded; but when weather or circumstance made it deserted, she would more often turn that way and end by standing where Charles had first seen her; there, it was supposed, she felt herself nearest to France.

All this, suitably distorted and draped in black, came back to Mrs. Poulteney. But she was then in the first possessive pleasure of her new toy, and as sympathetically disposed as it was in her sour and suspicious old nature to be. She did not, however, hesitate to take the toy to task.

"I am told, Miss Woodruff, that you are always to be seen in the same places when you go out." Sarah looked down before the accusing eyes. "You look to sea." Still Sarah was silent. "I am satisfied that you are in a state of repentance. Indeed I cannot believe that you should be anything else in your present circumstances."

Sarah took her cue. "I am grateful to you, ma'm."

"I am not concerned with your gratitude to me. There is One Above who has a prior claim."

The girl murmured, "How should I not know it?"

"To the ignorant it may seem that you are persevering in your sin."

55

"If they know my story, ma'm, they cannot think that."

"But they do think that. I am told they say you are looking for Satan's sails."

Sarah rose then and went to the window. It was early summer, and scent of syringa and lilac mingled with the blackbirds' songs. She gazed for a moment out over that sea she was asked to deny herself, then turned back to the old lady, who sat as implacably in her armchair as the Queen on her throne.

"Do you wish me to leave, ma'm?"

Mrs. Poulteney was inwardly shocked. Once again Sarah's simplicity took all the wind from her swelling spite. The voice, the other charms, to which she had become so addicted! Far worse, she might throw away the interest accruing to her on those heavenly ledgers. She moderated her tone.

"I wish you to show that this ... person is expunged from your heart. I know that he is. But you must show it."

"How am I to show it?"

"By walking elsewhere. By not exhibiting your shame. If for no other reason, because I request it."

Sarah stood with bowed head, and there was a silence. But then she looked Mrs. Poulteney in the eyes and for the first time since her arrival, she gave the faintest smile.

"I will do as you wish, ma'm."

It was, in chess terms, a shrewd sacrifice, since Mrs. Poulteney graciously went on to say that she did not want to deny her completely the benefits of the sea air and that she might on occasion walk by the sea; but not always by the sea—"and pray do not stand and stare so." It was, in short, a bargain struck between two obsessions. Sarah's offer to leave had let both women see the truth, in their different ways.

Sarah kept her side of the bargain, or at least that part of it that concerned the itinerary of her walks. She now went very rarely to the Cobb, though when she did, she still sometimes allowed herself to stand and stare, as on the day we have described. After all, the countryside around Lyme abounds in walks; and few of them do not give a view of the sea. If that had been all Sarah craved she had but to walk over the lawns of Marlborough House.

Mrs. Fairley, then, had a poor time of it for many months. No occasion on which the stopping and staring took place was omitted; but they were not frequent, and Sarah had by this time acquired a kind of ascendancy of suffering over Mrs. Poulteney that saved her from any serious criticism. And after all, as the spy and the mistress often reminded each other, poor "Tragedy" was mad.

You will no doubt have guessed the truth: that she was far

56

less mad than she seemed . . . or at least not mad in the way that was generally supposed. Her exhibition of her shame had a kind of purpose; and people with purposes know when they have been sufficiently attained and can be allowed to rest in abeyance for a while.

But one day, not a fortnight before the beginning of my story, Mrs. Fairley had come to Mrs. Poulteney with her creaking stays and the face of one about to announce the death of a close friend.

"I have something unhappy to communicate, ma'm."

This phrase had become as familiar to Mrs. Poulteney as a storm cone to a fisherman; but she observed convention.

"It cannot concern Miss Woodruff?"

"Would that it did not, ma'm." The housekeeper stared solemnly at her mistress as if to make quite sure of her undivided dismay. "But I fear it is my duty to tell you."

"We must never fear what is our duty."

"No, ma'm."

Still the mouth remained clamped shut; and a third party might well have wondered what horror could be coming. Nothing less than dancing naked on the altar of the parish church would have seemed adequate.

"She has taken to walking, ma'm, on Ware Commons."

Such an anticlimax! Yet Mrs. Poulteney seemed not to think so. Indeed her mouth did something extraordinary. It fell open.

10

And once, but once, she lifted her eyes,
And suddenly, sweetly, strangely blush'd
To find they were met by my own . . .

                                    TENNYSON, *Maud* (1855)

. . . with its green chasms between romantic rocks,
where the scattered forest trees and orchards of luxuriant growth declare that many a generation must have
passed away since the first partial falling of the cliff
prepared the ground for such a state, where a scene
so wonderful and so lovely is exhibited, as may more
than equal any of the resembling scenes of the far-
famed Isle of Wight . . .

                                    JANE AUSTEN, *Persuasion*

There runs, between Lyme Regis and Axmouth six miles to
the west, one of the strangest coastal landscapes in Southern
England. From the air it is not very striking; one notes
merely that whereas elsewhere on the coast the fields run to
the cliff edge, here they stop a mile or so short of it. The
cultivated chequer of green and red-brown breaks, with a
kind of joyous undiscipline, into a dark cascade of trees and
undergrowth. There are no roofs. If one flies low enough one
can see that the terrain is very abrupt, cut by deep chasms
and accented by strange bluffs and towers of chalk and flint,
which loom over the lush foliage around them like the walls
of ruined castles. From the air . . . but on foot this seemingly
unimportant wilderness gains a strange extension. People
have been lost in it for hours, and cannot believe, when they
see on the map where they were lost, that their sense of
isolation—and if the weather be bad, desolation—could have
seemed so great.

The Undercliff—for this land is really the mile-long slope
caused by the erosion of the ancient vertical cliff face—is
very steep. Flat places are as rare as visitors in it. But this

steepness in effect tilts it, and its vegetation, towards the sun; and it is this fact, together with the water from the countless springs that have caused the erosion, that lends the area its botanical strangeness—its wild arbutus and ilex and other trees rarely seen growing in England; its enormous ashes and beeches; its green Brazilian chasms choked with ivy and the liana of wild clematis; its bracken that grows seven, eight feet tall; its flowers that bloom a month earlier than any-where else in the district. In summer it is the nearest this country can offer to a tropical jungle. It has also, like all land that has never been worked or lived on by man, its mysteries, its shadows, its dangers—only too literal ones geologically, since there are crevices and sudden falls that can bring disaster, and in places where a man with a broken leg could shout all week and not be heard. Strange as it may seem, it was slightly less solitary a hundred years ago than it is today. There is not a single cottage in the Undercliff now; in 1867 there were several, lived in by gamekeepers, woodmen, a pigherd or two. The roedeer, sure proof of abundant soli-tude, then must have passed less peaceful days. Now the Undercliff has reverted to a state of total wildness. The cottage walls have crumbled into ivied stumps, the old branch paths have gone; no car road goes near it, the one remaining track that traverses it is often impassable. And it is so by Act of Parliament: a national nature reserve. Not all is lost to expedience.

It was this place, an English Garden of Eden on such a day as March 29th, 1867, that Charles had entered when he had climbed the path from the shore at Pinhay Bay; and it was this same place whose eastern half was called Ware Commons.

When Charles had quenched his thirst and cooled his brow with his wetted handkerchief he began to look seriously around him. Or at least he tried to look seriously around him; but the little slope on which he found himself, the prospect before him, the sounds, the scents, the unalloyed wildness of growth and burgeoning fertility, forced him into anti-science. The ground about him was studded gold and pale yellow with celandines and primroses and banked by the bridal white of densely blossoming sloe; where jubilantly green-tipped elders shaded the mossy banks of the little brook he had drunk from were clusters of moschatel and woodsorrel, most deli-cate of English spring flowers. Higher up the slope he saw the white heads of anemones, and beyond them deep green drifts of bluebell leaves. A distant woodpecker drummed in the branches of some high tree, and bullfinches whistled quietly over his head; newly arrived chiffchaffs and willow warblers sang in every bush and treetop. When he turned he saw the blue sea, now washing far below; and the whole extent of Lyme Bay reaching round, diminishing cliffs that dropped into the endless yellow saber of the Chesil Bank, whose remote tip touched that strange English Gibraltar, Portland Bill, a thin gray shadow wedged between azures.

Only one art has ever caught such scenes—that of the Renaissance; it is the ground that Botticelli's figures walk on, the air that includes Ronsard's songs. It does not matter what that cultural revolution's conscious aims and purposes, its cruelties and failures were; in essence the Renaissance was simply the green end of one of civilization's hardest winters. It was an end to chains, bounds, frontiers. Its device was the only device: What is, is good. It was all, in short, that Charles's age was not; but do not think that as he stood there he did not know this. It is true that to explain his obscure feeling of malaise, of inappropriateness, of limitation, he went back closer home—to Rousseau, and the childish myths of a Golden Age and the Noble Savage. That is, he tried to dismiss the inadequacies of his own time's approach to nature by supposing that one cannot reenter a legend. He told himself he was too pampered, too spoiled by civilization, ever to inhabit nature again; and that made him sad, in a not unpleasant bittersweet sort of way. After all, he was a Victorian. We could not expect him to see what we are only just beginning—and with so much more knowledge and the lessons of existentialist philosophy at our disposal—to realize ourselves: that the desire to hold and the desire to enjoy are mutually destructive. His statement to himself should have been, "I possess this now, therefore I am happy," instead of what it so Victorianly was: "I cannot possess this forever, and therefore am sad."

Science eventually regained its hegemony, and he began to search among the beds of flint along the course of the stream for his tests. He found a pretty fragment of fossil scallop, but the sea urchins eluded him. Gradually he moved through the trees to the west, bending, carefully quartering the ground with his eyes, moving on a few paces, then repeating the same procedure. Now and then he would turn over a likely-looking flint with the end of his ashplant. But he had no luck. An hour passed, and his duty towards Ernestina began to outweigh his lust for echinoderms. He looked at his watch, repressed a curse, and made his way back to where he had left his rucksack. Some way up the slope, with the declining sun on his back, he came on a path and set off for Lyme. The path climbed and curved slightly inward beside an ivy-grown stone wall and then—in the unkind manner of paths—forked without indication. He hesitated, then walked some fifty yards or so along the lower path, which lay sunk in a transverse gully, already deeply shadowed. But then he came to a solution to his problem—not knowing exactly how the land lay—for yet another path suddenly branched to his right, back towards the sea, up a steep small slope crowned with grass, and from which he could plainly orientate himself. He therefore pushed up through the strands of bramble—the path was seldom used—to the little green plateau.

It opened out very agreeably, like a tiny alpine meadow. The white scuts of three or four rabbits explained why the turf was so short.

Charles stood in the sunlight. Eyebright and birdsfoot starred the grass, and already vivid green clumps of marjoram reached up to bloom. Then he moved forward to the edge of the plateau.

And there, below him, he saw a figure.

For one terrible moment he thought he had stumbled on a corpse. But it was a woman asleep. She had chosen the strangest position, a broad, sloping ledge of grass some five feet beneath the level of the plateau, and which hid her from the view of any but one who came, as Charles had, to the very edge. The chalk walls behind this little natural balcony made it into a sun trap, for its widest axis pointed southwest. But it was not a sun trap many would have chosen. Its outer edge gave onto a sheer drop of some thirty or forty feet into an ugly tangle of brambles. A little beyond them the real cliff plunged down to the beach.

Charles's immediate instinct had been to draw back out of the woman's view. He did not see who she was. He stood at a loss, looking at but not seeing the fine landscape the place commanded. He hesitated, he was about to withdraw; but then his curiosity drew him forward again.

The girl lay in the complete abandonment of deep sleep, on her back. Her coat had fallen open over her indigo dress, unrelieved in its calico severity except by a small white collar at the throat. The sleeper's face was turned away from him, her right arm thrown back, bent in a childlike way. A scattered handful of anemones lay on the grass around it. There was something intensely tender and yet sexual in the way she lay; it awakened a dim echo of Charles of a moment from his time in Paris. Another girl, whose name now he could not even remember, perhaps had never known, seen sleeping so, one dawn, in a bedroom overlooking the Seine.

He moved round the curving lip of the plateau, to where he could see the sleeper's face better, and it was only then that he realized whom he had intruded upon. It was the French Lieutenant's Woman. Part of her hair had become loose and half covered her cheek. On the Cobb it had seemed to him a dark brown; now he saw that it had red tints, a rich warmth, and without the then indispensable gloss of feminine hair oil. The skin below seemed very brown, almost ruddy, in that light, as if the girl cared more for health than a fashionably pale and languid-cheeked complexion. A strong nose, heavy eyebrows ... the mouth he could not see. It irked him strangely that he had to see her upside down, since the land would not allow him to pass round for the proper angle.

He stood unable to do anything but stare down, tranced by this unexpected encounter, and overcome by an equally strange feeling—not sexual, but fraternal, perhaps paternal, a certainty of the innocence of this creature, of her being unfairly outcast, and which was in turn a factor of his intuition of her appalling loneliness. He could not imagine what, besides despair, could drive her, in an age where women were semistatic, timid, incapable of sustained physical effort, to this wild place.

He came at last to the very edge of the rampart above her, directly over her face, and there he saw that all the sadness he had so remarked before was gone; in sleep the face was gentle, it might even have had the ghost of a smile. It was precisely then, as he craned sideways down, that she awoke.

She looked up at once, so quickly that his step back was in vain. He was detected, and he was too much a gentleman to deny it. So when Sarah scrambled to her feet, gathering her coat about her, and stared back up at him from her ledge, he raised his wideawake and bowed. She said nothing, but fixed him with a look of shock and bewilderment, perhaps not untinged with shame. She had fine eyes, dark eyes.

They stood thus for several seconds, locked in a mutual incomprehension. She seemed so small to him, standing there below him, hidden from the waist down, clutching her collar, as if, should he take a step towards her, she would turn and fling herself out of his sight. He came to his sense of what was proper.

"A thousand apologies. I came upon you inadvertently." And then he turned and walked away. He did not look back, but scrambled down to the path he had left, and back to the fork, where he wondered why he had not had the presence of mind to ask which path he was to take, and waited half a minute to see if she was following him. She did not appear. Very soon he marched firmly away up the steeper path.

Charles did not know it, but in those brief poised seconds

above the waiting sea, in that luminous evening silence broken only by the waves' quiet wash, the whole Victorian Age was lost. And I do not mean he had taken the wrong path.

11

With the form conforming duly,
Senseless what it meaneth truly,
Go to church—the world require you,
To balls—the world require you too,
And marry—papa and mama desire you,
And your sisters and schoolfellows do.

A. H. CLOUGH, "Duty" (1841)

"Oh! no, what he!" she cried in scorn,
"I woulden gi'e a penny vor'n;
The best ov him's outzide in view;
His cwoat is gay enough, 'tis true,
But then the wold vo'k didden bring
En up to know a single thing . . ."

WILLIAM BARNES, Poems in the Dorset Dialect (1869)

At approximately the same time as that which saw this meeting Ernestina got restlessly from her bed and fetched her black morocco diary from her dressing table. She first turned rather sulkily to her entry of that morning, which was certainly not very inspired from a literary point of view: "Wrote letter to Mama. Did not see dearest Charles. Did not go out, tho' it is very fine. Did not feel happy."

It had been a very did-not sort of day for the poor girl, who had had only Aunt Tranter to show her displeasure to. There had been Charles's daffodils and jonquils, whose perfume she now inhaled, but even they had vexed her at first. Aunt Tranter's house was small, and she had heard Sam knock on the front door downstairs; she had heard the wicked and irreverent Mary open it—a murmur of voices and then a distinct, suppressed gurgle of laughter from the maid, a slammed door. The odious and abominable suspicion crossed her mind that Charles had been down there, flirting; and this touched on one of her deepest fears about him.

She knew he had lived in Paris, in Lisbon, and traveled much; she knew he was eleven years older than herself;

she knew he was attractive to women. His answers to her discreetly playful interrogations about his past conquests were always discreetly playful in return; and that was the rub. She felt he must be hiding something—a tragic French countess, a passionate Portuguese marquesa. Her mind did not allow itself to run to a Parisian *grisette* or an almond-eyed inn-girl at Cintra, which would have been rather nearer the truth. But in a way the matter of whether he had slept with other women worried her less than it might a modern girl. Of course Ernestina uttered her autocratic "I must not" just as soon as any such sinful speculation crossed her mind; but it was really Charles's heart of which she was jealous. That, she could not bear to think of having to share, either historically or presently. Occam's useful razor was unknown to her. Thus the simple fact that he had never really been in love became clear proof to Ernestina, on her darker days, that he had once been passionately so. His calm exterior she took for the terrible silence of a recent battlefield, Waterloo a month after; instead of for what it really was—a place without history.

When the front door closed, Ernestina allowed dignity to control her for precisely one and a half minutes, whereupon her fragile little hand reached out and peremptorily pulled the gilt handle beside her bed. A pleasantly insistent tinkle filtered up from the basement kitchen; and soon afterwards, there were footsteps, a knock, and the door opened to reveal Mary bearing a vase with a positive fountain of spring flowers. The girl came and stood by the bed, her face half hidden by the blossoms, smiling, impossible for a man to have been angry with—and therefore quite the reverse to Ernestina, who frowned sourly and reproachfully at this unwelcome vision of Flora.

Of the three young women who pass through these pages Mary was, in my opinion, by far the prettiest. She had infinitely the most life, and infinitely the least selfishness; and physical charms to match ... an exquisitely pure, if pink complexion, corn-colored hair and delectably wide gray-blue eyes, eyes that invited male provocation and returned it as gaily as it was given. They bubbled as the best champagne bubbles, irrepressibly; and without causing flatulence. Not even the sad Victorian clothes she had so often to wear could hide the trim, plump promise of her figure—indeed, "plump" is unkind. I brought up Ronsard's name just now; and her figure required a word from his vocabulary, one for which we have no equivalent in English: *rondelet*—all that is seductive in plumpness without losing all that is nice in slimness.

Mary's great-great-granddaughter, who is twenty-two years old this month I write in, much resembles her ancestor; and her face is known over the entire world, for she is one of the more celebrated younger English film actresses.

But it was not, I am afraid, the face for 1867. It had not, for instance, been at all the face for Mrs. Poulteney, to whom it had become familiar some three years previously. Mary was the niece of a cousin of Mrs. Fairley, who had wheedled Mrs. Poulteney into taking the novice into the unkind kitchen. But Marlborough House and Mary had suited each other as well as a tomb would a goldfinch; and when one day Mrs. Poulteney was somberly surveying her domain and saw from her upstairs window the disgusting sight of her stableboy soliciting a kiss, and not being very successfully resisted, the goldfinch was given an instant liberty; whereupon it flew to Mrs. Tranter's, in spite of Mrs. Poulteney's solemn warnings to that lady as to the foolhardiness of harboring such proven dissoluteness.

In Broad Street Mary was happy. Mrs. Tranter liked pretty girls; and pretty, laughing girls even better. Of course, Ernestina was her niece, and she worried for her more; but Ernestina she saw only once or twice a year, and Mary she saw every day. Below her mobile, flirtatious surface the girl had a gentle affectionateness; and she did not stint, she returned the warmth that was given. Ernestina did not know a dreadful secret of that house in Broad Street; there were times, if cook had a day off, when Mrs. Tranter sat and ate with Mary alone in the downstairs kitchen; and they were not the unhappiest hours in either of their lives.

Mary was not faultless; and one of her faults was a certain envy of Ernestina. It was not only that she ceased abruptly to be the tacit favorite of the household when the young lady from London arrived; but the young lady from London came also with trunkfuls of the latest London and Paris fashions, not the best recommendation to a servant with only three dresses to her name—and not one of which she really liked, even though the best of them she could really dislike only because it had been handed down by the young princess from the capital. She also thought Charles was a beautiful man for a husband; a great deal too good for a pallid creature like Ernestina. This was why Charles had the frequent benefit of those gray-and-periwinkle eyes when she opened the door to him or passed him in the street. In wicked fact the creature picked her exits and entrances to coincide with Charles's; and each time he raised his hat to her in the street she mentally cocked her nose at Ernestina; for she knew very well why Mrs. Tranter's niece went upstairs so abruptly after Charles's departures. Like all *soubrettes,* she dared to think things her young mistress did not; and knew it.

Having duly and maliciously allowed her health and cheerfulness to register on the invalid, Mary placed the flowers on the bedside commode.

"From Mr. Charles, Miss Tina. With 'er complimums." Mary spoke in a dialect notorious for its contempt of pronouns and suffixes.

"Place them on my dressing table. I do not like them so close."

Mary obediently removed them there and disobediently began to rearrange them a little before turning to smile at the suspicious Ernestina.

"Did he bring them himself?"

"No, miss."

"Where is Mr. Charles?"

"Doan know, miss. I didn' ask'un." But her mouth was pressed too tightly together, as if she wanted to giggle.

"But I heard you speak with the man."

"Yes, miss."

"What about?"

" 'Twas just the time o' day, miss."

"Is that what made you laugh?"

"Yes, miss. 'Tis the way 'e speaks, miss."

The Sam who had presented himself at the door had in fact borne very little resemblance to the mournful and indignant young man who had stropped the razor. He had thrust the handsome bouquet into the mischievous Mary's arms. "For the bootiful young lady hupstairs." Then dexterously he had placed his foot where the door had been about to shut and as dexterously produced from behind his back, in his other hand, while his now free one swept off his *à la mode* near-brimless topper, a little posy of crocuses. "And for the heven more lovely one down." Mary had blushed a deep pink; the pressure of the door on Sam's foot had mysteriously lightened. He watched her smell the yellow flowers; not politely, but genuinely, so that a tiny orange smudge of saffron appeared on the charming, impertinent nose.

"That there bag o' soot will be delivered as hordered." She bit her lips, and waited. "Hon one condition. No tick. Hit must be a-paid for at once."

" 'Ow much would'er cost then?"

The forward fellow eyed his victim, as if calculating a fair price; then laid a finger on his mouth and gave a profoundly unambiguous wink. It was this that had provoked that smothered laugh; and the slammed door.

Ernestina gave her a look that would have not disgraced Mrs. Poulteney. "You will kindly remember that he comes from London."

"Yes, miss."

"Mr. Smithson has already spoken to me of him. The man fancies himself a Don Juan."

"What's that then, Miss Tina?"

There was a certain eager anxiety for further information in Mary's face that displeased Ernestina very much.

"Never mind now. But if he makes advances I wish to be told at once. Now bring me some barley water. And be more discreet in future."

There passed a tiny light in Mary's eyes, something singularly like a flash of defiance. But she cast down her eyes and her flat little lace cap, bobbing a token curtsy, and left the room. Three flights down, and three flights up, as Ernestina, who had not the least desire for Aunt Tranter's wholesome but uninteresting barley water, consoled herself by remembering.

But Mary had in a sense won the exchange, for it reminded Ernestina, not by nature a domestic tyrant but simply a horrid spoiled child, that soon she would have to stop playing at mistress, and be one in real earnest. The idea brought pleasures, of course; to have one's own house, to be free of parents ... but servants were such a problem, as everyone said. Were no longer what they were, as everyone said. Were tiresome, in a word. Perhaps Ernestina's puzzlement and distress were not far removed from those of Charles, as he had sweated and stumbled his way along the shore. Life was the correct apparatus; it was heresy to think otherwise; but meanwhile the cross had to be borne, here and now.

It was to banish such gloomy forebodings, still with her in the afternoon, that Ernestina fetched her diary, propped herself up in bed and once more turned to the page with the sprig of jasmine.

In London the beginnings of a plutocratic stratification of society had, by the mid-century, begun. Nothing of course took the place of good blood; but it had become generally accepted that good money and good brains could produce artificially a passable enough facsimile of acceptable social standing. Disraeli was the type, not the exception, of his times. Ernestina's grandfather may have been no more than a well-to-do draper in Stoke Newington when he was young; but he died a very rich draper—much more than that, since he had moved commercially into central London, founded one of the West End's great stores and extended his business

67

into many departments besides drapery. Her father, indeed, had given her only what he had himself received: the best education that money could buy. In all except his origins he was impeccably a gentleman; and he had married discreetly above him, a daughter of one of the City's most successful solicitors, who could number an Attorney-General, no less, among his not-too-distant ancestors. Ernestina's qualms about her social status were therefore rather farfetched, even by Victorian standards; and they had never in the least troubled Charles.

"Do but think," he had once said to her, "how disgracefully plebeian a name Smithson is."

"Ah indeed—if you were only called Lord Brabazon Vavasour Vere de Vere—how much more I should love you!"

But behind her self-mockery lurked a fear.

He had first met her the preceding November, at the house of a lady who had her eye on him for one of her own covey of simperers. These young ladies had had the misfortune to be briefed by their parents before the evening began. They made the cardinal error of trying to pretend to Charles that paleontology absorbed them—he must give them the titles of the most interesting books on the subject—whereas Ernestina showed a gently acid little determination not to take him very seriously. She would, she murmured, send him any interesting specimens of coal she came across in her scuttle; and later she told him she thought he was very lazy. Why, pray? Because he could hardly enter any London drawing room without finding abundant examples of the objects of his interest.

To both young people it had promised to be just one more dull evening; and both, when they returned to their respective homes, found that it had not been so.

They saw in each other a superiority of intelligence, a lightness of touch, a dryness that pleased. Ernestina let it be known that she had found "that Mr. Smithson" an agreeable change from the dull crop of partners hitherto presented for her examination that season. Her mother made discreet inquiries; and consulted her husband, who made more; for no young male ever set foot in the drawing room of the house overlooking Hyde Park who had not been as well vetted as any modern security department vets its atomic scientists. Charles passed his secret ordeal with flying colors.

Now Ernestina had seen the mistake of her rivals: that no wife thrown at Charles's head would ever touch his heart. So when he began to frequent her mother's at homes and *soirées* he had the unusual experience of finding that there was no sign of the usual matrimonial trap; no sly hints from the mother of how much the sweet darling loved children or "secretly longed for the end of the season" (it was supposed that Charles would live permanently at Winsyatt, as soon as the obstacular uncle did his duty); or less sly ones from the father on the size of the fortune "my dearest girl" would bring to her husband. The latter were, in any case, conspicuously unnecessary; the Hyde Park house was fit for a duke to live in, and the absence of brothers and sisters said more than a thousand bank statements.

Nor did Ernestina, although she was very soon wildly determined, as only a spoiled daughter can be, to have Charles, overplay her hand. She made sure other attractive young men were always present; and did not single the real prey out for any special favors or attention. She was, on principle, never serious with him; without exactly saying so she gave him the impression that she liked him because he was fun—but of course she knew he would never marry. Then came an evening in January when she decided to plant the fatal seed.

She saw Charles standing alone; and on the opposite side of the room she saw an aged dowager, a kind of Mayfair equivalent of Mrs. Poulteney, whom she knew would be as congenial to Charles as castor oil to a healthy child. She went up to him.

"Shall you not go converse with Lady Fairwether?"

"I should rather converse with you."

"I will present you. And then you can have an eyewitness account of the goings-on in the Early Cretaceous era."

He smiled. "The Early Cretaceous is a period. Not an era."

"Never mind. I am sure it is sufficiently old. And I know how bored you are by anything that has happened in the last ninety million years. Come."

So they began to cross the room together; but halfway to the Early Cretaceous lady, she stopped, laid her hand a moment on his arm, and looked him in the eyes.

"If you are determined to be a sour old bachelor, Mr. Smithson, you must practice for your part."

She had moved on before he could answer; and what she had said might have sounded no more than a continuation of her teasing. But her eyes had for the briefest moment made it clear that she made an offer; as unmistakable, in its way, as those made by the women who in the London of the time haunted the doorways round the Haymarket.

What she did not know was that she had touched an increasingly sensitive place in Charles's innermost soul; his feeling that he was growing like his uncle at Winsyatt, that life was passing him by, that he was being, as in so many other things, overfastidious, lazy, selfish ... and worse. He had not traveled abroad those last two years; and he had realized that previously traveling had been a substitute for not having a wife. It took his mind off domestic affairs; it also allowed him to take an occasional woman into his bed, a pleasure he strictly forbade himself, perhaps remembering the black night of the soul his first essay in that field had caused, in England.

Traveling no longer attracted him; but women did, and he was therefore in a state of extreme sexual frustration, since his moral delicacy had not allowed him to try the simple expedient of a week in Ostend or Paris. He could never have allowed such a purpose to dictate the reason for a journey. He passed a very thoughtful week. Then one morning he woke up.

Everything had become simple. He loved Ernestina. He thought of the pleasure of waking up on just such a morning, cold, gray, with a powder of snow on the ground, and seeing that demure, sweetly dry little face asleep beside him—and by heavens (this fact struck Charles with a sort of amazement) legitimately in the eyes of both God and man beside him. A few minutes later he startled the sleepy Sam, who had crept up from downstairs at his urgent ringing, by saying: "Sam! I am an absolute one hundred per cent heaven forgive me damned fool!"

A day or two afterwards the unadulterated fool had an interview with Ernestina's father. It was brief, and very satisfactory. He went down to the drawing room, where Ernestina's mother sat in a state of the most poignant trepidation. She could not bring herself to speak to Charles, but pointed uncertainly in the direction of the conservatory. Charles opened the white doors to it and stood in the waft of the hot, fragrant air. He had to search for Ernestina, but at last he found her in one of the farthest corners, half screened behind a bower of stephanotis. He saw her glance at him, and then look hastily down and away. She held a pair of silver scissors, and was pretending to snip off some of the dead blooms of the heavily scented plant. Charles stood close behind her; coughed.

"I have come to bid my adieux." The agonized look she flashed at him he pretended, by the simple trick of staring at the ground, not to notice. "I have decided to leave England. For the rest of my life I shall travel. How else can a sour old bachelor divert his days?"

He was ready to go on in this vein. But then he saw that Ernestina's head was bowed and that her knuckles were drained white by the force with which she was gripping the table. He knew that normally she would have guessed his tease at once; and he understood that her slowness now sprang from a deep emotion, which communicated itself to him.

"But if I believed that someone cared for me sufficiently to share . . ."

He could not go on, for she had turned, her eyes full of tears. Their hands met, and he drew her to him. They did not kiss. They could not. How can you mercilessly imprison all natural sexual instinct for twenty years and then not expect the prisoner to be racked by sobs when the doors are thrown open?

A few minutes later Charles led Tina, a little recovered, down the aisle of hothouse plants to the door back to the drawing room. But he stopped a moment at a plant of jasmine and picked a sprig and held it playfully over her head.

"It isn't mistletoe, but it will do, will it not?"

And so they kissed, with lips as chastely asexual as children's. Ernestina began to cry again; then dried her eyes, and allowed Charles to lead her back into the drawing room, where her mother and father stood. No words were needed. Ernestina ran into her mother's opened arms, and twice as many tears as before began to fall. Meanwhile the two men stood smiling at each other; the one as if he had just concluded an excellent business deal, the other as if he was not quite sure which planet he had just landed on, but sincerely hoped the natives were friendly.

12

In what does the alienation of labor consist? First, that the work is external to the worker, that it is not a part of his nature, that consequently he does not fulfill himself in his work but denies himself, has a feeling of misery, not of well-being . . . The worker therefore feels himself at home only during his leisure, whereas at work he feels homeless.

MARX, *Economic and Political Manuscripts* (1844)

And was the day of my delight
As pure and perfect as I say?

TENNYSON, *In Memoriam* (1850)

Charles put his best foot forward, and thoughts of the mysterious woman behind him, through the woods of Ware Commons. He walked for a mile or more, until he came simultaneously to a break in the trees and the first outpost of civilization. This was a long thatched cottage, which stood slightly below his path. There were two or three meadows around it, running down to the cliffs, and just as Charles came out of the woodlands he saw a man hoying a herd of cows away from a low byre beside the cottage. There slipped into his mind an image: a deliciously cool bowl of milk. He had eaten nothing since the double dose of muffins. Tea and tenderness at Mrs. Tranter's called; but the bowl of milk shrieked . . . and was much closer at hand. He went down a steep grass slope and knocked on the back door of the cottage.

It was opened by a small barrel of a woman, her fat arms shiny with suds. Yes, he was welcome to as much milk as he could drink. The name of the place? The Dairy, it seemed, was all it was called. Charles followed her into the slant-roofed room that ran the length of the rear of the cottage. It was dark, shadowy, very cool; a slate floor; and heavy with the smell of ripening cheese. A line of scalding bowls, great copper pans on wooden trestles, each with its golden crust of cream, were ranged under the cheeses, which sat roundly, like squadrons of reserve moons, on the open rafters above. Charles remembered then to have heard of the place. Its cream and butter had a local reputation; Aunt Tranter had spoken of it. He mentioned her name; and the woman who ladled the rich milk from a churn by the door into just what he had imagined, a simple blue-and-white china bowl, glanced at him with a smile. He was less strange and more welcome.

As he was talking, or being talked to, by the woman on the grass outside the Dairy, her husband came back from driving out his cows. He was a bald, vast-bearded man with a distinctly saturnine cast to his face; a Jeremiah. He gave his wife a stern look. She promptly forewent her chatter and returned indoors to her copper. The husband was evidently a taciturn man, though he spoke quickly enough when Charles asked him how much he owed for the bowl of excellent milk. A penny, one of those charming heads of the young Victoria that still occasionally turn up in one's change, with all but that graceful head worn away by the century's use, passed hands.

Charles was about to climb back to the path. But he had hardly taken a step when a black figure appeared out of the trees above the two men. It was the girl. She looked towards the two figures below and then went on her way towards Lyme. Charles glanced back at the dairyman, who continued to give the figure above a dooming stare. He plainly did not allow delicacy to stand in the way of prophetic judgment.

"Do you know that lady?"

"Aye."

"Does she come this way often?"

"Often enough." The dairyman continued to stare. Then he said, "And she bëen't no lady. She be the French Loot'n'nt's Hoer."

Some moments passed before Charles grasped the meaning of that last word. And he threw an angry look at the bearded dairyman, who was a Methodist and therefore fond of calling a spade a spade, especially when the spade was somebody else's sin. He seemed to Charles to incarnate all the hypocritical gossip—and gossips—of Lyme. Charles could have believed many things of that sleeping face; but never that its owner was a whore.

A few seconds later he was himself on the cart track back to Lyme. Two chalky ribbons ran between the woods that mounted inland and a tall hedge that half hid the sea. Ahead moved the black and now bonneted figure of the girl; she walked not quickly, but with an even pace, without feminine

73

affectation, like one used to covering long distances. Charles set out to catch up, and after a hundred yards or so he came close behind her. She must have heard the sound of his nailed boots on the flint that had worn through the chalk, but she did not turn. He perceived that the coat was a little too large for her, and that the heels of her shoes were mudstained. He hesitated a moment then; but the memory of the surly look on the dissenting dairyman's face kept Charles to his original chivalrous intention: to show the poor woman that not everybody in her world was a barbarian.

"Madam!"

She turned, to see him hatless, smiling; and although her expression was one of now ordinary enough surprise, once again that face had an extraordinary effect on him. It was as if after each sight of it, he could not believe its effect, and had to see it again. It seemed to both envelop and reject him; as if he was a figure in a dream, both standing still and yet always receding.

"I owe you two apologies. I did not know yesterday that you were Mrs. Poulteney's secretary. I fear I addressed you in a most impolite manner."

She stared down at the ground. "It's no matter, sir."

"And just now when I seemed ... I was afraid lest you had been taken ill."

Still without looking at him, she inclined her head and turned to walk on.

"May I not accompany you? Since we walk in the same direction?"

She stopped, but did not turn. "I prefer to walk alone."

"It was Mrs. Tranter who made me aware of my error. I am—"

"I know who you are, sir."

He smiled at her timid abruptness. "Then ..."

Her eyes were suddenly on his, and with a kind of despair beneath the timidity.

"Kindly allow me to go on my way alone." His smile faltered. He bowed and stepped back. But instead of continuing on her way, she stared at the ground a moment. "And please tell no one you have seen me in this place."

Then, without looking at him again, she did turn and go on, almost as if she knew her request was in vain and she regretted it as soon as uttered. Standing in the center of the road, Charles watched her black back recede. All he was left with was the after-image of those eyes—they were abnormally large, as if able to see more and suffer more. And their directness of look—he did not know it, but it was the tract-delivery look he had received—contained a most peculiar element of rebuffal. Do not come near me, they said. *Noli me tangere.*

He looked round, trying to imagine why she should not wish it known that she came among these innocent woods. A man perhaps; some assignation? But then he remembered her story.

When Charles finally arrived in Broad Street, he decided to call at Mrs. Tranter's on his way to the White Lion to explain that as soon as he had bathed and changed into decent clothes he would . . .

The door was opened by Mary; but Mrs. Tranter chanced to pass through the hall—to be exact, deliberately came out into the hall—and insisted that he must not stand upon ceremony; and were not his clothes the best proof of his excuses? So Mary smilingly took his ashplant and his rucksack, and he was ushered into the little back drawing room, then shot with the last rays of the setting sun, where the invalid lay in a charmingly elaborate state of carmine-and-gray *déshabille.*

"I feel like an Irish navigator transported into a queen's boudoir," complained Charles, as he kissed Ernestina's fingers in a way that showed he would in fact have made a very poor Irish navvy.

She took her hand away. "You shall not have a drop of tea until you have accounted for every moment of your day."

He accordingly described everything that had happened to him; or almost everything, for Ernestina had now twice made it clear that the subject of the French Lieutenant's Woman was distasteful to her—once on the Cobb, and then again later at lunch afterwards when Aunt Tranter had given Charles very much the same information as the vicar of Lyme had given Mrs. Poulteney twelve months before. But Ernestina had reprimanded her nurse-aunt for boring Charles with dull tittle-tattle, and the poor woman—too often summonsed for provinciality not to be alert to it—had humbly obeyed.

Charles produced the piece of ammonitiferous rock he had brought for Ernestina, who put down her fireshield and attempted to hold it, and could not, and forgave Charles everything for such a labor of Hercules, and then was mock-angry with him for endangering life and limb.

"It is a most fascinating wilderness, the Undercliff. I had no idea such places existed in England. I was reminded of some of the maritime sceneries of Northern Portugal."

"Why, the man is tranced," cried Ernestina. "Now confess, Charles, you haven't been beheading poor innocent rocks—but dallying with the wood nymphs."

Charles showed here an unaccountable moment of embar-

75

rassment, which he covered with a smile. It was on the tip of his tongue to tell them about the girl; a facetious way of describing how he had come upon her entered his mind; and yet seemed a sort of treachery, both to the girl's real sorrow and to himself. He knew he would have been lying if he had dismissed those two encounters lightly; and silence seemed finally less a falsehood in that trivial room.

It remains to be explained why Ware Commons had appeared to evoke Sodom and Gomorrah in Mrs. Poulteney's face a fortnight before.

One needs no further explanation, in truth, than that it was the nearest place to Lyme where people could go and not be spied on. The area had an obscure, long and mischievous legal history. It had always been considered common land until the enclosure acts; then it was encroached on, as the names of the fields of the Dairy, which were all stolen from it, still attest. A gentleman in one of the great houses that lie behind the Undercliff performed a quiet *Anschluss*—with, as usual in history, the approval of his fellows in society. It is true that the more republican citizens of Lyme rose in arms—if an axe is an arm. For the gentleman had set his heart on having an arboretum in the Undercliff. It came to law, and then to a compromise: a right of way was granted, and the rare trees stayed unmolested. But the commonage was done for.

Yet there had remained locally a feeling that Ware Commons was public property. Poachers slunk in less guiltily than elsewhere after the pheasants and rabbits; one day it was discovered, horror of horrors, that a gang of gypsies had been living there, encamped in a hidden dell, for nobody knew how many months. These outcasts were promptly cast out; but the memory of their presence remained, and became entangled with that of a child who had disappeared about the same time from a nearby village. It was—forgive the pun—common knowledge that the gypsies had taken her, and thrown her into a rabbit stew, and buried her bones. Gypsies were not English; and therefore almost certain to be cannibals.

But the most serious accusation against Ware Commons had to do with far worse infamy: though it never bore that familiar rural name, the cart track to the Dairy and beyond to the wooded common was a *de facto* Lover's Lane. It drew courting couples every summer. There was the pretext of a bowl of milk at the Dairy; and many inviting little paths, as one returned, led up into the shielding bracken and hawthorn coverts.

76

That running sore was bad enough; a deeper darkness still existed. There was an antediluvian tradition (much older than Shakespeare) that on Midsummer's Night young people should go with lanterns, and a fiddler, and a keg or two of cider, to a patch of turf known as Donkey's Green in the heart of the woods and there celebrate the solstice with dancing. Some said that after midnight more reeling than dancing took place; and the more draconian claimed that there was very little of either, but a great deal of something else.

Scientific agriculture, in the form of myxomatosis, has only very recently lost us the Green forever, but the custom itself lapsed in relation to the lapse in sexual mores. It is many years since anything but fox or badger cubs tumbled over Donkey's Green on Midsummer's Night. But it was not so in 1867.

Indeed, only a year before, a committee of ladies, generaled by Mrs. Poulteney, had pressed the civic authorities to have the track gated, fenced and closed. But more democratic voices prevailed. The public right of way must be left sacrosanct; and there were even some disgusting sensualists among the Councilors who argued that a walk to the Dairy was an innocent pleasure; and the Donkey's Green Ball no more than an annual jape. But it is sufficient to say that among the more respectable townsfolk one had only to speak of a boy or a girl as "one of the Ware Commons kind" to tar them for life. The boy must thenceforth be a satyr; and the girl, a hedge-prostitute.

Sarah therefore found Mrs. Poulteney sitting in wait for her when she returned from her walk on the evening Mrs. Fairley had so nobly forced herself to do her duty. I said "in wait"; but "in state" would have been a more appropriate term. Sarah appeared in the private drawing room for the evening Bible-reading, and found herself as if faced with the muzzle of a cannon. It was very clear that any moment Mrs. Poulteney might go off, and with a very loud bang indeed.

Sarah went towards the lectern in the corner of the room, where the large "family" Bible—not what you may think of as a family Bible, but one from which certain inexplicable errors of taste in the Holy Writ (such as the Song of Solomon) had been piously excised—lay in its off-duty hours. But she saw that all was not well.

"Is something wrong, Mrs. Poulteney?"

"Something is very wrong," said the abbess. "I have been told something I can hardly believe."

"To do with me?"

77

"I should never have listened to the doctor. I should have listened to the dictates of my own common sense."

"What have I done?"

"I do not think you are mad at all. You are a cunning, wicked creature. You know very well what you have done."

"I will swear on the Bible—"

But Mrs. Poulteney gave her a look of indignation. "You will do nothing of the sort! That is blasphemy."

Sarah came forward, and stood in front of her mistress. "I must insist on knowing of what I am accused." Mrs. Poulteney told her.

To her amazement Sarah showed not the least sign of shame.

"But what is the sin in walking on Ware Commons?"

"The sin! You, a young woman, alone, in such a place!"

"But ma'm, it is nothing but a large wood."

"I know very well what it is. And what goes on there. And the sort of person who frequents it."

"No one frequents it. That is why I go there—to be alone."

"Do you contradict me, miss! Am I not to know what I speak of?"

The first simple fact was that Mrs. Poulteney had never set eyes on Ware Commons, even from a distance, since it was out of sight of any carriage road. The second simple fact is that she was an opium-addict—but before you think I am wildly sacrificing plausibility to sensation, let me quickly add that she did not know it. What we call opium she called laudanum. A shrewd, if blasphemous, doctor of the time called it Our-Lordanum, since many a nineteenth-century lady—and less, for the medicine was cheap enough (in the form of Godfrey's Cordial) to help all classes get through that black night of womankind—sipped it a good deal more frequently than Communion wine. It was, in short, a very near equivalent of our own age's sedative pills. Why Mrs. Poulteney should have been an inhabitant of the Victorian valley of the dolls we need not inquire, but it is to the point that laudanum, as Coleridge once discovered, gives vivid dreams.

I cannot imagine what Bosch-like picture of Ware Commons Mrs. Poulteney had built up over the years; what satanic orgies she divined behind every tree, what French abominations under every leaf. But I think we may safely say that it had become the objective correlative of all that went on in her own subconscious.

Her outburst reduced both herself and Sarah to silence.

Having discharged, Mrs. Poulteney began to change her tack.

"You have distressed me deeply."

"But how was I to tell? I am not to go to the sea. Very well, I don't go to the sea. I wish for solitude. That is all. That is not a sin. I will not be called a sinner for that."

"Have you never heard speak of Ware Commons?"

"As a place of the kind you imply—never."

Mrs. Poulteney looked somewhat abashed then before the girl's indignation. She recalled that Sarah had not lived in Lyme until recently; and that she could therefore, just conceivably, be ignorant of the obloquy she was inviting.

"Very well. But let it be plainly understood. I permit no one in my employ to go or to be seen near that place. You will confine your walks to where it is seemly. Do I make myself clear?"

"Yes. I am to walk in the paths of righteousness." For one appalling moment Mrs. Poulteney thought she had been the subject of a sarcasm; but Sarah's eyes were solemnly down, as if she had been pronouncing sentence on herself; and righteousness were synonymous with suffering.

"Then let us hear no more of this foolishness. I do this for your own good."

Sarah murmured, "I know." Then, "I thank you, ma'm."

No more was said. She turned to the Bible and read the passage Mrs. Poulteney had marked. It was the same one as she had chosen for that first interview—Psalm 119: "Blessed are the undefiled in the way, who walk in the law of the Lord." Sarah read in a very subdued voice, seemingly without emotion. The old woman sat facing the dark shadows at the far end of the room; like some pagan idol she looked, oblivious of the blood sacrifice her pitiless stone face demanded.

Later that night Sarah might have been seen—though I cannot think by whom, unless a passing owl—standing at the open window of her unlit bedroom. The house was silent, and the town as well, for people went to bed by nine in those days before electricity and television. It was now one o'clock. Sarah was in her nightgown, with her hair loose; and she was staring out to sea. A distant lantern winked faintly on the black waters out towards Portland Bill, where some ship sailed towards Bridport. Sarah had seen the tiny point of light; and not given it a second thought.

If you had gone closer still, you would have seen that her face was wet with silent tears. She was not standing at her window as part of her mysterious vigil for Satan's sails; but as a preliminary to jumping from it.

79

I will not make her teeter on the windowsill; or sway forward, and then collapse sobbing back onto the worn carpet of her room. We know she was alive a fortnight after this incident, and therefore she did not jump. Nor were hers the sobbing, hysterical sort of tears that presage violent action; but those produced by a profound conditional, rather than emotional, misery—slow-welling, unstoppable, creeping like blood through a bandage.

Who is Sarah?

Out of what shadows does she come?

13

> For the drift of the Maker is dark, an Isis hid by
> the veil . . .
>
> TENNYSON, *Maud* (1855)

I do not know. This story I am telling is all imagination. These characters I create never existed outside my own mind. If I have pretended until now to know my characters' minds and innermost thoughts, it is because I am writing in (just as I have assumed some of the vocabulary and "voice" of) a convention universally accepted at the time of my story: that the novelist stands next to God. He may not know all, yet he tries to pretend that he does. But I live in the age of Alain Robbe-Grillet and Roland Barthes; if this is a novel, it cannot be a novel in the modern sense of the word.

So perhaps I am writing a transposed autobiography; perhaps I now live in one of the houses I have brought into the fiction; perhaps Charles is myself disguised. Perhaps it is only a game. Modern women like Sarah exist, and I have never understood them. Or perhaps I am trying to pass off a concealed book of essays on you. Instead of chapter headings, perhaps I should have written "On the Horizontality of Existence," "The Illusions of Progress," "The History of the Novel

Form," "The Aetiology of Freedom," "Some Forgotten Aspects of the Victorian Age" . . . what you will.

Perhaps you suppose that a novelist has only to pull the right strings and his puppets will behave in a lifelike manner; and produce on request a thorough analysis of their motives and intentions. Certainly I intended at this stage (*Chap. Thirteen—unfolding of Sarah's true state of mind*) to tell all—or all that matters. But I find myself suddenly like a man in the sharp spring night, watching from the lawn beneath that dim upper window in Marlborough House; I know in the context of my book's reality that Sarah would never have brushed away her tears and leaned down and delivered a chapter of revelation. She would instantly have turned, had she seen me there just as the old moon rose, and disappeared into the interior shadows.

But I am a novelist, not a man in a garden—I can follow her where I like? But possibility is not permissibility. Husbands could often murder their wives—and the reverse—and get away with it. But they don't.

You may think novelists always have fixed plans to which they work, so that the future predicted by Chapter One is always inexorably the actuality of Chapter Thirteen. But novelists write for countless different reasons: for money, for fame, for reviewers, for parents, for friends, for loved ones; for vanity, for pride, for curiosity, for amusement: as skilled furniture makers enjoy making furniture, as drunkards like drinking, as judges like judging, as Sicilians like emptying a shotgun into an enemy's back. I could fill a book with reasons, and they would all be true, though not true of all. Only one same reason is shared by all of us: *we wish to create worlds as real as, but other than the world that is.* Or was. This is why we cannot plan. We know a world is an organism, not a machine. We also know that a genuinely created world must be independent of its creator; a planned world (a world that fully reveals its planning) is a dead world. It is only when our characters and events begin to disobey us that they begin to live. When Charles left Sarah on her cliff edge, I ordered him to walk straight back to Lyme Regis. But he did not; he gratuitously turned and went down to the Dairy.

Oh, but you say, come on—what I really mean is that the idea crossed my mind as I wrote that it might be more clever to have him stop and drink milk . . . and meet Sarah again. That is certainly one explanation of what happened; but I can only report—and I am the most reliable witness—that the idea seemed to me to come clearly from Charles, not myself. It is not only that he has begun to gain an autonomy;

81

I must respect it, and disrespect all my quasi-divine plans for him, if I wish him to be real.

In other words, to be free myself, I must give him, and Tina, and Sarah, even the abominable Mrs. Poulteney, their freedom as well. There is only one good definition of God: the freedom that allows other freedoms to exist. And I must conform to that definition.

The novelist is still a god, since he creates (and not even the most aleatory avant-garde modern novel has managed to extirpate its author completely); what has changed is that we are no longer the gods of the Victorian image, omniscient and decreeing; but in the new theological image, with freedom our first principle, not authority.

I have disgracefully broken the illusion? No. My characters still exist, and in a reality no less, or no more, real than the one I have just broken. Fiction is woven into all, as a Greek observed some two and a half thousand years ago. I find this new reality (or unreality) more valid; and I would have you share my own sense that I do not fully control these creatures of my mind, any more than you control—however hard you try, however much of a latterday Mrs. Poulteney you may be—your children, colleagues, friends, or even yourself.

But this is preposterous? A character is either "real" or "imaginary"? If you think that, *hypocrite lecteur,* I can only smile. You do not even think of your own past as quite real; you dress it up, you gild it or blacken it, censor it, tinker with it . . . fictionalize it, in a word, and put it away on a shelf—your book, your romanced autobiography. We are all in flight from the real reality. That is a basic definition of *Homo sapiens.*

So if you think all this unlucky (but it *is* Chapter Thirteen) digression has nothing to do with your Time, Progress, Society, Evolution and all those other capitalized ghosts in the night that are rattling their chains behind the scenes of this book . . . I will not argue. But I shall suspect you.

I report, then, only the outward facts: that Sarah cried in the darkness, but did not kill herself; that she continued, in spite of the express prohibition, to haunt Ware Commons. In a way, therefore, she had indeed jumped; and was living in a kind of long fall, since sooner or later the news must inevitably come to Mrs. Poulteney of the sinner's compounding of her sin. It is true Sarah went less often to the woods than she had become accustomed to, a deprivation at first made easy for her by the wetness of the weather those following two weeks. It is true also that she took some minimal precautions of a military kind. The cart track eventually ran out into a small lane, little better than a superior cart track itself, which curved down a broad combe called Ware Valley until it joined, on the outskirts of Lyme, the main carriage road to Sidmouth and Exeter. There was a small scatter of respectable houses in Ware Valley, and it was therefore a seemly place to walk. Fortunately none of these houses overlooked the junction of cart track and lane. Once there, Sarah had merely to look round to see if she was alone. One day she set out with the intention of walking into the woods. But as in the lane she came to the track to the Dairy she saw two people come round a higher bend. She walked straight on towards them, and once round the bend, watched to make sure that the couple did not themselves take the Dairy track; then retraced her footsteps and entered her sanctuary unobserved.

She risked meeting other promenaders on the track itself; and might always have risked the dairyman and his family's eyes. But this latter danger she avoided by discovering for herself that one of the inviting paths into the bracken above the track led round, out of sight of the Dairy, onto the path through the woods. This path she had invariably taken, until that afternoon when she recklessly—as we can now realize—emerged in full view of the two men.

The reason was simple. She had overslept, and she knew she was late for her reading. Mrs. Poulteney was to dine at Lady Cotton's that evening; and the usual hour had been put forward to allow her to prepare for what was always in essence, if not appearance, a thunderous clash of two brontosauri; with black velvet taking the place of iron cartilage, and quotations from the Bible the angry raging teeth; but no less dour and relentless a battle.

Also, Charles's down-staring face had shocked her; she felt the speed of her fall accelerate; when the cruel ground rushes up, when the fall is from such a height, what use are precautions?

14

> "My idea of good company, Mr. Elliot, is the company of clever, well-informed people, who have a great deal of conversation; that is what I call good company."
>
> "You are mistaken," said he, gently, "that is not good company—that is the best. Good company requires only birth, education, and manners, and with regard to education is not very nice."
>
> JANE AUSTEN, *Persuasion*

Visitors to Lyme in the nineteenth century, if they did not quite have to undergo the ordeal facing travelers to the ancient Greek colonies—Charles did not actually have to deliver a Periclean oration plus comprehensive world news summary from the steps of the Town Hall—were certainly expected to allow themselves to be examined and spoken to. Ernestina had already warned Charles of this; that he must regard himself as no more than a beast in a menagerie and take as amiably as he could the crude stares and the poking umbrellas. Thus it was that two or three times a week he had to go visiting with the ladies and suffer hours of excruciating boredom, whose only consolation was the little scene that took place with a pleasing regularity when they had got back to Aunt Tranter's house. Ernestina would anxiously search his eyes, glazed by clouds of platitudinous small talk, and say "Was it dreadful? Can you forgive me? Do you hate me?"; and when he smiled she would throw herself into his arms, as if he had miraculously survived a riot or an avalanche.

It so happened that the avalanche for the morning after Charles's discovery of the Undercliff was appointed to take place at Marlborough House. There was nothing fortuitous or spontaneous about these visits. There could not be, since the identities of visitors and visited spread round the little town with incredible rapidity; and that both made and maintained a rigorous sense of protocol. Mrs. Poulteney's interest in Charles was probably no greater than Charles's in her; but she would have been mortally offended if he had not been dragged in chains for her to place her fat little foot on—and pretty soon after his arrival, since the later the visit during a stay, the less the honor.

These "foreigners" were, of course, essentially counters in a game. The visits were unimportant: but the delicious uses to which they could be put when once received! *"Dear* Mrs. Tranter, she wanted me to be the first to meet . . ." and "I am most surprised that Ernestina has not called on you yet—she has spoiled us—already two calls . . ." and "I am sure it is an oversight—Mrs. Tranter is an affectionate old soul, but so absent-minded . . ." These, and similar mouthwatering opportunities for twists of the social dagger depended on a supply of "important" visitors like Charles. And he could no more have avoided his fate than a plump mouse dropping between the claws of a hungry cat—several dozen hungry cats, to be exact.

When Mrs. Tranter and her two young companions were announced on the morning following that woodland meeting, Sarah rose at once to leave the room. But Mrs. Poulteney, whom the thought of young happiness always made petulant, and who had in any case reason enough—after an evening of Lady Cotton—to be a good deal more than petulant, bade her stay. Ernestina she considered a frivolous young woman, and she was sure her intended would be a frivolous young man; it was almost her duty to embarrass them. She knew, besides, that such social occasions were like a hair shirt to the sinner. All conspired.

The visitors were ushered in. Mrs. Tranter rustled forward, effusive and kind. Sarah stood shyly, painfully out of place in the background; and Charles and Ernestina stood easily on the carpet behind the two elder ladies, who had known each other sufficient decades to make a sort of token embrace necessary. Then Ernestina was presented, giving the faintest suspicion of a curtsy before she took the reginal hand.

"How are you, Mrs. Poulteney? You look exceedingly well."

"At my age, Miss Freeman, spiritual health is all that counts."

"Then I have no fears for you."

Mrs. Poulteney would have liked to pursue this interesting subject, but Ernestina turned to present Charles, who bent over the old lady's hand.

"Great pleasure, ma'm. Charming house."

"It is too large for me. I keep it on for my dear husband's sake. I know he would have wished—he wishes it so."

And she stared past Charles at the house's chief icon, an oil painting done of Frederick only two years before he died in 1851, in which it was clear that he was a wise, Christian, dignified, good-looking sort of man—above all, superior to most. He had certainly been a Christian, and dignified in the extreme, but the painter had drawn on imagination for the other qualities. The long-departed Mr. Poulteney had been a total, though very rich, nonentity; and the only really significant act of his life had been his leaving it. Charles surveyed this skeleton at the feast with a suitable deference.

"Ah. Indeed. I understand. Most natural."

"*Their* wishes must be obeyed."

"Just so."

Mrs. Tranter, who had already smiled at Sarah, took her as an opportunity to break in upon this sepulchral *Introit*.

"My dear Miss Woodruff, it is a pleasure to see you." And she went and pressed Sarah's hand, and gave her a genuinely solicitous look, and said in a lower voice, "Will you come to see me—when dear Tina has gone?" For a second then, a rare look crossed Sarah's face. That computer in her heart had long before assessed Mrs. Tranter and stored the resultant tape. That reserve, that independence so perilously close to defiance which had become her mask in Mrs. Poulteney's presence, momentarily dropped. She smiled even, though sadly, and made an infinitesimal nod: if she could, she would.

Further introductions were then made. The two young ladies coolly inclined heads at one another, and Charles bowed. He watched closely to see if the girl would in any way betray their two meetings of the day before, but her eyes studiously avoided his. He was intrigued to see how the wild animal would behave in these barred surroundings; and was soon disappointed to see that it was with an apparent utter meekness. Unless it was to ask her to fetch something, or to pull the bell when it was decided that the ladies would like hot chocolate, Mrs. Poulteney ignored Sarah absolutely. So also, Charles was not pleased to note, did Ernestina. Aunt Tranter did her best to draw the girl into the conversation; but she sat slightly apart, with a kind of blankness of face, a withdrawnness, that could very well be taken for consciousness of her inferior status. He himself once or twice turned

86

politely to her for the confirmation of an opinion—but it was without success. She made the least response possible; and still avoided his eyes.

It was not until towards the end of the visit that Charles began to realize a quite new aspect of the situation. It became clear to him that the girl's silent meekness ran contrary to her nature; that she was therefore playing a part; and that the part was one of complete disassociation from, and disapprobation of, her mistress. Mrs. Poulteney and Mrs. Tranter respectively gloomed and bubbled their way through the schedule of polite conversational subjects—short, perhaps, in number, but endlessly long in process ... servants; the weather; impending births, funerals and marriages; Mr. Disraeli and Mr. Gladstone (this seemingly for Charles's benefit, though it allowed Mrs. Poulteney to condemn severely the personal principles of the first and the political ones of the second);* then on to last Sunday's sermon, the deficiencies of the local tradesmen and thence naturally back to servants. As Charles smiled and raised eyebrows and nodded his way through this familiar purgatory, he decided that the silent Miss Woodruff was laboring under a sense of injustice—and, very interestingly to a shrewd observer, doing singularly little to conceal it.

This was perceptive of Charles, for he had noticed something that had escaped almost everyone else in Lyme. But perhaps his deduction would have remained at the state of a mere suspicion, had not his hostess delivered herself of a characteristic Poulteneyism.

"That girl I dismissed—she has given you no further trouble?"

Mrs. Tranter smiled. "Mary? I would not part with her for the world."

"Mrs. Fairley informs me that she saw her only this

---

* Perhaps, in fairness to the lady, it might be said that in that spring of 1867 her blanket disfavor was being shared by many others. Mr. Gladraeli and Mr. Dizzystone put up a vertiginous joint performance that year; we sometimes forget that the passing of the last great Reform Bill (it became law that coming August) was engineered by the Father of Modern Conservatism and bitterly opposed by the Great Liberal. Tories like Mrs. Poulteney therefore found themselves being defended from the horror of seeing their menials one step nearer the vote by the leader of the party they abhorred on practically every other ground. Marx remarked, in one of his *New York Daily Tribune* articles, that in reality the British Whigs "represent something quite different from their professed liberal and enlightened principles. Thus they are in the same position as the drunkard brought up before the Lord Mayor, who declared that he represented the Temperance principle, but from some accident or other always got drunk on Sundays." The type is not extinct.

morning talking with a person." Mrs. Poulteney used "person" as two patriotic Frenchmen might have said "Nazi" during the occupation. "A young person. Mrs. Fairley did not know him."

Ernestina gave Charles a sharp, reproachful glance; for a wild moment he thought he was being accused himself—then realized.

He smiled. "Then no doubt it was Sam. My servant, madam," he added for Mrs. Poulteney's benefit.

Ernestina avoided his eyes. "I meant to tell you. I too saw them talking together yesterday."

"But surely . . . we are not going to forbid them to speak together if they meet?"

"There is a world of difference between what may be accepted in London and what is proper here. I think you should speak to Sam. The girl is too easily led."

Mrs. Tranter looked hurt. "Ernestina my dear . . . she may be high-spirited. But I've never had the least cause to—"

"My dear, kind aunt, I am well aware how fond you are of her."

Charles heard the dryness in her voice and came to the hurt Mrs. Tranter's defense.

"I wish that more mistresses were as fond. There is no surer sign of a happy house than a happy maidservant at its door."

Ernestina looked down at that, with a telltale little tightening of her lips. Good Mrs. Tranter blushed slightly at the compliment, and also looked down. Mrs. Poulteney had listened to this crossfire with some pleasure; and she now decided that she disliked Charles sufficiently to be rude to him.

"Your future wife is a better judge than you are of such matters, Mr. Smithson. I know the girl in question. I had to dismiss her. If you were older you would know that one cannot be too strict in such matters."

And she too looked down, her way of indicating that a subject had been pronounced on by her, and was therefore at a universal end.

"I bow to your far greater experience, madam."

But his tone was unmistakably cold and sarcastic.

The three ladies all sat with averted eyes: Mrs. Tranter out of embarrassment, Ernestina out of irritation with herself —for she had not meant to bring such a snub on Charles's head, and wished she had kept silent; and Mrs. Poulteney out of being who she was. It was thus that a look unseen by these ladies did at last pass between Sarah and Charles. It was very brief, but it spoke worlds; two strangers had recognized they shared a common enemy. For the first time she did not look through him, but at him; and Charles resolved that he would have his revenge on Mrs. Poulteney, and teach Ernestina an evidently needed lesson in common humanity.

He remembered, too, his recent passage of arms with Ernestina's father on the subject of Charles Darwin. Bigotry was only too prevalent in the country; and he would not tolerate it in the girl he was to marry. He would speak to Sam; by heavens, yes, he would speak to Sam.

How he spoke, we shall see in a moment. But the general tenor of that conversation had, in fact, already been forestalled, since Mrs. Poulteney's "person" was at that moment sitting in the downstairs kitchen at Mrs. Tranter's.

Sam *had* met Mary in Coombe Street that morning; and innocently asked if the soot might be delivered in an hour's time. He knew, of course, that the two ladies would be away at Marlborough House.

The conversation in that kitchen was surprisingly serious, really a good deal more so than that in Mrs. Poulteney's drawing room. Mary leaned against the great dresser, with her pretty arms folded, and a strand of the corn-colored hair escaping from under her dusting cap. Now and then she asked questions, but Sam did most of the talking, though it was mainly to the scrubbed deal of the long table. Only very occasionally did their eyes meet, and then by mutual accord they looked shyly away from each other.

15

. . . as regards the laboring classes, the half-savage manners of the last generation have been exchanged for a deep and almost universally pervading sensuality . . .

Report from the Mining Districts (1850)

Or in the light of deeper eyes
Is matter for a flying smile.

TENNYSON, *In Memoriam* (1850)

When the next morning came and Charles took up his ungentle probing of Sam's Cockney heart, he was not in fact betraying Ernestina, whatever may have been the case with Mrs. Poulteney. They had left shortly following the exchange described above, and Ernestina had been very silent on the walk downhill to Broad Street. Once there she had seen to it that she was left alone with Charles; and no sooner had the door shut on her aunt's back than she burst into tears (without the usual preliminary self-accusations) and threw herself into his arms. It was the first disagreement that had ever darkened their love, and it horrified her: that her sweet gentle Charles should be snubbed by a horrid old woman, and all because of a fit of pique on her part. When he had dutifully patted her back and dried her eyes, she said as much. Charles stole a kiss on each wet eyelid as a revenge, and forthwith forgave her.

"And my sweet, silly Tina, why should we deny to others what has made us both so happy? What if this wicked maid and my rascal Sam should fall in love? Are we to throw stones?"

She smiled up at him from her chair. "This is what comes of trying to behave like a grown-up."

He knelt beside her and took her hand. "Sweet child. You will always be that to me." She bent her head to kiss his hand, and he in turn kissed the top of her hair.

She murmured, "Eighty-eight days. I cannot bear the thought."

"Let us elope. And go to Paris."

"Charles . . . what wickedness!"

She raised her head, and he kissed her on the lips. She sank back against the corner of the chair, dewy-eyed, blushing, her heart beating so fast that she thought she would faint; too frail for such sudden changes of emotion. He retained her hand, and pressed it playfully.

"If the worthy Mrs. P. could see us now?"

She covered her face with her hands, and began to laugh, choked giggles that communicated themselves to Charles and forced him to get to his feet and go to the window, and pretend to be dignified—but he could not help looking back, and caught her eyes between her fingers. There were more choked sounds in the silent room. To both came the same insight: the wonderful new freedoms their age brought, how wonderful it was to be thoroughly modern young people, with a thoroughly modern sense of humor, a millennium away from . . .

"Oh Charles . . . oh Charles . . . do you remember the Early Cretaceous lady?"

That set them off again; and thoroughly mystified poor Mrs. Tranter, who had been on hot coals outside, sensing

90

that a quarrel must be taking place. She at last plucked up courage to enter, to see if she could mend. Tina, still laughing, ran to her at the door and kissed her on both cheeks.

"Dear, dear aunt. You are not too fond. I am a horrid, spoiled child. And I do not want my green walking dress. May I give it to Mary?"

Thus it was that later that same day Ernestina figured, and sincerely, in Mary's prayers. I doubt if they were heard, for instead of getting straight into bed after she had risen from her knees, as all good prayer-makers should, Mary could not resist trying the green dress on one last time. She had only a candle's light to see by, but candlelight never did badly by any woman. That cloud of falling golden hair, that vivacious green, those trembling shadows, that shy, delighted, self-surprised face ... if her God was watching, He must have wished Himself the Fallen One that night.

"I have decided, Sam, that I do not need you." Charles could not see Sam's face, for his eyes were closed. He was being shaved. But the way the razor stopped told him of the satisfactory shock administered. "You may return to Kensington." There was a silence that would have softened the heart of any less sadistic master. "You have nothing to say?"

"Yes, sir. Be 'appier 'ere."

"I have decided you are up to no good. I am well aware that that is your natural condition. But I prefer you to be up to no good in London. Which is more used to up-to-no-gooders."

"I ain't done nothink, Mr. Charles."

"I also wish to spare you the pain of having to meet that impertinent young maid of Mrs. Tranter's." There was an audible outbreath. Charles cautiously opened an eye. "Is that not kind of me?"

Sam stared stonily over his master's head. "She 'as made halopogies. I'ave haccepted them."

"What! From a mere milkmaid? Impossible."

Charles had to close his eye then in a hurry, to avoid a roughly applied brushful of lather.

"It was higgerance, Mr. Charles. Sheer higgerance."

"I see. Then matters are worse than I thought. You must certainly decamp." But Sam had had enough. He let the lather stay where it was, until Charles was obliged to open his eyes and see what was happening. What was happening was that Sam stood in a fit of the sulks; or at least with the semblance of it.

"Now what is wrong?"

" 'Er, sir."

"*Ursa?* Are you speaking Latin now? Never mind, my wit is beyond you, you bear. Now I want the truth. Yesterday you were not prepared to touch the young lady with a bargee's tool of trade? Do you deny that?"

"I was provoked."

"Ah, but where is the *primum mobile?* Who provoked first?"

But Charles now saw he had gone too far. The razor was trembling in Sam's hand; not with murderous intent, but with suppressed indignation. Charles reached out and took it away from him; pointed it at him.

"In twenty-four hours, Sam? In twenty-four hours?"

Sam began to rub the washstand with the towel that was intended for Charles's cheeks. There was a silence; and when he spoke it was with a choked voice.

"We're not 'orses. We're 'ooman beings."

Charles smiled then, and stood, and went behind his man, and hand to his shoulder made him turn.

"Sam, I apologize. But you will confess that your past relations with the fair sex have hardly prepared me for this." Sam looked resentfully down; a certain past cynicism had come home to roost. "Now this girl—what is her name?— Mary?—this charming Miss Mary may be great fun to tease and be teased by—let me finish—but I am told she is a gentle trusting creature at heart. And I will not have that heart broken."

"Cut off me harms, Mr. Charles!"

"Very well. I believe you, without the amputation. But you will not go to the house again, or address the young woman in the street, until I have spoken with Mrs. Tranter and found whether she permits your attentions."

Sam, whose eyes had been down, looked up then at his master; and he grinned ruefully, like some dying young soldier on the ground at his officer's feet.

"I'm a Derby duck, sir. I'm a bloomin' Derby duck."

A Derby duck, I had better add, is one already cooked— and therefore quite beyond hope of resurrection.

16

Maud in the light of her youth and her grace,
Singing of Death, and of Honor that cannot die,
Till I well could weep for a time so sordid and mean,
And myself so languid and base.

TENNYSON, *Maud* (1855)

Never, believe me, I knew of the feelings between men and women,
Till in some village fields in holidays now getting stupid,
One day sauntering "long and listless," as Tennyson has it,
Long and listless strolling, ungainly in hobbadiboyhood,
Chanced it my eye fell aside on a capless, bonnetless maiden . . .

A. H. CLOUGH, *The Bothie of Tober-na-Vuolich* (1848)

Five uneventful days passed after the last I have described.
For Charles, no opportunities to continue his exploration of
the Undercliff presented themselves. On one day there was a
long excursion to Sidmouth; the mornings of the others were
taken up by visits or other more agreeable diversions, such as
archery, then a minor rage among the young ladies of England—the dark green *de rigueur* was so becoming, and so
delightful the tamed gentlemen walking to fetch the arrows
from the butts (where the myopic Ernestina's seldom landed,
I am afraid) and returning with pretty jokes about Cupid and
hearts and Maid Marian.

As for the afternoons, Ernestina usually persuaded him to
stay at Aunt Tranter's; there were very serious domestic
matters to discuss, since the Kensington house was far too
small and the lease of the Belgravia house, into which they
would eventually move, did not revert into Charles's hands
for another two years. The little *contretemps* seemed to have

93

changed Ernestina; she was very deferential to Charles, so dutiful-wifely that he complained he was beginning to feel like a Turkish pasha—and unoriginally begged her to contradict him about something lest he forget theirs was to be a Christian marriage.

Charles suffered this sudden access of respect for his every wish with good humor. He was shrewd enough to realize that Ernestina had been taken by surprise; until the little disagreement she had perhaps been more in love with marriage than with her husband-to-be; now she had recognized the man, as well as the state. Charles, it must be confessed, found this transposition from dryness to moistness just a shade cloying at times; he was happy to be adulated, fussed over, consulted, deferred to. What man is not? But he had had years of very free bachelorhood, and in his fashion was also a horrid, spoiled child. It was still strange to him to find that his mornings were not his own; that the plans of an afternoon might have to be sacrificed to some whim of Tina's. Of course he had duty to back him up; husbands were expected to do such things, therefore he must do them—just as he must wear heavy flannel and nailed boots to go walking in the country.

And the evenings! Those gaslit hours that had to be filled, and without benefit of cinema or television! For those who had a living to earn this was hardly a great problem: when you have worked a twelve-hour day, the problem of what to do after your supper is easily solved. But pity the unfortunate rich; for whatever license was given them to be solitary before the evening hours, convention demanded that then they must be bored in company. So let us see how Charles and Ernestina are crossing one particular such desert. Aunt Tranter, at least, they are spared, as the good lady has gone to take tea with an invalid spinster neighbor; an exact facsimile, in everything but looks and history, of herself.

Charles is gracefully sprawled across the sofa, two fingers up his cheek, two others and the thumb under his chin, his elbow on the sofa's arm, and staring gravely across the Axminster carpet at Tina, who is reading, a small red morocco volume in her left hand and her right hand holding her fireshield (an object rather like a long-paddled Ping-Pong bat, covered in embroidered satin and maroon-braided round the edges, whose purpose is to prevent the heat from the crackling coals daring to redden that chastely pale complexion), which she beats, a little irregularly, to the very regular beat of the narrative poem she is reading.

It is a best seller of the 1860s: the Honorable Mrs. Caroline Norton's *The Lady of La Garaye,* of which *The*

Edinburgh Review, no less, has pronounced: "The poem is a pure, tender, touching tale of pain, sorrow, love, duty, piety and death"—surely as pretty a string of key mid-Victorian adjectives and nouns as one could ever hope to light on (and much too good for me to invent, let me add). You may think that Mrs. Norton was a mere insipid poetastrix of the age. Insipid her verse is, as you will see in a minute; but she was a far from insipid person. She was Sheridan's granddaughter for one thing; she had been, so it was rumored, Melbourne's mistress—her husband had certainly believed the rumor strongly enough to bring an unsuccessful *crim. con.* action against the great statesman; and she was an ardent feminist—what we would call today a liberal.

The lady of the title is a sprightly French lord's sprightly wife who has a crippling accident out hunting and devotes the rest of her excessively somber life to good works—more useful ones than Lady Cotton's, since she founds a hospital. Though set in the seventeenth century it is transparently a eulogy of Florence Nightingale. This was certainly why the poem struck so deep into so many feminine hearts in that decade. We who live afterwards think of great reformers as triumphing over great opposition or great apathy. Opposition and apathy the real Lady of the Lamp had certainly had to contend with; but there is an element in sympathy, as I have pointed out elsewhere, that can be almost as harmful. It was very far from the first time that Ernestina had read the poem; she knew some of it almost by heart. Each time she read it (she was overtly reading it again now because it was Lent) she felt elevated and purified, a better young woman. I need only add here that she had never set foot in a hospital, or nursed a sick cottager, in her life. Her parents would not have allowed her to, of course; but she had never even *thought* of doing such a thing.

Ah, you say, but women were chained to their role at that time. But remember the date of this evening: April 6th, 1867. At Westminster only one week before John Stuart Mill had seized an opportunity in one of the early debates on the Reform Bill to argue that now was the time to give women equal rights at the ballot box. His brave attempt (the motion was defeated by 196 to 73, Disraeli, the old fox, abstaining) was greeted with smiles from the average man, guffaws from *Punch* (one joke showed a group of gentlemen besieging a female Cabinet minister, haw haw haw), and disapproving frowns from a sad majority of educated women, who maintained that their influence was best exerted from the home. Nonetheless, March 30th, 1867, is the point from which we can date the beginning of feminine emancipation in

England; and Ernestina, who had giggled at the previous week's *Punch* when Charles showed it to her, cannot be completely exonerated.

But we started off on the Victorian home evening. Let us return to it. Listen. Charles stares, a faint opacity in his suitably solemn eyes, at Ernestina's grave face.

"Shall I continue?"

"You read most beautifully."

She clears her throat delicately, raises the book again. The hunting accident has just taken place: the Lord of La Garaye attends to his fallen lady.

> "He parts the masses of her golden hair,
> He lifts her, helpless, with a shuddering care,
>
> He looks into her face with awestruck eyes;—
> She dies—the darling of his soul—she dies!"

Ernestina's eyes flick gravely at Charles. His eyes are shut, as if he is picturing to himself the tragic scene. He nods solemnly; he is all ears.

Ernestina resumes.

> "You might have heard, through that thought's fearful shock,
> The beating of his heart like some huge clock;
> And then the strong pulse falter and stand still,
> When lifted from that fear with sudden thrill,
> Which from those blanched lips low and trembling came:
> 'Oh! Claud!' she said: no more—but never yet
> Through all the loving days since first they met,
> Leaped his heart's blood with such a yearning vow
> That she was all in all to him, as now."

She has read the last line most significantly. Again she glanced up at Charles. His eyes are still closed, but he is clearly too moved even to nod. She takes a little breath, her eyes still on her gravely reclined fiancé, and goes on.

> " 'Oh! Claud—the pain!' 'Oh! Gertrude, my beloved!'
> Then faintly o'er her lips a wan smile moved,
> Which dumbly spoke of comfort from his tone—
> You've gone to sleep, you hateful mutton-bone!"

A silence. Charles's face is like that of a man at a funeral. Another breath and fierce glance from the reader.

"Ah! happy they who in their grief or pain
Yearn not for some familiar face in vain—
CHARLES!"

The poem suddenly becomes a missile, which strikes
Charles a glancing blow on the shoulder and lands on the
floor behind the sofa.

"Yes?" He sees Ernestina on her feet, her hands on her
hips, in a *very* untypical way. He sits up and murmurs, "Oh
dear."

"You are caught, sir. You have no excuse."

But sufficient excuses or penance Charles must have made,
for the very next lunchtime he had the courage to complain
when Ernestina proposed for the nineteenth time to discuss
the furnishings of his study in the as yet unfound house.
Leaving his very comfortable little establishment in Kensington was not the least of Charles's impending sacrifices; and he
could bear only just so much reminding of it. Aunt Tranter
backed him up, and he was accordingly granted an afternoon
for his "wretched grubbing" among the stones.

He knew at once where he wished to go. He had had no
thought except for the French Lieutenant's Woman when he
found her on that wild cliff meadow; but he had just had
enough time to notice, at the foot of the little bluff whose
flat top was the meadow, considerable piles of fallen flint. It
was certainly this which made him walk that afternoon to the
place. The new warmth, the intensification of love between
Ernestina and himself had driven all thought, or all but the
most fleeting, casual thought, of Mrs. Poulteney's secretary
from his conscious mind.

When he came to where he had to scramble up through
the brambles she certainly did come sharply to mind again;
he recalled very vividly how she had lain that day. But when
he crossed the grass and looked down at her ledge, it was
empty; and very soon he had forgotten her. He found a way
down to the foot of the bluff and began to search among the
scree for his tests. It was a colder day than when he had been
there before. Sun and clouds rapidly succeeded each other in
proper April fashion, but the wind was out of the north. At
the foot of the south-facing bluff, therefore, it was agreeably
warm; and an additional warmth soon came to Charles when
he saw an excellent test, seemingly not long broken from its
flint matrix, lying at his feet.

Forty minutes later, however, he had to resign himself to
the fact that he was to have no further luck, at least among

the flints below the bluff. He regained the turf above and walked towards the path that led back into the woods. And there, a dark movement!

She was halfway up the steep little path, too occupied in disengaging her coat from a recalcitrant bramble to hear Charles's turf-silenced approach. As soon as he saw her he stopped. The path was narrow and she had the right of way. But then she saw him. They stood some fifteen feet apart, both clearly embarrassed, though with very different expressions. Charles was smiling; and Sarah stared at him with profound suspicion.

"Miss Woodruff!"

She gave him an imperceptible nod, and seemed to hesitate, as if she would have turned back if she could. But then she realized he was standing to one side for her and made hurriedly to pass him. Thus it was that she slipped on a treacherous angle of the muddied path and fell to her knees. He sprang forward and helped her up; now she was totally like a wild animal, unable to look at him, trembling, dumb.

Very gently, with his hand on her elbow, he urged her forward on to the level turf above the sea. She wore the same black coat, the same indigo dress with the white collar. But whether it was because she had slipped, or he held her arm, or the colder air, I do not know, but her skin had a vigor, a pink bloom, that suited admirably the wild shyness of her demeanor. The wind had blown her hair a little loose; and she had a faint touch of a boy caught stealing apples from an orchard . . . a guilt, yet a mutinous guilt. Suddenly she looked at Charles, a swift sideways and upward glance from those almost exophthalmic dark-brown eyes with their clear whites: a look both timid and forbidding. It made him drop her arm.

"I dread to think, Miss Woodruff, what would happen if you should one day turn your ankle in a place like this."

"It does not matter."

"But it would most certainly matter, my dear young lady. From your request to me last week I presume you don't wish Mrs. Poulteney to know you come here. Heaven forbid that I should ask for your reasons. But I must point out that if you were in some way disabled I am the only person in Lyme who could lead your rescuers to you. Am I not?"

"She knows. She would guess."

"She knows you come here—to this very place?"

She stared at the turf, as if she would answer no more questions; begged him to go. But there was something in that face, which Charles examined closely in profile, that made him determine not to go. All in it had been sacrificed, he now

98

realized, to the eyes. They could not conceal an intelligence, an independence of spirit; there was also a silent contradiction of any sympathy; a determination to be what she was. Delicate, fragile, arched eyebrows were then the fashion, but Sarah's were strong, or at least unusually dark, almost the color of her hair, which made them seem strong, and gave her a faintly tomboyish air on occasion. I do not mean that she had one of those masculine, handsome, heavy-chinned faces popular in the Edwardian Age—the Gibson Girl type of beauty. Her face was well modeled, and completely feminine; and the suppressed intensity of her eyes was matched by the suppressed sensuality of her mouth, which was wide—and once again did not correspond with current taste, which veered between pretty little almost lipless mouths and childish cupid's bows. Charles, like most men of his time, was still faintly under the influence of Lavater's *Physiognomy*. He noted that mouth, and was not deceived by the fact that it was pressed unnaturally tight.

Echoes, that one flashed glance from those dark eyes had certainly roused in Charles's mind; but they were not English ones. He associated such faces with foreign women—to be frank (much franker than he would have been to himself) with foreign beds. This marked a new stage of his awareness of Sarah. He had realized she was more intelligent and independent than she seemed; he now guessed darker qualities.

To most Englishmen of his age such an intuition of Sarah's real nature would have been repellent; and it did very faintly repel—or at least shock—Charles. He shared enough of his contemporaries' prejudices to suspect sensuality in any form; but whereas they would, by one of those terrible equations that take place at the behest of the superego, have made Sarah vaguely responsible for being born as she was, he did not. For that we can thank his scientific hobbies. Darwinism, as its shrewder opponents realized, let open the floodgates to something far more serious than the undermining of the Biblical account of the origins of man; its deepest implications lay in the direction of determinism and behaviorism, that is, towards philosophies that reduce morality to a hypocrisy and duty to a straw hut in a hurricane. I do not mean that Charles completely exonerated Sarah; but he was far less inclined to blame her than she might have imagined.

Partly then, his scientific hobbies ... but Charles had also the advantage of having read—very much in private, for the book had been prosecuted for obscenity—a novel that had appeared in France some ten years before; a novel profoundly deterministic in its assumptions, the celebrated *Madame*

Bovary. And as he looked down at the face beside him, it was suddenly, out of nowhere, that Emma Bovary's name sprang into his mind. Such allusions are comprehensions; and temptations. That is why, finally, he did not bow and withdraw.

At last she spoke.

"I did not know you were here."

"How should you?"

"I must return."

And she turned. But he spoke quickly.

"Will you permit me to say something first? Something I have perhaps, as a stranger to you and your circumstances, no right to say." She stood with bowed head, her back to him. "May I proceed?"

She was silent. He hesitated a moment, then spoke.

"Miss Woodruff, I cannot pretend that your circumstances have not been discussed in front of me . . . by Mrs. Tranter. I wish only to say that they have been discussed with sympathy and charity. She believes you are not happy in your present situation, which I am given to understand you took from force of circumstance rather than from a more congenial reason. I have known Mrs. Tranter only a very short time. But I count it not the least of the privileges of my forthcoming marriage that it has introduced me to a person of such geniuine kindness of heart. I will come to the point. I am confident—"

He broke off as she looked quickly round at the trees behind them. Her sharper ears had heard a sound, a branch broken underfoot. But before he could ask her what was wrong, he too heard men's low voices. But by then she had already acted; gathering up her skirt she walked swiftly over the grass to the east, some forty yards; and there disappeared behind a thicket of gorse that had crept out a little over the turf. Charles stood dumbfounded, a mute party to her guilt.

The men's voices sounded louder. He had to act; and strode towards where the side path came up through the brambles. It was fortunate that he did, for just as the lower path came into his sight, so also did two faces, looking up; and both sharply surprised. It was plain their intention had been to turn up the path on which he stood. Charles opened his mouth to bid them good day; but the faces disappeared with astonishing quickness. He heard a hissed voice—"Run for 'un, Jem!"— and the sound of racing footsteps. A few moments later there was an urgent low whistle, and the excited whimper of a dog. Then silence.

He waited a minute, until he was certain they had gone, then he walked round to the gorse. She stood pressed sideways against the sharp needles, her face turned away.

"They have gone. Two poachers, I fancy."

She nodded, but continued to avoid his eyes. The gorse was in full bloom, the cadmium-yellow flowers so dense they almost hid the green. The air was full of their honeyed musk.

He said, "I think that was not necessary."

"No gentleman who cares for his good name can be seen with the scarlet woman of Lyme."

And that too was a step; for there was a bitterness in her voice. He smiled at her averted face.

"I think the only truly scarlet things about you are your cheeks."

Her eyes flashed round at him then, as if he were torturing some animal at bay. Then she turned away again.

Charles said gently, "Do not misunderstand me. I deplore your unfortunate situation. As I appreciate your delicacy in respect of my reputation. But it is indifferent to the esteem of such as Mrs. Poulteney."

She did not move. He continued smiling, at ease in all his travel, his reading, his knowledge of a larger world.

"My dear Miss Woodruff, I have seen a good deal of life. And I have a long nose for bigots ... whatever show of solemn piety they present to the world. Now will you please leave your hiding place? There is no impropriety in our meeting in this chance way. And you must allow me to finish what I was about to say."

He stepped aside and she walked out again onto the cropped turf. He saw that her eyelashes were wet. He did not force his presence on her, but spoke from some yards behind her back.

"Mrs. Tranter would like—is most anxious to help you, if you wish to change your situation."

Her only answer was to shake her head.

"No one is beyond help ... who inspires sympathy in others." He paused. The sharp wind took a wisp of her hair and blew it forward. She nervously smoothed it back into place. "I am merely saying what I know Mrs. Tranter would wish to say herself."

Charles was not exaggerating; for during the gay lunch that followed the reconciliation, Mrs. Poulteney and Sarah had been discussed. Charles had been but a brief victim of the old lady's power; and it was natural that they should think of her who was a permanent one. Charles determined, now that he had rushed in so far where less metropolitan angels might have feared to tread, to tell Sarah their conclusion that day.

"You should leave Lyme ... this district. I understand you have excellent qualifications. I am sure a much happier use could be found for them elsewhere." Sarah made no response. "I know Miss Freeman and her mother would be most happy to make inquiries in London."

She walked away from him then, to the edge of the cliff meadow; and stared out to sea a long moment; then turned to look at him still standing by the gorse: a strange, glistening look, so direct that he smiled: one of those smiles the smiler knows are weak, but cannot end.

She lowered her eyes. "I thank you. But I cannot leave this place."

He gave the smallest shrug. He felt baffled, obscurely wronged. "Then once again I have to apologize for intruding on your privacy. I shall not do so again."

He bowed and turned to walk away. But he had not gone two steps before she spoke.

"I . . . I know Mrs. Tranter wishes to be kind."

"Then permit her to have her wish."

She looked at the turf between them.

"To be spoken to again as if . . . as if I am not whom I am . . . I am most grateful. But such kindness . . ."

"Such kindness?"

"Such kindness is crueler to me than—"

She did not finish the sentence, but turned to the sea. Charles felt a great desire to reach out and take her shoulders and shake her; tragedy is all very well on the stage, but it can seem mere perversity in ordinary life. And that, in much less harsh terms, is what he then said.

"What you call my obstinacy is my only succor."

"Miss Woodruff, let me be frank. I have heard it said that you are . . . not altogether of sound mind. I think that is very far from true. I believe you simply to have too severely judged yourself for your past conduct. Now why in heaven's name must you always walk alone? Have you not punished yourself enough? You are young. You are able to gain your living. You have no family ties, I believe, that confine you to Dorset."

"I have ties."

"To this French gentleman?" She turned away, as if that subject was banned. "Permit me to insist—these matters are like wounds. If no one dares speak of them, they fester. If he does not return, he was not worthy of you. If he returns, I cannot believe that he will be so easily put off, should he not find you in Lyme Regis, as not to discover where you are and follow you there. Now is that not common sense?"

There was a long silence. He moved, though still several feet away, so that he could see the side of her face. Her expression was strange, almost calm, as if what he had said had confirmed some deep knowledge in her heart.

She remained looking out to sea, where a russet-sailed and westward-headed brig could be seen in a patch of sunlight some five miles out. She spoke quietly, as if to the distant ship.

"He will never return."

"You *fear* he will never return?"

"I know he will never return."

"I do not take your meaning."

She turned then and looked at Charles's puzzled and solicitous face. For a long moment she seemed almost to enjoy his bewilderment. Then she looked away.

"I have long since received a letter. The gentleman is . . ." and again she was silent, as if she wished she had not revealed so much. Suddenly she was walking, almost running, across the turf towards the path.

"Miss Woodruff!"

She took a step or two more, then turned; and again those eyes both repelled and lanced him. Her voice had a pent-up harshness, yet as much implosive as directed at Charles.

"He is married!"

"Miss Woodruff!"

But she took no notice. He was left standing there. His amazement was natural. What was unnatural was his now quite distinct sense of guilt. It was as if he had shown a callous lack of sympathy, when he was quite sure he had done his best. He stared after her several moments after she had disappeared. Then he turned and looked at the distant brig, as if that might provide an answer to this enigma. But it did not.

17

The boats, the sands, the esplanade,
    The laughing crowd;
    Light-hearted, loud
Greetings from some not ill-endowed:

The evening sunlit cliffs, the talk,
    Hailings and halts,
    The keen sea-salts,
The band, the Morgenblätter Waltz.

Still, when at night I drew inside
    Forward she came,
    Sad, but the same . . .
        HARDY, "At a Seaside Town in 1869"

That evening Charles found himself seated between Mrs.
Tranter and Ernestina in the Assembly Rooms. The Lyme
Assembly Rooms were perhaps not much, compared to those
at Bath and Cheltenham; but they were pleasing, with their
spacious proportions and windows facing the sea. Too pleasing, alas, and too excellent a common meeting place not to
be sacrificed to that Great British God, Convenience; and
they were accordingly long ago pulled down, by a Town
Council singleminded in its concern for the communal bladder, to make way for what can very fairly claim to be the
worst-sited and ugliest public lavatory in the British Isles.

You must not think, however, that the Poulteney contingent in Lyme objected merely to the frivolous architecture
of the Assembly Rooms. It was what went on there that
really outraged them. The place provoked whist, and gentlemen with cigars in their mouths, and balls, and concerts. In
short, it encouraged pleasure; and Mrs. Poulteney and her

kind knew very well that the only building a decent town could allow people to congregate in was a church. When the Assembly Rooms were torn down in Lyme, the heart was torn out of the town; and no one has yet succeeded in putting it back.

Charles and his ladies were in the doomed building for a concert. It was not, of course—it being Lent—a secular concert. The programme was unrelievedly religious. Even that shocked the narrower-minded in Lyme, who professed, at least in public, a respect for Lent equal to that of the most orthodox Muslim for Ramadan. There were accordingly some empty seats before the fern-fringed dais at one end of the main room, where the concerts were held.

Our broader-minded three had come early, like most of the rest of the audience; for these concerts were really enjoyed—in true eighteenth-century style—as much for the company as for the music. It gave the ladies an excellent opportunity to assess and comment on their neighbors' finery; and of course to show off their own. Even Ernestina, with all her contempt for the provinces, fell a victim to this vanity. At least here she knew she would have few rivals in the taste and luxury of her clothes; and the surreptitious glances at her little "plate" hat (no stuffy old bonnets for her) with its shamrock-and-white ribbons, her *vert espérance* dress, her mauve-and-black pelisse, her Balmoral boots, were an agreeable compensation for all the boredom inflicted at other times.

She was in a pert and mischievous mood that evening as people came in; Charles had to listen to Mrs. Tranter's commentary—places of residence, relatives, ancestry—with one ear, and to Tina's *sotto voce* wickednesses with the other. The John-Bull-like lady over there, he learned from the aunt, was "Mrs. Tomkins, the kindest old soul, somewhat hard of hearing, that house above Elm House, her son is in India"; while another voice informed him tersely, "A perfect gooseberry." According to Ernestina, there were far more gooseberries than humans patiently, because gossipingly, waiting for the concert to begin. Every decade invents such a useful noun-and-epithet; in the 1860s "gooseberry" meant "all that is dreary and old-fashioned"; today Ernestina would have called those worthy concert-goers square ... which was certainly Mrs. Tomkins's shape, at least from the back.

But at last the distinguished soprano from Bristol appeared, together with her accompanist, the even more distinguished Signor Ritornello (or some such name, for if a man was a pianist he must be Italian) and Charles was free to examine his conscience.

At least he began in the spirit of such an examination; as if it was his duty to do so, which hid the awkward fact that it was also his pleasure to do so. In simple truth he had become a little obsessed with Sarah . . . or at any rate with the enigma she presented. He had—or so he believed—fully intended, when he called to escort the ladies down Broad Street to the Assembly Rooms, to tell them of his meeting—though of course on the strict understanding that they must speak to no one about Sarah's wanderings over Ware Commons. But somehow the moment had not seemed opportune. There was first of all a very material dispute to arbitrate upon—Ernestina's folly in wearing grenadine when it was still merino weather, since "Thou shalt not wear grenadine till May" was one of the nine hundred and ninety-nine commandments her parents had tacked on to the statutory ten. Charles killed concern with compliment; but if Sarah was not mentioned, it was rather more because he had begun to feel that he had allowed himself to become far too deeply engaged in conversation with her—no, he had lost all sense of proportion. He had been very foolish, allowing a misplaced chivalry to blind his common sense; and the worst of it was that it was all now deucedly difficult to explain to Ernestina.

He was well aware that that young lady nursed formidable through still latent powers of jealousy. At worst, she would find his behavior incomprehensible and be angry with him; at best, she would only tease him—but it was a poor "at best." He did not want to be teased on this subject. Charles could perhaps have trusted himself with fewer doubts to Mrs. Tranter. She, he knew, certainly shared his charitable concern; but duplicity was totally foreign to her. He could not ask her not to tell Ernestina; and if Tina should learn of the meeting through her aunt, then he would be in very hot water indeed.

On his other feelings, his mood toward Ernestina that evening, he hardly dared to dwell. Her humor did not exactly irritate him, but it seemed unusually and unwelcomely artificial, as if it were something she had put on with her French hat and her new pelisse; to suit them rather than the occasion. It also required a response from him . . . a corresponding twinkle in his eyes, a constant smile, which he obliged her with, but also artificially, so that they seemed enveloped in a double pretense. Perhaps it was the gloom of so much Handel and Bach, or the frequency of the discords between the prima donna and her aide, but he caught himself stealing glances at the girl beside him—looking at her as if he saw her for the first time, as if she were a total stranger to him. She was very pretty, charming . . . but was not that face a little characterless, a little monotonous with its one set paradox of demureness and dryness? If you took away those two qualities, what remained? A vapid selfishness. But this cruel thought no sooner entered Charles's head than he dismissed it. How could the only child of rich parents be anything else? Heaven knows—why else had he fallen for her?—Ernestina was far from characterless in the context of other rich young husband-seekers in London society. But was that the only context—the only market for brides? It was a fixed article of Charles's creed that he was not like the great majority of his peers and contemporaries. That was why he had traveled so much; he found English society too hidebound, English solemnity too solemn, English thought too moralistic, English religion too bigoted. So? In this vital matter of the woman with whom he had elected to share his life, had he not been only too conventional? Instead of doing the most intelligent thing had he not done the most obvious?

What then would have been the most intelligent thing? To have waited.

Under this swarm of waspish self-inquiries he began to feel sorry for himself—a brilliant man trapped, a Byron tamed; and his mind wandered back to Sarah, to visual images, attempts to recollect that face, that mouth, that generous mouth. Undoubtedly it awoke some memory in him, too tenuous, perhaps too general, to trace to any source in his past; but it unsettled him and haunted him, by calling to some hidden self he hardly knew existed. He said it to himself: It is the stupidest thing, but that girl attracts me. It seemed clear to him that it was not Sarah in herself who attracted him—how could she, he was betrothed—but some emotion, some possibility she symbolized. She made him aware of a deprivation. His future had always seemed to him of vast potential; and now suddenly it was a fixed voyage to a known place. She had reminded him of that.

Ernestina's elbow reminded him gently of the present. The singer required applause, and Charles languidly gave his share. Placing her own hands back in their muff, Ernestina delivered a sidelong, humorous *moue*, half intended for his absentmindedness, half for the awfulness of the performance. He smiled at her. She was so young, such a child. He could not be angry with her. After all, she was only a woman. There were so many things she must never understand: the richness of male life, the enormous difficulty of being one to whom the world was rather more than dress and home and children.

All would be well when she was truly his; in his bed and in his bank . . . and of course in his heart, too.

Sam, at that moment, was thinking the very opposite; how many things his fraction of Eve *did* understand. It is difficult to imagine today the enormous differences then separating a lad born in the Seven Dials and a carter's daughter from a remote East Devon village. Their coming together was fraught with almost as many obstacles as if he had been an Eskimo and she, a Zulu. They had barely a common language, so often did they not understand what the other had just said.

Yet this distance, all those abysses unbridged and then unbridgeable by radio, television, cheap travel and the rest, was not wholly bad. People knew less of each other, perhaps, but they felt more free of each other, and so were more individual. The entire world was not for them only a push or a switch away. Strangers were strange, and sometimes with an exciting, beautiful strangeness. It may be better for humanity that we should communicate more and more. But I am a heretic, I think our ancestors' isolation was like the greater space they enjoyed: it can only be envied. The world is only too literally too much with us now.

Sam could, did give the appearance, in some back taproom, of knowing all there was to know about city life—and then some. He was aggressively contemptuous of anything that did not emanate from the West End of London, that lacked its go. But deep down inside, it was another story. There he was a timid and uncertain person—not uncertain about what he wanted to be (which was far removed from what he was) but about whether he had the ability to be it.

Now Mary was quite the reverse at heart. She was certainly dazzled by Sam to begin with: he was very much a superior being, and her teasing of him had been pure self-defense before such obvious cultural superiority: that eternal city ability to leap the gap, find shortcuts, force the pace. But she had a basic solidity of character, a kind of artless self-confidence, a knowledge that she would one day make a good wife and a good mother; and she knew, in people, what was what ... the difference in worth, say, between her mistress and her mistress's niece. After all, she was a peasant; and peasants live much closer to real values than town helots.

Sam first fell for her because she was a summer's day after the drab dollymops and gays* who had constituted his past sexual experience. Self-confidence in that way he did not

* A "dollymop" was a maidservant who went in for spare-time prostitution. A "gay," a prostitute—it is the significance in Leech's famous cartoon of 1857, in which two sad-faced women stand in the rain "not a hundred miles from the Haymarket." One turns to the other: "Ah! Fanny! How long have you been *gay?*"

lack—few Cockneys do. He had fine black hair over very blue eyes and a fresh complexion. He was slim, very slightly built; and all his movements were neat and trim, though with a tendency to a certain grandiose exaggeration of one or two of Charles's physical mannerisms that he thought particularly gentlemanly. Women's eyes seldom left him at the first glance, but from closer acquaintance with London girls he had never got much beyond a reflection of his own cynicism. What had really knocked him acock was Mary's innocence. He found himself like some boy who flashes a mirror—and one day does it to someone far too gentle to deserve such treatment. He suddenly wished to be what he was with her; and to discover what she was.

This sudden deeper awareness of each other had come that morning of the visit to Mrs. Poulteney. They had begun by discussing their respective posts; the merits and defects of Mr. Charles and Mrs. Tranter. She thought he was lucky to serve such a lovely gentleman. Sam demurred; and then, to his own amazement, found himself telling this mere milkmaid something he had previously told only to himself.

His ambition was very simple: he wanted to be a haberdasher. He had never been able to pass such shops without stopping and staring in the windows; criticizing or admiring them, as the case might require. He believed he had a flair for knowing the latest fashion. He had traveled abroad with Charles, he had picked up some foreign ideas in the haberdashery field . . .

All this (and incidentally, his profound admiration for Mr. Freeman) he had got out somewhat incoherently—and the great obstacles: no money, no education. Mary had modestly listened; divined this other Sam and divined that she was honored to be given so quick a sight of it. Sam felt he was talking too much. But each time he looked nervously up for a sneer, a giggle, the least sign of mockery of his absurd pretensions, he saw only a shy and wide-eyed sympathy, a begging him to go on. His listener felt needed, and a girl who feels needed is already a quarter way in love.

The time came when he had to go. It seemed to him that he had hardly arrived. He stood, and she smiled at him, a little mischievous again. He wanted to say that he had never talked so freely—well, so seriously—to anyone before about himself. But he couldn't find the words.

"Well. Dessay we'll meet tomorrow mornin'."

"Happen so."

"Dessay you've got a suitor an' all."

"None I really likes."

"I bet you 'ave. I 'eard you 'ave."

109

" 'Tis all talk in this ol' place. Us izzen 'lowed to look at a man an' we'm courtin'."

He fingered his bowler hat. "Like that heverywhere." A silence. He looked her in the eyes. "I ain't so bad?"

"I never said 'ee wuz."

Silence. He worked all the way round the rim of his bowler.

"I know lots o' girls. All sorts. None like you."

"Taren't so awful hard to find."

"I never 'ave. Before." There was another silence. She would not look at him, but at the edge of her apron. " 'Ow about London then? Fancy seein' London?"

She grinned then, and nodded—very vehemently.

"Expec' you will. When they're a-married orf hupstairs. I'll show yer round."

"Would 'ee?"

He winked then, and she clapped her hand over her mouth. Her eyes brimmed at him over her pink cheeks.

"All they fashional Lunnon girls, 'ee woulden want to go walkin' out with me."

"If you 'ad the clothes, you'd do. You'd do very nice."

"Doan believe 'ee."

"Cross my 'eart."

Their eyes met and held for a long moment. He bowed elaborately and swept his hat to cover his left breast.

"A demang, madymosselle."

"What's that then?"

"It's French for Coombe Street, tomorrow mornin'— where yours truly will be waitin'."

She turned then, unable to look at him. He stepped quickly behind her and took her hand and raised it to his lips. She snatched it away, and looked at it as if his lips might have left a sooty mark. Another look flashed between them. She bit her pretty lips. He winked again; and then he went.

Whether they met that next morning, in spite of Charles's express prohibition, I do not know. But later that day, when Charles came out of Mrs. Tranter's house, he saw Sam waiting, by patently contrived chance, on the opposite side of the street. Charles made the Roman sign of mercy, and Sam uncovered, and once again placed his hat reverentially over his heart—as if to a passing bier, except that his face bore a wide grin.

Which brings me to this evening of the concert nearly a week later, and why Sam came to such differing conclusions about the female sex from his master's; for he was in that kitchen again. Unfortunately there was now a duenna present—Mrs. Tranter's cook. But the duenna was fast asleep

110

in her Windsor chair in front of the opened fire of her range. Sam and Mary sat in the darkest corner of the kitchen. They did not speak. They did not need to. Since they were holding hands. On Mary's part it was but self-protection, since she had found that it was only thus that she could stop the hand trying to feel its way round her waist. Why Sam, in spite of that, and the silence, should have found Mary so understanding is a mystery no lover will need explaining.

18

Who can wonder that the laws of society should at times be forgotten by those whom the eye of society habitually overlooks, and whom the heart of society often appears to discard?

DR. JOHN SIMON, *City Medical Report* (1849)

I went, and knelt, and scooped my hand
As if to drink, into the brook,
And a faint figure seemed to stand
Above me, with the bygone look.

HARDY, "On a Midsummer Eve"

Two days passed during which Charles's hammers lay idle in his rucksack. He banned from his mind thoughts of the tests lying waiting to be discovered: and thoughts, now associated with them, of women lying asleep on sunlit ledges. But then, Ernestina having a migraine, he found himself unexpectedly with another free afternoon. He hesitated a while; but the events that passed before his eyes as he stood at the bay window of his room were so few, so dull. The inn sign—a white lion with the face of an unfed Pekinese and a distinct resemblance, already remarked on by Charles, to Mrs. Poulteney—stared glumly up at him. There was little wind, little sunlight . . . a high gray canopy of cloud, too high to threaten rain. He had intended to write letters, but he found himself not in the mood.

To tell the truth he was not really in the mood for anything; strangely there had come ragingly upon him the old travel-lust that he had believed himself to have grown out of those last years. He wished he might be in Cadiz, Naples, the Morea, in some blazing Mediterranean spring not only for the Mediterranean spring itself, but to be free, to have endless weeks of travel ahead of him, sailed-towards islands, mountains, the blue shadows of the unknown.

Half an hour later he was passing the Dairy and entering the woods of Ware Commons. He could have walked in some other direction? Yes, indeed he could. But he had sternly forbidden himself to go anywhere near the cliff-meadow; if he met Miss Woodruff, he would do, politely but firmly, what he ought to have done at that last meeting—that is, refuse to enter into conversation with her. In any case, it was evident that she resorted always to the same place. He felt sure that he would not meet her if he kept well clear of it.

Accordingly, long before he came there he turned northward, up the general slope of the land and through a vast grove of ivyclad ash trees. They were enormous, these trees, among the largest of the species in England, with exotic-looking colonies of polypody in their massive forks. It had been their size that had decided the encroaching gentleman to found his arboretum in the Undercliff; and Charles felt dwarfed, pleasantly dwarfed as he made his way among them towards the almost vertical chalk faces he could see higher up the slope. He began to feel in a better humor, especially when the first beds of flint began to erupt from the dog's mercury and arum that carpeted the ground. Almost at once he picked up a test of *Echinocorys scutata*. It was badly worn away ... a mere trace remained of one of the five sets of converging pinpricked lines that decorate the perfect shell. But it was better than nothing and thus encouraged, Charles began his bending, stopping search.

Gradually he worked his way up to the foot of the bluffs where the fallen flints were thickest, and the tests less likely to be corroded and abraded. He kept at this level, moving westward. In places the ivy was dense—growing up the cliff face and the branches of the nearest trees indiscriminately, hanging in great ragged curtains over Charles's head. In one place he had to push his way through a kind of tunnel of such foliage; at the far end there was a clearing, where there had been a recent fall of flints. Such a place was most likely to yield tests; and Charles set himself to quarter the area, bounded on all sides by dense bramble thickets, methodically. He had been at this task perhaps ten minutes, with no sound but the lowing of a calf from some distant field above and

112

inland; the clapped wings and cooings of the wood pigeons; and the barely perceptible wash of the tranquil sea far through the trees below. He heard then a sound as of a falling stone. He looked, and saw nothing, and presumed that a flint had indeed dropped from the chalk face above. He searched on for another minute or two; and then, by one of those inexplicable intuitions, perhaps the last remnant of some faculty from our paleolithic past, knew he was not alone. He glanced sharply round.

She stood above him, where the tunnel of ivy ended, some forty yards away. He did not know how long she had been there; but he remembered that sound of two minutes before. For a moment he was almost frightened; it seemed uncanny that she should appear so silently. She was not wearing nailed boots, but she must even so have moved with great caution. To surprise him; therefore she had deliberately followed him.

"Miss Woodruff!" He raised his hat. "How come you here?"

"I saw you pass."

He moved a little closer up the scree towards her. Again her bonnet was in her hand. Her hair, he noticed, was loose, as if she had been in wind; but there had been no wind. It gave her a kind of wildness, which the fixity of her stare at him aggravated. He wondered why he had ever thought she was not indeed slightly crazed.

"You have something . . . to communicate to me?"

Again that fixed stare, but not through him, very much down at him. Sarah had one of those peculiar female faces that vary very much in their attractiveness; in accordance with some subtle chemistry of angle, light, mood. She was dramatically helped at this moment by an oblique shaft of wan sunlight that had found its way through a small rift in the clouds, as not infrequently happens in a late English afternoon. It lit her face, her figure standing before the entombing greenery behind her; and her face was suddenly very beautiful, truly beautiful, exquisitely grave and yet full of an inner, as well as outer, light. Charles recalled that it was just so that a peasant near Gavarnie, in the Pyrenees, had claimed to have seen the Virgin Mary standing on a *déboulis* beside his road . . . only a few weeks before Charles once passed that way. He was taken to the place; it had been most insignificant. But if such a figure as this had stood before him!

However, this figure evidently had a more banal mission. She delved into the pockets of her coat and presented to him, one in each hand, two excellent *Micraster* tests. He climbed close enough to distinguish them for what they were. Then he looked up in surprise at her unsmiling face. He remembered—he had talked briefly of paleontology, of the importance of sea urchins, at Mrs. Poulteney's that morning. Now he stared again at the two small objects in her hands.

"Will you not take them?"

She wore no gloves, and their fingers touched. He examined the two tests; but he thought only of the touch of those cold fingers.

"I am most grateful. They are in excellent condition."

"They are what you seek?"

"Yes indeed."

"They were once marine shells?"

He hesitated, then pointed to the features of the better of the two tests: the mouth, the ambulacra, the anus. As he talked, and was listened to with a grave interest, his disapproval evaporated. The girl's appearance was strange; but her mind—as two or three questions she asked showed—was very far from deranged. Finally he put the two tests carefully in his own pocket.

"It is most kind of you to have looked for them."

"I had nothing better to do."

"I was about to return. May I help you back to the path?"

But she did not move. "I wished also, Mr. Smithson, to thank you . . . for your offer of assistance."

"Since you refused it, you leave me the more grateful."

There was a little pause. He moved up past her and parted the wall of ivy with his stick, for her to pass back. But she stood still, and still facing down the clearing.

"I should not have followed you."

He wished he could see her face, but he could not.

"I think it is better if I leave."

She said nothing, and he turned towards the ivy. But he could not resist a last look back at her. She was staring back over her shoulder at him, as if body disapproved of face and turned its back on such shamelessness; because her look, though it still suggested some of the old universal reproach, now held an intensity that was far more of appeal. Her eyes were anguished . . . and anguishing; an outrage in them, a weakness abominably raped. They did not accuse Charles of the outrage, but of not seeing that it had taken place. A long moment of locked eyes; and then she spoke to the ground between them, her cheeks red.

"I have no one to turn to."

"I hoped I had made it clear that Mrs. Tranter—"

"Has the kindest heart. But I do not need kindness."

There was a silence. He still stood parting the ivy.

"I am told the vicar is an excellently sensible man."

"It was he who introduced me to Mrs. Poulteney."

Charles stood by the ivy, as if at a door. He avoided her eyes; sought, sought for an exit line.

"If I can speak on your behalf to Mrs. Tranter, I shall be most happy . . . but it would be most improper of me to . . ."

"Interest yourself further in my circumstances."

"That is what I meant to convey, yes." Her reaction was to look away; he had reprimanded her. Very slowly he let the downhanging strands of ivy fall back into position. "You haven't reconsidered my suggestion—that you should leave this place?"

"If I went to London, I know what I should become." He stiffened inwardly. "I should become what so many women who have lost their honor become in great cities." Now she turned fully towards him. Her color deepened. "I should become what some already call me in Lyme."

It was outrageous, most unseemly. He murmured, "My dear Miss Woodruff . . ." His own cheeks were now red as well.

"I am weak. How should I not know it?" She added bitterly, "I have sinned."

This new revelation, to a stranger, in such circumstances—it banished the good the attention to his little lecture on fossil sea urchins had done her in his eyes. But yet he felt the two tests in his pockets; some kind of hold she had on him; and a Charles in hiding from himself felt obscurely flattered, as a clergyman does whose advice is sought on a spiritual problem.

He stared down at the iron ferrule of his ashplant.

"Is this the fear that keeps you at Lyme?"

"In part."

"That fact you told me the other day as you left. Is anyone else apprised of it?"

"If they knew, they would not have missed the opportunity of telling me."

There was a longer silence. Moments like modulations come in human relationships: when what has been until then an objective situation, one perhaps described by the mind to itself in semiliterary terms, one it is sufficient merely to classify under some general heading (man with alcoholic problems, woman with unfortunate past, and so on) becomes subjective; becomes unique; becomes, by empathy, instantaneously shared rather than observed. Such a metamorphosis took place in Charles's mind as he stared at the bowed head of the sinner before him. Like most of us when such moments come—who has not been embraced by a drunk?—he sought for a hasty though diplomatic restoration of the *status quo*.

"I am most sorry for you. But I must confess I don't understand why you should seek to ... as it were ... make me your confidant."

She began then—as if the question had been expected—to speak rapidly; almost repeating a speech, a litany learned by heart.

"Because you have traveled. Because you are educated. Because you are a gentleman. Because ... because, I do not know, I live among people the world tells me are kind, pious, Christian people. And they seem to me crueler than the cruelest heathens, stupider than the stupidest animals. I cannot believe that the truth is so. That life is without understanding or compassion. That there are not spirits generous enough to understand what I have suffered and why I suffer ... and that, whatever sins I have committed, it is not right that I should suffer so much." There was silence. Unprepared for this articulate account of her feelings, this proof, already suspected but not faced, of an intelligence beyond convention, Charles said nothing. She turned away and went on in a quieter voice. "My only happiness is when I sleep. When I wake, the nightmare begins. I feel cast on a desert island, imprisoned, condemned, and I know not what crime it is for."

Charles looked at her back in dismay, like a man about to be engulfed by a landslide; as if he would run, but could not; would speak, but could not.

Her eyes were suddenly on his. "Why am I born what I am? Why am I not born Miss Freeman?" But the name no sooner passed her lips than she turned away, conscious that she had presumed too much.

"That question were better not asked."

"I did not mean to ..."

"Envy is forgivable in your—"

"Not envy. Incomprehension."

"It is beyond my powers—the powers of far wiser men than myself—to help you here."

"I do not—I *will* not believe that."

Charles had known women—frequently Ernestina herself—contradict him playfully. But that was in a playful context. A woman did not contradict a man's opinion when he was being serious unless it were in carefully measured terms. Sarah seemed almost to assume some sort of equality of intellect with him; and in precisely the circumstances where she should have been most deferential if she wished to encompass her end. He felt insulted, he felt ... he could not say. The logical conclusion of his feelings should have been that he raised his hat with a cold finality and walked away in

116

his stout nailed boots. But he stood where he was, as if he had taken root. Perhaps he had too fixed an idea of what a siren looked like and the circumstances in which she appeared—long tresses, a chaste alabaster nudity, a mermaid's tail, matched by an Odysseus with a face acceptable in the best clubs. There were no Doric temples in the Undercliff; but here was a Calypso.

She murmured, "Now I have offended you."

"You bewilder me, Miss Woodruff. I do not know what you can expect of me that I haven't already offered to try to effect for you. But you must surely realize that any greater intimacy . . . however innocent in its intent . . . between us is quite impossible in my present circumstances."

There was a silence; a woodpecker laughed in some green recess, mocking those two static bipeds far below.

"Would I have . . . thrown myself on your mercy in this way if I were not desperate?"

"I don't doubt your despair. But at least concede the impossibility of your demand." He added, "Whose exact nature I am still ignorant of."

"I should like to tell you of what happened eighteen months ago."

A silence. She looked to see his reaction. Again Charles stiffened. The invisible chains dropped, and his conventional side triumphed. He drew himself up, a monument to suspicious shock, rigidly disapproving; yet in his eyes a something that searched hers . . . an explanation, a motive . . . he thought she was about to say more, and was on the point of turning through the ivy with no more word. But as if she divined his intention, she did, with a forestalling abruptness, the most unexpected thing. She sank to her knees.

Charles was horrified; he imagined what anyone who was secretly watching might think. He took a step back, as if to keep out of view. Strangely, she seemed calm. It was not the kneeling of a hysteric. Only the eyes were more intense: eyes without sun, bathed in an eternal moonlight.

"Miss Woodruff!"

"I beg you. I am not yet mad. But unless I am helped I shall be."

"Control yourself. If we were seen . . ."

"You are my last resource. You are not cruel, I know you are not cruel."

He stared at her, glanced desperately round, then moved forward and made her stand, and led her, a stiff hand under her elbow, under the foliage of the ivy. She stood before him with her face in her hands; and Charles had, with the atrocious swiftness of the human heart when it attacks the human brain, to struggle not to touch her.

"I don't wish to seem indifferent to your troubles. But you must see I have . . . I have no choice."

She spoke in a rapid, low voice. "All I ask is that you meet me once more. I will come here each afternoon. No one will see us." He tried to expostulate, but she was not to be stopped. "You are kind, you understand what is beyond the understanding of any in Lyme. Let me finish. Two days ago I was nearly overcome by madness. I felt I had to see you, to speak to you. I know where you stay. I would have come there to ask for you, had not . . . had not some last remnant of sanity mercifully stopped me at the door."

"But this is unforgivable. Unless I mistake, you now threaten me with a scandal."

She shook her head vehemently. "I would rather die than you should think that of me. It is that . . . I do not know how to say it, I seem driven by despair to contemplate these dreadful things. They fill me with horror at myself. I do not know where to turn, what to do, I have no one who can . . . please . . . can you not understand?"

Charles's one thought now was to escape from the appalling predicament he had been landed in; from those remorselessly sincere, those naked eyes.

"I must go. I am expected in Broad Street."

"But you will come again?"

"I cannot—"

"I walk here each Monday, Wednesday, Friday. When I have no other duties."

"What you are suggesting is—I must insist that Mrs. Tranter . . ."

"I could not tell the truth before Mrs. Tranter."

"Then it can hardly be fit for a total stranger—and not of your sex—to hear."

"A total stranger . . . and one not of one's sex . . . is often the least prejudiced judge."

"Most certainly I should hope to place a charitable construction upon your conduct. But I must repeat that I find myself amazed that you should . . ."

But she was still looking up at him then; and his words tailed off into silence. Charles, as you will have noticed, had more than one vocabulary. With Sam in the morning, with Ernestina across a gay lunch, and here in the role of Alarmed Propriety . . . he was almost three different men; and there will be others of him before we are finished. We may explain it biologically by Darwin's phrase: *cryptic coloration,* survival by learning to blend with one's surroundings—

with the unquestioned assumptions of one's age or social caste. Or we can explain this flight to formality sociologically. When one was skating over so much thin ice—ubiquitous economic oppression, terror of sexuality, the flood of mechanistic science—the ability to close one's eyes to one's own absurd stiffness was essential. Very few Victorians chose to question the virtues of such cryptic coloration; but there was that in Sarah's look which did. Though direct, it was a timid look. Yet behind it lay a very modern phrase: Come clean, Charles, come clean. It took the recipient off balance. Ernestina and her like behaved always as if habited in glass: infinitely fragile, even when they threw books of poetry. They encouraged the mask, the safe distance; and this girl, behind her façade of humility forbade it. He looked down in his turn.

"I ask but one hour of your time."

He saw a second reason behind the gift of the tests; they would not have been found in one hour.

"If I should, albeit with the greatest reluctance—"

She divined, and interrupted in a low voice. "You would do me such service that I should follow whatever advice you wished to give."

"It must certainly be that we do not continue to risk—"

Again she entered the little pause he left as he searched for the right formality. "That—I understand. And that you have far more pressing ties."

The sun's rays had disappeared after their one brief illumination. The day drew to a chilly close. It was as if the road he walked, seemingly across a plain, became suddenly a brink over an abyss. He knew it as he stared at her bowed head. He could not say what had lured him on, what had gone wrong in his reading of the map, but both lost and lured he felt. Yet now committed to one more folly.

She said, "I cannot find the words to thank you. I shall be here on the days I said." Then, as if the clearing was her drawing room, "I must not detain you longer."

Charles bowed, hesitated, one last poised look, then turned. A few seconds later he was breaking through the further curtain of ivy and stumbling on his downhill way, a good deal more like a startled roebuck than a worldly English gentleman.

He came to the main path through the Undercliff and strode out back towards Lyme. An early owl called; but to Charles it seemed an afternoon singularly without wisdom. He should have taken a firmer line, should have left earlier, should have handed back the tests, should have suggested— no, commanded—other solutions to her despair. He felt outwitted, inclined almost to stop and wait for her. But his feet strode on all the faster.

He knew he was about to engage in the forbidden, or rather the forbidden was about to engage in him. The farther he moved from her, in time and distance, the more clearly he saw the folly of his behavior. It was as if, when she was before him, he had become blind: had not seen her for what she was, a woman most patently dangerous—not consciously so, but prey to intense emotional frustration and no doubt social resentment.

Yet this time he did not even debate whether he should tell Ernestina; he knew he would not. He felt as ashamed as if he had, without warning her, stepped off the Cobb and set sail for China.

19

As many more individuals of each species are born than can possibly survive; and as, consequently, there is a frequently recurring struggle for existence, it follows that any being, if it vary however slightly in any manner profitable to itself, under the complex and sometimes varying conditions of life, will have a better chance of surviving, and thus be *naturally selected*.

DARWIN, *The Origin of Species* (1859)

The China-bound victim had in reality that evening to play host at a surprise planned by Ernestina and himself for Aunt Tranter. The two ladies were to come and dine in his sitting room at the White Lion. A dish of succulent first lobsters was prepared, a fresh-run salmon boiled, the cellars of the inn ransacked; and that doctor we met briefly one day at Mrs. Poulteney's was pressed into establishing the correct balance of the sexes.

One of the great characters of Lyme, he was generally supposed to be as excellent a catch in the river Marriage as the salmon he sat down to that night had been in the river Axe. Ernestina teased her aunt unmercifully about him, accusing that quintessentially mild woman of heartless cruelty to a poor lonely man pining for her hand. But since this tragic figure had successfully put up with his poor loneliness for sixty years or more, one may doubt the pining as much as the heartless cruelty.

Dr. Grogan was, in fact, as confirmed an old bachelor as Aunt Tranter a spinster. Being Irish, he had to the full that strangely eunuchistic Hibernian ability to flit and flirt and flatter womankind without ever allowing his heart to become entangled. A dry little kestrel of a man, sharp, almost fierce on occasion, yet easy to unbend when the company was to his taste, he added a pleasant astringency to Lyme society; for when he was with you you felt he was always hovering a little, waiting to pounce on any foolishness—and yet, if he liked you, it was always with a tonic wit and the humanity of a man who had lived and learned, after his fashion, to let live. There was, too, something faintly dark about him, for he had been born a Catholic; he was, in terms of our own time, not unlike someone who had been a Communist in the 1930s—accepted now, but still with the devil's singe on him. It was certain—would Mrs. Poulteney have ever allowed him into her presence otherwise?—that he was now (like Disraeli) a respectable member of the Church of England. It must be so, for (unlike Disraeli) he went scrupulously to matins every Sunday. That a man might be so indifferent to religion that he would have gone to a mosque or a synagogue, had that been the chief place of worship, was a deceit beyond the Lymers' imagination. Besides he was a very good doctor, with a sound knowledge of that most important branch of medicine, his patients' temperament. With those that secretly wanted to be bullied, he bullied; and as skillfully chivvied, cosseted, closed a blind eye, as the case required.

Nobody in Lyme liked good food and wine better; and the repast that Charles and the White Lion offered meeting his approval, he tacitly took over the role of host from the younger man. He had studied at Heidelberg, and practiced in London, and knew the world and its absurdities as only an intelligent Irishman can; which is to say that where his knowledge or memory failed him, his imagination was always ready to fill the gap. No one believed all his stories; or wanted any the less to hear them. Aunt Tranter probably knew them as well as anyone in Lyme, for the doctor and she were old friends, and she must have known how little consistent each telling was with the previous; yet she laughed

121

most—and at times so immoderately that I dread to think what might have happened had the pillar of the community up the hill chanced to hear.

It was an evening that Charles would normally have enjoyed; not least perhaps because the doctor permitted himself little freedoms of language and fact in some of his tales, especially when the plump salmon lay in anatomized ruins and the gentlemen proceeded to a decanter of port, that were not quite *comme il faut* in the society Ernestina had been trained to grace. Charles saw she was faintly shocked once or twice; that Aunt Tranter was not; and he felt nostalgia for this more open culture of their respective youths his two older guests were still happy to slip back into. Watching the little doctor's mischievous eyes and Aunt Tranter's jolliness he had a whiff of corollary nausea for his own time: its stifling propriety, its worship not only of the literal machine in transport and manufacturing but of the far more terrible machine now erecting in social convention.

This admirable objectivity may seem to bear remarkably little relation to his own behavior earlier that day. Charles did not put it so crudely to himself; but he was not quite blind to his inconsistency, either. He told himself, now swinging to another tack, that he had taken Miss Woodruff altogether too seriously—in his stumble, so to speak, instead of in his stride. He was especially solicitous to Ernestina, no longer *souffrante,* but a little lacking in her usual vivacity, though whether that was as a result of the migraine or the doctor's conversational Irish reel, it was hard to say. And yet once again it bore in upon him, as at the concert, that there was something shallow in her—that her acuteness was largely constituted, intellectually as alphabetically, by a mere cuteness. Was there not, beneath the demure knowingness, something of the automaton about her, of one of those ingenious girl-machines from Hoffmann's Tales?

But then he thought: she is a child among three adults—and pressed her hand gently beneath the mahogany table. She was charming when she blushed.

The two gentlemen, the tall Charles with his vague resemblance to the late Prince Consort and the thin little doctor, finally escorted the ladies back to their house. It was half past ten, the hour when the social life of London was just beginning; but here the town was well into its usual long sleep. They found themselves, as the door closed in their smiling faces, the only two occupants of Broad Street.

The doctor put a finger on his nose. "Now for you, sir, I prescribe a copious toddy dispensed by my own learned hand." Charles put on a polite look of demurral. "Doctor's orders, you know. *Dulce est desipere,* as the poet says. It is sweet to sip in the proper place."

Charles smiled. "If you promise the grog to be better than the Latin, then with the greatest pleasure."

Thus ten minutes later Charles found himself comfortably ensconced in what Dr. Grogan called his "cabin," a bow-fronted second-floor study that looked out over the small bay between the Cobb Gate and the Cobb itself; a room, the Irishman alleged, made especially charming in summer by the view it afforded of the nereids who came to take the waters. What nicer—in both senses of the word—situation could a doctor be in than to have to order for his feminine patients what was so pleasant also for his eye? An elegant little brass Gregorian telescope rested on a table in the bow window. Grogan's tongue flickered wickedly out, and he winked.

"For astronomical purposes only, of course."

Charles craned out of the window, and smelled the salt air, and saw on the beach some way to his right the square black silhouettes of the bathing-machines from which the nereids emerged. But the only music from the deep that night was the murmur of the tide on the shingle; and somewhere much farther out, the dimly raucous cries of the gulls roosting on the calm water. Behind him in the lamp-lit room he heard the small chinks that accompanied Grogan's dispensing of his "medicine." He felt himself in suspension between the two worlds, the warm, neat civilization behind his back, the cool, dark mystery outside. We all write poems; it is simply that poets are the ones who write in words.

The grog was excellent, the Burmah cheroot that accompanied it a pleasant surprise; and these two men still lived in a world where strangers of intelligence shared a common landscape of knowledge, a community of information, with a known set of rules and attached meanings. What doctor today knows the classics? What amateur can talk comprehensibly to scientists? These two men's was a world without the tyranny of specialization; and I would not have you—nor would Dr. Grogan, as you will see—confuse progress with happiness.

For a while they said nothing, sinking back gratefully into that masculine, more serious world the ladies and the occasion had obliged them to leave. Charles had found himself curious to know what political views the doctor held; and by way of getting to the subject asked whom the two busts that sat whitely among his host's books might be of.

The doctor smiled. *"Quisque suos patimur manes."* Which is Virgil, and means something like "We make our destinies by our choice of gods."

Charles smiled back. "I recognize Bentham, do I not?"

"You do. And the other lump of Parian is Voltaire."

"Therefore I deduce that we subscribe to the same party."

The doctor quizzed him. "Has an Irishman a choice?"

Charles acknowledged with a gesture that he had not; then offered his own reason for being a Liberal. "It seems to me that Mr. Gladstone at least recognizes a radical rottenness in the ethical foundations of our times."

"By heavens, I'm not sitting with a socialist, am I?"

Charles laughed. "Not as yet."

"Mind you, in this age of steam and cant, I could forgive a man anything—except Vital Religion."

"Ah yes indeed."

"I was a Benthamite as a young man. Voltaire drove me out of Rome, the other man out of the Tory camp. But this new taradiddle now—the extension of franchise. That's not for me. I don't give a fig for birth. A duke, heaven knows a king, can be as stupid as the next man. But I thank Mother Nature I shall not be alive in fifty years' time. When a government begins to fear the mob, it is as much as to say it fears itself." His eyes twinkled. "Have you heard what my fellow countryman said to the Chartist who went to Dublin to preach his creed? 'Brothers,' the Chartist cried, 'is not one man as good as another?' 'Faith, Mr. Speaker, you're right,' cries back Paddy, 'and a divilish bit better too!' " Charles smiled, but the doctor raised a sharp finger. "You smile, Smithson. But hark you—Paddy was right. That was no bull. That 'divilish bit better' will be the ruin of this country. You mark my words."

"But are your two household gods quite free of blame? Who was it preached the happiness of the greatest number?"

"I do not dispute the maxim. But the way we go about it. We got by very well without the Iron Civilizer" (by which he meant the railway) "when I was a young man. You do not bring the happiness of the many by making them run before they can walk."

Charles murmured a polite agreement. He had touched exactly that same sore spot with his uncle, a man of a very different political complexion. Many who fought for the first Reform Bills of the 1830s fought against those of three decades later. They felt an opportunism, a twofacedness had cancered the century, and given birth to a menacing spirit of envy and rebellion. Perhaps the doctor, born in 1801, was really a fragment of Augustan humanity; his sense of progress depended too closely on an ordered society—order being whatever allowed him to be exactly as he always had been, which made him really much closer to the crypto-Liberal Burke than the crypto-Fascist Bentham. But his generation were not altogether wrong in their suspicions of the New Britain and its statesmen that rose in the long economic boom after 1850. Many younger men, obscure ones like Charles, celebrated ones like Matthew Arnold, agreed with them. Was not the supposedly converted Disraeli later heard, on his deathbed, to mutter the prayers for the dead in Hebrew? And was not Gladstone, under the cloak of noble oratory, the greatest master of the ambiguous statement, the brave declaration qualified into cowardice, in modern political history? Where the highest are indecipherable, the worst ... but clearly the time had come to change the subject. Charles asked the doctor if he was interested in paleontology.

"No, sir. I had better own up. I did not wish to spoil that delightful dinner. But I am emphatically a neo-ontologist." He smiled at Charles from the depths of his boxwing chair. "When we know more of the living, that will be the time to pursue the dead."

Charles accepted the rebuke; and seized his opportunity. "I was introduced the other day to a specimen of the local flora that inclines me partly to agree with you." He paused cunningly. "A very strange case. No doubt you know more of it than I do." Then sensing that his oblique approach might suggest something more than a casual interest, he added quickly, "I think her name is Woodruff. She is employed by Mrs. Poulteney."

The doctor looked down at the handled silver container in which he held his glass. "Ah yes. Poor 'Tragedy.'"

"I am being indiscreet? She is perhaps a patient."

"Well, I attend Mrs. Poulteney. And I would not allow a bad word to be said about *her*."

Charles glanced cautiously at him; but there was no mistaking a certain ferocity of light in the doctor's eyes, behind his square-rimmed spectacles. The younger man looked down with a small smile.

Dr. Grogan reached out and poked his fire. "We know more about the fossils out there on the beach than we do about what takes place in that girl's mind. There is a clever German doctor who has recently divided melancholia into several types. One he calls natural. By which he means, one is born with a sad temperament. Another he calls occasional, by which he means, springing from an occasion. This, you understand, we all suffer from at times. The third class he calls obscure melancholia. By which he really means, poor man, that he doesn't know what the devil it is that causes it."

125

"But she had an occasion, did she not?"

"Oh now come, is she the first young woman who has been jilted? I could tell you of a dozen others here in Lyme."

"In such brutal circumstance?"

"Worse, some of them. And today they're as merry as crickets."

"So you class Miss Woodruff in the obscure category?"

The doctor was silent a few moments. "I was called in—all this, you understand, in strictest confidence—I was called in to see her . . . a tenmonth ago. Now I could see what was wrong at once—weeping without reason, not talking, a look about the eyes. Melancholia as plain as measles. I knew her story, I know the Talbots, she was governess there when it happened. And I think, well the cause is plain—six weeks, six *days* at Marlborough House is enough to drive any normal being into Bedlam. Between ourselves, Smithson, I'm an old heathen. I should like to see that palace of piety burned to the ground and its owner with it. I'll be damned if I wouldn't dance a jig on the ashes."

"I think I might well join you."

"And begad we wouldn't be the only ones." The doctor took a fierce gulp of his toddy. "The whole town would be out. But that's neither here nor the other place. I did what I could for the girl. But I saw there was only one cure."

"Get her away."

The doctor nodded vehemently. "A fortnight later, Grogan's coming into his house one afternoon and this colleen's walking towards the Cobb. I have her in, I talk to her, I'm as gentle to her as if she's my favorite niece. And it's like jumping a jarvey over a ten-foot wall. Not-on, my goodness, Smithson, didn't she show me not-on! And it wasn't just the talking I tried with her. I have a colleague in Exeter, a darling man and a happy wife and four little brats like angels, and he was just then looking out for a governess. I told her so."

"And she wouldn't leave!"

"Not an inch. It's this, you see. Mrs. Talbot's a dove, she would have had the girl back at the first. But no, she goes to a house she must know is a living misery, to a mistress who never knew the difference between servant and slave, to a post like a pillow of furze. And there she is, she won't be moved. You won't believe this, Smithson. But you could offer that girl the throne of England—and a thousand pounds to a penny she'd shake her head."

"But . . . I find this incomprehensible. What you tell me she refused is precisely what we had considered. Ernestina's mother—"

"Will be wasting her time, my dear fellow, with all respect to the lady." He smiled grimly at Charles, then stopped to top up their glasses from the grog-kettle on the hob. "But the good Doctor Hartmann describes somewhat similar cases. He says of one, now, a very striking thing. A case of a widow, if I recall, a young widow, Weimar, husband a cavalry officer, died in some accident on field exercises. You see there are parallels. This woman went into deep mourning. Very well. To be expected. But it went on and on, Smithson, year after year. Nothing in the house was allowed to be changed. The dead man's clothes still hung in his wardrobe, his pipe lay beside his favorite chair, even some letters that came addressed to him after his death ... there ..." the doctor pointed into the shadows behind Charles ... "there on the same silver dish, unopened, yellowing, year after year." He paused and smiled at Charles. "Your ammonites will never hold such mysteries as that. But this is what Hartmann says."

He stood over Charles, and directed the words into him with pointed finger. *"It was as if the woman had become addicted to melancholia as one becomes addicted to opium. Now do you see how it is? Her sadness becomes her happiness. She wants to be a sacrificial victim, Smithson. Where you and I flinch back, she leaps forward. She is possessed, you see."* He sat down again. "Dark indeed. Very dark."

There was a silence between the two men. Charles threw the stub of his cheroot into the fire. For a moment it flamed. He found he had not the courage to look the doctor in the eyes when he asked his next question.

"And she has confided the real state of her mind to no one?"

"Her closest friend is certainly Mrs. Talbot. But she tells me the girl keeps mum even with her. I flatter myself ... but I most certainly failed."

"And if ... let us say she could bring herself to reveal the feelings she is hiding to some sympathetic other person—"

"She would be cured. But she does not want to be cured. It is as simple as if she refused to take medicine."

"But presumably in such a case you would ..."

"How do you force the soul, young man? Can you tell me that?" Charles shrugged his impotence. "Of course not. And I will tell you something. It is better so. Understanding never grew from violation."

"She is then a hopeless case?"

"In the sense you intend, yes. Medicine can do nothing. You must not think she is like us men, able to reason clearly, examine her motives, understand why she behaves as she does. One must see her as a being in a mist. All we can do is wait and hope that the mists rise. Then perhaps ..." he fell silent. Then added, without hope, "Perhaps."

At that very same moment, Sarah's bedroom lies in the black silence shrouding Marlborough House. She is asleep, turned to the right, her dark hair falling across her face and almost hiding it. Again you notice how peaceful, how untragic, the features are: a healthy young woman of twenty-six or -seven, with a slender, rounded arm thrown out, over the bedclothes, for the night is still and the windows closed ... thrown out, as I say, and resting over another body.

Not a man. A girl of nineteen or so, also asleep, her back to Sarah, yet very close to her, since the bed, though large, is not meant for two people.

A thought has swept into your mind; but you forget we are in the year 1867. Suppose Mrs. Poulteney stood suddenly in the door, lamp in hand, and came upon those two affectionate bodies lying so close, so together, there. You imagine perhaps that she would have swollen, an infuriated black swan, and burst into an outraged anathema; you see the two girls, dressed only in their piteous shifts, cast from the granite gates.

Well, you would be quite wrong. Since we know Mrs. Poulteney dosed herself with laudanum every night, it was very unlikely that the case should have been put to the test. But if she had after all stood there, it is almost certain that she would simply have turned and gone away—more, she might even have closed the door quietly enough not to wake the sleepers.

Incomprehensible? But some vices were then so unnatural that they did not exist. I doubt if Mrs. Poulteney had ever heard of the word "lesbian"; and if she had, it would have commenced with a capital, and referred to an island in Greece. Besides, it was to her a fact as rock-fundamental as that the world was round or that the Bishop of Exeter was Dr. Phillpotts that women did not feel carnal pleasure. She knew, of course, that the lower sort of female apparently enjoyed a certain kind of male caress, such as that monstrous kiss she had once seen planted on Mary's cheeks, but this she took to be the result of feminine vanity and feminine weakness. Prostitutes, as Lady Cotton's most celebrated good work could but remind her, existed; but they were explicable as creatures so depraved that they overcame their innate woman's disgust at the carnal in their lust for money. That indeed had been her first assumption about Mary; the girl, since she giggled after she was so grossly abused by the stableboy, was most patently a prostitute in the making.

But what of Sarah's motives? As regards lesbianism, she was as ignorant as her mistress; but she did not share Mrs. Poulteney's horror of the carnal. She knew, or at least suspected, that there was a physical pleasure in love. Yet she was, I think, as innocent as makes no matter. It had begun, this sleeping with Millie, soon after the poor girl had broken down in front of Mrs. Poulteney. Dr. Grogan recommended that she be moved out of the maids' dormitory and given a room with more light. It so happened that there was a long unused dressing room next to Sarah's bedroom; and Millie was installed in it. Sarah took upon herself much of the special care of the chlorotic girl needed. She was a plowman's daughter, fourth of eleven children who lived with their parents in a poverty too bitter to describe, her home a damp, cramped, two-room cottage in one of those valleys that radiates west from bleak Eggardon. A fashionable young London architect now has the place and comes there for weekends, and loves it, so wild, so out-of-the-way, so picturesquely rural; and perhaps this exorcizes the Victorian horrors that took place there. I hope so; those visions of the contented country laborer and his brood made so fashionable by George Morland and his kind (Birket Foster was the arch criminal by 1867) were as stupid and pernicious a sentimentalization, therefore a suppression of reality, as that in our own Hollywood films of "real" life. One look at Millie and her ten miserable siblings should have scorched the myth of the Happy Swain into ashes; but so few gave that look. Each age, each guilty age, builds high walls round its Versailles; and personally I hate those walls most when they are made by literature and art.

One night, then, Sarah heard the girl weeping. She went into her room and comforted her, which was not too difficult, for Millie was a child in all but her years; unable to read or write and as little able to judge the other humans around her as a dog; if you patted her, she understood—if you kicked her, then that was life. It was a bitterly cold night, and Sarah had simply slipped into the bed and taken the girl in her arms, and kissed her, and quite literally patted her. To her Millie was like one of the sickly lambs she had once, before her father's social ambitions drove such peasant procedures from their way of life, so often brought up by hand. And heaven knows the simile was true also for the plowman's daughter.

From then on, the lamb would come two or three times a week and look desolate. She slept badly, worse than Sarah, who sometimes went solitary to sleep, only to wake in the dawn to find the girl beside her—so meekly-gently did Millie, at some intolerable midnight hour, slip into her place. She was afraid of the dark, poor girl; and had it not been for Sarah, would have asked to go back to the dormitory up-stairs.

This tender relationship was almost mute. They rarely if ever talked, and if they did, of only the most trivial domestic things. They knew it was that warm, silent co-presence in the darkness that mattered. There must have been something sexual in their feelings? Perhaps; but they never went beyond the bounds that two sisters would. No doubt here and there in another milieu, in the most brutish of the urban poor, in the most emancipated of the aristocracy, a truly orgastic lesbianism existed then; but we may ascribe this very com-mon Victorian phenomenon of women sleeping together far more to the desolating arrogance of contemporary man than to a more suspect motive. Besides, in such wells of loneliness is not any coming together closer to humanity than perver-sity?

So let them sleep, these two innocents; and let us return to that other more rational, more learned and altogether more nobly gendered pair down by the sea.

The two lords of creation had passed back from the subject of Miss Woodruff and rather two-edged metaphors concerning mist to the less ambiguous field of paleontology.

"You must admit," said Charles, "that Lyell's findings are fraught with a much more than intrinsic importance. I fear the clergy have a tremendous battle on their hands."

Lyell, let me interpose, was the father of modern geology. Already Buffon, in the famous *Epoques de la Nature* of 1778, had exploded the myth, invented by Archbishop Ussher in the seventeenth century and recorded solemnly in count-less editions of the official English Bible, that the world had been created at nine o'clock on October 26th, 4004 B.C. But even the great French naturalist had not dared to push the origin of the world back further than some 75,000 years. Lyell's *Principles of Geology*, published between 1830 and 1833—and so coinciding very nicely with reform elsewhere—had hurled it back millions. His is a largely unremembered, but an essential name; he gave the age, and countless scien-tists in other fields, the most meaningful space. His discov-eries blew like a great wind, freezing to the timid, but invigorating to the bold, through the century's stale meta-physical corridors. But you must remember that at the time of which I write few had even heard of Lyell's masterwork, fewer believed its theories, and fewer still accepted all their implications. Genesis is a great lie; but it is also a great

130

poem; and a six-thousand-year-old womb is much warmer than one that stretches for two thousand million.

Charles was therefore interested—both his future father-in-law and his uncle had taught him to step very delicately in this direction—to see whether Dr. Grogan would confirm or dismiss his solicitude for the theologians. But the doctor was unforthcoming. He stared into his fire and murmured, "They have indeed."

There was a little silence, which Charles broke casually, as if really to keep the conversation going.

"Have you read this fellow Darwin?"

Grogan's only reply was a sharp look over his spectacles. Then he got to his feet and taking the camphine lamp, went to a bookshelf at the back of the narrow room. In a moment he returned and handed a book to Charles. It was *The Origin of Species.* He looked up at the doctor's severe eyes.

"I did not mean to imply—"

"Have you read it?"

"Yes."

"Then you should know better than to talk of a great man as 'this fellow.' "

"From what you said—"

"This book is about the living, Smithson. Not the dead."

The doctor rather crossly turned to replace the lamp on its table. Charles stood.

"You are quite right. I apologize."

The little doctor eyed him sideways.

"Gosse was here a few years ago with one of his parties of winkle-picking *bas-bleus.* Have you read his *Omphalos?*"

Charles smiled. "I found it central to nothing but the sheerest absurdity."

And now Grogan, having put him through both a positive and a negative test, smiled bleakly in return.

"I told him as much at the end of his lecture here. Ha! Didn't I just." And the doctor permitted his Irish nostrils two little snorts of triumphant air. "I fancy that's one bag of fundamentalist wind that will think twice before blowing on this part of the Dorset littoral again."*

* *Omphalos: an attempt to untie the geological knot* is now forgotten; which is a pity, as it is one of the most curious—and unintentionally comic—books of the whole era. The author was a Fellow of the Royal Society and the leading marine biologist of his day; yet his fear of Lyell and his followers drove him in 1857 to advance a theory in which the anomalies between science and the Biblical account of Creation are all neatly removed at one fine blow: Gosse's ingenious argument being that on the day God created Adam he also created all fossil and extinct forms of life along with him—which must surely rank as the most incomprehensible cover-up operation ever attributed

131

He eyed Charles more kindly.

"A Darwinian?"

"Passionately."

Grogan then seized his hand and gripped it; as if he were Crusoe, and Charles, Man Friday; and perhaps something passed between them not so very unlike what passed unconsciously between those two sleeping girls half a mile away. They knew they were like two grains of yeast in a sea of lethargic dough—two grains of salt in a vast tureen of insipid broth.

Our two *carbonari* of the mind—has not the boy in man always adored playing at secret societies?—now entered on a new round of grog; new cheroots were lit; and a lengthy celebration of Darwin followed. They ought, one may think, to have been humbled by the great new truths they were discussing; but I am afraid the mood in both of them—and in Charles especially, when he finally walked home in the small hours of the morning—was one of exalted superiority, intellectual distance above the rest of their fellow creatures.

Unlit Lyme was the ordinary mass of mankind, most evidently sunk in immemorial sleep; while Charles the naturally selected (the adverb carries both its senses) was pure intellect, walking awake, free as a god, one with the unslumbering stars and understanding all.

All except Sarah, that is.

to divinity by man. Even the date of *Omphalos*—just two years before *The Origin*—could not have been more unfortunate. Gosse was, of course, immortalized half a century later in his son Edmund's famous and exquisite memoir.

20

Are God and Nature then at strife,
That Nature lends such evil dreams?
So careful of the type she seems,
So careless of the single life . . .

TENNYSON, *In Memoriam* (1850)

Finally, she broke the silence and spelled it out to
Dr. Burkley. Kneeling, the physician indicated her
ghastly skirt with a trembling hand. "Another dress?"
he suggested diffidently.

"No," she whispered fiercely. "Let them see what
they've done."

WILLIAM MANCHESTER, *The Death of a President*

She stood obliquely in the shadows at the tunnel of ivy's
other end. She did not look round; she had seen him climbing
up through the ash trees. The day was brilliant, steeped in
azure, with a warm southwesterly breeze. It had brought out
swarms of spring butterflies, those brimstones, orange-tips and
green-veined whites we have lately found incompatible with
high agricultural profit and so poisoned almost to extinction;
they had danced with Charles all along his way past the
Dairy and through the woods; and now one, a brilliant fleck
of sulphur, floated in the luminous clearing behind Sarah's
dark figure.

Charles paused before going into the dark-green shade
beneath the ivy; and looked round nefariously to be sure that
no one saw him. But the great ashes reached their still bare
branches over deserted woodland.

She did not turn until he was close, and even then she
would not look at him; instead, she felt in her coat pocket
and silently, with downcast eyes, handed him yet another
test, as if it were some expiatory offering. Charles took it, but
her embarrassment was contagious.

"You must allow me to pay for these tests what I should
pay at Miss Anning's shop."

133

Her head rose then, and at last their eyes met. He saw that she was offended; again he had that unaccountable sensation of being lanced, of falling short, of failing her. But this time it brought him to his senses, that is, to the attitude he had decided to adopt; for this meeting took place two days after the events of the last chapters. Dr. Grogan's little remark about the comparative priority to be accorded the dead and the living had germinated, and Charles now saw a scientific as well as a humanitarian reason in his adventure. He had been frank enough to admit to himself that it contained, besides the impropriety, an element of pleasure; but now he detected a clear element of duty. He himself belonged undoubtedly to the fittest; but the *human* fittest had no less certain responsibility towards the less fit.

He had even recontemplated revealing what had passed between himself and Miss Woodruff to Ernestina; but alas, he foresaw only too vividly that she might put foolish female questions, questions he could not truthfully answer without moving into dangerous waters. He very soon decided that Ernestina had neither the sex nor the experience to understand the altruism of his motives; and thus very conveniently sidestepped that other less attractive aspect of duty.

So he parried Sarah's accusing look. "I am rich by chance, you are poor by chance. I think we are not to stand on such ceremony."

This indeed was his plan: to be sympathetic to Sarah, but to establish a distance, to remind her of their difference of station . . . though lightly, of course, with an unpretentious irony.

"They are all I have to give."

"There is no reason why you should give me anything."

"You have come."

He found her meekness almost as disconcerting as her pride.

"I have come because I have satisfied myself that you do indeed need help. And although I still don't understand why you should have honored me by interesting me in your . . ." he faltered here, for he was about to say "case," which would have betrayed that he was playing the doctor as well as the gentleman: ". . . Your predicament, I have come prepared to listen to what you wished me . . . did you not? . . . to hear."

She looked up at him again then. He felt flattered. She getured timidly towards the sunlight.

"I know a secluded place nearby. May we go there?"

He indicated willingness, and she moved out into the sun and across the stony clearing where Charles had been searching when she first came upon him. She walked lightly and surely, her skirt gathered up a few inches by one hand, while the other held the ribbons of her black bonnet. Following her, far less nimbly, Charles noted the darns in the heels of her black stockings, the worndown backs of her shoes; and also the red sheen in her dark hair. He guessed it was beautiful hair when fully loose; rich and luxuriant; and though it was drawn tightly back inside the collar of her coat, he wondered whether it was not a vanity that made her so often carry her bonnet in her hand.

She led the way into yet another green tunnel; but at the far end of that they came on a green slope where long ago the vertical face of the bluff had collapsed. Tussocks of grass provided foothold; and she picked her way carefully, in zigzag fashion, to the top. Laboring behind her, he glimpsed the white-ribboned bottoms of her pantalettes, which came down to just above her ankles; a lady would have mounted behind, not ahead of him.

Sarah waited above for Charles to catch up. He walked after her then along the top of the bluff. The ground sloped sharply up to yet another bluff some hundred yards above them; for these were the huge subsident "steps" that could be glimpsed from the Cobb two miles away. Their traverse brought them to a steeper shoulder. It seemed to Charles dangerously angled; a slip, and within a few feet one would have slithered helplessly over the edge of the bluff below. By himself he might have hesitated. But Sarah passed quietly on and over, as if unaware of the danger. On the far side of this shoulder the land flattened for a few yards, and there was her "secluded place."

It was a little south-facing dell, surrounded by dense thickets of brambles and dogwood; a kind of minute green amphitheater. A stunted thorn grew towards the back of its arena, if one can use that term of a space not fifteen feet across, and someone—plainly not Sarah—had once heaved a great flat-topped block of flint against the tree's stem, making a rustic throne that commanded a magnificent view of the treetops below and the sea beyond them. Charles, panting slightly in his flannel suit and more than slightly perspiring, looked round him. The banks of the dell were carpeted with primroses and violets, and the white stars of wild strawberry. Poised in the sky, cradled to the afternoon sun, it was charming, in all ways protected.

"I must congratulate you. You have a genius for finding eyries."

"For finding solitude."

She offered the flint seat beneath the little thorn tree.

"I am sure that is your chair."

135

But she turned and sat quickly and gracefully sideways on a hummock several feet in front of the tree, so that she faced the sea; and so, as Charles found when he took the better seat, that her face was half hidden from him—and yet again, by some ingenuous coquetry, so that he must take note of her hair. She sat very upright, yet with head bowed, occupied in an implausible adjustment to her bonnet. Charles watched her, with a smile in his mind, if not on his lips. He could see that she was at a loss how to begin; and yet the situation was too *al fresco*, too informally youthful, as if they were a boy and his sister, for the shy formality she betrayed.

She put the bonnet aside, and loosened her coat, and sat with her hands folded; but still she did not speak. Something about the coat's high collar and cut, especially from the back, was masculine—it gave her a touch of the air of a girl coachman, a female soldier—a touch only, and which the hair effortlessly contradicted. With a kind of surprise Charles realized how shabby clothes did not detract from her; in some way even suited her, and more than finer clothes might have done. The last five years had seen a great emancipation in women's fashions, at least in London. The first artificial aids to a well-shaped bosom had begun to be commonly worn; eyelashes and eyebrows were painted, lips salved, hair "dusted" and tinted ... and by most fashionable women, not just those of the *demi-monde*. Now with Sarah there was none of all this. She seemed totally indifferent to fashion; and survived in spite of it, just as the simple primroses at Charles's feet survived all the competition of exotic conservatory plants.

So Charles sat silent, a little regal with this strange supplicant at his feet; and not overmuch inclined to help her. But she would not speak. Perhaps it was out of a timid modesty, yet he began very distinctly to sense that he was being challenged to coax the mystery out of her; and finally he surrendered.

"Miss Woodruff, I detest immorality. But morality without mercy I detest rather more. I promise not to be too severe a judge."

She made a little movement of her head. But still she hesitated. Then, with something of the abruptness of a disinclined bather who hovers at the brink, she plunged into her confession. "His name was Varguennes. He was brought to Captain Talbot's after the wreck of his ship. All but two of the others were drowned. But you have been told this?"

"The mere circumstance. Not what he was like."

"The first thing I admired in him was his courage. I did not then know that men can be both very brave and very

136

false." She stared out to sea, as if that was the listener, not Charles behind her. "His wound was most dreadful. His flesh was torn from his hip to his knee. If gangrene had intervened, he would have lost his leg. He was in great pain, those first days. Yet he never cried. Not the smallest groan. When the doctor dressed his wound he would clench my hand. So hard that one day I nearly fainted."

"He spoke no English?"

"A few words. Mrs. Talbot knew French no better than he did English. And Captain Talbot was called away on duty soon after he first came. He told us he came from Bordeau. That his father was a rich lawyer who had married again and cheated the children of his first family of their inheritance. Varguennes had gone to sea in the wine commerce. At the time of his wreck he said he was first officer. But all he said was false. I don't know who he really was. He seemed a gentleman. That is all."

She spoke as one unaccustomed to sustained expression, with odd small pauses between each clipped, tentative sentence; whether to allow herself to think ahead or to allow him to interrupt, Charles could not tell.

He murmured, "I understand."

"Sometimes I think he had nothing to do with the shipwreck. He was the devil in the guise of a sailor." She looked down at her hands. "He was very handsome. No man had ever paid me the kind of attentions that he did—I speak of when he was mending. He had no time for books. He was worse than a child. He must have conversation, people about him, people to listen to him. He told me foolish things about myself. That he could not understand why I was not married. Such things. I foolishly believed him."

"He made advances, in short?"

"You must understand we talked always in French. Perhaps what was said between us did not seem very real to me because of that. I have never been to France, my knowledge of the spoken tongue is not good. Very often I did not comprehend perfectly what he was saying. The blame is not all his. Perhaps I heard what he did not mean. He would mock me. But it seemed without offense." She hesitated a moment. "I ... I took pleasure in it. He called me cruel when I would not let him kiss my hand. A day came when I thought myself cruel as well."

"And you were no longer cruel."

"Yes."

A crow floated close overhead, its black feathers gleaming, splintering hesitantly in the breeze before it slipped away in sudden alarm.

"I understand."

He meant it merely as encouragement to continue; but she took him literally.

"You cannot, Mr. Smithson. Because you are not a woman. Because you are not a woman who was born to be a farmer's wife but educated to be something . . . better. My hand has been several times asked in marriage. When I was in Dorchester, a rich grazier—but that is nothing. You were not born a woman with a natural respect, a love of intelligence, beauty, learning . . . I don't know how to say it, I have no right to desire these things, but my heart craves them and I cannot believe it is all vanity . . ." She was silent a moment. "And you were not ever a governess, Mr. Smithson, a young woman without children paid to look after children. You cannot know that the sweeter they are the more intolerable the pain is. You must not think I speak of mere envy. I loved little Paul and Virginia, I feel for Mrs. Talbot nothing but gratitude and affection—I would *die* for her or her children. But to live each day in scenes of domestic happiness, the closest spectator of a happy marriage, home, adorable children." She paused. "Mrs. Talbot is my own age exactly." She paused again. "It came to seem to me as if I were allowed to live in paradise, but forbidden to enjoy it."

"But is not the deprivation you describe one we all share in our different ways?" She shook her head with a surprising vehemence. He realized he had touched some deep emotion in her.

"I meant only to suggest that social privilege does not necessarily bring happiness."

"There is no likeness between a situation where happiness is at least possible and one where . . ." again she shook her head.

"But you surely can't pretend that all governesses are unhappy—or remain unmarried?"

"All like myself."

He left a silence, then said, "I interrupted your story. Forgive me."

"And you will believe I speak not from envy?"

She turned then, her eyes intense, and he nodded. Plucking a little spray of milkwort from the bank beside her, blue flowers like microscopic cherubs' genitals, she went on.

"Varguennes recovered. It came to within a week of the time when he should take his leave. By then he had declared his attachment to me."

"He asked you to marry him?"

She found difficulty in answering. "There was talk of marriage. He told me he was to be promoted captain of a

138

wine ship when he returned to France. That he had expectations of recovering the patrimony he and his brother had lost." She hesitated, then came out with it. "He wished me to go with him back to France."

"Mrs. Talbot was aware of this?"

"She is the kindest of women. And the most innocent. If Captain Talbot had been there ... but he was not. I was ashamed to tell her in the beginning. And afraid, at the end." She added, "Afraid of the advice I knew she must give me." She began to defoliate the milkwort. "Varguennes became insistent. He made me believe that his whole happiness depended on my accompanying him when he left—more than that, that my happiness depended on it as well. He had found out much about me. How my father had died in a lunatic asylum. How I was without means, without close relatives. How for many years I had felt myself in some mysterious way condemned—and I knew not why—to solitude." She laid the milkwort aside, and clenched her fingers on her lap. "My life has been steeped in loneliness, Mr. Smithson. As if it has been ordained that I shall never form a friendship with an equal, never inhabit my own home, never see the world except as the generality to which I must be the exception. Four years ago my father was declared bankrupt. All our possessions were sold. Ever since then I have suffered from the illusion that even things—mere chairs, tables, mirrors—conspire to increase my solitude. You will never own us, they say, we shall never be yours. But always someone else's. I know this is madness, I know in the manufacturing cities poverties and solitude exist in comparison to which I live in comfort and luxury. But when I read of the Unionists' wild acts of revenge, part of me understands. Almost envies them, for they know where and how to wreak their revenge. And I am powerless." Something new had crept into her voice, an intensity of feeling that in part denied her last sentence. She added, more quietly, "I fear I don't explain myself well."

"I'm not sure that I can condone your feelings. But I understand them perfectly."

"Varguennes left, to take the Weymouth packet. Mrs. Talbot supposed, of course, that he would take it as soon as he arrived there. But he told me he should wait until I joined him. I did not promise him. On the contrary—I swore to him that ... but I was in tears. He said finally he should wait one week. I said I would never follow him. But as one day passed, and then another, and he was no longer there to talk to, the sense of solitude I spoke of just now swept back over me. I felt I would drown in it, far worse, that I had let a spar that might have saved me drift out of reach. I was overcome

139

by despair. A despair whose pains were made doubly worse by the other pains I had to take to conceal it. When the fifth day came, I could endure it no longer."

"But I gather all this was concealed from Mrs. Talbot— were not your suspicions aroused by that? It is hardly the conduct of a man with honorable intentions."

"Mr. Smithson, I know my folly, my blindness to his real character, must seem to a stranger to my nature and circumstances at that time so great that it cannot be but criminal. I can't hide that. Perhaps I always knew. Certainly some deep flaw in my soul wished my better self to be blinded. And then we had begun by deceiving. Such a path is difficult to reascend, once engaged upon."

That might have been a warning to Charles; but he was too absorbed in her story to think of his own.

"You went to Weymouth?"

"I deceived Mrs. Talbot with a tale of a school friend who had fallen gravely ill. She believed me to be going to Sherborne. Both journeys require one to go to Dorchester. Once there, I took the omnibus to Weymouth."

But Sarah fell silent then and her head bowed, as if she could not bring herself to continue.

"Spare yourself, Miss Woodruff. I can guess—"

She shook her head. "I come to the event I must tell. But I do not know how to tell it." Charles too looked at the ground. In one of the great ash trees below a hidden missel thrush was singing, wild-voiced beneath the air's blue peace. At last she went on. "I found a lodging house by the harbor. Then I went to the inn where he had said he would take a room. He was not there. But a message awaited me, giving the name of another inn. I went there. It was not . . . a respectable place. I knew that by the way my inquiry for him was answered. I was told where his room was and expected to go up to it. I insisted he be sent for. He came down. He seemed overjoyed to see me, he was all that a lover should be. He apologized for the humbleness of the place. He said it was less expensive than the other, and used often by French seamen and merchants. I was frightened and he was very kind. I had not eaten that day and he had food prepared . . ."

She hesitated, then went on, "It was noisy in the common rooms, so we went to a sitting room. I cannot tell you how, but I knew he was changed. Though he was so attentive, so full of smiles and caresses, I knew that if I hadn't come he would have been neither surprised nor long saddened. I knew then I had been for him no more than an amusement during his convalescence. The veil before my eyes dropped. I saw he

140

was insincere ... a liar. I saw marriage with him would have been marriage to a worthless adventurer. I saw all this within five minutes of that meeting." As if she heard a self-recriminatory bitterness creep into her voice again, she stopped; then continued in a lower tone. "You may wonder how I had not seen it before. I believe I had. But to see something is not the same as to acknowledge it. I think he was a little like the lizard that changes color with its surroundings. He appeared far more a gentleman in a gentleman's house. In that inn, I saw him for what he was. And I knew his color there was far more natural than the other."

She stared out to sea for a moment. Charles fancied a deeper pink now suffused her cheeks, but her head was turned away.

"In such circumstances I know a ... a respectable woman would have left at once. I have searched my soul a thousand times since that evening. All I have found is that no one explanation of my conduct is sufficient. I was first of all as if frozen with horror at the realization of my mistake—and yet so horrible was it ... I tried to see worth in him, respectability, honor. And then I was filled with a kind of rage at being deceived. I told myself that if I had not suffered such unendurable loneliness in the past I shouldn't have been so blind. Thus I blamed circumstances for my situation. I had never been in such a situation before. Never in such an inn, where propriety seemed unknown and the worship of sin as normal as the worship of virtue is in a nobler building. I cannot explain. My mind was confused. Perhaps I believed I owed it to myself to appear mistress of my destiny. I had run away to this man. Too much modesty must seem absurd ... almost a vanity." She paused. "I stayed. I ate the supper that was served. I drank the wine he pressed on me. It did not intoxicate me. I think it made me see more clearly ... is that possible?"

She turned imperceptibly for his answer; almost as if he might have disappeared, and she wanted to be sure, though she could not look, that he had not vanished into thin air.

"No doubt."

"It seemed to me that it gave me strength and courage ... as well as understanding. It was not the devil's instrument. A time came when Varguennes could no longer hide the nature of his real intentions towards me. Nor could I pretend to surprise. My innocence was false from the moment I chose to stay. Mr. Smithson, I am not seeking to defend myself. I know very well that I could still, even after the door closed on the maid who cleared away our supper, I could still have left. I could pretend to you that he overpowered me, that he had drugged me . . . what you will. But it is not so. He was a man without scruples, a man of caprice, of a passionate selfishness. But he would never violate a woman against her will."

And then, at the least expected moment, she turned fully to look at Charles. Her color was high, but it seemed to him less embarrassment than a kind of ardor, an anger, a defiance; as if she were naked before him, yet proud to be so.

"I gave myself to him."

He could not bear her eyes then, and glanced down with the faintest nod of the head.

"I see."

"So I am a doubly dishonored woman. By circumstances. And by choice."

There was silence. Again she faced the sea.

He murmured, "I did not ask you to tell me these things."

"Mr. Smithson, what I beg you to understand is not that I did this shameful thing, but why I did it. Why I sacrificed a woman's most precious possession for the transient gratification of a man I did not love." She raised her hands to her cheeks. "I did it so that I should never be the same again. I did it so that people *should* point at me, *should* say, there walks the French Lieutenant's Whore—oh yes, let the word be said. So that they should know I have suffered, and suffer, as others suffer in every town and village in this land. I could not marry that man. So I married shame. I do not mean that I knew what I did, that it was in cold blood that I let Varguennes have his will of me. It seemed to me then as if I threw myself off a precipice or plunged a knife into my heart. It was a kind of despair, Mr. Smithson. I know it was wicked . . . blasphemous, but I knew no other way to break out of what I was. If I had left that room, and returned to Mrs. Talbot's, and resumed my former existence, I know that by now I should be truly dead . . . and by my own hand. What has kept me alive is my shame, my knowing that I am truly not like other women. I shall never have children, a husband, and those innocent happinesses they have. And they will never understand the reason for my crime." She paused, as if she was seeing what she said clearly herself for the first time. "Sometimes I almost pity them. I think I have a freedom they cannot understand. No insult, no blame, can touch me. Because I have set myself beyond the pale. I am nothing, I am hardly human any more. I am the French Lieutenant's Whore."

Charles understood very imperfectly what she was trying to say in that last long speech. Until she had come to her strange decision at Weymouth, he had felt much more sympathy for her behavior than he had shown; he could imagine the slow, tantalizing agonies of her life as a governess; how easily she might have fallen into the clutches of such a plausible villain as Varguennes; but this talk of freedom beyond the pale, of marrying shame, he found incomprehensible. And yet in a way he understood, for Sarah had begun to weep towards the end of her justification. Her weeping she hid, or tried to hide; that is, she did not sink her face in her hands or reach for a handkerchief, but sat with her face turned away. The real reason for her silence did not dawn on Charles at first.

But then some instinct made him stand and take a silent two steps over the turf, so that he could see the profile of that face. He saw the cheeks were wet, and he felt unbearably touched; disturbed; beset by a maze of crosscurrents and swept hopelessly away from his safe anchorage of judicial, and judicious, sympathy. He saw the scene she had not detailed: her giving herself. He was at one and the same time Varguennes enjoying her and the man who sprang forward and struck him down; just as Sarah was to him both an innocent victim and a wild, abandoned woman. Deep in himself he forgave her her unchastity; and glimpsed the dark shadows where he might have enjoyed it himself.

Such a sudden shift of sexual key is impossible today. A man and a woman are no sooner in any but the most casual contact than they consider the possibility of a physical relationship. We consider such frankness about the real drives of human behavior healthy, but in Charles's time private minds did not admit the desires banned by the public mind; and when the consciousness was sprung on by these lurking tigers it was ludicrously unprepared.

And then too there was that strangely Egyptian quality among the Victorians; that claustrophilia we see so clearly evidenced in their enveloping, mummifying clothes, their narrow-windowed and -corridored architecture, their fear of the open and of the naked. Hide reality, shut out nature. The revolutionary art movement of Charles's day was of course the Pre-Raphaelite: they at least were making an attempt to admit nature and sexuality, but we have only to compare the pastoral background of a Millais or a Ford Madox Brown with that in a Constable or a Palmer to see how idealized, how décor-conscious the former were in their approach to external reality. Thus to Charles the openness of Sarah's confession—both so open in itself and in the open sunlight—seemed less to present a sharper reality than to offer a glimpse of an ideal world. It was not strange because it was more real, but because it was less real; a mythical world where naked beauty mattered far more than naked truth.

Charles stared down at her for a few hurtling moments, then turned and resumed his seat, his heart beating, as if he had just stepped back from the brink of the bluff. Far out to sea, above the southernmost horizon, there had risen gently into view an armada of distant cloud. Cream, amber, snowy, like the gorgeous crests of some mountain range, the towers and ramparts stretched as far as the eye could see ... and yet so remote—as remote as some abbey of Thélème, some land of sinless, swooning idyll, in which Charles and Sarah and Ernestina could have wandered ...

I do not mean to say Charles's thoughts were so specific, so disgracefully Mohammedan. But the far clouds reminded him of his own dissatisfaction; of how he would have liked to be sailing once again through the Tyrrhenian; or riding, arid scents in his nostrils, towards the distant walls of Avila; or approaching some Greek temple in the blazing Aegean sunshine. But even then a figure, a dark shadow, his dead sister, moved ahead of him, lightly, luringly, up the ashlar steps and into the broken columns' mystery.

21

Forgive me! forgive me!
 Ah, Marguerite, fain
Would these arms reach to clasp thee:—
 But see! 'tis in vain.

In the void air towards thee
 My strain'd arms are cast.
But a sea rolls between us—
 Our different past.
        MATTHEW ARNOLD, "Parting" (1853)

A minute's silence. By a little upward movement of the head she showed she had recovered. She half turned.

"May I finish? There is little more to add."

"Pray do not distress yourself."

She bowed in promise, then went on. "He left the next day. There was a ship. He had excuses. His family difficulties, his long stay from home. He said he would return at once. I knew he was lying. But I said nothing. Perhaps you think I should have returned to Mrs. Talbot and pretended that I had indeed been at Sherborne. But I could not hide my feelings, Mr. Smithson. I was in a daze of despair. It was enough to see my face to know some life-changing event had taken place in my absence. And I could not lie to Mrs. Talbot. I did not wish to lie."

"Then you told her what you have just told me?"

She looked down at her hands. "No. I told her that I had met Varguennes. That he would return one day to marry me. I spoke thus . . . not out of pride. Mrs. Talbot had the heart to understand the truth—I mean to forgive me—but I could not tell her that it was partly her own happiness that had driven me."

"When did you learn that he was married?"

"A month later. He made himself out an unhappy husband. He spoke still of love, of an arrangement . . . it was no shock. I felt no pain. I replied without anger. I told him my affection for him had ceased, I wished never to see him again."

"And you have concealed it from everyone but myself?"

She waited a long time before answering. "Yes. For the reason I said."

"To punish yourself?"

"To be what I must be. An outcast."

Charles remembered Dr. Grogan's commonsensical reaction to his own concern for her. "But my dear Miss Woodruff, if every woman who'd been deceived by some unscrupulous member of my sex were to behave as you have—I fear the country would be full of outcasts."

"It is."

"Now come, that's absurd."

"Outcasts who are afraid to seem so."

He stared at her back; and recalled something else that Dr. Grogan had said—about patients who refused to take medicine. But he determined to make one more try. He leaned forward, his hands clasped.

"I can very well understand how unhappy some circumstances must seem to a person of education and intelligence. But should not those very qualities enable one to triumph—"

Now she stood, abruptly, and moved towards the edge of the bluff. Charles hastily followed and stood beside her, ready to seize her arm—for he saw his uninspired words of counsel had had the very contrary effect to that intended. She stared out to sea, and something in the set of her face suggested to him that she felt she had made a mistake; that he was trite, a

145

mere mouther of convention. There *was* something male about her there. Charles felt himself an old woman; and did not like the feeling.

"Forgive me. I ask too much, perhaps. But I meant well."

She lowered her head, acknowledging the implicit apology; but then resumed her stare out to sea. They were now more exposed, visible to anyone in the trees below.

"And please step back a little. It is not safe here."

She turned and looked at him then. There was once again a kind of penetration of his real motive that was disconcertingly naked. We can sometimes recognize the looks of a century ago on a modern face; but never those of a century to come. A moment, then she walked past him back to the thorn. He stood in the center of the little arena.

"What you have told me does but confirm my previous sentiment. You must leave Lyme."

"If I leave here I leave my shame. Then I am lost."

She reached up and touched a branch of the hawthorn. He could not be sure, but she seemed deliberately to press her forefinger down; a second later she was staring at a crimson drop of blood. She looked at it a moment, then took a handkerchief from her pocket and surreptitiously dabbed the blood away.

He left a silence, then sprang it on her.

"Why did you refuse Dr. Grogan's help last summer?" Her eyes flashed round at him accusingly, but he was ready for that reaction. "Yes—I asked him his opinion. You cannot deny that I had a right to."

She turned away again. "Yes. You had right."

"Then you must answer me."

"Because I did not choose to go to him for help. I mean nothing against him. I know he wished to help."

"And was not his advice the same as mine?"

"Yes."

"Then with respect I must remind you of your promise to me."

She did not answer. But that was an answer. Charles went some steps closer to where she stood staring into the thorn branches.

"Miss Woodruff?"

"Now you know the truth—can you still tender that advice?"

"Most certainly."

"Then you forgive me my sin?"

This brought up Charles a little short. "You put far too high a value on my forgiveness. The essential is that you forgive yourself your sin. And you can never do that here."

"You did not answer my question, Mr. Smithson."

"Heaven forbid I should pronounce on what only Our Maker can decide. But I am convinced, we are all convinced that you have done sufficient penance. You are forgiven."

"And may be forgotten."

The dry finality of her voice puzzled him a moment. Then he smiled. "If you mean by that that your friends here intend no practical assistance—"

"I did not mean that. I know they mean kindly. But I am like this thorn tree, Mr. Smithson. No one reproaches it for growing here in this solitude. It is when it walks down Broad Street that it offends society."

He made a little puff of protest. "But my dear Miss Woodruff, you cannot tell me it is your duty to offend society." He added, "If that is what I am to infer."

She half turned. "But is it not that society wishes to remove me to another solitude?"

"What you question now is the justice of existence."

"And that is forbidden?"

"Not forbidden. But fruitless."

She shook her head. "There are fruit. Though bitter."

But it was said without contradiction, with a deep sadness, almost to herself. Charles was overcome, as by a backwash from her wave of confession, by a sense of waste. He perceived that her directness of look was matched by a directness of thought and language—that what had on occasion struck him before as a presumption of intellectual equality (therefore a suspect resentment against man) was less an equality than a proximity, a proximity like a nakedness, an intimacy of thought and feeling hitherto unimaginable to him in the context of a relationship with a woman.

He did not think this subjectively, but objectively: here, if only some free man had the wit to see it, is a remarkable woman. The feeling was not of male envy: but very much of human loss. Abruptly he reached out his hand and touched her shoulder in a gesture of comfort; and as quickly turned away. There was a silence.

As if she sensed his frustration, she spoke. "You think then that I should leave?"

At once he felt released and turned eagerly back to her.

"I beg you to. New surroundings, new faces . . . and have no worries as regards the practical considerations. We await only your decision to interest ourselves on your behalf."

"May I have a day or two to reflect?"

"If it so be you feel it necessary." He took his chance; and grasped the normality she made so elusive. "And I propose that we now put the matter under Mrs. Tranter's auspices. If

147

you will permit, I will see to it that her purse is provided for any needs you may have."

Her head bowed; she seemed near tears again. She murmured, "I don't deserve such kindness. I . . ."

"Say no more. I cannot think of money better spent."

A delicate tinge of triumph was running through Charles. It had been as Grogan prophesied. Confession had brought cure—or at least a clear glimpse of it. He turned to pick up his ashplant by the block of flint.

"I must come to Mrs. Tranter's?"

"Excellent. There will of course be no necessity to speak of our meetings."

"I shall say nothing."

He saw the scene already; his polite but not too interested surprise, followed by his disinterested insistence that any pecuniary assistance desirable should be to his charge. Ernestina might very well tease him about it—but that would ease his conscience. He smiled at Sarah.

"You have shared your secret. I think you will find it to be an unburdening in many other ways. You have very considerable natural advantages. You have nothing to fear from life. A day will come when these recent unhappy years may seem no more than that cloud-stain over there upon Chesil Bank. You shall stand in sunlight—and smile at your own past sorrows." He thought he detected a kind of light behind the doubt in her eyes; for a moment she was like a child, both reluctant and yet willing to be cozened—or homilized—out of tears. His smile deepened. He added lightly, "And now had we better not descend?"

She seemed as if she would like to say something, no doubt reaffirm her gratitude, but his stance of brisk waiting made her, after one last lingering look into his eyes, move past him.

She led the way down as neat-footedly as she had led it up. Looking down on her back, he felt tinges of regret. Not to see her thus again . . . regret and relief. A remarkable young woman. He would not forget her; and it seemed some consolation that he would not be allowed to. Aunt Tranter would be his future spy.

They came to the base of the lower cliff, and went through the first tunnel of ivy, over the clearing, and into the second green corridor—and then!

There came from far below, from the main path through the Undercliff, the sound of a stifled peal of laughter. Its effect was strange—as if some wood spirit had been watching their clandestine meeting and could now no longer bottle up her—for the laugh was unmistakably female—mirth at their foolish confidence in being unseen.

Charles and Sarah stopped as of one accord. Charles's growing relief was instantaneously converted into a shocked alarm. But the screen of ivy was dense, the laugh had come from two or three hundred yards away; they could not have been seen. Unless as they came down the slope . . . a moment, then she swiftly raised a finger to her lips, indicated that he should not move, and then herself stole along to the end of the tunnel. Charles watched her crane forward and stare cautiously down towards the path. Then her face turned sharply back to him. She beckoned—he was to go to her, but with the utmost quietness; and simultaneously that laugh came again. It was quieter this time, yet closer. Whoever had been on the path had left it and was climbing up through the ash trees toward them.

Charles trod cautiously towards Sarah, making sure of each place where he had to put his wretchedly unstealthy boots. He felt himself flushing, most hideously embarrassed. No explanation could hold water for a moment. However he was seen with Sarah, it must be *in flagrante delicto*.

He came to where she stood, and where the ivy was fortunately at its thickest. She had turned away from the interlopers and stood with her back against a tree trunk, her eyes cast down as if in mute guilt for having brought them both to this pass. Charles looked through the leaves and down the slope of the ash grove—and his blood froze. Coming up towards them, as if seeking their same cover, were Sam and Mary. Sam had his arm round the girl's shoulders. He carried his hat, and she her bonnet; she wore the green walking dress given her by Ernestina—indeed, the last time Charles had seen it it had been on Ernestina—and her head lay back a little against Sam's cheek. They were young lovers as plain as the ashes were old trees; as greenly erotic as the April plants they trod on.

Charles drew back a little but kept them in view. As he watched Sam drew the girl's face round and kissed her. Her arm came up and they embraced; and then holding hands, stood shyly apart a little. Sam led the girl to where a bank of grass had managed to establish itself between the trees. Mary sat and lay back, and Sam leaned beside her, looking down at her; then he touched her hair aside from her cheeks and bent and kissed her tenderly on the eyes.

Charles felt pierced with a new embarrassment: he glanced at Sarah, to see if she knew who the intruders were. But she stared at the hart's-tongue ferns at her feet, as if

149

they were merely sheltering from some shower of rain. Two minutes, then three passed. Embarrassment gave way to a degree of relief—it was clear that the two servants were far more interested in exploring each other than their surroundings. He glanced again at Sarah. Now she too was watching, from round her tree trunk. She turned back, her eyes cast down. But then without warning she looked up at him.

A moment.

Then she did something as strange, as shocking, as if she had thrown off her clothes.

She smiled.

It was a smile so complex that Charles could at the first moment only stare at it incredulously. It was so strangely timed! He felt she had almost been waiting for such a moment to unleash it upon him—this revelation of her humor, that her sadness was not total. And in those wide eyes, so somber, sad and direct, was revealed an irony, a new dimension of herself—one little Paul and Virginia would have been quite familiar with in days gone by, but never till now bestowed on Lyme.

Where are your pretensions now, those eyes and gently curving lips seemed to say; where is your birth, your science, your etiquette, your social order? More than that, it was not a smile one could stiffen or frown at; it could only be met with a smile in return, for it excused Sam and Mary, it excused all; and in some way too subtle for analysis, undermined all that had passed between Charles and herself till then. It lay claim to a far profounder understanding, acknowledgment of that awkward equality melting into proximity than had been consciously admitted. Indeed, Charles did not consciously smile in return; he found himself smiling; only with his eyes, but smiling. And excited, in some way too obscure and general to be called sexual, to the very roots of his being; like a man who at last comes, at the end of a long high wall, to the sought-for door ... but only to find it locked.

For several moments they stood, the woman who was the door, the man without the key; and then she lowered her eyes again. The smile died. A long silence hung between them. Charles saw the truth: he really did stand with one foot over the precipice. For a moment he thought he would, he must plunge. He knew if he reached out his arm she would meet with no resistance ... only a passionate reciprocity of feeling. The red in his cheeks deepened, and at last he whispered.

"We must never meet alone again."

She did not raise her head, but gave the smallest nod of

assent; and then with an almost sullen movement she turned away from him, so that he could not see her face. He looked again through the leaves. Sam's head and shoulders were bent over the invisible Mary. Long moments passed, but Charles remained watching, his mind still whirling down that precipice, hardly aware that he was spying, yet infected, as each moment passed, with more of the very poison he was trying to repel.

Mary saved him. Suddenly she pushed Sam aside and laughing, ran down the slope back towards the path; poising a moment, her mischievous face flashed back at Sam, before she raised her skirts and skittered down, a thin line of red petticoat beneath the viridian, through the violets and the dog's mercury. Sam ran after her. Their figures dwindled between the gray stems; dipped, disappeared, a flash of green, a flash of blue; a laugh that ended in a little scream; then silence.

Five minutes passed, during which the hidden pair spoke not a word to each other. Charles remained staring fixedly down the hill, as if it were important that he should keep such intent watch. All he wanted, of course, was to avoid looking at Sarah. At last he broke the silence.

"You had better go." She bowed her head. "I will wait a half-hour." She bowed her head again, and then moved past him. Their eyes did not meet.

Only when she was out among the ash trees did she turn and look back for a moment at him. She could not have seen his face, but she must have known he was watching. And her face had its old lancing look again. Then she went lightly on down through the trees.

22

I too have felt the load I bore
In a too strong emotion's sway;
I too have wished, no woman more,
This starting, feverish heart, away.

I too have longed for trenchant force
And will like a dividing spear;
Have praised the keen, unscrupulous course,
Which knows no doubt, which feels no fear.

But in the world I learnt, what there
Thou too will surely one day prove,
That will, that energy, though rare,
And yet far, far less rare than love.

MATTHEW ARNOLD, "A Farewell" (1853)

Charles's thoughts on his own eventual way back to Lyme were all variations on that agelessly popular male theme: "You've been playing with fire, my boy." But it was precisely that theme, by which I mean that the tenor of his thoughts matched the verbal tenor of the statement. He had been very foolish, but his folly had not been visited on him. He had run an absurd risk; and escaped unscathed. And so now, as the great stone claw of the Cobb came into sight far below, he felt exhilarated.

And how should he have blamed himself very deeply? From the outset his motives had been the purest; he had cured her of her madness; and if something impure had for a moment threatened to infiltrate his defenses, it had been but mint sauce to the wholesome lamb. He would be to blame, of course, if he did not now remove himself, and for good, from the fire. That, he would take very good care to do. After all, he was not a moth infatuated by a candle; he was a highly intelligent being, one of the fittest, and endowed with total free will. If he had not been sure of that latter safeguard,

152

would he ever have risked himself in such dangerous waters? I am mixing metaphors—but that was how Charles's mind worked.

And so, leaning on free will quite as much as on his ashplant, he descended the hill to the town. All sympathetic physical feelings towards the girl he would henceforth rigorously suppress, by free will. Any further solicitation of a private meeting he would adamantly discountenance, by free will. All administration of his interest should be passed to Aunt Tranter, by free will. And he was therefore permitted, obliged rather, to continue to keep Ernestina in the dark, by the same free will. By the time he came in sight of the White Lion, he had free-willed himself most convincingly into a state of self-congratulation . . . and one in which he could look at Sarah as an object of his past.

A remarkable young woman, a remarkable young woman. And baffling. He decided that that was—had been, rather—her attraction: her unpredictability. He did not realize that she had two qualities as typical of the English as his own admixture of irony and convention. I speak of passion and imagination. The first quality Charles perhaps began dimly to perceive; the second he did not. He could not, for those two qualities of Sarah's were banned by the epoch, equated in the first case with sensuality and in the second with the merely fanciful. This dismissive double equation was Charles's greatest defect—and here he stands truly for his age.

There was still deception in the flesh, or Ernestina, to be faced. But Charles, when he arrived at his hotel, found that family had come to his aid.

A telegram awaited him. It was from his uncle at Winsyatt. His presence was urgently requested "for most important reasons." I am afraid Charles smiled as soon as he read it; he very nearly kissed the orange envelope. It removed him from any immediate further embarrassment; from the need for further lies of omission. It was most marvelously convenient. He made inquiries . . . there was a train early the next morning from Exeter, then the nearest station to Lyme, which meant that he had a good pretext for leaving at once and staying there overnight. He gave orders for the fastest trap in Lyme to be procured. He would drive himself. He felt inclined to make such an urgent rush of it as to let a note to Aunt Tranter's suffice. But that would have been too cowardly. So telegram in hand, he walked up the street.

The good lady herself was full of concern, since telegrams for her meant bad news. Ernestina, less superstitious, was plainly vexed. She thought it "too bad" of Uncle Robert to act

153

the grand vizir in this way. She was sure it was nothing; a whim, an old man's caprice, worse—an envy of young love.

She had, of course, earlier visited Winsyatt, accompanied by her parents; and she had not fallen for Sir Robert. Perhaps it was because she felt herself under inspection; or because the uncle had sufficient generations of squirearchy behind him to possess, by middle-class London standards, really rather bad manners—though a kinder critic might have said agreeably eccentric ones; perhaps because she considered the house such an old barn, so *dreadfully* old-fashioned in its furnishings and hangings and pictures; because the said uncle so doted on Charles and Charles was so *provokingly* nephew-ish in return that Ernestina began to feel *positively* jealous; but above all, because she was frightened.

Neighboring ladies had been summoned to meet her. It was all very well knowing *her* father could buy up all *their* respective fathers and husbands lock, stock and barrel; she felt herself looked down on (though she was simply envied) and snubbed in various subtle ways. Nor did she much relish the prospect of eventually living at Winsyatt, though it allowed her to dream of one way at least in which part of her vast marriage portion should be spent exactly as she insisted— in a comprehensive replacement of all those absurd scrolly wooden chairs (Carolean and almost priceless), gloomy cupboards (Tudor), moth-eaten tapestries (Gobelins), and dull paintings (including two Claudes and a Tintoretto) that did not meet her approval.

Her distaste for the uncle she had not dared to communicate to Charles; and her other objections she hinted at with more humor than sarcasm. I do not think she is to be blamed. Like so many daughters of rich parents, before and since, she had been given no talent except that of conventional good taste ... that is, she knew how to spend a great deal of money in dressmakers', milliners' and furniture shops. That was her province; and since it was her only real one, she did not like it encroached upon.

The urgent Charles put up with her muted disapproval and pretty poutings, and assured her that he would fly back with as much speed as he went. He had in fact a fairly good idea what his uncle wanted him so abruptly for; the matter had been tentatively broached when he was there with Tina and her parents ... most tentatively since his uncle was a shy man. It was the possibility that Charles and his bride might share Winsyatt with him—they could "fit up" the east wing. Charles knew his uncle did not mean merely that they should come and stay there on occasion, but that Charles should settle down and start learning the business of running the estate. Now this appealed to him no more than it would have, had he realized, to Ernestina. He knew it would be a poor arrangement, that his uncle would alternate between doting and disapproving ... and that Ernestina needed educating into Winsyatt by a less trammeled early marriage. But his uncle had hinted privately to him at something beyond this: that Winsyatt was too large for a lonely old man, that he didn't know if he wouldn't be happier in a smaller place. There was no shortage of suitable smaller places in the environs ... indeed, some figured on the Winsyatt rent roll. There was one such, an Elizabethan manor house in the village of Winsyatt, almost in view of the great house.

Charles guessed now that the old man was feeling selfish; and that he was called to Winsyatt to be offered either the manor house or the great house. Either would be agreeable. It did not much matter to him which it should be, provided his uncle was out of the way. He felt certain that the old bachelor could now be maneuvered into either house, that he was like a nervous rider who had come to a jump and wanted to be led over it.

Accordingly, at the end of the brief trio in Broad Street, Charles asked for a few words alone with Ernestina; and as soon as Aunt Tranter had retired, he told her what he suspected.

"But why should he have not discussed it sooner?"

"Dearest, I'm afraid that is Uncle Bob to the life. But tell me what I am to say."

"Which should you prefer?"

"Whichever you choose. Neither, if needs be. Though he would be hurt ..."

Ernestina uttered a discreet curse against rich uncles. But a vision of herself, Lady Smithson in a Winsyatt appointed to her taste, did cross her mind, perhaps because she was in Aunt Tranter's not very spacious back parlor. After all, a title needs a setting. And if the horrid old man were safely from under the same roof ... and he was old. And dear Charles. And her parents, to whom she owed ...

"This house in the village—is it not the one we passed in the carriage?"

"Yes, you remember, it had all those picturesque old gables—"

"Picturesque to look at from the outside."

"Of course it would have to be done up."

"What did you call it?"

"The villagers call it the Little House. But only by comparison. It's many years since I was in it, but I fancy it is a good deal larger than it looks."

155

"I know those old houses. Dozens of wretched little rooms. I think the Elizabethans were all dwarfs."

He smiled (though he might have done better to correct her curious notion of Tudor architecture), and put his arm round her shoulders. "Then Winsyatt itself?"

She gave him a straight little look under her arched eyebrows.

"Do you wish it?"

"You know what it is to me."

"I may have my way with new decorations?"

"You may raze it to the ground and erect a second Crystal Palace, for all I care."

"Charles! Be serious!"

She pulled away. But he soon received a kiss of forgiveness, and went on his way with a light heart. For her part, Ernestina went upstairs and drew out her copious armory of catalogues.

23

Portion of this yew
Is a man my grandsire knew . . .
HARDY, "Transformations"

The chaise, its calash down to allow Charles to enjoy the spring sunshine, passed the gatehouse. Young Hawkins stood by the opened gates, old Mrs. Hawkins beamed coyly at the door of the cottage. And Charles called to the under-coachman who had been waiting at Chippenham and now drove with Sam beside him on the box, to stop a moment. A special relationship existed between Charles and the old woman. Without a mother since the age of one, he had had to put up with a series of substitutes as a little boy; in his stays at Winsyatt he had attached himself to this same Mrs. Hawkins, technically in those days the head laundrymaid, but by right of service and popularity second only below stairs to the august housekeeper herself. Perhaps Charles's affection for Aunt Tranter was an echo of his earlier memories of the simple woman—a perfect casting for Baucis—who now hobbled down the path to the garden gate to greet him.

He had to answer all her eager inquiries about the forthcoming marriage; and to ask in his turn after her children. She seemed more than ordinarily solicitous for him, and he detected in her eye that pitying shadow the kind-hearted poor sometimes reserve for the favored rich. It was a shadow he knew of old, bestowed by the innocent-shrewd country woman on the poor motherless boy with the wicked father—for gross rumors of Charles's surviving parent's enjoyment of the pleasures of London life percolated down to Winsyatt. It seemed singularly out of place now, that mute sympathy, but Charles permitted it with an amused tolerance. It came from love of him, as the neat gatehouse garden, and the parkland beyond, and the clumps of old trees—each with a well-loved name, Carson's Stand, Ten-pine Mound, Ramillies (planted in celebration of that battle), the Oak-and-Elm, the Muses' Grove and a dozen others, all as familiar to Charles as the names of the parts of his body—and the great avenue of limes, the iron railings, as all in his view of the domain came that day also, or so he felt, from love of him. At last he smiled down at the old laundrymaid.

"I must get on. My uncle expects me."

Mrs. Hawkins looked for a moment as if she would not let herself be so easily dismissed; but the servant overcame the substitute mother. She contented herself with touching his hand as it lay on the chaise door.

"Aye, Mr. Charles. He expects you."

The coachman flicked the rump of the leading horse with his whip and the chaise pulled off up the gentle incline and into the fenestrated shadow of the still-leafless limes. After a while the drive became flat, again the whip licked lazily onto the bay haunch, and the two horses, remembering the manger was now near, broke into a brisk trot. The swift gay crunch of the ironbound wheels, the slight screech of an insufficiently greased axle, the old affection revived by Mrs. Hawkins, his now certainty of being soon in real possession of this landscape, all this evoked in Charles that ineffable feeling of fortunate destiny and right order which his stay in Lyme had vaguely troubled. This piece of England belonged to him, and he belonged to it; its responsibilities were his, and its prestige, and its centuries-old organization.

They passed a group of his uncle's workers: Ebenezer the smith, beside a portable brazier, hammering straight one of the iron rails that had been bent. Behind him, two woodmen, passing the time of day; and a fourth very old man, who still wore the smock of his youth and an ancient billycock ... old Ben, the smith's father, now one of the dozen or more aged pensioners of the estate allowed to live there, as free in all his outdoor comings and goings as the master himself; a kind of living file, and still often consulted, of the last eighty years or more of Winsyatt history.

These four turned as the chaise went past, and raised arms, and the billycock. Charles waved seigneurially back. He knew all their lives, as they knew his. He even knew how the rail had been bent . . . the great Jonas, his uncle's favorite bull, had charged Mrs. Tomkins's landau. "Her own d——d fault"—his uncle's letter had said—"for painting her mouth scarlet." Charles smiled, remembering the dry inquiry in his answer as to why such an attractive widow should be calling at Winsyatt unchaperoned . . .

But it was the great immutable rural peace that was so delicious to reenter. The miles of spring sward, the background of Wiltshire downland, the distant house now coming into view, cream and gray, with its huge cedars, the famous copper beech (all copper beeches are famous) by the west wing, the almost hidden stable row behind, with its little wooden tower and clock like a white exclamation mark between the intervening branches. It was symbolic, that stable clock; though nothing—despite the telegram—was ever really urgent at Winsyatt, green todays flowed into green tomorrows, the only real hours were the solar hours, and though, except at haymaking and harvest, there were always too many hands for too little work, the sense of order was almost mechanical in its profundity, in one's feeling that it could not be disturbed, that it would always remain thus: benevolent and divine. Heaven—and Millie—knows there were rural injustices and poverties as vile as those taking place in Sheffield and Manchester; but they shunned the neighborhood of the great houses of England, perhaps for no better reason than that the owners liked well-tended peasants as much as well-tended fields and livestock. Their comparative kindness to their huge staffs may have been no more than a side-product of their pursuit of the pleasant prospect; but the underlings gained thereby. And the motives of "intelligent" modern management are probably no more altruistic. One set of kind exploiters went for the Pleasant Prospect; the others go for Higher Productivity.

As the chaise emerged from the end of the avenue of limes, where the railed pasture gave way to smoother lawns and shrubberies, and the drive entered its long curve up to the front of the house—a Palladian structure not too ruthlessly improved and added to by the younger Wyatt—Charles felt himself truly entering upon his inheritance. It seemed to him to explain all his previous idling through life, his dallying with religion, with science, with travel; he had been waiting for this moment . . . his call to the throne, so to speak. The

158

absurd adventure in the Undercliff was forgotten. Immense duties, the preservation of this peace and order, lay ahead, as they had lain ahead of so many young men of his family in the past. Duty—that was his real wife, his Ernestina and his Sarah, and he sprang out of the chaise to welcome her as joyously as a boy not half his real age.

He was greeted in return, however, by an empty hall. He broke into the dayroom, or drawing room, expecting to see his uncle smilingly on his feet to meet him. But that room was empty, too. And something was strange in it, puzzling Charles a moment. Then he smiled. There were new curtains—and the carpets, yes, they were new as well. Ernestina would not be pleased, to have had the choice taken out of her hands—but what surer demonstration could there be of the old bachelor's intention gracefully to hand on the torch?

Yet something else had also changed. It was some moments before Charles realized what it was. The immortal bustard had been banished; where its glass case had last stood was now a cabinet of china.

But still he did not guess.

Nor did he—but in this case, how could he?—guess what had happened to Sarah when she left him the previous afternoon. She had walked quickly back through the woods until she came to the place where she normally took the higher path that precluded any chance of her being seen from the Dairy. An observer would have seen her hesitate, and then, if he had had as sharp hearing as Sarah herself, have guessed why: a sound of voices from the Dairy cottage some hundred yards away down through the trees. Slowly and silently Sarah made her way forward until she came to a great holly bush, through whose dense leaves she could stare down at the back of the cottage. She remained standing some time, her face revealing nothing of what passed through her mind. Then some development in the scene below, outside the cottage, made her move . . . but not back into the cover of the woods. Instead she walked boldly from out behind the holly tree and along the path that joined the cart track above the cottage. Thus she emerged in full view of the two women at the cottage door, one of whom carried a basket and was evidently about to set off on her way home.

Sarah's dark figure came into view. She did not look down towards the cottage, towards those two surprised pairs of eyes, but went swiftly on her way until she passed behind the hedge of one of the fields that ran above the Dairy.

One of the women below was the dairyman's wife. The other was Mrs. Fairley.

24

I once heard it suggested that the typical Victorian
saying was, "You must remember he is your uncle . . ."

G. M. YOUNG, *Victorian Essays*

"It is monstrous. Monstrous. I cannot believe he has not lost
his senses."

"He has lost his sense of proportion. But that is not quite
the same thing."

"But at this juncture!"

"My dear Tina, Cupid has a notorious contempt for other
people's convenience."

"You know very well that Cupid has nothing to do with
it."

"I am afraid he has everything to do with it. Old hearts
are the most susceptible."

"It is my fault. I know he disapproves of me."

"Come now, that is nonsense."

"It is not nonsense. I know perfectly well that for him I am
a draper's daughter."

"My dear child, contain yourself."

"It is for you I am so angry."

"Very well—then let me be angry on my own behalf."

There was silence then, which allows me to say that the
conversation above took place in Aunt Tranter's rear parlor.
Charles stood at the window, his back to Ernestina, who had
very recently cried, and who now sat twisting a lace handkerchief in a vindictive manner.

"I know how much you love Winsyatt."

How Charles would have answered can only be conjec-
tured, for the door opened at that moment and Aunt Tranter
appeared, a pleased smile of welcome on her face.

"You are back so soon!" It was half past nine of the same day we saw Charles driving up to Winsyatt House.

Charles smiled thinly. "Our business was soon . . . finished."

"Something terrible and disgraceful has happened." Aunt Tranter looked with alarm at the tragic and outraged face of her niece, who went on: "Charles had been disinherited."

"Disinherited!"

"Ernestina exaggerates. It is simply that my uncle has decided to marry. If he should be so fortunate as to have a son and heir . . ."

"Fortunate . . . !" Ernestina slipped Charles a scalding little glance. Aunt Tranter looked in consternation from one face to the other.

"But . . . who is the lady?"

"Her name is Mrs. Tomkins, Mrs. Tranter. A widow."

"And young enough to bear a dozen sons."

Charles smiled. "Hardly that. But young enough to bear sons."

"You know her?"

Ernestina answered before Charles could, "That is what is so disgraceful. Only two months ago his uncle made fun of the woman to Charles in a letter. And now he is groveling at her feet."

"My dear Ernestina!"

"I will not be calm! It is too much. After all these years . . ."

Charles took a deep breath, and turned to Aunt Tranter. "I understand she has excellent connections. Her husband was colonel in the Fortieth Hussars and left her handsomely provided for. There is no suspicion of fortune hunting." Ernestina's smoldering look up at him showed plainly that in her mind there was every suspicion. "I am told she is a very attractive woman."

"No doubt she rides to hounds."

He smiled bleakly at Ernestina, who was referring to a black mark she had earlier gained in the monstrous uncle's book. "No doubt. But that is not yet a crime."

Aunt Tranter plumped down on a chair and looked again from one young face to the other, searching, as ever in such situations, for some ray of hope.

"But is he not too old to have children?"

Charles managed a gentle smile for her innocence. "He is sixty-seven, Mrs. Tranter. That is not too old."

"Even though she is young enough to be his granddaughter."

"My dear Tina, all one has in such circumstances is one's

dignity. I must beg you for my sake not to be bitter. We must accept the event with as good a grace as possible."

She looked up and saw how nervously stern he was; that she must play a different role. She ran to him, and catching his hand, raised it to her lips. He drew her to him and kissed the top of her head, but he was not deceived. A shrew and a mouse may look the same; but they are not the same; and though he could not find a word to describe Ernestina's reception of his shocking and unwelcome news, it was not far removed from "unladylike." He had leaped straight from the trap bringing him back from Exeter into Aunt Tranter's house; and expected a gentle sympathy, not a sharp rage however flatteringly it was intended to resemble his own feelings. Perhaps that was it—that she had not divined that a gentleman could never reveal the anger she ascribed to him. But there seemed to him something only too reminiscent of the draper's daughter in her during those first minutes; of one who had been worsted in a business deal, and who lacked a traditional imperturbability, that fine aristocratic refusal to allow the setbacks of life ever to ruffle one's style.

He handed Ernestina back to the sofa from which she had sprung. An essential reason for his call, a decision he had come to on his long return, he now perceived must be left for discussion on the morrow. He sought for some way to demonstrate the correct attitude; and could find none better than that of lightly changing the subject.

"And what great happenings have taken place in Lyme today?"

As if reminded, Ernestina turned to her aunt. "Did you get news of her?" And then, before Aunt Tranter could answer, she looked up at Charles, "There *has* been an event. Mrs. Poulteney has dismissed Miss Woodruff."

Charles felt his heart miss a beat. But any shock his face may have betrayed passed unnoticed in Aunt Tranter's eagerness to tell *her* news: for that is why she had been absent when Charles arrived. The dismissal had apparently taken place the previous evening; the sinner had been allowed one last night under the roof of Marlborough House. Very early that same morning a porter had come to collect her box—and had been instructed to take it to the White Lion. Here Charles quite literally blanched, but Aunt Tranter allayed his fears in the very next sentence.

"That is the depot for the coaches, you know." The Dorchester to Exeter omnibuses did not descend the steep hill to Lyme, but had to be picked up at a crossroads some four miles inland on the main road to the west. "But Mrs. Hunnicott spoke to the man. He is most positive that Miss

162

Woodruff was not there. The maid said she had left very early at dawn, and gave only the instructions as to her box."

"And since?"

"Not a sign."

"You saw the vicar?"

"No, but Miss Trimble assures me he went to Marlborough House this forenoon. He was told Mrs. Poulteney was unwell. He spoke to Mrs. Fairley. All she knew was that some disgraceful matter had come to Mrs. Poulteney's knowledge, that she was deeply shocked and upset . . ." The good Mrs. Tranter broke off, apparently almost as distressed at her ignorance as at Sarah's disappearance. She sought her niece's and Charles's eyes. "What can it be—what *can* it be?"

"She ought never to have been employed at Marlborough House. It was like offering a lamb to a wolf." Ernestina looked at Charles for confirmation of her opinion. Feeling far less calm than he looked, he turned to Aunt Tranter.

"There is no danger of . . ."

"That is what we all fear. The vicar has sent men to search along towards Charmouth. She walks there, on the cliffs."

"And they have . . . ?"

"Found nothing."

"Did you not say she once worked for—"

"They have sent there. No word of her."

"Grogan—has he not been called to Marlborough House?" He skillfully made use of his introduction of the name, turning to Ernestina. "That evening when we took grog—he mentioned her. I know he is concerned for her situation."

"Miss Trimble saw him talking with the vicar at seven o'clock. She said he looked most agitated. Angry. That was her word." Miss Trimble kept a ladies' trinket shop at the bottom of Broad Street—and was therefore admirably placed to be the general information center of the town. Aunt Tranter's gentle face achieved the impossible—and looked harshly severe. "I shall not call on Mrs. Poulteney, however ill she is."

Ernestina covered her face in her hands. "Oh, what a cruel day it's been!"

Charles stared down at the two ladies. "Perhaps I should call on Grogan."

"Oh Charles—what can you do? There are men enough to search."

That, of course, had not been in Charles's mind. He guessed that Sarah's dismissal was not unconnected with her wanderings in the Undercliff—and his horror, of course, was that she might have been seen there with him. He stood in an agony of indecision. It became imperative to discover how

163

much was publicly known about the reason for her dismissal. He suddenly found the atmosphere of the little sitting room claustrophobic. He had to be alone. He had to consider what to do. For if Sarah was still living—but who could tell what wild decision she might have made in her night of despair, while he was quietly sleeping in his Exeter hotel?—but if she still breathed, he guessed where she was; and it oppressed him like a shroud that he was the only person in Lyme to know. And yet dared not reveal his knowledge.

A few minutes later he was striding down the hill to the White Lion. The air was mild, but the sky was overcast. Idle fingers of wet air brushed his cheeks. There was thunder in the offing, as in his heart.

25

O young lord-lover, what sighs are those,
For one that will never be thine?

TENNYSON, *Maud* (1855)

It was his immediate intention to send Sam with a message for the Irish doctor. He phrased it to himself as he walked— "Mrs. Tranter is deeply concerned" ... "If any expense should be incurred in forming a search party" ... or better, "If I can be of any assistance, financial or otherwise"—such sentences floated through his head. He called to the undeaf ostler as he entered the hotel to fetch Sam out of the taproom and send him upstairs. But he no sooner entered his sitting room when he received his third shock of that eventful day.

A note lay on the round table. It was sealed with black wax. The writing was unfamiliar: *Mr. Smithson, at the White Lion.* He tore the folded sheet open. There was no heading, no signature.

I beg you to see me one last time. I will wait this afternoon and tomorrow morning. If you do not come, I shall never trouble you again.

Charles read the note twice, three times; then stared out at the dark air. He felt infuriated that she should so carelessly risk his reputation; relieved at this evidence that she was still alive; and outraged again at the threat implicit in that last sentence. Sam came into the room, wiping his mouth with his handkerchief, an unsubtle hint that he had been interrupted at his supper. As his lunch had consisted of a bottle of ginger beer and three stale Abernethy biscuits, he may be forgiven. But he saw at a glance that his master was in no better a mood than he had been ever since leaving Winsyatt.

"Go down and find out who left me this note."

"Yes, Mr. Charles."

Sam left, but he had not gone six steps before Charles was at the door. "Ask whoever took it in to come up."

"Yes, Mr. Charles."

The master went back into his room; and there entered his mind a brief image of that ancient disaster he had found recorded in the blue lias and brought back to Ernestina—the ammonites caught in some recession of water, a micro-catastrophe of ninety million years ago. In a vivid insight, a flash of black lightning, he saw that all life was parallel: that evolution was not vertical, ascending to a perfection, but horizontal. Time was the great fallacy; existence was without history, was always now, was always this being caught in the same fiendish machine. All those painted screens erected by man to shut out reality—history, religion, duty, social position, all were illusions, mere opium fantasies.

He turned as Sam came through the door with the same ostler Charles had just spoken to. A boy had brought the note. At ten o'clock that morning. The ostler knew the boy's face, but not his name. No, he had not said who the sender was. Charles impatiently dismissed him; and then as impatiently asked Sam what he found to stare at.

"Wasn't starin' at nuffin', Mr. Charles."

"Very well. Tell them to send me up some supper. Anything, anything."

"Yes, Mr. Charles."

"And I do not want to be disturbed again. You may lay out my things now."

Sam went into the bedroom next to the sitting room, while Charles stood at the window. As he looked down, he saw in the light from the inn windows a small boy run up the far side of the street, then cross the cobbles below his own window and go out of sight. He nearly threw up the sash and called out, so sharp was his intuition that this was the messenger again. He stood in a fever of embarrassment. There was a long enough pause for him to begin to believe that he was wrong. Sam appeared from the bedroom and made his way to the door out. But then there was a knock. Sam opened the door.

It was the ostler, with the idiot smile on his face of one who this time has made no mistake. In his hand was a note.

" 'Twas the same boy, sir. I asked 'un, sir. 'E sez 'twas the same woman as before, sir, but 'e doan' know 'er name. Us all calls 'er the—"

"Yes, yes. Give me the note."

Sam took it and passed it to Charles, but with a certain dumb insolence, a dry knowingness beneath his mask of manservitude. He flicked his thumb at the ostler and gave him a secret wink, and the ostler withdrew. Sam himself was about to follow, but Charles called him back. He paused, searching for a sufficiently delicate and plausible phrasing.

"Sam, I have interested myself in an unfortunate woman's case here. I wished . . . that is, I still wish to keep the matter from Mrs. Tranter. You understand?"

"Perfeckly, Mr. Charles."

"I hope to establish the person in a situation more suited . . . to her abilities. Then of course I shall tell Mrs. Tranter. It is a little surprise. A little return for Mrs. Tranter's hospitality. She is concerned for her."

Sam had assumed a demeanor that Charles termed to himself "Sam the footman"; a profoundly respectful obedience to his master's behests. It was so remote from Sam's real character that Charles was induced to flounder on.

"So—though it is not important at all—you will speak of this to no one."

"O' course not, Mr. Charles." Sam looked as shocked as a curate accused of gambling.

Charles turned away to the window, received unawares a look from Sam that gained its chief effect from a curious swift pursing of the mouth accompanied by a nod, and then opened the second note as the door closed on the servant.

Je vous ai attendu toute la journée. Je vous prie—une femme à genoux vous supplie de l'aider dans son désespoir. Je passerai la nuit en prières pour votre venue. Je serai dès l'aube à la petite grange près de la mer atteinte par le premier sentier à gauche après la ferme.

No doubt for lack of wax, this note was unsealed, which explained why it was couched in governess French. It was written, scribbled, in pencil, as if composed in haste at some cottage door or in the Undercliff—for Charles knew that that was where she must have fled. The boy no doubt was some poor fisherman's child from the Cobb—a path from the Undercliff descended to it, obviating the necessity of passing through the town itself. But the folly of the procedure, the risk!

The French! Varguennes!

Charles crumpled the sheet of paper in his clenched hand. A distant flash of lightning announced the approach of the storm; and as he looked out of the window the first heavy, sullen drops splashed and streaked down the pane. He wondered where she was; and a vision of her running sodden through the lightning and rain momentarily distracted him from his own acute and self-directed anxiety. But it was too much! After such a day!

I am overdoing the exclamation marks. But as Charles paced up and down, thoughts, reactions, reactions to reactions spurted up angrily thus in his mind. He made himself stop at the bay window and stare out over Broad Street; and promptly remembered what she had said about thorn trees walking therein. He span round and clutched his temples; then went into his bedroom and peered at his face in the mirror.

But he knew only too well he was awake. He kept saying to himself, I must do something, I must act. And a kind of anger at his weakness swept over him—a wild determination to make some gesture that would show he was more than an ammonite stranded in a drought, that he could strike out against the dark clouds that enveloped him. He must talk to someone, he must lay bare his soul.

He strode back into his sitting room and pulled the little chain that hung from the gasolier, turning the pale-green flame into a white incandescence, and then sharply tugged the bellcord by the door. And when the old waiter came, Charles sent him peremptorily off for a gill of the White Lion's best cobbler, a velvety concoction of sherry and brandy that caused many a Victorian unloosing of the stays.

Not much more than five minutes later, the astonished Sam, bearing the supper tray, was halted in midstairs by the sight of his master, with somewhat flushed cheeks, striding down to meet him in his Inverness cape. Charles halted a stair above him, lifted the cloth that covered the brown soup, the mutton and boiled potatoes, and then passed on down without a word.

"Mr. Charles?"

"Eat it yourself."

And the master was gone—in marked contrast to Sam, who stayed where he was, his tongue thrusting out his left cheek and his eyes fiercely fixed on the banister beside him.

167

26

Let me tell you, my friends, that the whole thing depends
On an ancient manorial right.

LEWIS CARROLL, *The Hunting of the Snark* (1876)

The effect of Mary on the young Cockney's mind had indeed
been ruminative. He loved Mary for herself, as any normal
young man in his healthy physical senses would; but he also
loved her for the part she played in his dreams—which was
not at all the sort of part girls play in young men's dreams in
our own uninhibited, and unimaginative, age. Most often he
saw her prettily caged behind the counter of a gentleman's
shop. From all over London, as if magnetized, distinguished
male customers homed on that seductive face. The street
outside was black with their top hats, deafened by the wheels
of their carriages and hansoms. A kind of magical samovar,
whose tap was administered by Mary, dispensed an endless
flow of gloves, scarves, stocks, hats, gaiters, Oxonians (a kind
of shoe then in vogue) and collars—Piccadilly's, Shake-
spere's, Dog-collar's, Dux's—Sam had a fixation on collars, I
am not sure it wasn't a fetish, for he certainly saw Mary
putting them round her small white neck before each admiring duke and lord. During this charming scene Sam himself
was at the till, the recipient of the return golden shower.

He was well aware that this was a dream. But Mary, so to
speak, underlined the fact; what is more, sharpened the
hideous features of the demon that stood so squarely in the
way of its fulfillment. Its name? Short-of-the-ready. Perhaps
it was this ubiquitous enemy of humankind that Sam was
still staring at in his master's sitting room, where he had
made himself comfortable—having first watched Charles
safely out of sight down Broad Street, with yet another
mysterious pursing of the lips—as he toyed with his second
supper: a spoonful or two of soup, the choicer hearts of the

mutton slices, for Sam had all the instincts, if none of the finances, of a swell. But now again he was staring into space past a piece of mutton anointed with caper sauce, which he held poised on his fork, though oblivious to its charms.

Mal (if I may add to your stock of useless knowledge) is an Old English borrowing from Old Norwegian and was brought to us by the Vikings. It originally meant "speech," but since the only time the Vikings went in for that rather womanish activity was to demand something at axeblade, it came to mean "tax" or "payment in tribute." One branch of the Vikings went south and founded the Mafia in Sicily; but another—and by this time *mal* was spelled *mail*—were busy starting their own protection rackets on the Scottish border. If one cherished one's crops or one's daughter's virginity one paid mail to the neighborhood chieftains; and the victims, in the due course of an expensive time, called it black mail.

If not exactly engaged in etymological speculation, Sam was certainly thinking of the meaning of the word; for he had guessed at once who the "unfortunate woman" was. Such an event as the French Lieutenant's Woman's dismissal was too succulent an item not to have passed through every mouth in Lyme in the course of the day; and Sam had already overheard a conversation in the taproom as he sat at his first and interrupted supper. He knew who Sarah was, since Mary had mentioned her one day. He also knew his master and his manner; he was not himself; he was up to something; he was on his way to somewhere other than Mrs. Tranter's house. Sam laid down the fork and its morsel and began to tap the side of his nose; a gesture not unknown in the ring at Newmarket, when a bow-legged man smells a rat masquerading as a racehorse. But the rat here, I am afraid, was Sam—and what he smelled was a sinking ship.

Downstairs at Winsyatt they knew very well what was going on; the uncle was out to spite the nephew. With the rural working class's innate respect for good husbandry they despised Charles for not visiting more often—in short, for not buttering up Sir Robert at every opportunity. Servants in those days were regarded as little more than furniture, and their masters frequently forgot they had both ears and intelligences; certain abrasive exchanges between the old man and his heir had not gone unnoticed and undiscussed. And though there was a disposition among the younger female staff to feel sorry for the handsome Charles, the sager part took a kind of ant's-eye view of the frivolous grasshopper and his come-uppance. They had worked all their lives for their wages; and they were glad to see Charles punished for his laziness.

169

Besides, Mrs. Tomkins, who was very much as Ernestina suspected, an upper-middle-class adventuress, had shrewdly gone out of her way to ingratiate herself with the housekeeper and the butler; and those two worthies had set their *imprimatur*—or *ducatur in matrimonium*—upon the plump and effusive widow; who furthermore had, upon being shown a long-unused suite in the before-mentioned east wing, remarked to the housekeeper how excellent a nursery the rooms would make. It was true that Mrs. Tomkins had a son and two daughters by her first marriage; but in the housekeeper's opinion—graciously extended to Mr. Benson, the butler—Mrs. Tomkins was as good as expecting again.

"It could be daughters, Mrs. Trotter."

"She's a trier, Mr. Benson. You mark my words. She's a trier."

The butler sipped his dish of tea, then added, "And tips well." Which Charles, as one of the family, did not.

The general substance of all this had come to Sam's ears, while he waited down in the servants' hall for Charles. It had not come pleasantly in itself or pleasantly inasmuch as Sam, as the servant of the grasshopper, had to share part of the general judgment on him; and all this was not altogether unconnected with a kind of second string Sam had always kept for his bow: a *faute de mieux* dream in which he saw himself in the same exalted position at Winsyatt that Mr. Benson now held. He had even casually planted this seed—and one pretty certain to germinate, if he chose—in Mary's mind. It was not nice to see one's tender seedling, even if it was not the most cherished, so savagely uprooted.

Charles himself, when they left Winsyatt, had not said a word to Sam, so officially Sam knew nothing about his blackened hopes. But his master's blackened face was as good as knowledge.

And now this.

Sam at last ate his congealing mutton, and chewed it, and swallowed it; and all the time his eyes stared into the future.

Charles's interview with his uncle had not been stormy, since both felt guilty—the uncle for what he was doing, the nephew for what he had failed to do in the past. Charles's reaction to the news, delivered bluntly but with telltale averted eyes, had been, after the first icy shock, stiffly polite.

"I can only congratulate you, sir, and wish you every happiness."

His uncle, who had come upon him soon after we left Charles in the drawing room, turned away to a window, as if to gain heart from his green acres. He gave a brief account

170

of his passion. He had been rejected at first: that was three weeks ago. But he was not the man to turn tail at the first refusal. He had sensed a certain indecision in the lady's voice. A week before he had taken train to London and "galloped straight in again"; the obstinate hedge was triumphantly cleared. "She said 'no' again, Charles, but she was weeping. I knew I was over." It had apparently taken two or three days more for the definitive "Yes" to be spoken.

"And then, my dear boy, I knew I had to face you. You are the very first to be told."

But Charles remembered then that pitying look from old Mrs. Hawkins; all Winsyatt had the news by now. His uncle's somewhat choked narration of his amorous saga had given him time to absorb the shock. He felt whipped and humiliated; a world less. But he had only one defense: to take it calmly, to show the stoic and hide the raging boy.

"I appreciate your punctiliousness, Uncle."

"You have every right to call me a doting old fool. Most of my neighbors will."

"Late choices are often the best."

"She's a lively sort of woman, Charles. Not one of your damned niminy-piminy modern misses." For one sharp moment Charles thought this was a slight on Ernestina—as it was, but not intended. His uncle went obliviously on. "She says what she thinks. Nowadays some people consider that signifies a woman's a thruster. But she's not." He enlisted the agreement of his parkland. "Straight as a good elm."

"I never for a moment supposed she could be anything else."

The uncle cast a shrewd look at him then; just as Sam played the meek footman with Charles, so did Charles sometimes play the respectful nephew with the old man.

"I would rather you were angry than . . ." he was going to say a cold fish, but he came and put his arm round Charles's shoulder; for he had tried to justify his decision by working up anger against Charles—and he was too good a sportsman not to know it was a mean justification. "Charles, now damn it, it must be said. This brings an alteration to your prospects. Though at my age, heaven knows . . ." that "bullfinch" he did refuse. "But if it should happen, Charles, I wish you to know that whatever may come of the marriage, you will not go unprovided for. I can't give you the Little House; but I wish emphatically that you take it as yours for as long as you live. I should like that to be my wedding gift to Ernestina and yourself—and the expenses of doing the place up properly, of course."

"That is most generous of you. But I think we have more

or less decided to go into the Belgravia house when the lease falls in."

"Yes, yes, but you must have a place in the country. I will not have this business coming between us, Charles. I shall break it off tomorrow if—"

Charles managed a smile. "Now you are being absurd. You might well have married many years ago."

"That may be. But the fact is I didn't."

He went nervously to the wall and placed a picture back into alignment. Charles was silent; perhaps he felt less hurt at the shock of the news than at the thought of all his foolish dream of possession as he drove up to Winsyatt. And the old devil should have written. But to the old devil that would have been a cowardice. He turned from the painting.

"Charles, you're a young fellow, you spend half your life traveling about. You don't know how deuced lonely, bored, I don't know what it is, but half the time I feel I might as well be dead."

Charles murmured, "I had no idea . . ."

"No, no, I don't mean to accuse you. You have your own life to lead." But he did still, secretly, like so many men without children, blame Charles for falling short of what he imagined all sons to be—dutiful and loving to a degree ten minutes' real fatherhood would have made him see was a sentimental dream. "All the same there are things only a woman can bring one. The old hangings in this room, now. Had you noticed? Mrs. Tomkins called them gloomy one day. And damn it, I'm blind, they *were* gloomy. Now that's what a woman does. Makes you see what's in front of your nose." Charles felt tempted to suggest that spectacles performed the same function a great deal more cheaply, but he merely bowed his head in understanding. Sir Robert rather unctuously waved his hand. "What say you to these new ones?"

Charles then had to grin. His uncle's aesthetic judgments had been confined for so long to matters such as the depth of a horse's withers and the superiority of Joe Manton over any other gunmaker known to history that it was rather like hearing a murderer ask his opinion of a nursery rhyme.

"A great improvement."

"Just so. Everyone says the same."

Charles bit his lip. "And when am I going to meet the lady?"

"Indeed, I was coming to that. She is most anxious to get to know you. And Charles, most delicate in the matter of . . . well, the . . . how shall I put it?"

"Limitations of my prospects?"

172

"Just so. She confessed last week she first refused me for that very reason." This was, Charles realized, supposed to be a commendation, and he showed a polite surprise. "But I assured her you had made an excellent match. And would understand and approve my choice of partner . . . for my last years."

"You haven't yet answered my question, Uncle."

Sir Robert looked a little ashamed. "She is visiting family in Yorkshire. She is related to the Daubenys, you know."

"Indeed."

"I go to join her there tomorrow."

"Ah."

"And I thought it best to get it over man to man. But she is most anxious to meet you." His uncle hesitated, then with a ludicrous shyness reached in his waistcoat pocket and produced a locket. "She gave me this last week."

And Charles stared at a miniature, framed in gold and his uncle's heavy fingers, of Mrs. Bella Tomkins. She looked disagreeably young; firm-lipped; and with assertive eyes—not at all unattractive, even to Charles. There was, curiously, some faint resemblance to Sarah in the face; and a subtle new dimension was added to Charles's sense of humiliation and dispossession. Sarah was a woman of profound inexperience, and this was a woman of the world; but both in their very different ways—his uncle was right—stood apart from the great niminy-piminy flock of women in general. For a moment he felt himself like a general in command of a weak army looking over the strong dispositions of the enemy; he foresaw only too clearly the result of a confrontation between Ernestina and the future Lady Smithson. It would be a rout.

"I see I have further reason to congratulate you."

"She's a fine woman. A splendid woman. Worth waiting for, Charles." His uncle dug him in the ribs. "You'll be jealous. Just see if you won't." He gazed fondly again at the locket, then closed it reverentially and replaced it in his pocket. And then, as if to counteract the soft sop, he briskly made Charles accompany him to the stables to see his latest brood mare, bought for "a hundred guineas less than she was worth"; and which seemed a totally unconscious but distinct equine parallel in his mind to his other new acquisition.

They were both English gentlemen; and they carefully avoided further discussion of, if not further reference to (for Sir Robert was too irrepressibly full of his own good luck not to keep on harking back), the subject uppermost in both their minds. But Charles insisted that he must return to Lyme and his fiancée that evening; and his uncle, who in former days would, at such a desertion, have sunk into a black gloom, made no great demur now. Charles promised to discuss the matter of the Little House with Ernestina, and to bring her to meet the other bride-to-be as soon as could be conveniently arranged. But all his uncle's last-minute warmth and hand-shaking could not disguise the fact that the old man was relieved to see the back of him.

Pride had buoyed Charles up through the three or four hours of his visit; but his driving away was a sad business. Those lawns, pastures, railings, landscaped groves seemed to slip through his fingers as they slipped slowly past his eyes. He felt he never wanted to see Winsyatt again. The morning's azure sky was overcast by a high veil of cirrus, harbinger of that thunderstorm we have already heard in Lyme, and his mind soon began to plummet into a similar climate of morose introspection.

This latter was directed not a little against Ernestina. He knew his uncle had not been very impressed by her fastidious little London ways; her almost total lack of interest in rural life. To a man who had devoted so much of his life to breeding she must have seemed a poor new entry to such fine stock as the Smithsons. And then one of the bonds between uncle and nephew had always been their bachelorhood—perhaps Charles's happiness had opened Sir Robert's eyes a little: if he, why not I? And then there was the one thing about Ernestina his uncle had thoroughly approved of: her massive marriage portion. But that was precisely what allowed him to expropriate Charles with a light conscience.

But above all, Charles now felt himself in a very displeasing position of inferiority as regards Ernestina. His income from his father's estate had always been sufficient for his needs; but he had not increased the capital. As the future master of Winsyatt he could regard himself as his bride's financial equal; as a mere *rentier* he must become her financial dependent. In disliking this, Charles was being a good deal more fastidious than most young men of his class and age. To them dowry-hunting (and about this time, dollars began to be as acceptable as sterling) was as honorable a pursuit as fox-hunting or gaming. Perhaps that was it: he felt sorry for himself and yet knew very few would share his feeling. It even exacerbated his resentment that circumstances had not made his uncle's injustice even greater: if he had spent more time at Winsyatt, say, or if he had never met Ernestina in the first place . . .

But it was Ernestina, and the need once again to show the stiff upper lip, that was the first thing to draw him out of his misery that day.

27

How often I sit, poring o'er
  My strange distorted youth,
Seeking in vain, in all my store,
  One feeling based on truth; . . .
So constant as my heart would be,
  So fickle as it must,
'Twere well for others and for me
  'Twere dry as summer dust.
Excitements come, and act and speech
Flow freely forth:—but no,
Nor they, nor aught beside can reach
  The buried world below.

A. H. CLOUGH, Poem (1840)

The door was opened by the housekeeper. The doctor, it
seemed, was in his dispensary; but if Charles would like to
wait upstairs ... so, divested of his hat and his Inverness
cape he soon found himself in that same room where he had
drunk the grog and declared himself for Darwin. A fire
burned in the grate; and evidence of the doctor's solitary
supper, which the housekeeper hastened to clear, lay on the
round table in the bay window overlooking the sea. Charles
very soon heard feet on the stairs. Grogan came warmly into
the room, hand extended.

"This *is* a pleasure, Smithson. That stupid woman now
has she not given you something to counteract the rain?"

"Thank you ..." he was going to refuse the brandy decanter, but changed his mind. And when he had the glass in his
hand, he came straight out with his purpose. "I have something private and very personal to discuss. I need your
advice."

A little glint showed in the doctor's eyes then. He had had
other well-bred young men come to him shortly before their
marriage. Sometimes it was gonorrhea, less often syphilis;

sometimes it was mere fear, masturbation phobia; a widespread theory of the time maintained that the wages of self-abuse was impotence. But usually it was ignorance; only a year before a miserable and childless young husband had come to see Dr. Grogan, who had had gravely to explain that new life is neither begotten nor born through the navel.

"Do you now? Well I'm not sure I have any left—I've given a vast amount of it away today. Mainly concerning what should be executed upon that damned old bigot up in Marlborough House. You've heard what she's done?"

"That is precisely what I wish to talk to you about."

The doctor breathed a little inward sigh of relief; and he once again jumped to the wrong conclusion.

"Ah, of course—Mrs. Tranter is worried? Tell her from me that all is being done that can be done. A party is out searching. I have offered five pounds to the man who brings her back ..." his voice went bitter "... or finds the poor creature's body."

"She is alive. I've just received a note from her."

Charles looked down before the doctor's amazed look. And then, at first addressing his brandy glass, he began to tell the truth of his encounters with Sarah—that is, almost all the truth, for he left undescribed his own more secret feelings. He managed, or tried, to pass some of the blame off on Dr. Grogan and their previous conversation; giving himself a sort of scientific status that the shrewd little man opposite did not fail to note. Old doctors and old priests share one thing in common: they get a long nose for deceit, whether it is overt or, as in Charles's case, committed out of embarrassment. As he went on with his confession, the end of Dr. Grogan's nose began metaphorically to twitch; and this invisible twitching signified very much the same as Sam's pursing of his lips. The doctor let no sign of his suspicions appear. Now and then he asked questions, but in general he let Charles talk his increasingly lame way to the end of his story. Then he stood up.

"Well, first things first. We must get those poor devils back." The thunder was now much closer and though the curtains had been drawn, the white shiver of lightning trembled often in their weave behind Charles's back.

"I came as soon as I could."

"Yes, you are not to blame for that. Now let me see ..." The doctor was already seated at a small desk in the rear of the room. For a few moments there was no sound in it but the rapid scratch of his pen. Then he read what he had written to Charles.

" 'Dear Forsyth, News has this minute reached me that Miss Woodruff is safe. She does not wish her whereabouts

176

disclosed, but you may set your mind at rest. I hope to have further news of her tomorrow. Please offer the enclosed to the party of searchers when they return.' Will that do?"

"Excellently. Except that the enclosure must be mine." Charles produced a small embroidered purse, Ernestina's work, and set three sovereigns on the green cloth desk beside Grogan, who pushed two away. He looked up with a smile.

"Mr. Forsyth is trying to abolish the demon alcohol. I think one piece of gold is enough." He placed the note and the coin in an envelope, sealed it, and then went to arrange for the letter's speedy delivery.

He came back, talking. "Now the girl—what's to be done about her? You have no notion where she is at the moment?"

"None at all. Though I am sure she will be where she indicated tomorrow morning."

"But of course you cannot be there. In your situation you cannot risk any further compromise."

Charles looked at him, then down at the carpet.

"I am in your hands."

The doctor stared thoughtfully at Charles. He had just set a little test to probe his guest's mind. And it had revealed what he had expected. He turned and went to the bookshelves by his desk and then came back with the same volume he had shown Charles before: Darwin's great work. He sat before him across the fire; then with a small smile and a look at Charles over his glasses, he laid his hand, as if swearing on a Bible on *The Origin of Species*.

"Nothing that has been said in this room or that remains to be said shall go beyond its walls." Then he put the book aside.

"My dear Doctor, that was not necessary."

"Confidence in the practitioner is half of medicine."

Charles smiled wanly. "And the other half?"

"Confidence in the patient." But he stood before Charles could speak. "Well now—you came for my advice, did you not?" He eyed Charles almost as if he was going to box with him; no longer the bantering, but the fighting Irishman. Then he began to pace his "cabin," his hands tucked under his frock coat.

"I am a young woman of superior intelligence and some education. I think the world has done badly by me. I am not in full command of my emotions. I do foolish things, such as throwing myself at the head of the first handsome rascal who is put in my path. What is worse, I have fallen in love with being a victim of fate. I put out a very professional line in the way of looking melancholy. I have tragic eyes. I weep without explanation. Et cetera. Et cetera. And now ..." the

177

little doctor waved his hand at the door, as if invoking magic "... enter a young god. Intelligent. Good-looking. A perfect specimen of that class my education has taught me to admire. I see he is interested in me. The sadder I seem, the more interested he appears to be. I kneel before him, he raises me to my feet. He treats me like a lady. Nay, more than that. In a spirit of Christian brotherhood he offers to help me escape from my unhappy lot."

Charles made to interrupt, but the doctor silenced him.

"Now I am very poor. I can use none of the wiles the more fortunate of my sex employ to lure mankind into their power." He raised his forefinger. "I have but one weapon. The pity I inspire in this kindhearted man. Now pity is a thing that takes a devil of a lot of feeding. I have fed this Good Samaritan my past and he has devoured it. So what can I do? I must make him pity my present. One day, when I am walking where I have been forbidden to walk, I seize my chance. I show myself to someone I know will report my crime to the one person who will not condone it. I get myself dismissed from my position. I disappear, under the strong presumption that it is in order to throw myself off the nearest clifftop. And then, *in extremis* and *de profundis*—or rather *de altis*—I cry to my savior for help." He left a long pause then, and Charles's eyes slowly met his. The doctor smiled, "I present what is partly hypothesis, of course."

"But your specific accusation—that she invited her own ..."

The doctor sat and poked the fire into life. "I was called early this morning to Marlborough House. I did not know why—merely that Mrs. P. was severely indisposed. Mrs. Fairley—the housekeeper, you know—told me the gist of what had happened." He paused and fixed Charles's unhappy eyes. "Mrs. Fairley was yesterday at the dairy out there on Ware Cleeves. The girl walked flagrantly out of the woods under her nose. Now that woman is a very fair match to her mistress, and I'm sure she did her subsequent duty with all the mean appetite of her kind. But I am convinced, my dear Smithson, that she was deliberately invited to do it."

"You mean ..." The doctor nodded. Charles gave him a terrible look, then revolted. "I cannot believe it. It is not possible she should—"

He did not finish the sentence. The doctor murmured, "It is possible. Alas."

"But only a person of ..." he was going to say "warped mind," but he stood abruptly and went to the window, parted the curtains, stared a blind moment out into the teeming

178

night. A livid flash of sheet lightning lit the Cobb, the beach, the torpid sea. He turned.

"In other words, I have been led by the nose."

"Yes, I think you have. But it required a generous nose. And you must remember that a deranged mind is not a criminal mind. In this case you must think of despair as a disease, no more or less. That girl, Smithson, has a cholera, a typhus of the intellectual faculties. You must think of her like that. Not as some malicious schemer."

Charles came back into the room. "And what do you suppose her final intention to be?"

"I very much doubt if she knows. She lives from day to day. Indeed she must. No one of foresight could have behaved as she has."

"But she cannot seriously have supposed that someone in my position . . ."

"As a man who is betrothed?" The doctor smiled grimly. "I have known many prostitutes. I hasten to add: in pursuance of my own profession, not theirs. And I wish I had a guinea for every one I have heard gloat over the fact that a majority of their victims are husbands and fathers." He stared into the fire, into his past. " 'I am cast out. But I shall be revenged.' "

"You make her sound like a fiend—she is not so." He had spoken too vehemently, and turned quickly away. "I cannot believe this of her."

"That, if you will permit a man old enough to be your father to say so, is because you are half in love with her."

Charles spun round and stared at the doctor's bland face.

"I do *not* permit you to say that." Grogan bowed his head. In the silence, Charles added, "It is highly insulting to Miss Freeman."

"It is indeed. But who is making the insult?"

Charles swallowed. He could not bear these quizzical eyes, and he started down the long, narrow room as if to go. But before he could reach the door, Grogan had him by the arm and made him turn, and seized the other arm—and he was fierce, a terrier at Charles's dignity.

"Man, man, are we not both believers in science? Do we not both hold that truth is the one great principle? What did Socrates die for? A keeping social face? A homage to decorum? Do you think in my forty years as a doctor I have not learned to tell when a man is in distress? And because he is hiding the truth from himself? Know thyself, Smithson, *know* thyself!"

The mixture of ancient Greek and Gaelic fire in Grogan's

soul seared Charles. He stood staring down at the doctor, then looked aside, and returned to the fireside, his back to his tormentor. There was a long silence. Grogan watched him intently.

At last Charles spoke.

"I am not made for marriage. My misfortune is to have realized it too late."

"Have you read Malthus?" Charles shook his head. "For him the tragedy of *Homo sapiens* is that the least fit to survive breed the most. So don't say you aren't made for marriage, my boy. And don't blame yourself for falling for that girl. I think I know why that French sailor ran away. He knew she had eyes a man could drown in."

Charles swivelled round in agony. "On my most sacred honor, nothing improper has passed between us. You must believe that."

"I believe you. But let me put you through the old catechism. Do you wish to hear her? Do you wish to see her? Do you wish to touch her?"

Charles turned away again and sank into the chair, his face in his hands. It was no answer, yet it said everything. After a moment, he raised his face and stared into the fire.

"Oh my dear Grogan, if you knew the mess my life was in ... the waste of it ... the uselessness of it. I have no moral purpose, no real sense of duty to anything. It seems only a few months ago that I was twenty-one—full of hopes ... all disappointed. And now to get entangled in this miserable business ..."

Grogan moved beside him and gripped his shoulder. "You are not the first man to doubt his choice of bride."

"She understands so little of what I really am."

"She is—what?—a dozen years younger than yourself? And she has known you not six months. How could she understand you as yet? She is hardly out of the schoolroom."

Charles nodded gloomily. He could not tell the doctor his real conviction about Ernestina: that she would never understand him. He felt fatally disabused of his own intelligence. It had let him down in his choice of a life partner; for like so many Victorian, and perhaps more recent, men Charles was to live all his life under the influence of the ideal. There are some men who are consoled by the idea that there are women less attractive than their wives; and others who are haunted by the knowledge that there are more attractive. Charles now saw only too well which category he belonged to.

He murmured, "It is not her fault. It cannot be."

180

"I should think not. A pretty young innocent girl like that."

"I shall honor my vows to her."

"Of course."

A silence.

"Tell me what to do."

"First tell me your real sentiments as regards the other."

Charles looked up in despair; then down to the fire, and tried at last to tell the truth.

"I cannot say, Grogan. In all that relates to her, I am an enigma to myself. I do not love her. How could I? A woman so compromised, a woman you tell me is mentally diseased. But ... it is as if ... I feel like a man possessed against his will—against all that is better in his character. Even now her face rises before me, denying all you say. There is something in her. A knowledge, an apprehension of nobler things than are compatible with either evil or madness. Beneath the dross ... I cannot explain."

"I did not lay evil at her door. But despair."

No sound, but a floorboard or two that creaked as the doctor paced. At last Charles spoke again.

"What do you advise?"

"That you leave matters entirely in my hands."

"You will go to see her?"

"I shall put on my walking boots. I shall tell her you have been unexpectedly called away. And you *must* go away, Smithson."

"It so happens I have urgent business in London."

"So much the better. And I suggest that before you go you lay the whole matter before Miss Freeman."

"I had already decided upon that." Charles got to his feet. But still that face rose before him. "And she—what will you do?"

"Much depends upon her state of mind. It may well be that all that keeps her sane at the present juncture is her belief that you feel sympathy—perhaps something sweeter—for her. The shock of your not appearing may, I fear, produce a graver melancholia. I am afraid we must anticipate that." Charles looked down. "You are not to blame that upon yourself. If it had not been you, it would have been some other. In a way, such a state of affairs will make things easier. I shall know what course to take."

Charles stared at the carpet. "An asylum."

"That colleague I mentioned—he shares my views on the treatment of such cases. We shall do our best. You would be prepared for a certain amount of expense?"

"Anything to be rid of her—without harm to her."

"I know a private asylum in Exeter. My friend Spencer has patients there. It is conducted in an intelligent and enlightened manner. I should not recommend a public institution at this stage."

"Heaven forbid. I have heard terrible accounts of them."

"Rest assured. This place is a model of its kind."

"We are not talking of committal?"

For there had arisen in Charles's mind a little ghost of treachery: to discuss her so clinically, to think of her locked in some small room . . .

"Not at all. We are talking of a place where her spiritual wounds can heal, where she will be kindly treated, kept occupied—and will have the benefit of Spencer's excellent experience and care. He has had similar cases. He knows what to do."

Charles hesitated, then stood and held out his hand. In his present state he needed orders and prescriptions, and as soon as he had them, he felt better.

"I feel you have saved my life."

"Nonsense, my dear fellow."

"No, it is not nonsense. I shall be in debt to you for the rest of my days."

"Then let me inscribe the name of your bride on the bill of credit."

"I shall honor the debt."

"And give the charming creature time. The best wines take the longest to mature, do they not?"

"I fear that in my own case the same is true of a very inferior vintage."

"Bah. Poppycock." The doctor clapped him on the shoulder. "And by the bye, I think you read French?"

Charles gave a surprised assent. Grogan sought through his shelves, found a book, and then marked a passage in it with a pencil before passing it to his guest.

"You need not read the whole trial. But I should like you to read this medical evidence that was brought by the defense."

Charles stared at the volume. "A purge?"

The little doctor had a gnomic smile.

"Something of the kind."

182

28

Assumptions, hasty, crude, and vain,
Full oft to use will Science deign;
The corks the novice plies today
The swimmer soon shall cast away.

    A. H. CLOUGH, Poem (1840)

Again I spring to make my choice;
Again in tones of ire
I hear a God's tremendous voice—
"Be counsel'd, and retire!"

    MATTHEW ARNOLD, "The Lake" (1853)

The trial of Lieutenant Emile de La Roncière in 1835 is psychiatrically one of the most interesting of early nineteenth-century cases. The son of the martinet Count de La Roncière, Emile was evidently a rather frivolous—he had a mistress and got badly into debt—yet not unusual young man for his country, period and profession. In 1834 he was attached to the famous cavalry school at Saumur in the Loire valley. His commanding officer was the Baron de Morell, who had a highly strung daughter of sixteen, named Marie. In those days commanding officers' houses served in garrison as a kind of mess for their subordinates. One evening the Baron, as stiffnecked as Emile's father, but a good deal more influential, called the lieutenant up to him and, in the presence of his brother officers and several ladies, furiously ordered him to leave the house. The next day La Roncière was presented with a vicious series of poison-pen letters threatening the Morell family. All displayed an uncanny knowledge of the most intimate details of the life of the household, and all—the first absurd flaw in the prosecution case—were signed with the lieutenant's initials.

183

Worse was to come. On the night of September 24th, 1834, Marie's English governess, a Miss Allen, was woken by her sixteen-year-old charge, who told in tears how La Roncière, in full uniform, had just forced his way through the window into her adjacent bedroom, bolted the door, made obscene threats, struck her across the breasts and bitten her hand, then forced her to raise her night-chemise and wounded her in the upper thigh. He had then escaped by the way he had come.

The very next morning another lieutenant supposedly favored by Marie de Morell received a highly insulting letter, again apparently from La Roncière. A duel was fought. La Roncière won, but the severely wounded adversary and his second refused to concede the falsity of the poison-pen charge. They threatened La Roncière that his father would be told if he did not sign a confession of guilt; once that was done, the matter would be buried. After a night of agonized indecision, La Roncière foolishly agreed to sign.

He then asked for leave and went to Paris, in the belief that the affair would be hushed up. But signed letters continued to appear in the Morells' house. Some claimed that Marie was pregnant, others that her parents would soon both be murdered, and so on. The Baron had had enough. La Roncière was arrested.

The number of circumstances in the accused's favor was so large that we can hardly believe today that he should have been brought to trial, let alone convicted. To begin with, it was common knowledge in Saumur that Marie had been piqued by La Roncière's obvious admiration for her handsome mother, of whom the daughter was extremely envious. Then the Morell mansion was surrounded by sentries on the night of the attempted rape; not one had noticed anything untoward, even though the bedroom concerned was on the top floor and reachable only by a ladder it would have required at least three men to carry and "mount"—therefore a ladder that would have left traces in the soft soil beneath the window ... and the defense established that there had been none. Furthermore, the glazier brought in to mend the pane broken by the intruder testified that all the broken glass had fallen *outside* the house and that it was in any case impossible to reach the window catch through the small aperture made. Then the defense asked why during the assault Marie had never once cried for help; why the light-sleeping Miss Allen had not been woken by the scuffling; why she and Marie then *went back to sleep* without waking Madame de Morell, who slept through the whole incident on the floor below; why the thigh wound was not examined until *months* after the incident (and was then pronounced to be a light scratch, now fully healed); why Marie went to a ball only two evenings later and led a perfectly normal life until the arrest was finally made—when she promptly had a nervous breakdown (again, the defense showed that it was far from the first in her young life); how the letters could still appear in the house, even when the penniless La Roncière was in jail awaiting trial; why any poison-pen letter-writer in his senses should not only not disguise his writing (which was easily copiable) but sign his name; why the letters showed an accuracy of spelling and grammar (students of French will be pleased to know that La Roncière invariably forgot to make his past participles agree) conspicuously absent from genuine correspondence produced for comparison; why twice he even failed to spell his own name correctly; why the incriminating letters appeared to be written on paper—the greatest contemporary authority witnessed as much—identical to a sheaf found in Marie's escritoire. Why and why and why, in short. As a final doubt, the defense also pointed out that a similar series of letters had been found previously in the Morells' Paris house, and at a time when La Roncière was on the other side of the world, doing service in Cayenne.

But the ultimate injustice at the trial (attended by Hugo, Balzac and George Sand among many other celebrities) was the court's refusal to allow any cross-examination of the prosecution's principal witness: Marie de Morell. She gave her evidence in a cool and composed manner; but the president of the court, under the cannon-muzzle eyes of the Baron and an imposing phalanx of distinguished relations, decided that her "modesty" and her "weak nervous state" forbade further interrogation.

La Roncière was found guilty and sentenced to ten years' imprisonment. Almost every eminent jurist in Europe protested, but in vain. We can see why he was condemned, or rather, by what he was condemned: by social prestige, by the myth of the pure-minded virgin, by psychological ignorance, by a society in full reaction from the pernicious notions of freedom disseminated by the French Revolution.

But now let me translate the pages that the doctor had marked. They come from the *Observations Médico-psychologiques* of a Dr. Karl Matthaei, a well-known German physician of his time, written in support of an abortive appeal against the La Roncière verdict. Matthaei had already had the intelligence to write down the dates on which the more obscene letters, culminating in the attempted rape, had occurred. They fell into a clear monthly—or menstrual—pattern. After analyzing the evidence brought before the court, the Herr Doktor proceeds, in a somewhat moralistic tone, to explain the mental illness we today call hysteria—the assumption, that is, of symptoms of disease or disability in order to gain the attention and sympathy of others: a neurosis or psychosis almost invariably caused, as we now know, by sexual repression.

If I glance back over my long career as a doctor, I recall many incidents of which girls have been the heroines, although their participation seemed for long impossible . . .

Some forty years ago, I had among my patients the family of a lieutenant-general of cavalry. He had a small property some six miles from the town where he was in garrison, and he lived there, riding into town when his duties called. He had an exceptionally pretty daughter of sixteen years' age. She wished fervently that her father lived in the town. Her exact reasons were never discovered, but no doubt she wished to have the company of the officers and the pleasures of society there. To get her way, she chose a highly criminal procedure: she set fire to the country home. A wing of it was burned to the ground. It was rebuilt. New attempts at arson were made: and one day once again part of the house went up in flames. No less than thirty attempts at arson were committed subsequently. However nearly one came upon the arsonist, his identity was never discovered. Many people were apprehended and interrogated. The one person who was never suspected was that beautiful young innocent daughter. Several years passed; and then finally she was caught in the act; and condemned to life imprisonment in a house of correction.

In a large German city, a charming young girl of a distinguished family found her pleasure in sending anonymous letters whose purpose was to break up a recent happy marriage. She also spread vicious scandals concerning another young lady, widely admired for her talents and therefore an object of envy. These letters continued for several years. No shadow of suspicion fell on the authoress, though many other people were accused. At last she gave herself away, and was accused, and confessed to her crime . . . She served a long sentence in prison for her evil.

Again, at the very time and in this very place where I write,* the police are investigating a similar affair . . .

It may be objected that Marie de Morell would not have inflicted pain on herself to attain her ends. But her suffering was very slight compared to that in other cases from the annals of medicine. Here are some very remarkable instances.

Professor Herholdt of Copenhagen knew an attractive young woman of excellent education and well-to-do parents. He, like many of his colleagues, was completely deceived by her. She applied the greatest skill and perseverance to her deceits, and over a course of several years. She even tortured herself in the most atrocious manner. She plunged some hundreds of needles into the flesh of various parts of her body: and when inflammation or sup-

* Hanover, 1836.

186

puration had set in she had them removed by incision. She refused to urinate and had her urine removed each morning by means of a catheter. She herself introduced air into her bladder, which escaped when the instrument was inserted. For a year and a half she rested dumb and without movement, refused food, pretended spasms, fainting fits, and so on. Before her tricks were discovered, several famous doctors, some from abroad, examined her and were horror-struck to see such suffering. Her unhappy story was in all the news-papers, and no one doubted the authenticity of her case. Finally, in 1826, the truth was discovered. The sole motives of this clever fraud (*cette adroite trompeuse*) were to become an object of ad-miration and astonishment to men, and to make a fool of the most learned, famous and perceptive of them. The history of this case, so important from the psychological point of view, may be found in Herholdt: *Notes on the illness of Rachel Hertz between 1807 and 1826.*

At Lüneburg, a mother and daughter hit on a scheme whose aim was to draw a lucrative sympathy upon themselves—a scheme they pursued to the end with an appalling determination. The daughter complained of unbearable pain in one breast, lamented and wept, sought the help of the professions, tried all their remedies. The pain continued; a cancer was suspected. She herself elected without hesitation to have the breast extirpated; it was found to be per-fectly healthy. Some years later, when sympathy for her had less-ened, she took up her old role. The other breast was removed, and was found to be as healthy as the first. When once again sympathy began to dry up, she complained of pain in the hand. She wanted that too to be amputated. But suspicion was aroused. She was sent to hospital, accused of false pretenses, and finally dispatched to prison.

Lentin, in his *Supplement to a practical knowledge of medicine* (Hanover, 1798) tells this story, of which he was a witness. From a girl of no great age were drawn, by the medium of forceps after previous incision of the bladder and its neck, no less than one hundred and four stones in ten months. The girl herself introduced the stones into her bladder, even though the subsequent operations caused her great loss of blood and atrocious pain. Before this, she had had vomiting, convulsions and violent symptoms of many kinds. She showed a rare skill in her deceptions.

After such examples, which it would be easy to extend, who would say that it is impossible for a girl, in order to attain a de-sired end, to inflict pain upon herself?*

---

* I cannot leave the story of La Roncière—which I have taken from the same 1835 account that Dr. Grogan handed Charles—without add-ing that in 1848, some years after the lieutenant had finished his time, one of the original prosecuting counsel had the belated honesty to sus-pect that he had helped procure a gross miscarriage of justice. He was by then in a position to have the case reopened. La Roncière was com-pletely exonerated and rehabilitated. He resumed his military career and might, at that very hour Charles was reading the black climax of his life, have been found leading a pleasant enough existence as mili-tary governor of Tahiti. But his story has an extraordinary final twist. Only quite recently has it become known that he at least partly deserved

Those latter pages were the first Charles read. They came as a brutal shock to him, for he had no idea that such perversions existed—and in the pure and sacred sex. Nor, of course, could he see mental illness of the hysteric kind for what it is: a pitiable striving for love and security. He turned to the beginning of the account of the trial and soon found himself drawn fatally on into that. I need hardly say that he identified himself almost at once with the miserable Emile de La Roncière; and towards the end of the trial he came upon a date that sent a shiver down his spine. The day that other French lieutenant was condemned was the very same day that Charles had come into the world. For a moment, in that silent Dorset night, reason and science dissolved; life was a dark machine, a sinister astrology, a verdict at birth and without appeal, a zero over all.

He had never felt less free.

And he had never felt less sleepy. He looked at his watch. It lacked ten minutes of four o'clock. All was peace now outside. The storm had passed. Charles opened a window and breathed in the cold but clean spring air. Stars twinkled faintly overhead, innocently, disclaiming influence, either sinister or beneficent. And where was she? Awake also, a mile or two away, in some dark woodland darkness.

The effects of the cobbler and Grogan's brandy had long worn off, leaving Charles only with a profound sense of guilt. He thought he recalled a malice in the Irish doctor's eyes, a storing-up of this fatuous London gentleman's troubles that would soon be whispered and retailed all over Lyme. Was it not notorious that his race could not keep a secret?

How puerile, how undignified his behavior had been! He had lost not only Winsyatt that previous day, but all his self-respect. Even that last phrase was a tautology; he had, quite simply, lost respect for everything he knew. Life was a pit in Bedlam. Behind the most innocent faces lurked the vilest iniquities. He was Sir Galahad shown Guinevere to be a whore.

the hysterical Mlle de Morell's revenge on him. He had indeed entered her bedroom on that September night of 1834; but not through the window. Having earlier seduced the governess Miss Allen (perfide Albion!), he made a much simpler entry from her adjoining bedroom. The purpose of his visit was not amatory, but in fulfillment of a bet he had made with some brother officers, to whom he had boasted of having slept with Marie. He was challenged to produce proof in the form of a lock of hair—but not from the girl's head. The wound in Marie's thigh was caused by a pair of scissors; and the wound to her self-esteem becomes a good deal more explicable. An excellent discussion of this bizarre case may be found in René Floriot, Les Erreurs Judiciaires, Paris, 1968.

To stop the futile brooding—if only he could *act!*—he picked up the fatal book and read again some of the passages in Matthaei's paper on hysteria. He saw fewer parallels now with Sarah's conduct. His guilt began to attach itself to its proper object. He tried to recollect her face, things she had said, the expression in her eyes as she had said them; but he could not grasp her. Yet it came to him that he knew her better, perhaps, than any other human being did. That account of their meetings he had given Grogan . . . *that* he could remember, and almost word for word. Had he not, in his anxiety to hide his own real feelings, misled Grogan? Exaggerated her strangeness? Not honestly passed on what she had actually said?

Had he not condemned her to avoid condemning himself?

Endlessly he paced his sitting room, searching his soul and his hurt pride. Suppose she was what she had represented herself to be—a sinner, certainly, but also a woman of exceptional courage, refusing to turn her back on her sin? And now finally weakened in her terrible battle with her past and crying for help?

Why had he allowed Grogan to judge her for him?

Because he was more concerned to save appearances than his own soul. Because he had no more free will than an ammonite. Because he was a Pontius Pilate, a worse than he, not only condoning the crucifixion but encouraging, nay, even causing—did not all spring from that second meeting, when she had wanted to leave, but had had discussion of her situation forced upon her?—the events that now led to its execution.

He opened the window again. Two hours had passed since he had first done so. Now a faint light spread from the east. He stared up at the paling stars.

Destiny.

Those eyes.

Abruptly he turned.

If he met Grogan, he met him. His conscience must explain his disobedience. He went into his bedroom. And there, with an outward sour gravity reflecting the inward, self-awed and indecipherable determination he had come to, he began to change his clothes.

189

29

For a breeze of morning moves,
And the planet of Love is on high . . .

TENNYSON, *Maud* (1855)

It is a part of special prudence never to do anything
because one has an inclination to do it; but because
it is one's duty, or is reasonable.

MATTHEW ARNOLD, *Notebooks* (1868)

The sun was just redly leaving the insubstantial dove-gray
waves of the hills behind the Chesil Bank when Charles, not
dressed in the clothes but with all the facial expression of an
undertaker's mute, left the doors of the White Lion. The sky
was without cloud, washed pure by the previous night's storm
and of a deliciously tender and ethereal blue; the air as sharp
as lemon-juice, yet as clean and cleansing. If you get up at
such an hour in Lyme today you will have the town to
yourself. Charles, in that earlier-rising age, was not quite so
fortunate; but the people who were about had that pleasant
lack of social pretension, that primeval classlessness of dawn
population: simple people setting about their day's work. One
or two bade Charles a cheery greeting; and got very perempt-
tory nods and curt raisings of the ashplant in return. He
would rather have seen a few symbolic corpses littering the
streets than those bright faces; and he was glad when he left
the town behind him and entered the lane to the Undercliff.

But his gloom (and a self-suspicion I have concealed, that
his decision was really based more on the old sheepstealer's
adage, on a dangerous despair, than on the nobler movings of
his conscience) had an even poorer time of it there; the
quick walking sent a flood of warmth through him, a warmth
from inside complemented by the warmth from without
brought by the sun's rays. It seemed strangely distinct, this

190

undefiled dawn sun. It had almost a smell, as of warm stone, a sharp dust of photons streaming down through space. Each grass-blade was pearled with vapor. On the slopes above his path the trunks of the ashes and sycamores, a honey gold in the oblique sunlight, erected their dewy green vaults of young leaves; there was something mysteriously religious about them, but of a religion before religion; a druid balm, a green sweetness over all ... and such an infinity of greens, some almost black in the further recesses of the foliage; from the most intense emerald to the palest pomona. A fox crossed his path and strangely for a moment stared, as if Charles was the intruder; and then a little later, with an uncanny similarity, with the same divine assumption of possession, a roe deer looked up from its browsing; and stared in its small majesty before quietly turning tail and slipping away into the thickets. There is a painting by Pisanello in the National Gallery that catches exactly such a moment: St. Hubert in an early Renaissance forest, confronted by birds and beasts. The saint is shocked, almost as if the victim of a practical joke, all his arrogance dowsed by a sudden drench of Nature's profoundest secret: the universal parity of existence.

It was not only these two animals that seemed fraught with significance. The trees were dense with singing birds—blackcaps, whitethroats, thrushes, blackbirds, the cooing of woodpigeons, filling that windless dawn with the serenity of evening; yet without any of its sadness, its elegaic quality. Charles felt himself walking through the pages of a bestiary, and one of such beauty, such minute distinctness, that every leaf in it, each small bird, each song it uttered, came from a perfect world. He stopped a moment, so struck was he by this sense of an exquisitely particular universe, in which each was appointed, each unique. A tiny wren perched on top of a bramble not ten feet from him and trilled its violent song. He saw its glittering black eyes, the red and yellow of its song-gaped throat—a midget ball of feathers that yet managed to make itself the Announcing Angel of evolution: I am what I am, thou shalt not pass my being now. He stood as Pisanello's saint stood, astonished perhaps more at his own astonishment at this world's existing so close, so within reach of all that suffocating banality of ordinary day. In those few moments of defiant song, any ordinary hour or place—and therefore the vast infinity of all Charles's previous hours and places—seemed vulgarized, coarsened, made garish. The appalling ennui of human reality lay cleft to the core; and the heart of all life pulsed there in the wren's triumphant throat.

It seemed to announce a far deeper and stranger reality than the pseudo-Linnaean one that Charles had sensed on the beach that earlier morning—perhaps nothing more original than a priority of existence over death, of the individual over the species, of ecology over classification. We take such priorities for granted today; and we cannot imagine the hostile implications to Charles of the obscure message the wren was announcing. For it was less a profounder reality he seemed to see than universal chaos, looming behind the fragile structure of human order.

There was a more immediate bitterness in this natural eucharist, since Charles felt in all ways excommunicated. He was shut out, all paradise lost. Again, he was like Sarah—he could stand here in Eden, but not enjoy it, and only envy the wren its ecstasy.

He took the path formerly used by Sarah, which kept him out of sight of the Dairy. It was well that he did, since the sound of a pail being clattered warned him that the dairyman or his wife was up and about. So he came into the woods and went on his way with due earnestness. Some paranoiac transference of guilt now made him feel that the trees, the flowers, even the inanimate things around him were watching him. Flowers became eyes, stones had ears, the trunks of the reproving trees were a numberless Greek chorus.

He came to where the path forked, and took the left branch. It ran down through dense undergrowth and over increasingly broken terrain, for here the land was beginning to erode. The sea came closer, a milky blue and infinitely calm. But the land leveled out a little over it, where a chain of small meadows had been won from the wilderness; a hundred yards or so to the west of the last of these meadows, in a small gulley that eventually ran down to the cliff-edge, Charles saw the thatched roof of a barn. The thatch was mossy and derelict, which added to the already forlorn appearance of the little stone building, nearer a hut than its name would suggest. Originally it had been some grazier's summer dwelling; now it was used by the dairyman for storing hay; today it is gone without trace, so badly has this land deteriorated during the last hundred years.

Charles stood and stared down at it. He had expected to see the figure of a woman there, and it made him even more nervous that the place seemed so deserted. He walked down towards it, but rather like a man going through a jungle renowned for its tigers. He expected to be pounced on; and he was far from sure of his skill with his gun.

There was an old door, closed. Charles walked round the little building. To the east, a small square window; he peered through it into the shadows, and the faint musty-sweet smell

192

of old hay crept up his nostrils. He could see the beginning of a pile of it at the end of the barn opposite the door. He walked round the other walls. She was not there. He stared back the way he had come, thinking that he must have preceded her. But the rough land lay still in the early morning peace. He hesitated, took out his watch, and waited two or three minutes more, at a loss what to do. Finally he pushed open the door of the barn.

He made out a rough stone floor, and at the far end two or three broken stalls, filled with the hay that was still to be used. But it was difficult to see that far end, since sunlight lanced brilliantly in through the small window. Charles advanced to the slanting bar of light; and then stopped with a sudden dread. Beyond the light he could make out something hanging from a nail in an old stallpost: a black bonnet. Perhaps because of his reading the previous night he had an icy premonition that some ghastly sight lay below the partition of worm-eaten planks beyond the bonnet, which hung like an ominously slaked vampire over what he could not yet see. I do not know what he expected: some atrocious mutilation, a corpse ... he nearly turned and ran out of the barn and back to Lyme. But the ghost of a sound drew him forward. He craned fearfully over the partition.

30

> But the more these conscious illusions of the ruling classes are shown to be false and the less they satisfy common sense, the more dogmatically they are asserted and the more deceitful, moralizing and spiritual becomes the language of established society.
>
> MARX, *German Ideology* (1845–1846)

Sarah had, of course, arrived home—though "home" is a sarcasm in the circumstances—before Mrs. Fairley. She had played her usual part in Mrs. Poulteney's evening devotions; and she had then retired to her own room for a few minutes. Mrs. Fairley seized her chance; and the few minutes were all she needed. She came herself and knocked on the door of Sarah's bedroom. Sarah opened it. She had her usual mask of resigned sadness, but Mrs. Fairley was brimming with triumph.

"The mistress is waiting. At once, if you please."

Sarah looked down and nodded faintly. Mrs. Fairley thrust a look, sardonic and as sour as verjuice, at that meek head, and rustled venomously away. She did not go downstairs however, but waited around a corner until she heard the door of Mrs. Poulteney's drawing room open and close on the secretary-companion. Then she stole silently to the door and listened.

Mrs. Poulteney was not, for once, established on her throne; but stood at the window, placing all her eloquence in her back.

"You wish to speak to me?"

But Mrs. Poulteney apparently did not, for she neither moved nor uttered a sound. Perhaps it was the omission of her customary title of "madam" that silenced her; there was a something in Sarah's tone that made it clear the omission was deliberate. Sarah looked from the black back to an occasional table that lay between the two women. An envelope lay conspicuously on it. The minutest tightening of her lips—into a determination or a resentment, it was hard to say which—was her only reaction to this freezing majesty, who if the truth be known was slightly at a loss for the best way of crushing this serpent she had so regrettably taken to her bosom. Mrs. Poulteney elected at last for one blow of the axe.

"A month's wages are in that packet. You will take it in lieu of notice. You will depart this house at your earliest convenience tomorrow morning."

Sarah now had the effrontery to use Mrs. Poulteney's weapon in return. She neither moved nor answered; until that lady, outraged, deigned to turn and show her white face, upon which burnt two pink spots of repressed emotion.

"Did you not hear me, miss?"

"Am I not to be told why?"

"Do you dare to be impertinent!"

"I dare to ask to know why I am dismissed."

"I shall write to Mr. Forsyth. I shall see that you are locked away. You are a public scandal."

This impetuous discharge had some effect. Two spots began to burn in Sarah's cheeks as well. There was a silence, a visible swelling of the already swollen bosom of Mrs. Poulteney.

"I *command* you to leave this room at once."

"Very well. Since all I have ever experienced in it is hypocrisy, I shall do so with the greatest pleasure."

With this Parthian shaft Sarah turned to go. But Mrs. Poulteney was one of those actresses who cannot bear not to have the last line of the scene; or perhaps I do her an injustice, and she was attempting, however unlikely it might seem from her tone of voice, to do a charity.

"Take your wages!"

Sarah turned on her, and shook her head. "You may keep them. And if it is possible with so small a sum of money, I suggest you purchase some instrument of torture. I am sure Mrs. Fairley will be pleased to help you use it upon all those wretched enough to come under your power."

For an absurd moment Mrs. Poulteney looked like Sam: that is, she stood with her grim purse of a mouth wide open.

"You . . . shall . . . answer . . . for . . . that."

"Before God? Are you so sure you will have His ear in the world to come?"

For the first time in their relationship, Sarah smiled at Mrs. Poulteney: a very small but a knowing, and a telling, smile. For a few moments the mistress stared incredulously at her—indeed almost pathetically at her, as if Sarah was Satan himself come to claim his own. Then with a crablike clutching and motion she found her way to her chair and collapsed into it in a not altogether simulated swoon. Sarah stared at her a few moments, then very unfairly—to one named Fairley—took three or four swift steps to the door and opened it. The hastily erect housekeeper stood there with alarm, as if she thought Sarah might spring at her. But Sarah stood aside and indicated the gasping, throat-clutching Mrs. Poulteney, which gave Mrs. Fairley her chance to go to her aid.

"You wicked Jezebel—you have murdered her!"

Sarah did not answer. She watched a few more moments as Mrs. Fairley administered sal volatile to her mistress, then turned and went to her room. She went to her mirror, but did not look at herself; she slowly covered her face with her hands, and then very slowly raised her eyes from the fingers. What she saw she could not bear. Two moments later she was kneeling by her bed and weeping silently into the worn cover.

She should rather have prayed? But she believed she was praying.

31

When panting sighs the bosom fill,
And hands by chance united thrill
At once with one delicious pain
The pulses and the nerves of twain;
When eyes that erst could meet with ease,
Do seek, yet, seeking, shyly shun
Ecstatic conscious unison,—
The sure beginnings, say, be these,
Prelusive to the strain of love
Which angels sing in heaven above?

Or is it but the vulgar tune,
Which all that breathe beneath the moon
So accurately learn—so soon?

A. H. CLOUGH, Poem (1844)

And now she was sleeping.

That was the disgraceful sight that met Charles's eyes as he finally steeled himself to look over the partition. She lay curled up like a small girl under her old coat, her feet drawn up from the night's cold, her head turned from him and resting on a dark-green Paisley scarf; as if to preserve her one great jewel, her loosened hair, from the hayseed beneath. In that stillness her light, even breathing was both visible and audible; and for a moment that she should be sleeping there so peacefully seemed as wicked a crime as any Charles had expected.

Yet there rose in him, and inextinguishably, a desire to protect. So sharply it came upon him, he tore his eyes away and turned, shocked at this proof of the doctor's accusation, for he knew his instinct was to kneel beside her and comfort her . . . worse, since the dark privacy of the barn, the girl's posture, suggested irresistibly a bedroom. He felt his heart beating as if he had run a mile. The tiger was in him, not in her. A moment passed and then he retraced his steps silently but quickly to the door. He looked back, he was about to go; and then he heard his own voice say her name. He had not intended it to speak. Yet it spoke.

"Miss Woodruff."

No answer.

He said her name again, a little louder, more himself, now that the dark depths had surged safely past.

There was a tiny movement, a faint rustle; and then her head appeared, almost comically, as she knelt hastily up and peeped over the partition. He had a vague impression, through the motes, of shock and dismay.

"Oh forgive me, forgive me . . ."

The head bobbed down out of sight. He withdrew into the sunlight outside. Two herring gulls flew over, screaming raucously. Charles moved out of sight of the fields nearer the Dairy. Grogan, he did not fear; or expect yet. But the place was too open; the dairyman might come for hay . . . though why he should when his fields were green with spring grass Charles was too nervous to consider.

"Mr. Smithson?"

He moved round back to the door, just in time to prevent her from calling, this time more anxiously, his name again. They stood some ten feet apart, Sarah in the door, Charles by the corner of the building. She had performed a hurried toilet, put on her coat, and held her scarf in her hand as if she had used it for a brush. Her eyes were troubled, but her features were still softened by sleep, though flushed at the rude awakening.

There was a wildness about her. Not the wildness of lunacy or hysteria—but that same wildness Charles had sensed in the wren's singing . . . a wildness of innocence, almost an eagerness. And just as the sharp declension of that dawn walk had so confounded—and compounded—his earnest autobiographical gloom, so did that intensely immediate face confound and compound all the clinical horrors bred in Charles's mind by the worthy doctors Matthaei and Grogan. In spite of Hegel, the Victorians were not a dialectically minded age; they did not think naturally in opposites, of positives and negatives as aspects of the same whole. Paradoxes troubled rather than pleased them. They were not the people for existentialist moments, but for chains of cause and effect; for positive all-explaining theories, carefully studied and studiously applied. They were busy erecting, of course; and we have been busy demolishing for so long that now erection seems as ephemeral an activity as bubble-blowing. So Charles was inexplicable to himself. He managed a very unconvincing smile.

"May we not be observed here?"

She followed his glance towards the hidden Dairy.

"It is Axminster market. As soon as he has milked he will be gone."

But she moved back inside the barn. He followed her in, and they stood, still well apart, Sarah with her back to him.

"You have passed the night here?"

She nodded. There was a silence.

"Are you not hungry?"

Sarah shook her head; and silence flowed back again. But this time she broke it herself.

"You know?"

"I was away all yesterday. I could not come."

More silence. "Mrs. Poulteney has recovered?"

"I understand so."

"She was most angry with me."

"It is no doubt for the best. You were ill placed in her house."

"Where am I not ill placed?"

He remembered he must choose his words with care.

"Now come . . . you must not feel sorry for yourself." He moved a step or two closer. "There has been great concern. A search party was out looking for you last night. In the storm."

Her face turned as if he might have been deceiving her. She saw that he was not; and he in his turn saw by her surprise that she was not deceiving him when she said, "I did not mean to cause such trouble."

"Well . . . never mind. I daresay they enjoyed the excitement. But it is clear that you must now leave Lyme."

She bowed her head. His voice had been too stern. He hesitated, then stepped forward and laid his hand on her shoulder comfortingly.

"Do not fear. I come to help you do that."

He had thought by his brief gesture and assurance to take the first step towards putting out the fire the doctor had told him he had lit; but when one is oneself the fuel, firefighting is a hopeless task. Sarah was all flame. Her eyes were all flame as she threw a passionate look back at Charles. He withdrew his hand, but she caught it and before he could stop her raised it towards her lips. He snatched it away in alarm then; and she reacted as if he had struck her across the face.

"My dear Miss Woodruff, pray control yourself. I—"

"I cannot."

The words were barely audible, but they silenced Charles. He tried to tell himself that she meant she could not control

198

her gratitude for his charity . . . he tried, he tried. But there came on him a fleeting memory of Catullus: "Whenever I see you, sound fails, my tongue falters, thin fire steals through my limbs, an inner roar, and darkness shrouds my ears and eyes." Catullus was translating Sappho here; and the Sapphic remains the best clinical description of love in European medicine.

Sarah and Charles stood there, prey—if they had but known it—to precisely the same symptoms; admitted on the one hand, denied on the other; though the one who denied found himself unable to move away. Four or five seconds of intense repressed emotion passed. Then Sarah could quite literally stand no more. She fell to her knees at his feet. The words rushed out.

"I have told you a lie, I made sure Mrs. Fairley saw me, I knew she would tell Mrs. Poulteney."

What control Charles had felt himself gaining now slipped from his grasp again. He stared down aghast at the upraised face before him. He was evidently being asked for forgiveness; but he himself was asking for guidance, since the doctors had failed him again. The distinguished young ladies who had gone in for house-burning and anonymous letter-writing had all, with a nice deference to black-and-white moral judgments, waited to be caught before confession.

Tears had sprung in her eyes. A fortune coming to him, a golden world; and against that, a minor exudation of the lachrymatory glands, a trembling drop or two of water, so small, so transitory, so brief. Yet he stood like a man beneath a breaking dam, instead of a man above a weeping woman.

"But why . . . ?"

She looked up then, with an intense earnestness and supplication; with a declaration so unmistakable that words were needless; with a nakedness that made any evasion—any other "My dear Miss Woodruff!"—impossible.

He slowly reached out his hands and raised her. Their eyes remained on each other's, as if they were both hypnotized. She seemed to him—or those wide, those drowning eyes seemed—the most ravishingly beautiful he had ever seen. What lay behind them did not matter. The moment overcame the age.

He took her into his arms, saw her eyes close as she swayed into his embrace; then closed his own and found her lips. He felt not only their softness but the whole close substance of her body; her sudden smallness, fragility, weakness, tenderness . . .

He pushed her violently away.

199

An agonized look, as if he was the most debased criminal caught in his most abominable crime. Then he turned and rushed through the door—into yet another horror. It was not Doctor Grogan.

32

And her, white-muslined, waiting there
In the porch with high-expectant heart,
While still the thin mechanic air
    Went on inside.

                    HARDY, "The Musical Box"

Ernestina had, that previous night, not been able to sleep. She knew perfectly well which windows in the White Lion were Charles's, and she did not fail to note that his light was still on long after her aunt's snores began to creep through the silent house. She felt hurt and she felt guilty in about equal parts—that is, to begin with. But when she had stolen from her bed for quite the sixteenth time to see if the light still burned, and it *did*, her guilt began to increase. Charles was very evidently, and justly, displeased with her.

Now when, after Charles's departure, Ernestina had said to herself—and subsequently to Aunt Tranter—that she really didn't care a fig for Winsyatt, you may think that sour grapes would have been a more appropriate horticultural metaphor. She had certainly wooed herself into graciously accepting the role of chatelaine when Charles left for his uncle's, had even begun drawing up lists of "Items to be attended to" ... but the sudden death of *that* dream had come as a certain relief. Women who run great houses need a touch of the general about them; and Ernestina had no military aspirations whatever. She liked every luxury, and to be waited on, hand if not foot; but she had a very sound bourgeois sense of proportion. Thirty rooms when fifteen were sufficient was to her a folly. Perhaps she got this comparative thrift from her father, who secretly believed that "aristocrat" was a synonym of "vain ostentation," though this did not stop him basing a not inconsiderable part of his business on that fault, or running a London house many a nobleman would have been glad of— *or* pouncing on the first chance of a title that offered for his dearly beloved daughter. To give him his due, he might have turned down a viscount as excessive; a baronetcy was so eminently proper.

I am not doing well by Ernestina, who was after all a victim of circumstances; of an illiberal environment. It is, of course, its essentially schizophrenic outlook on society that makes the middle class such a peculiar mixture of yeast and dough. We tend nowadays to forget that it has always been the great revolutionary class; we see much more the doughy aspect, the bourgeoisie as the heartland of reaction, the universal insult, forever selfish and conforming. Now this Janus-like quality derives from the class's one saving virtue, which is this: that alone of the three great castes of society it sincerely and habitually despises itself. Ernestina was certainly no exception here. It was not only Charles who heard an unwelcome acidity in her voice; she heard it herself. But her tragedy (and one that remains ubiquitous) was that she misapplied this precious gift of self-contempt and so made herself a victim of her class's perennial lack of faith in itself. Instead of seeing its failings as a reason to reject the entire class system, she saw them as a reason to seek a higher. She cannot be blamed, of course; she had been hopelessly well trained to view society as so many rungs on a ladder; thus reducing her own to a mere step to something supposedly better.

Thus ("I am shameful, I have behaved like a draper's daughter") it was, in the small hours, that Ernestina gave up the attempt to sleep, rose and pulled on her *peignoir,* and then unlocked her diary. Perhaps Charles would see that *her* window was also still penitentially bright in the heavy darkness that followed the thunderstorm. Meanwhile, she set herself to composition.

I cannot sleep. Dearest C. is displeased with me—I was so very upset at the dreadful news from Winsyatt. I wished to cry, I was so *very* vexed, but I foolishly said many angry, spiteful things—which I ask God to forgive me, remembering I said them out of love for dearest C. and not wickedness. I did weep *most terribly* when he went away. Let this be a lesson to me to take the beautiful words of the Marriage Service to my conscience, to honor and *obey* my *dearest* Charles even when my feelings would drive me to contradict him. Let me earnestly and humbly learn to bend my horrid, spiteful willfulness to his much greater wisdom, let me cherish his judgment and chain myself to his heart, for "The sweet of true Repentance is the gate to Holy Bliss."

You may have noted a certain lack of Ernestina's normal dryness in this touching paragraph; but Charles was not alone

201

in having several voices. And just as she hoped he might see the late light in her room, so did she envisage a day when he might coax her into sharing this intimate record of her prenuptial soul. She wrote partly for his eyes—as, like every other Victorian woman, she wrote partly for *His* eyes. She went relieved to bed, so totally and suitably her betrothed's chastened bride in spirit that she leaves me no alternative but to conclude that she must, in the end, win Charles back from his infidelity.

And she was still fast asleep when a small drama took place four floors below her. Sam had not got up quite as early as his master that morning. When he went into the hotel kitchen for his tea and toasted cheese—one thing few Victorian servants did was eat less than their masters, whatever their lack of gastronomic propriety—the boots greeted him with the news that his master had gone out; and that Sam was to pack and strap and be ready to leave at noon. Sam hid his shock. Packing and strapping was but half an hour's work. He had more pressing business.

He went immediately to Aunt Tranter's house. What he said we need not inquire, except that it must have been penetrated with tragedy, since when Aunt Tranter (who kept uncivilized rural hours) came down to the kitchen only a minute later, she found Mary slumped in a collapse of tears at the kitchen table. The deaf cook's sarcastic uplift of her chin showed there was little sympathy there. Mary was interrogated; and Aunt Tranter soon elicited, in her briskly gentle way, the source of misery; and applied a much kinder remedy than Charles had. The maid might be off till Ernestina had to be attended to; since Miss Ernestina's heavy brocade curtains customarily remained drawn until ten, that was nearly three hours' grace. Aunt Tranter was rewarded by the most grateful smile the world saw that day. Five minutes later Sam was to be seen sprawling in the middle of Broad Street. One should not run full tilt across cobbles, even to a Mary.

33

It would be difficult to say who was more shocked—the
master frozen six feet from the door, or the servants no less
frozen some thirty yards away. So astounded were the latter
that Sam did not even remove his arm from round Mary's
waist. What broke the tableau was the appearance of the
fourth figure: Sarah, wildly, in the doorway. She withdrew so
swiftly that the sight was barely more than subliminal. But it
was enough. Sam's mouth fell open and his arm dropped
from Mary's waist.

"What the devil are you doing here?"

"Out walkin', Mr. Charles."

"I thought I left instructions to—"

"I done it, sir. S'all ready."

Charles knew he was lying. Mary had turned away, with a
delicacy that became her. Charles hesitated, then strode up to
Sam, through whose mind flashed visions of dismissal, assault
. . .

"We didn't know, Mr. Charles. 'Onest we didn't."

Mary flashed a shy look back at Charles: there was shock
in it, and fear, but the faintest touch of a sly admiration. He
addressed her.

"Kindly leave us alone a moment." The girl bobbed and
began to walk quickly out of earshot. Charles eyed Sam, who
reverted to his humblest footman self and stared intently at
his master's boots. "I have come here on that business I
mentioned."

"Yes, sir."

Charles dropped his voice. "At the request of the physician
who is treating her. He is fully aware of the circumstances."

"Yes, sir."

"Which must on no account be disclosed."

"I hunderstand, Mr. Charles."

"Does she?"

Sam looked up. "Mary won't say nuffink, sir. On my life."

Now Charles looked down. He was aware that his cheeks were deep red. "Very well. I . . . I thank you. And I'll see that . . . here." He fumbled for his purse.

"Oh no, Mr. Charles." Sam took a small step back, a little overdramatically to convince a dispassionate observer. "Never."

Charles's hand came to a mumbling stop. A look passed between master and servant. Perhaps both knew a shrewd sacrifice had just been made.

"Very well. I will make it up to you. But not a word."

"On my slombest hoath, Mr. Charles."

With this dark superlative (most solemn and best) Sam turned and went after his Mary, who now waited, her back discreetly turned, some hundred yards off in the gorse and bracken.

Why their destination should have been the barn, one can only speculate; it may have already struck you as curious that a sensible girl like Mary should have burst into tears at the thought of a mere few days' absence. But let us leave Sam and Mary as they reeenter the woods, walk a little way in shocked silence, then covertly catch each other's eyes—and dissolve into a helpless paralysis of silent laughter; and return to the scarlet-faced Charles.

He watched them out of sight, then glanced back at the uninformative barn. His behavior had rent his profoundest being, but the open air allowed him to reflect a moment. Duty, as so often, came to his aid. He had flagrantly fanned the forbidden fire. Even now the other victim might be perishing in its flames, casting the rope over the beam . . . He hesitated, then marched back to the barn and Sarah.

She stood by the window's edge, hidden from view from outside, as if she had tried to hear what had passed between Charles and Sam. He stood by the door.

"You must forgive me for taking an unpardonable advantage of your unhappy situation." He paused, then went on. "And not only this morning." She looked down. He was relieved to see that she seemed abashed, no longer wild. "The last thing I wished was to engage your affections. I have behaved very foolishly. Very foolishly. It is I who am wholly to blame." She stared at the rough stone floor between them, the prisoner awaiting sentence. "The damage is done, alas. I must ask you now to help me repair it." Still she refused his invitation to speak. "Business calls me to London. I do not

204

know for how long." She looked at him then, but only for a moment. He stumbled on. "I think you should go to Exeter. I beg you to take the money in this purse—as a loan, if you wish ... until you can find a suitable position ... and if you should need any further pecuniary assistance ..." His voice tailed off. It had become progressively more formal. He knew he must sound detestable. She turned her back on him.

"I shall never see you again."

"You cannot expect me to deny that."

"Though seeing you is all I live for."

The terrible threat hung in the silence that followed. He dared not bring it into the open. He felt like a man in irons; and his release came as unexpectedly as to a condemned prisoner. She looked round, and patently read his thought.

"If I had wished to kill myself, I have had reason enough before now." She looked out of the window. "I accept your loan ... with gratitude."

His eyes closed in a moment of silent thanksgiving. He placed the purse—not the one Ernestina had embroidered for him—on a ledge by the door.

"You will go to Exeter?"

"If that is your advice."

"It most emphatically is."

She bowed her head.

"And I must tell you something else. There is talk in the town of committing you to an institution." Her eyes flashed round. "The idea emanates from Marlborough House, no doubt. You need not take it seriously. For all that, you may save yourself embarrassment if you do not return to Lyme." He hesitated, then said, "I understand a party is to come shortly searching for you again. That is why I came so early."

"My box ..."

"I will see to that. I will have it sent to the depot at Exeter. It occurred to me that if you have the strength, it might be wiser to walk to Axmouth Cross. That would avoid ..." scandal for them both. But he knew what he was asking. Axmouth was seven miles away; and the Cross, where the coaches passed, two miles farther still.

She assented.

"And you will let Mrs. Tranter know as soon as you have found a situation?"

"I have no references."

"You may give Mrs. Talbot's name. And Mrs. Tranter's. I will speak to her. And you are not to be too proud to call on her for further financial provision, should it be necessary. I shall see to that as well before I leave."

"It will not be necessary." Her voice was almost inaudible. "But I thank you."

"I think it is I who have to thank you."

She glanced up into his eyes. The lance was still there, the seeing him whole.

"You are a very remarkable person, Miss Woodruff. I feel deeply ashamed not to have perceived it earlier."

She said, "Yes, I am a remarkable person."

But she said it without pride; without sarcasm; with no more than a bitter simplicity. And the silence flowed back. He bore it as long as he could, then took out his half hunter, a very uninspired hint that he must leave. He felt his clumsiness, his stiffness, her greater dignity than his; perhaps he still felt her lips.

"Will you not walk with me back to the path?"

He would not let her, at this last parting, see he was ashamed. If Grogan appeared, it would not matter now. But Grogan did not appear. Sarah preceded him, through the dead bracken and living gorse in the early sunlight, the hair glinting; silent, not once turning. Charles knew very well that Sam and Mary might be watching, but it now seemed better that they should see him openly with her. The way led up through trees and came at last to the main path. She turned. He stepped beside her, his hand out.

She hesitated, then held out her own. He gripped it firmly, forbidding any further folly.

He murmured, "I shall never forget you."

She raised her face to his, with an imperceptible yet searching movement of her eyes; as if there was something he must see, it was not too late: a truth beyond his truths, an emotion beyond his emotions, a history beyond all his conceptions of history. As if she could say worlds; yet at the same time knew that if he could not apprehend those words without her saying them . . .

It lasted a long moment. Then he dropped his eyes, and her hand.

A minute later he looked back. She stood where he had left her, watching him. He raised his hat. She made no sign.

Ten minutes later still, he stopped at a gateway on the seaward side of the track to the Dairy. It gave a view down across fields towards the Cobb. In the distance below a short figure mounted the fieldpath towards the gate where Charles stood. He drew back a little, hesitated a moment . . . then went on his own way along the track to the lane that led down to the town.

206

34

And the rotten rose is ript from the wall.
HARDY, "During Wind and Rain"

"You have been walking."

His second change of clothes was thus proved a vain pretense.

"I needed to clear my mind. I slept badly."

"So did I." She added, "You said you were fatigued beyond belief."

"I was."

"But you stayed up until after one o'clock."

Charles turned somewhat abruptly to the window. "I had many things to consider."

Ernestina's part in this stiff exchange indicates a certain failure to maintain in daylight the tone of her nocturnal self-adjurations. But besides the walking she also knew, via Sam, Mary and a bewildered Aunt Tranter, that Charles planned to leave Lyme that day. She had determined not to demand an explanation of this sudden change of intention; let his lordship give it in his own good time.

And then, when he had finally come, just before eleven, and while she sat primly waiting in the back parlor, he had had the unkindness to speak at length in the hall to Aunt Tranter, *and* inaudibly, which was the worst of all. Thus she inwardly seethed.

Perhaps not the least of her resentments was that she had taken especial pains with her toilet that morning, and he had not paid her any compliment on it. She wore a rosepink "breakfast" dress with bishop sleeves—tight at the delicate armpit, then pleating voluminously in a froth of gauze to the constricted wrist. It set off her fragility very prettily; and the white ribbons in her smooth hair and a delicately pervasive fragrance of lavender water played their part. She was a sugar Aphrodite, though with faintly bruised eyes, risen from a bed of white linen. Charles might have found it rather easy to be cruel. But he managed a smile and sitting beside her, took one of her hands, and patted it.

"My dearest, I must ask forgiveness. I am not myself. And I fear I've decided I must go to London."

"Oh Charles!"

"I wish it weren't so. But this new turn of events makes it imperative I see Montague at once." Montague was the solicitor, in those days before accountants, who looked after Charles's affairs.

"Can you not wait till I return? It is only ten more days."

"I shall return to bring you back."

"But cannot Mr. Montague come here?"

"Alas no, there are so many papers. Besides, that is not my only purpose. I must inform your father of what has happened."

She removed her hand from his arm.

"But what is it to do with him?"

"My dear child, it has everything to do with him. He has entrusted you to my care. Such a grave alteration in my prospects—"

"But you have still your own income!"

"Well . . . of course, yes, I shall always be comfortably off. But there are other things. The title . . ."

"I had forgotten that. Of course. It's quite impossible that I should marry a mere commoner." She glanced back at him with an appropriately sarcastic firmness.

"My sweet, be patient. These things have to be said—you bring a great sum of money with you. Of course our private affections are the paramount consideration. However, there is a . . . well, a legal and contractual side to matrimony which—"

"Fiddlesticks!"

"My dearest Tina . . ."

"You know perfectly well they would allow me to marry a Hottentot if I wanted."

"That may be so. But even the most doting parents prefer to be informed—"

"How many rooms has the Belgravia house?"

"I have no idea." He hesitated, then added, "Twenty, I daresay."

"And you mentioned one day that you had two and a half thousand a year. To which my dowry will bring—"

"Whether our changed circumstances are still sufficient for comfort is not at issue."

"Very well. Suppose Papa tells you you cannot have my hand. What then?"

"You choose to misunderstand. I know my duty. One cannot be too scrupulous at such a juncture."

This exchange has taken place without their daring to look at each other's faces. She dropped her head, in a very plain and mutinous disagreement. He rose and stood behind her.

"It is no more than a formality. But such formalities matter."

She stared obstinately down.

"I am weary of Lyme. I see you less here than in town."

He smiled. "That is absurd."

"It seems less."

A sullen little line had set about her mouth. She would not be mollified. He went and stood in front of the fireplace, his arm on the mantelpiece, smiling down at her; but it was a smile without humor, a mask. He did not like her when she was willful; it contrasted too strongly with her elaborate clothes, all designed to show a total inadequacy outside the domestic interior. The thin end of the sensible clothes wedge had been inserted in society by the disgraceful Mrs. Bloomer a decade and a half before the year of which I write; but that early attempt at the trouser suit had been comprehensively defeated by the crinoline—a small fact of considerable significance in our understanding of the Victorians. They were offered sense; and chose a six-foot folly unparalleled in the most folly-ridden of minor arts.

However, in the silence that followed Charles was not meditating on the idiocy of high fashion, but on how to leave without more to-do. Fortunately for him Tina had at the same time been reflecting on her position: it was after all rather maidservantish (Aunt Tranter had explained why Mary was not able to answer the waking bell) to make such a fuss about a brief absence. Besides, male vanity lay in being obeyed; female, in using obedience to have the ultimate victory. A time would come when Charles should be made to pay for his cruelty. Her little smile up at him was repentant.

"You will write every day?"

He reached down and touched her cheek. "I promise."

"And return as soon as you can?"

"Just as soon as I can expedite matters with Montague."

"I shall write to Papa with strict orders to send you straight back."

Charles seized his opportunity. "And I shall bear the letter, if you write it at once. I leave in an hour."

She stood then and held out her hands. She wished to be kissed. He could not bring himself to kiss her on the mouth. So he grasped her shoulders and lightly embraced her on both temples. He then made to go. But for some odd reason he stopped. Ernestina stared demurely and meekly in front of her—at his dark blue cravat with its pearl pin. Why Charles could not get away was not immediately apparent; in fact two hands were hooded firmly in his lower waistcoat pockets. He understood the price of his release, and paid it. No worlds fell, no inner roar, no darkness shrouded eyes and ears, as he stood pressing his lips upon hers for several seconds. But Ernestina was very prettily dressed; a vision, perhaps more a tactile impression, of a tender little white body entered Charles's mind. Her head turned against his shoulder, she nestled against him; and as he patted and stroked and murmured a few foolish words, he found himself most suddenly embarrassed. There was a distinct stir in his loins. There had always been Ernestina's humor, her odd little piques and whims of emotion, a promise of certain buried wildnesses . . . a willingness to learn perversity, one day to bite timidly but deliciously on forbidden fruit. What Charles unconsciously felt was perhaps no more than the ageless attraction of shallow-minded women: that one may make of them what one wants. What he felt consciously was a sense of pollution: to feel carnal desire now, when he had touched another woman's lips that morning!

He kissed Ernestina rather hastily on the crown of her head, gently disengaged her fingers from their holds, kissed them in turn, then left.

He still had an ordeal, since Mary was standing by the door with his hat and gloves. Her eyes were down, but her cheeks were red. He glanced back at the closed door of the room he had left as he drew on his gloves.

"Sam has explained the circumstances of this morning?"

"Yes, sir."

"You . . . understand?"

"Yes, sir."

He took off a glove again and felt in his waistcoat pocket. Mary did not take a step back, though she lowered her head still further.

"Oh sir, I doan' want that."

But she already had it. A moment later she had closed the door on Charles. Very slowly she opened her small—and I'm afraid, rather red—hand and stared at the small golden coin in its palm. Then she put it between her white teeth and bit it, as she had always seen her father do, to make sure it was not brass; not that she could tell one from the other by bite, but biting somehow proved it *was* gold; just as being on the Undercliff proved it was sin.

What can an innocent country virgin know of sin? The question requires an answer. Meanwhile, Charles can get up to London on his own.

35

In you resides my single power.
Of sweet continuance here.

HARDY, "Her Immortality"

At the infirmary many girls of 14 years of age, and
even girls of 13, up to 17 years of age, have been
brought in pregnant to be confined here. The girls
have acknowledged that their ruin has taken place
. . . in going or returning from their (agricultural)
work. Girls and boys of this age go five, six, or seven
miles to work, walking in droves along the roads and
by-lanes. I have myself witnessed gross indecencies between boys and girls of 14 to 16 years of age. I saw
once a young girl insulted by some five or six boys on
the roadside. Other older persons were about 20 or
30 yards off, but they took no notice. The girl was calling out, which caused me to stop. I have also seen
boys bathing in the brooks, and girls between 13 and
19 looking on from the bank.

Children's Employment Commission Report (1867)

What are we faced with in the nineteenth century? An age
where woman was sacred; and where you could buy a thir-
teen-year-old girl for a few pounds—a few shillings, if you
wanted her for only an hour or two. Where more churches
were built than in the whole previous history of the country;
and where one in sixty houses in London was a brothel (the
modern ratio would be nearer one in six thousand). Where
the sanctity of marriage (and chastity before marriage) was
proclaimed from every pulpit, in every newspaper editorial
and public utterance; and where never—or hardly ever—
have so many great public figures, from the future king
down, led scandalous private lives. Where the penal system
was progressively humanized; and flagellation so rife that a
Frenchman set out quite seriously to prove that the Marquis
de Sade must have had English ancestry. Where the female

211

body had never been so hidden from view; and where every sculptor was judged by his ability to carve naked women. Where there is not a single novel, play or poem of literary distinction that ever goes beyond the sensuality of a kiss, where Dr. Bowdler (the date of whose death, 1825, reminds us that the Victorian ethos was in being long before the strict threshold of the age) was widely considered a public benefactor; and where the output of pornography has never been exceeded. Where the excretory functions were never referred to; and where the sanitation remained—the flushing lavatory came late in the age and remained a luxury well up to 1900—so primitive that there can have been few houses, and few streets, where one was not constantly reminded of them. Where it was universally maintained that women do not have orgasms; and yet every prostitute was taught to simulate them. Where there was an enormous progress and liberation in every other field of human activity; and nothing but tyranny in the most personal and fundamental.

At first sight the answer seems clear—it is the business of sublimation. The Victorians poured their libido into those other fields; as if some genie of evolution, feeling lazy, said to himself: We need some progress, so let us dam and divert this one great canal and see what happens.

While conceding a partial truth to the theory of sublimation, I sometimes wonder if this does not lead us into the error of supposing the Victorians were not in fact highly sexed. But they were quite as highly sexed as our own century—and, in spite of the fact that *we* have sex thrown at us night and day (as the Victorians had religion), far more preoccupied with it than we really are. They were certainly preoccupied by love, and devoted far more of their arts to it than we do ours. Nor can Malthus and the lack of birth-control appliances* quite account for the fact that they bred like rabbits and worshiped fertility far more ardently than we do. Nor does our century fall behind in the matter of progress and liberalization; and yet we can hardly maintain that that is because *we* have so much sublimated energy to spare. I have seen the Naughty Nineties represented as a reaction to many decades of abstinence; I believe it was merely the publication of what had hitherto been private, and I suspect we are in reality dealing with a human constant: the difference is a vocabulary, a degree of metaphor.

* The first sheaths (of sausage skin) were on sale in the late eighteenth century. Malthus, of all people, condemned birth-control techniques as "improper," but agitation for their use began in the 1820s. The first approach to a modern "sex manual" was Dr. George Drysdale's somewhat obliquely entitled *The Elements of Social Science; or Physical, Sexual and Natural Religion. An Exposition of the true*

212

The Victorians chose to be serious about something we treat rather lightly, and the way they expressed their seriousness was not to *talk openly* about sex, just as part of our way is the very reverse. But these "ways" of being serious are mere conventions. The fact behind them remains constant.

I think, too, there is another common error: of equating a high degree of sexual ignorance with a low degree of sexual pleasure. I have no doubt that when Charles's and Sarah's lips touched, very little amatory skill was shown on either side; but I would not deduce any lack of sexual excitement from that. In any case, a much more interesting ratio is between the desire and the ability to fulfill it. Here again we may believe we come off much better than our great-grandparents. But the desire is conditioned by the frequency it is evoked: our world spends a vast amount of its time inviting us to copulate, while our reality is as busy in frustrating us. We are not so frustrated as the Victorians? Perhaps. But if you can only enjoy one apple a day, there's a great deal to be said against living in an orchard of the wretched things; you might even find apples sweeter if you were allowed only one a week.

So it seems very far from sure that the Victorians did not experience a much keener, because less frequent, sexual pleasure than we do; and that they were not dimly aware of this, and so chose a convention of suppression, repression and silence to maintain the keenness of the pleasure. In a way, by transferring to the public imagination what they left to the private, we are the more Victorian—in the derogatory sense

Cause and only Cure of the Three Primary Evils: Poverty, Prostitution and Celibacy. It appeared in 1854, and was widely read and translated. Here is Drysdale's practical advice, with its telltale final parenthesis: "Impregnation is avoided either by the withdrawal of the penis immediately before ejaculation takes place (which is very frequently practiced by married and unmarried men); by the use of the sheath (which is also very frequent, but more so on the Continent than in this country); by the introduction of a piece of sponge into the vagina . . . ; or by the injection of tepid water into the vagina immediately after coition.

"The first of these modes is physically injurious, and is apt to produce nervous disorder and sexual enfeeblement and congestion . . . The second, namely the sheath, dulls the enjoyment, and frequently produces impotence in the man and disgust in both parties, so that it also is injurious.

"These objections do not, I believe, apply to the third, namely, the introduction of a sponge or some other substance to guard the mouth of the womb. This could easily be done by the woman, and would scarcely, it appears to me, interfere at all in the sexual pleasures, nor have any prejudicial effect on the health of either party. (Any preventive means, to be satisfactory, must be used by the *woman*, as it spoils the passion and impulsiveness of the venereal act, if the man has to think of them.)"

of the word—century, since we have, in destroying so much of the mystery, the difficulty, the aura of the forbidden, destroyed also a great deal of the pleasure. Of course we cannot measure comparative degrees of pleasure; but it may be luckier for us than for the Victorians that we cannot. And in addition their method gave them a bonus of surplus energy. That secrecy, that gap between the sexes which so troubled Charles when Sarah tried to diminish it, certainly produced a greater force, and very often a greater frankness, in every other field.

All of which appears to have led us a long way from Mary, though I recall now that she was very fond of apples. But what she was not was an innocent country virgin, for the very simple reason that the two adjectives were incompatible in her century. The causes are not hard to find.

The vast majority of witnesses and reporters, in every age, belong to the educated class; and this has produced, throughout history, a kind of minority distortion of reality. The prudish puritanity we lend to the Victorians, and rather lazily apply to all classes of Victorian society, is in fact a middle-class view of the middle-class ethos. Dickens's working-class characters are all very funny (or very pathetic) and an incomparable range of grotesques, but for the cold reality we need to go elsewhere—to Mayhew, the great Commission Reports and the rest; and nowhere more than in this sexual aspect of their lives, which Dickens (who lacked a certain authenticity in his own) and his compeers so totally bowdlerized. The hard—I would rather call it soft, but no matter—fact of Victorian rural England was that what a simpler age called "tasting before you buy" (premarital intercourse, in our current jargon) *was the rule, not the exception.* Listen to this evidence, from a lady still living. She was born in 1883. Her father was Thomas Hardy's doctor.

The life of the farm laborer was very different in the Nineteenth Century to what it is now. For instance, among the Dorset peasants, conception before marriage was perfectly normal, and the marriage did not take place until the pregnancy was obvious . . . The reason was the low wages paid to the workers, and the need to ensure extra hands in the family to earn.*

* An additional economic reason was the diabolical system of paying all unmarried men—even though they did a man's work in every other way—half the married man's rate. This splendid method of ensuring the labor force—at the cost cited below—disappeared only with the general use of farm machinery. It might be added that Dorset, the scene of the Tolpuddle Martyrdom, was notoriously the most disgracefully exploited rural area in England.

Here is the Reverend James Fraser, writing in this same year of

I have now come under the shadow, the very relevant shadow, of the great novelist who towers over this part of England of which I write. When we remember that Hardy was the first to try to break the Victorian middle-class seal over the supposed Pandora's box of sex, not the least interesting (and certainly the most paradoxical) thing about him is his fanatical protection of the seal of his own and his immediate ancestors' sex life. Of course that was, and would still remain, his inalienable right. But few literary secrets—this one was not unearthed until the 1950s—have remained so well kept. It, and the reality of Victorian rural England I have tried to suggest in this chapter, answer Edmund Gosse's famous reproof: "What has Providence done to Mr. Hardy that he should rise up in the arable land of Wessex and shake his fist at his Creator?" He might as reasonably have inquired why the Atreids should have shaken their bronze fists skywards at Mycenae.

This is not the place to penetrate far into the shadows beside Egdon Heath. What is definitely known is that in 1867 Hardy, then twenty-seven years old, returned to Dorset from his architectural studies in London and fell profoundly in love with his sixteen-year-old cousin Tryphena. They became engaged. Five years later, and incomprehensibly, the engagement was broken. Though not absolutely proven, it now seems clear that the engagement was broken by the revelation to Hardy of a very sinister skeleton in the family cupboard: Tryphena was not his cousin, but his illegitimate half-sister's illegitimate daughter. Countless poems of Hardy's hint at it: "At the wicket gate," "She did not turn," "Her immortality"* and many others; and that there were several

1867: "Modesty must be an unknown virtue, decency an unimaginable thing, where, in one small chamber, with the beds lying as thickly as they can be packed, father, mother, young men, lads, grown and growing girls—two and sometimes three generations—are herded promiscuously; where every operation of the toilette and of nature, dressings, undressings, births, deaths—is performed by each within the sight and hearing of all—where the whole atmosphere is sensual and human nature is degraded into something below the level of the swine . . . Cases of incest are anything but uncommon. We complain of the antenuptial unchastity of our women, of the loose talk and conduct of the girls who work in the fields, of the light way in which maidens part with their honor, and how seldom either a parent's or a brother's blood boils with shame—here, in cottage herding, is the sufficient account and history of it all . . ."

And behind all this loomed even grimmer figures, common to every ghetto since time began; scrofula, cholera, endemic typhoid and tuberculosis.

* Not the greatest, but one of the most revealing poems, in this context, that Hardy ever wrote. Its first version may be dated to 1897. Gosse's key question was asked in the course of a review of *Jude the Obscure* in January 1896.

recent illegitimacies on the maternal side in his family *is* proven. Hardy himself was born "five months from the altar." The pious have sometimes maintained that he broke his engagement for class reasons—he was too much the rising young master to put up with a simple Dorset girl. It is true he did marry above himself in 1874—to the disastrously insensitive Lavinia Gifford. But Tryphena was an exceptional young woman; she became the headmistress of a Plymouth school at the age of twenty, having passed out fifth from her teachers' training college in London. It is difficult not to accept that some terrible family secret was what really forced them to separate. It was a fortunate secret, of course, in one way, since never was an English genius so devoted and indebted to one muse and one muse only. It gives us all his greatest love elegies. It gave us Sue Bridehead and Tess, who are pure Tryphena in spirit; and *Jude the Obscure* is even tacitly dedicated to her in Hardy's own preface—"The scheme was laid down in 1890 ... some of the circumstances being suggested by the death of a woman ..." Tryphena, by then married to another man, had died in that year.

This tension, then—between lust and renunciation, undying recollection and undying repression, lyrical surrender and tragic duty, between the sordid facts and their noble use— energizes and explains one of the age's greatest writers; and beyond him, structures the whole age itself. It is this I have digressed to remind you of.

So let us descend to our own sheep. You will guess now why Sam and Mary were on their way to the barn; and as it was not the first time they had gone there, you will perhaps understand better Mary's tears ... and why she knew a little more about sin than one might have suspected at first sight of her nineteen-year-old face; or *would* have suspected, had one passed through Dorchester later that same year, from the face of a better educated though three years younger girl in the real world; who stands, inscrutable for eternity now, beside the pale young architect newly returned from his dreary five years in the capital and about to become ("Till the flame had eaten her breasts, and mouth and hair") the perfect emblem of his age's greatest mystery.

36

But on her forehead sits a fire:
She sets her forward countenance
And leaps into the future chance,
Submitting all things to desire.

TENNYSON, *In Memoriam* (1850)

Exeter, a hundred years ago, was a great deal farther from
the capital than it is today; and it therefore still provided for
itself some of the wicked amenities all Britain now flocks to
London to enjoy. It would be an exaggeration to say that the
city had a red light quarter in 1867; for all that it had a
distinctly louche area, rather away from the center of the
town and the carbolic presence of the Cathedral. It occupied
a part of the city that slopes down towards the river, once, in
the days (already well past in 1867) when it was a considerable port, the heart of Exeter life. It consisted of a warren of
streets still with many Tudor houses, badly lit, malodorous,
teeming. There were brothels there, and dance halls and gin
places; but rather more frequent were variously undone girls
and women—unmarried mothers, mistresses, a whole population in retreat from the claustrophobic villages and small
towns of Devon. It was notoriously a place to hide, in short;
crammed with cheap lodging houses and inns like that one
described by Sarah in Weymouth, safe sanctuaries from the
stern moral tide that swept elsewhere through the life of the
country. Exeter was, in all this, no exception—all the larger
provincial towns of the time had to find room for this
unfortunate army of female wounded in the battle for universal masculine purity.

In a street on the fringe of this area there stood a row of
Georgian terrace houses. No doubt they had when built
enjoyed a pleasant prospect down towards the river. But

217

warehouses had gone up and blocked that view; the houses had most visibly lost self-confidence in their natural elegance. Their woodwork lacked paint, their roofs tiles, the door panels were split. One or two were still private residences; but a central block of five, made shabbily uniform by a blasphemous application of dull brown paint to the original brick, declared themselves in a long wooden sign over the central doorway of the five to be a hotel—Endicott's Family Hotel, to be precise. It was owned, and administered (as the wooden sign also informed passers-by) by Mrs. Martha Endicott, whose chief characteristic may be said to have been a sublime lack of curiosity about her clientèle. She was a thoroughly Devon woman; that is, she did not see intending guests, but only the money their stay would represent. She classified those who stood in her little office off the hall accordingly: ten-shillinger, twelve-shillinger, fifteener, and so on ... the prices referring to the charge per week. Those accustomed to being fifteen shillings down every time they touch a bell in a modern hotel must not think that her hotel was cheap; the normal rent for a cottage in those days was a shilling a week, two at most. Very nice little houses in Exeter could have been rented for six or seven shillings; and ten shillings a week for the cheapest room made Endicott's Family, though without any obvious justification beyond the rapacity of the proprietress, on the choice side.

It is a gray evening turning into night. Already the two gaslamps on the pavement opposite have been pulled to brightness by the lamplighter's long pole and illumine the raw brick of the warehouse walls. There are several lights on in the rooms of the hotel; brighter on the ground floor, softer above, since as in so many Victorian houses the gaspipes had been considered too expensive to be allowed upstairs, and there oil lamps are still in use. Through one ground-floor window, by the main door, Mrs. Endicott herself can be seen at a table by a small coal fire, poring over her Bible—that is, her accounts ledger; and if we traverse diagonally up from that window to another in the endmost house to the right, a darkened top-floor window, whose murrey curtains are still not drawn, we can just see a good example of a twelve-and-sixer—though here I mean the room, not the guest.

It is really two rooms, a small sitting room and an even smaller bedroom, both made out of one decent-sized Georgian room. The walls are papered in an indeterminate pattern of minute bistre flowers. There is a worn carpet, a round-topped tripod table covered by a dark green rep cloth, on the corners of which someone had once attempted—evidently the very first attempt—to teach herself embroidery; two awk-

218

ward armchairs, overcarved wood garnished by a tired puce velvet, a dark-brown mahogany chest of drawers. On the wall, a foxed print of Charles Wesley, and a very bad watercolor of Exeter Cathedral—received in reluctant part payment, some years before, from a lady in reduced circumstances.

Apart from a small clatter of appliances beneath the tiny barred fire, now a sleeping ruby, that was the inventory of the room. Only one small detail saved it: the white marble surround of the fireplace, which was Georgian, and showed above graceful nymphs with cornucopias of flowers. Perhaps they had always had a faint air of surprise about their classical faces; they certainly seemed to have it now, to see what awful changes a mere hundred years could work in a nation's culture. They had been born into a pleasant pine-paneled room; now they found themselves in a dingy cell.

They must surely, if they had been capable, have breathed a sigh of relief when the door opened and the hitherto absent occupant stood silhouetted in the doorway. That strange-cut coat, that black bonnet, that indigo dress with its small white collar . . . but Sarah came briskly, almost eagerly in.

This was not her arrival at the Endicott Family. How she had come there—several days before—was simple. The name of the hotel had been a sort of joke at the academy where she studied as a girl in Exeter; the adjective was taken as a noun, and it was supposed that the Endicotts were so multiplied that they required a whole hotel to themselves.

Sarah had found herself standing at the Ship, where the Dorchester omnibuses ended their run. Her box was waiting; had arrived the previous day. A porter asked her where she was to go. She had a moment of panic. No ready name came to her mind except that dim remembered joke. A something about the porter's face when he heard her destination must have told her she had not chosen the most distinguished place to stay in Exeter. But he humped her box without argument and she followed him down through the town to the quarter I have already mentioned. She was not taken by the appearance of the place—in her memory (but she had only seen it once) it was homelier, more dignified, more open . . . however, beggars cannot be choosers. It relieved her somewhat that her solitary situation evoked no comment. She paid over a week's room money in advance, and that was evidently sufficient recommendation. She had intended to take the cheapest room, but when she found that only one room was offered for ten shillings but one and a half for the extra half-crown, she had changed her mind.

She came swiftly inside the room and shut the door. A

match was struck and applied to the wick of the lamp, whose milk-glass diffuser, once the "chimney" was replaced, gently repelled the night. Then she tore off her bonnet and shook her hair loose in her characteristic way. She lifted the canvas bag she was carrying onto the table, evidently too anxious to unpack it to be bothered to take off her coat. Slowly and carefully she lifted out one after the other a row of wrapped objects and placed them on the green cloth. Then she put the basket on the floor, and started to unwrap her purchases.

She began with a Staffordshire teapot with a pretty colored transfer of a cottage by a stream and a pair of lovers (she looked closely at the lovers); and then a Toby jug, not one of those garish-colored monstrosities of Victorian manufacture, but a delicate little thing in pale mauve and primrose-yellow, the jolly man's features charmingly lacquered by a soft blue glaze (ceramic experts may recognize a Ralph Wood). Those two purchases had cost Sarah ninepence in an old china shop; the Toby was cracked, and was to be recracked in the course of time, as I can testify, having bought it myself a year or two ago for a good deal more than the three pennies Sarah was charged. But unlike her, I fell for the Ralph Wood part of it. She fell for the smile.

Sarah had, though we have never seen it exercised, an aesthetic sense; or perhaps it was an emotional sense—a reaction against the dreadful décor in which she found herself. She did not have the least idea of the age of her little Toby. But she had a dim feeling that it had been much used, had passed through many hands ... and was now hers. *Was now hers*—she set it on the mantelpiece and, still in her coat, stared at it with a childlike absorption, as if not to lose any atom of this first faint taste of ownership.

Her reverie was broken by footsteps in the passage outside. She threw a brief but intense look at the door. The footsteps passed on. Now Sarah took off her coat and poked the fire into life; then set a blackened kettle on the hob. She turned again to her other purchases: a twisted paper of tea, another of sugar, a small metal can of milk she set beside the teapot. Then she took the remaining three parcels and went into the bedroom: a bed, a marble washstand, a small mirror, a sad scrap of carpet, and that was all.

But she had eyes only for her parcels. The first contained a nightgown. She did not try it against herself, but laid it on the bed; and then unwrapped her next parcel. It was a dark-green shawl, merino fringed with emerald-green silk. This she held in a strange sort of trance—no doubt at its sheer expense, for it cost a good deal more than all her other purchases put together. At last she pensively raised and

220

touched its fine soft material against her cheek, staring down at the nightgown; and then in the first truly feminine gesture I have permitted her, moved a tress of her brown-auburn hair forward to lie on the green cloth; a moment later she shook the scarf out—it was wide, more than a yard across, and twisted it round her shoulders. More staring, this time into the mirror; and then she returned to the bed and arranged the scarf round the shoulders of the laid-out nightgown.

She unwrapped the third and smallest parcel; but this was merely a roll of bandage, which, stopping a moment to stare back at the green-and-white arrangement on the bed, she carried back into the other room and put in a drawer of the mahogany chest, just as the kettle lid began to rattle.

Charles's purse had contained ten sovereigns, and this alone—never mind what else may have been involved—was enough to transform Sarah's approach to the external world. Each night since she had first counted those ten golden coins, she had counted them again. Not like a miser, but as one who goes to see some film again and again—out of an irresistible pleasure in the story, in certain images . . .

For days, when she first arrived in Exeter, she spent nothing, only the barest amounts, and then from her own pitiful savings, on sustenance; but stared at shops: at dresses, at chairs, tables, groceries, wines, a hundred things that had come to seem hostile to her, taunters, mockers, so many two-faced citizens of Lyme, avoiding her eyes when she passed before them and grinning when she had passed behind. This was why she had taken so long to buy a teapot. You can make do with a kettle; and her poverty had inured her to not having, had so profoundly removed from her the appetite to buy that, like some sailor who has subsisted for weeks on half a biscuit a day, she could not eat all the food that was now hers for the asking. Which does not mean she was unhappy; very far from it. She was simply enjoying the first holiday of her adult life.

She made the tea. Small golden flames, reflected, gleamed back from the pot in the hearth. She seemed waiting in the quiet light and crackle, the firethrown shadows. Perhaps you think she must, to be so changed, so apparently equanimous and contented with her lot, have heard from or of Charles. But not a word. And I no more intend to find out what was going on in her mind as she firegazed than I did on that other occasion when her eyes welled tears in the silent night of Marlborough House. After a while she roused herself and went to the chest of drawers and took from a top compart-

ment a teaspoon and a cup without a saucer. Having poured
her tea at the table, she unwrapped the last of her parcels. It
was a small meat pie. Then she began to eat, and without
any delicacy whatsoever.

37

Respectability has spread its leaden mantle over the
whole country . . . and the man wins the race who
can worship that great goddess with the most undivided devotion.

LESLIE STEPHEN, *Sketches from Cambridge* (1865)

The bourgeoisie . . . compels all nations, on pain of
extinction, to adopt the bourgeois mode of produc-
tion; it compels them to introduce what it calls civilization into their midst, that is, to become bourgeois
themselves. In one word, it creates a world after its
own image.

MARX, *Communist Manifesto* (1848)

Charles's second formal interview with Ernestina's father was
a good deal less pleasant than the first, though that was in no
way the fault of Mr. Freeman. In spite of his secret feeling
about the aristocracy—that they were so many drones—he
was, in the more outward aspects of his life, a snob. He made
it his business—and one he looked after as well as his
flourishing other business—to seem in all ways a gentleman.
Consciously he believed he was a perfect gentleman; and
perhaps it was only in his obsessive determination to appear
one that we can detect a certain inner doubt.

These new recruits to the upper middle class were in a
tiresome position. If they sensed themselves recruits socially,
they knew very well that they were powerful captains in their
own world of commerce. Some chose another version of
cryptic coloration and went in very compehensively (like Mr.
Jorrocks) for the pursuits, property and manners of the true
country gentleman. Others—like Mr. Freeman—tried to re-
define the term. Mr. Freeman had a newly built mansion in
the Surrey pinewoods, but his wife and daughter lived there a
good deal more frequently than he did. He was in his way a
forerunner of the modern rich commuter, except that he

spent only his weekends there—and then rarely but in summer. And where his modern homologue goes in for golf, or roses, or gin and adultery, Mr. Freeman went in for earnestness.

Indeed, Profit and Earnestness (in that order) might have been his motto. He had thrived on the great social-economic change that took place between 1850 and 1870—the shift of accent from manufactory to shop, from producer to customer. That first great wave of conspicuous consumption had suited his accounting books very nicely; and by way of compensation—and in imitation of an earlier generation of Puritan profiteers, who had also preferred hunting sin to hunting the fox—he had become excessively earnest and Christian in his private life. Just as some tycoons of our own time go in for collecting art, covering excellent investment with a nice patina of philanthropy, Mr. Freeman contributed handsomely to the Society for the Propagation of Christian Knowledge and similar militant charities. His apprentices, improvers and the rest were atrociously lodged and exploited by our standards; but by those of 1867, Freeman's was an exceptionally advanced establishment, a model of its kind. When he went to heaven, he would have a happy labor force behind him; and his heirs would have the profit therefrom.

He was a grave headmasterly man, with intense gray eyes, whose shrewdness rather tended to make all who came under their survey feel like an inferior piece of Manchester goods. He listened to Charles's news, however, without any sign of emotion, though he nodded gravely when Charles came to the end of his explanation. A silence followed. The interview took place in Mr. Freeman's study in the Hyde Park house. It gave no hint of his profession. The walls were lined by suitably solemn-looking books; a bust of Marcus Aurelius (or was it Lord Palmerston in his bath?); one or two large but indeterminate engravings, whether of carnivals or battles it was hard to establish, though they managed to give the impression of an inchoate humanity a very great distance from present surroundings.

Mr. Freeman cleared his throat and stared at the red and gilt morocco of his desk; he seemed about to pronounce, but changed his mind.

"This is most surprising. Most surprising."

More silence followed, in which Charles felt half irritated and half amused. He saw he was in for a dose of the solemn papa. But since he had invited it, he could only suffer in the silence that followed, and swallowed, that unsatisfactory response. Mr. Freeman's private reaction had in fact been more that of a businessman than of a gentleman, for the

223

thought which had flashed immediately through his mind was that Charles had come to ask for an increase in the marriage portion. That he could easily afford; but a terrible possibility had simultaneously occurred to him—that Charles had known all along of his uncle's probable marriage. The one thing he loathed was to be worsted in an important business deal—and this, after all, was one that concerned the object he most cherished.

Charles at last broke the silence. "I need hardly add that this decision of my uncle's comes as a very great surprise to myself as well."

"Of course, of course."

"But I felt it my duty to apprise you of it at once—and in person."

"Most correct of you. And Ernestina . . . she knows?"

"She was the first I told. She is naturally influenced by the affections she has done me the honor of bestowing on me." Charles hesitated, then felt in his pocket. "I bear a letter to you from her." He stood and placed it on the desk, where Mr. Freeman stared at it with those shrewd gray eyes, evidently preoccupied with other thoughts.

"You have still a very fair private income, have you not?"

"I cannot pretend to have been left a pauper."

"To which we must add the possibility that your uncle may not be so fortunate as eventually to have an heir?"

"That is so."

"And the certainty that Ernestina does not come to you without due provision?"

"You have been most generous."

"And one day I shall be called to eternal rest."

"My dear sir, I—"

The gentleman had won. Mr. Freeman stood. "Between ourselves we may say these things. I shall be very frank with you, my dear Charles. My principal consideration is my daughter's happiness. But I do not need to tell you of the prize she represents in financial terms. When you asked my permission to solicit her hand, not the least of your recommendations in my eyes was my assurance that the alliance would be mutual respect and mutual worth. I have your assurance that your changed circumstances have come on you like a bolt from the blue. No stranger to your moral rectitude could possibly impute to you an ignoble motive. That is my only concern."

"As it is most emphatically mine, sir."

More silence followed. Both knew what was really being said: that malicious gossip must now surround the marriage. Charles would be declared to have had wind of his loss of

224

prospects before his proposal; Ernestina would be sneered at for having lost the title she could so easily have bought elsewhere.

"I had better read the letter. Pray excuse me."

He raised his solid gold letter-knife and slit the envelope open. Charles went to a window and stared out at the trees of Hyde Park. There beyond the chain of carriages in the Bayswater Road, he saw a girl—a shopgirl or maid by the look of her—waiting on a bench before the railings; and even as he watched a red-jacketed soldier came up. He saluted— and she turned. It was too far to see her face, but the eagerness of her turn made it clear that the two were lovers. The soldier took her hand and pressed it momentarily to his heart. Something was said. Then she slipped her hand under his arm and they began to walk slowly towards Oxford Street. Charles became lost in this little scene; and started when Mr. Freeman came beside him, the letter in hand. He was smiling.

"Perhaps I should read what she says in a postscript." He adjusted his silver-rimmed spectacles. " 'If you listen to Charles's nonsense for one moment, I shall make him elope with me to Paris.' " He looked drily up at Charles. "It seems we are given no alternative."

Charles smiled faintly. "But if you should wish for further time to reflect . . ."

Mr. Freeman placed his hand on the scrupulous one's shoulder. "I shall tell her that I find her intended even more admirable in adversity than in good fortune. And I think the sooner you return to Lyme the better it will be."

"You do me great kindness."

"In making my daughter so happy, you do me an even greater one. Her letter is not all in such frivolous terms." He took Charles by the arm and led him back into the room. "And my dear Charles . . ." this phrase gave Mr. Freeman a certain pleasure, ". . . I do not think the necessity to regulate one's expenditure a little when first married is altogether a bad thing. But should circumstances . . . you know what I mean."

"Most kind . . ."

"Let us say no more."

Mr. Freeman took out his keychain and opened a drawer of his desk and placed his daughter's letter inside, as if it were some precious state document; or perhaps he knew rather more about servants than most Victorian employers. As he relocked the desk he looked up at Charles, who now had the disagreeable impression that he had himself become an employee—a favored one, to be sure, but somehow now

225

in this commercial giant's disposal. Worse was to follow; perhaps, after all, the gentleman had not alone determined Mr. Freeman's kindness.

"May I now, since the moment is convenient, open my heart to you on another matter that concerns Ernestina and yourself?"

Charles bowed in polite assent, but Mr. Freeman seemed for a moment at a loss for words. He rather fussily replaced his letter-knife in its appointed place, then went to the window they had so recently left. Then he turned.

"My dear Charles, I count myself a fortunate man in every respect. Except one." He addressed the carpet. "I have no son." He stopped again, then gave his son-in-law a probing look. "I understand that commerce must seem abhorrent to you. It is not a gentleman's occupation."

"That is mere cant, sir. You are yourself a living proof that it is so."

"Do you mean that? Or are you perhaps but giving me another form of cant?"

The iron-gray eyes were suddenly very direct. Charles was at a loss for a moment. He opened his hands. "I see what any intelligent man must—the great utility of commerce, its essential place in our nation's—"

"Ah yes. That is just what every politician says. They have to, because the prosperity of our country depends on it. But would you like it to be said of you that you were ... in trade?"

"The possibility has never arisen."

"But say it should arise?"

"You mean ... I ..."

At last he realized what his father-in-law was driving at; and seeing his shock, the father-in-law hastily made way for the gentleman.

"Of course I don't mean that you should bother yourself with the day-to-day affairs of my enterprise. That is the duty of my superintendents, my clerks and the rest. But my business is prospering, Charles. Next year we shall open emporia in Bristol and Birmingham. They are but the beginning. I cannot offer you a geographical or political empire. But I am convinced that one day an empire of sorts will come to Ernestina and yourself." Mr. Freeman began to walk up and down. "When it seemed clear that your future duties lay in the administration of your uncle's estate I said nothing. But you have energy, education, great ability ..."

"But my ignorance of what you so kindly suggest is ... well, very nearly total."

226

Mr. Freeman waved the objection aside. "Matters like probity, the capacity to command respect, to judge men shrewdly—all those are of far greater import. And I do not believe you poor in such qualities."

"I'm not sure I know fully what you are suggesting."

"I suggest nothing immediate. In any case for the next year or two you have your marriage to think of. You will not want outside cares and interests at such a time. But should a day come when it would ... amuse you to know more of the great commerce you will one day inherit through Ernestina, nothing would bring me ... or my wife, may I add ... greater pleasure than to further that interest."

"The last thing I wish is to appear ungrateful, but ... that is, it seems so disconsonant with my natural proclivities, what small talents I have ..."

"I am suggesting no more than a partnership. In practical terms, nothing more onerous to begin with than an occasional visit to the office of management, a most general supervision of what is going on. I think you would be surprised at the type of man I now employ in the more responsible positions. One need be by no means ashamed to know them."

"I assure you my hesitation is in no way due to social considerations."

"Then it can only be caused by your modesty. And there, my dear young man, you misjudge yourself. That day I mentioned must come—I shall be no longer there. To be sure, you may dispose of what I have spent my life building up. You may find good managers to look after it for you. But I know what I am talking about. A successful enterprise needs an active owner just as much as a good army needs a general. Not all the good soldiers in the world will help unless *he* is there to command the battle."

Charles felt himself, under the first impact of this attractive comparison, like Jesus of Nazareth tempted by Satan. He too had had his days in the wilderness to make the proposition more tempting. But he was a gentleman; and gentlemen cannot go into trade. He sought for a way of saying so; and failed. In a business discussion indecision is a sign of weakness. Mr. Freeman seized his chance.

"You will never get me to agree that we are all descended from monkeys. I find that notion blasphemous. But I thought much on some of the things you said during our little disagreement. I would have you repeat what you said, what was it, about the purpose of this theory of evolution. A species must change ... ?"

227

"In order to survive. It must adapt itself to changes in the environment."

"Just so. Now that I can believe. I am twenty years older than you. Moreover, I have spent my life in a situation where if one does not—and very smartly—change oneself to meet the taste of the day, then one does not survive. One goes bankrupt. Times are changing, you know. This is a great age of progress. And progress is like a lively horse. Either one rides it, or it rides one. Heaven forbid I should suggest that being a gentleman is an insufficient pursuit in life. That it can never be. But this is an age of doing, *great* doing, Charles. You may say these things do not concern you—are beneath you. But ask yourself whether they ought to concern you. That is all I propose. You must reflect on this. There is no need for a decision yet. No need at all." He paused. "But you will not reject the idea out of hand?"

Charles did indeed by this time feel like a badly stitched sample napkin, in all ways a victim of evolution. Those old doubts about the futility of his existence were only too easily reawakened. He guessed now what Mr. Freeman really thought of him: he was an idler. And what he proposed for him: that he should earn his wife's dowry. He would have liked to be discreetly cold, but there was a warmth in Mr. Freeman's voice behind the vehemence, an assumption of relationship. It was to Charles as if he had traveled all his life among pleasant hills; and now came to a vast plain of tedium—and unlike the more famous pilgrim, he saw only Duty and Humiliation down there below—most certainly not Happiness or Progress.

He managed a look into those waiting, and penetrating, commercial eyes.

"I confess myself somewhat overwhelmed."

"I ask no more than that you should give the matter thought."

"Most certainly. Of course. Most serious thought."

Mr. Freeman went and opened the door. He smiled. "I fear you have one more ordeal. Mrs. Freeman awaits us, agog for all the latest tittle-tattle of Lyme."

A few moments later the two men were moving down a wide corridor to the spacious landing that overlooked the grand hall of the house. Little in it was not in the best of contemporary taste. Yet as they descended the sweep of stairs towards the attendant footman, Charles felt obscurely debased; a lion caged. He had, with an acute unexpectedness, a poignant flash of love for Winsyatt, for its "wretched" old paintings and furniture; its age, its security, its *savoir-vivre*. The abstract idea of evolution was entrancing; but its prac-

228

tice seemed as fraught with ostentatious vulgarity as the
freshly gilded Corinthian columns that framed the door on
whose threshold he and his tormentor now paused a second—
"Mr. Charles Smithson, madam"—before entering.

38

Sooner or later I too may passively take the print
Of the golden age—why not? I have neither hope nor trust;
May make my heart as a millstone, set my face as a flint,
Cheat and be cheated, and die: who knows? we are ashes and dust.

TENNYSON, *Maud* (1855)

When Charles at last found himself on the broad steps of the
Freeman town mansion, it was already dusk, gas-lamped and
crisp. There was a faint mist, compounding the scent of the
spring verdure from the Park across the street and the old
familiar soot. Charles breathed it in, acrid and essential
London, and decided to walk. The hansom that had been
called for him was dismissed.

He walked with no very clear purpose, in the general
direction of his club in St. James; at first beside the railings
of Hyde Park, those heavy railings whose fall before a mob
(and under the horrified eyes of his recent interlocutor) only
three weeks later was to precipitate the passing of the great
Reform Bill. He turned then down Park Lane. But the press
of traffic there was disagreeable. Mid-Victorian traffic jams
were quite as bad as modern ones—and a good deal noisier,
since every carriage wheel had an iron tire to grate on the
granite setts. So taking what he imagined would prove a
shortcut, he plunged into the heart of Mayfair. The mist
thickened, not so much as to obscure all, but sufficiently to
give what he passed a slightly dreamlike quality; as if he was
a visitor from another world, a Candide who could see
nothing but obvious explanations, a man suddenly deprived of
his sense of irony.

To be without such a fundamental aspect of his psyche was
almost to be naked; and this perhaps best describes what
Charles felt. He did not now really know what had driven
him to Ernestina's father; the whole matter could have been

dealt with by letter. If his scrupulousness now seemed absurd, so did all this talk of poverty, of having to regulate one's income. In those days, and especially on such a fog-threatening evening, the better-off traveled by carriage; pedestrians must be poor. Thus almost all those Charles met were of the humbler classes; servants from the great Mayfair houses, clerks, shop-people, beggars, street sweepers (a much commoner profession when the horse reigned), hucksters, urchins, a prostitute or two. To all of them, he knew, a hundred pounds a year would have been a fortune; and he had just been commiserated with for having to scrape by on twenty-five times that sum.

Charles was no early socialist. He did not feel the moral enormity of his privileged economic position, because he felt himself so far from privileged in other ways. The proof was all around him. By and large the passers and passed did not seem unhappy with their lots, unless it was the beggars, and they had to look miserable to succeed. But he *was* unhappy; alien and unhappy; he felt that the enormous apparatus rank required a gentleman to erect around himself was like the massive armor that had been the death warrant of so many ancient saurian species. His step slowed at this image of a superseded monster. He actually stopped, poor living fossil, as the brisker and fitter forms of life jostled busily before him, like pond amoeba under a microscope, along a small row of shops that he had come upon.

Two barrel-organists competed with one another, and a banjo-man with both. Mashed-potato men, trotter-sellers ("Penny a trotter, you won't find 'otter"), hot chestnuts. An old woman hawking fusees; another with a basket of daffodils. Watermen, turncocks, dustmen with their backlap caps, mechanics in their square pillboxes; and a plague of small ragamuffins sitting on doorsteps, on curbs, leaning against the carriage posts, like small vultures. One such lad interrupted his warming jog—like most of the others, he was barefooted—to whistle shrill warning to an image-boy, who ran, brandishing his sheaf of colored prints, up to Charles as he stood in the wings of this animated stage.

Charles turned hastily away and sought a darker street. A harsh little voice sped after him, chanting derisive lines from a vulgar ballad of the year:

> "Why don'cher come 'ome, Lord Marmaduke,
> An' 'ave an 'ot supper wiv me?
> An' when we've bottomed a jug o' good stout
> We'll riddle-dee-ro-di-dee, ooooh,
> We'll riddle-dee-ro-di-ree."

Which reminded Charles, when at last he was safely escaped from the voice and its accompanying jeers, of that other constituent of London air—not as physical, but as unmistakable as the soot—the perfume of sin. It was less the miserable streetwomen he saw now and then, women who watched him pass without soliciting him (he had too obviously the air of a gentleman and they were after lesser prey) than the general anonymity of the great city; the sense that all could be hidden here, all go unobserved.

Lyme was a town of sharp eyes; and this was a city of the blind. No one turned and looked at him. He was almost invisible, he did not exist, and this gave him a sense of freedom, but a terrible sense, for he had in reality lost it—it was like Winsyatt, in short. All in his life was lost; and all reminded him that it was lost.

A man and a woman who hurried past spoke French; were French. And then Charles found himself wishing he were in Paris—from that, that he were abroad ... traveling. Again! *If I could only escape, if I could only escape* ... he murmured the words to himself a dozen times; then metaphorically shook himself for being so impractical, so romantic, so dutiless.

He passed a mews, not then a fashionable row of bijou "maisonettes" but noisily in pursuit of its original function: horses being curried and groomed, equipages being drawn out, hooves clacking as they were backed between shafts, a coachman whistling noisily as he washed the sides of his carriage, all in preparation for the evening's work. An astounding theory crossed Charles's mind: the lower orders were secretly happier than the upper. They were not, as the radicals would have one believe, the suffering infrastructure groaning under the opulent follies of the rich; but much more like happy parasites. He remembered having come, a few months before, on a hedgehog in the gardens of Winsyatt. He had tapped it with his stick and made it roll up; and between its erect spines he had seen a swarm of disturbed fleas. He had been sufficiently the biologist to be more fascinated than revolted by this interrelation of worlds; as he was now sufficiently depressed to see who was the hedgehog: an animal whose only means of defense was to lie as if dead and erect its prickles, its aristocratic sensibilities.

A little later he came to an ironmonger's, and stood outside staring through the windows at the counter, at the ironmonger in his bowler and cotton apron, counting candles to a ten-year-old girl who stared up at him, her red fingers already holding high the penny to be taken.

Trade. Commerce. And he flushed, remembering what had been offered. He saw now it was an insult, a contempt for his class, that had prompted the suggestion. Freeman must know he could never go into business, play the shopkeeper. He should have rejected the suggestion icily at its very first mention; but how could he, when all his wealth was to come from that very source? And here we come near the real germ of Charles's discontent: this feeling that he was now the bought husband, his in-law's puppet. Never mind that such marriages were traditional in his class; the tradition had sprung from an age when polite marriage was a publicly accepted business contract that neither husband nor wife was expected to honor much beyond its terms: money for rank. But marriage now was a chaste and sacred union, a Christian ceremony for the creation of pure love, not pure convenience. Even if he had been cynic enough to attempt it, he knew Ernestina would never allow such love to become a secondary principle in their marriage. Her constant test would be that he loved her, and only her. From that would follow the other necessities: his gratitude for her money, this being morally blackmailed into a partnership . . .

And as if by some fatal magic he came to a corner. Filling the end of a dark side street was a tall lit façade. He had thought by now to be near Piccadilly; but this golden palace at the end of a sepia chasm was to his north, and he realized that he had lost his sense of direction and come out upon Oxford Street . . . and yes, fatal coincidence, upon that precise Oxford Street occupied by Mr. Freeman's great store. As if magnetized he walked down the side street towards it, out into Oxford Street, so that he could see the whole length of the yellow-tiered giant (its windows had been lately changed to the new plate glass), with its crowded arrays of cottons, laces, gowns, rolls of cloths. Some of the cylinders and curlicues of new aniline color seemed almost to stain the air around them, so intense, so *nouveau riche* were they. On each article stood the white ticket that announced its price. The store was still open, and people passed through its doors. Charles tried to imagine himself passing through them, and failed totally. He would rather have been the beggar crouched in the doorway beside him.

It was not simply that the store no longer seemed what it had been before to him—a wry joke, a goldmine in Australia, a place that hardly existed in reality. It now showed itself full of power; a great engine, a behemoth that stood waiting to suck in and grind all that came near it. To so many men, even then, to have stood and known that that huge building, and others like it, and its gold, its power, all lay easily in his

232

grasp, must have seemed a heaven on earth. Yet Charles stood on the pavement opposite and closed his eyes, as if he hoped he might obliterate it forever.

To be sure there was something base in his rejection—a mere snobbism, a letting himself be judged and swayed by an audience of ancestors. There was something lazy in it; a fear of work, of routine, of concentration on detail. There was something cowardly in it, as well—for Charles, as you have probably noticed, was frightened by other human beings and especially by those below his own class. The idea of being in contact with all those silhouetted shadows he saw thronging before the windows and passing in and out of the doors across the street—it gave him a nausea. It was an impossibility.

But there was one noble element in his rejection: a sense that the pursuit of money was an insufficient purpose in life. He would never be a Darwin or a Dickens, a great artist or scientist; he would at worst be a dilettante, a drone, a what-you-will that lets others work and contributes nothing. But he gained a queer sort of momentary self-respect in his nothingness, a sense that choosing to be nothing—to have nothing but prickles—was the last saving grace of a gentleman; his last freedom, almost. It came to him very clearly: If I ever set foot in that place I am done for.

This dilemma may seem a very historical one to you; and I hold no particular brief for the Gentleman, in 1969 far more of a dying species than even Charles's pessimistic imagination might have foreseen on that long-ago April evening. Death is not in the nature of things; it is the nature of things. But what dies is the form. The matter is immortal. There runs through this succession of superseded forms we call existence a certain kind of afterlife. We can trace the Victorian gentleman's best qualities back to the parfit knights and *preux chevaliers* of the Middle Ages; and trace them forward into the modern gentleman, that breed we call scientists, since that is where the river has undoubtedly run. In other words, every culture, however undemocratic, or however egalitarian, needs a kind of self-questioning, ethical élite, and one that is bound by certain rules of conduct, some of which may be very unethical, and so account for the eventual death of the form, though their hidden purpose is good: to brace or act as structure for the better effects of their function in history.

Perhaps you see very little link between the Charles of 1267 with all his newfangled French notions of chastity and chasing after Holy Grails, the Charles of 1867 with his loathing of trade, and the Charles of today, a computer scientist deaf to the screams of the tender humanists who begin to discern their own redundancy. But there is a link: they all rejected or reject the notion of *possession* as the purpose of life, whether it be of a woman's body, or of high profit at all costs, or of the right to dictate the speed of progress. The scientist is but one more form; and will be superseded.

Now all this is the great and timeless relevance of the New Testament myth of the Temptation in the Wilderness. All who have insight and education have automatically their own wilderness; and at some point in their life they will have their temptation. Their rejection may be foolish; but it is never evil. You have just turned down a tempting offer in commercial applied science in order to continue your academic teaching? Your last exhibition did not sell as well as the previous one, but you are determined to keep to your new style? You have just made some decision in which your personal benefit, your chance of possession, has not been allowed to interfere? Then do not dismiss Charles's state of mind as a mere conditioning of futile snobbery. See him for what he is: a man struggling to overcome history. And even though he does not realize it.

There pressed on Charles more than the common human instinct to preserve personal identity; there lay behind him all those years of thought, speculation, self-knowledge. His whole past, the best of his past self, seemed the price he was asked to pay; he could not believe that all he had wanted to be was worthless, however much he might have failed to match reality to the dream. He had pursued the meaning of life, more than that, he believed—poor clown—that at times he had glimpsed it. Was it his fault that he lacked the talent to communicate those glimpses to other men? That to an outside observer he seemed a dilettante, a hopeless amateur? At least he had gained the knowledge that the meaning of life was not to be found in Freeman's store.

But underlying all, at least in Charles, was the doctrine of the survival of the fittest, and most especially an aspect of it he had discussed—and it had been a discussion bathed in optimism—with Grogan that night in Lyme: that a human being cannot but see his power of self-analysis as a very special privilege in the struggle to adapt. Both men had seen proof there that man's free will was not in danger. If one had to change to survive—as even the Freemans conceded—then at least one was granted a choice of methods. So much for the theory—the practice, it now flooded in on Charles, was something other.

He was trapped. He could not be, but he was.

He stood for a moment against the vast pressures of his

age; then felt cold, chilled to his innermost marrow by an icy rage against Mr. Freeman and Freemanism.

He raised his stick to a passing hansom. Inside he sank back into the musty leather seat and closed his eyes; and in his mind there appeared a consoling image. Hope? Courage? Determination? I am afraid not. He saw a bowl of milk punch and a pint of champagne.

39

> Now, what if I am a prostitute, what business has so- ciety to abuse me? Have I received any favors at the hands of society? If I am a hideous cancer in society, are not the causes of the disease to be sought in the rottenness of the carcass? Am I not its legitimate child; no bastard, Sir?
> From a letter in *The Times* (February 24th, 1858) *

Milk punch and champagne may not seem a very profound philosophical conclusion to such soul-searching; but they had been perennially prescribed at Cambridge as a solution to all known problems, and though Charles had learned a good deal more about the problems since leaving the university he had not bettered the solution. Fortunately his club, like so many English gentlemen's clubs, was founded on the very simple and profitable presumption that a man's student days are his best. It had all the amenities of a rich college without any of its superfluous irritations (such as dons, deans and examinations). It pandered, in short, to the adolescent in man. It also provided excellent milk punch.

It so happened that the first two fellow members Charles set eyes on when he entered the smoking room had also been his fellow students; one was the younger son of a bishop and a famous disgrace to his father. The other was what Charles had until recently expected to be: a baronet. Born with a large lump of Northumberland in his pocket, Sir Thomas

---

* The substance of this famous and massively sarcastic letter, al- legedly written by a successful prostitute, but more probably by some- one like Henry Mayhew, may be read in *Human Documents of the Victorian Golden Age.*

Burgh had proved far too firm a rock for history to move. The immemorial pursuits of his ancestors had been hunting, shooting, drinking and whoring; and he still pursued them with a proper sense of tradition. He had in fact been a leader of the fast set into which Charles had drifted during his time at Cambridge. His escapades, of both the Mytton and the Casanova kind, were notorious. There had been several moves to get him ejected from the club; but since he provided its coal from one of his mines, and at a rate that virtually made a present of it, wiser counsels always prevailed. Besides, there was something honest about his manner of life. He sinned without shame, but also without hypocrisy. He was generous to a fault; half the younger members of the club had at one time or another been in his debt—and his loans were a gentleman's loans, indefinitely prolongable and without interest. He was always the first to start a book when there was something to bet on; and in a way he reminded all but the most irredeemably sober members of their less sober days. He was stocky, short, perpetually flushed by wine and weather; and his eyes had that splendid innocence, that opaque blue candor of the satanically fallen. These eyes crinkled when they saw Charles enter.

"Charley! Now what the devil are you doing out of the matrimonial lock up?"

Charles smiled, not without a certain sense of wan foolishness. "Good evening, Tom. Nathaniel, how are you?" Eternal cigar in mouth, the thorn in the unlucky bishop's side raised a languid hand. Charles turned back to the baronet. "On parole, you know. The dear girl's down in Dorset taking the waters."

Tom winked. "While you take spirit—and spirits, eh? But I hear she's the rose of the season. Nat says. He's green, y'know. Demmed Charley, he says. Best girl and best match— ain't fair, is it, Nat?" The bishop's son was notoriously short of money and Charles guessed it was not Ernestina's looks he was envied. Nine times out of ten he would at this point have moved on to the newspapers or joined some less iniquitous acquaintance. But today he stayed where he was. Would they "discuss" a punch and bubbly? They would. And so he sat with them.

"And how's the esteemed uncle, Charles?" Sir Tom winked again, but in a way so endemic to his nature that it was impossible to take offense. Charles murmured that he was in the best of health.

"How goes he for hounds? Ask him if he needs a brace of the best Northumberland. Real angels, though I says it wot

236

bred 'em. Tornado—you recall Tornado? His grandpups."
Tornado had spent a clandestine term in Sir Tom's rooms
one summer at Cambridge.

"I recall him. So do my ankles."

Sir Tom grinned broadly. "Aye, he took a fancy to you.
Always bit what he loved. Dear old Tornado—God rest his
soul." And he downed his tumbler of punch with a sadness
that made his two companions laugh. Which was cruel, since
the sadness was perfectly genuine.

In such talk did two hours pass—and two more bottles of
champagne, and another bowl of punch, and sundry chops
and kidneys (the three gentlemen moved on to the dining
room) which required a copious washing-down of claret,
which in turn needed purging by a decanter or two of port.

Sir Tom and the bishop's son were professional drinkers
and took more than Charles. Outwardly they seemed by the
end of the second decanter more drunk than he. But in fact
his façade was sobriety, while theirs was drunkenness, exactly the reverse of the true comparative state, as became clear
when they wandered out of the dining room for what Sir
Tom called vaguely "a little drive round town." Charles was
the one who was unsteady on his feet. He was not too far
gone not to feel embarrassed; somehow he saw Mr.
Freeman's gray assessing eyes on him, though no one as
closely connected with trade as Mr. Freeman would ever
have been allowed in that club.

He was helped into his cape and handed his hat, gloves,
and cane; and then he found himself in the keen outside
air—the promised fog had not materialized, though the mist
remained—staring with an intense concentration at the coat
of arms on the door of Sir Tom's town brougham. Winsyatt
meanly stabbed him again, but then the coat of arms swayed
towards him. His arms were taken, and a moment later he
found himself sitting beside Sir Tom and facing the bishop's
son. He was not too drunk to note an exchanged wink
between his two friends; but too drunk to ask what it meant.
He told himself he did not care. He was glad he was drunk,
that everything swam a little, that everything past and to
come was profoundly unimportant. He had a great desire to
tell them both about Mrs. Bella Tomkins and Winsyatt; but
he was not drunk enough for that, either. A gentleman
remains a gentleman, even in his cups. He turned to Tom.

"Tom ... Tom, dear old fellow, you're a damn' lucky
fellow."

"So are you, my Charley boy. We're all damn lucky
fellows."

237

"Where we going?"

"Where damn lucky fellows always go of a jolly night. Eh, Nat, ain't that so?"

There was a silence then, as Charles tried dimly to make out in which direction they were heading. This time he did not see the second wink exchanged. The key words in Sir Tom's last sentence slowly registered. He turned solemnly.

"Jolly night?"

"We're going to old Ma Terpsichore's, Charles. Worship at the muses' shrine, don't y'know?"

Charles stared at the smiling face of the bishop's son.

"Shrine?"

"So to speak, Charles."

"Metonymia. Venus for *puella,"* put in the bishop's son.

Charles stared at them, then abruptly smiled. "Excellent idea." But then he resumed his rather solemn stare out of the window. He felt he ought to stop the carriage and say good night to them. He remembered, in a brief flash of proportion, what their reputation was. Then there came out of nowhere Sarah's face; that face with its closed eyes tended to his, the kiss . . . so much fuss about nothing. He saw what all his troubles were caused by: he needed a woman, he needed intercourse. He needed a last debauch, as he sometimes needed a purge. He looked round at Sir Tom and the bishop's son. The first was sprawled back in his corner, the second had put his legs up across his seat. The top hats of both were cocked at flyly dissolute angles. This time the wink went among all three.

Soon they were in the press of carriages heading for that area of Victorian London we have rather mysteriously—since it was central in more ways than one—dropped from our picture of the age: an area of casinos (meeting places rather than gaming rooms), assembly cafés, cigar "divans" in its more public parts (the Haymarket and Regent Street) and very nearly unrelieved brothel in all the adjoining back streets. They passed the famous Oyster Shop in the Haymarket ("Lobsters, Oysters, Pickled and Kippered Salmon") and the no less celebrated Royal Albert Potato Can, run by the Khan, khan indeed of the baked-potato sellers of London, behind a great scarlet-and-brass stand that dominated and proclaimed the vista. They passed (and the bishop's son took his lorgnette out of its shagreen case) the crowded daughters of folly, the great whores in their carriages, the lesser ones in their sidewalk droves . . . from demure little milky-faced millinery girls to brandy-cheeked viragoes. A torrent of color —of fashion, for here unimaginable things were allowed. Women dressed as Parisian bargees, in bowler and trousers,

238

as sailors, as señoritas, as Sicilian peasant girls; as if the entire casts of the countless neighboring penny-gaffs had poured out into the street. Far duller the customers—the numerically equal male sex, who, stick in hand and "weed" in mouth, eyed the evening's talent. And Charles, though he wished he had not drunk so much, and so had to see everything twice over, found it delicious, gay, animated, and above all, unFreemanish.

Terpsichore, I suspect, would hardly have bestowed her patronage on the audience of whom our three in some ten minutes formed part; for they were not alone. Some six or seven other young men, and a couple of old ones, one of whom Charles recognized as a pillar of the House of Lords, sat in the large salon, appointed in the best Parisian taste, and reached through a narrow and noisome alley off a street some little way from the top of the Haymarket. At one end of the chandeliered room was a small stage hidden by deep red curtains, on which were embroidered in gold two pairs of satyrs and nymphs. One showed himself eminently in a state to take possession of his shepherdess; and the other had already been received. In black letters on a gilt cartouche above the curtains was written *Carmina Priapea XLIV*

> Velle quid hanc dicas, quamvis sim ligneus, hastam,
>   oscula dat medio si qua puella mihi?
> augure non opus est: "in me," mihi credite, dixit,
>   "utetur veris viribus hasta rudis."*

The copulatory theme was repeated in various folio prints in gilt frames that hung between the curtained windows. Already a loose-haired girl in Camargo petticoats was serving the waiting gentlemen with Roederer's champagne. In the background a much rouged but more seemingly dressed lady of some fifty years of age cast a quiet eye over her clientèle. In spite of her very different profession she had very much the mind of Mrs. Endicott down in Exeter, albeit her assessments were made in guineas rather than shillings.

Such scenes as that which followed have probably changed less in the course of history than those of any other human activity; what was done before Charles that night was done

---

*It is the god Priapus who speaks: small wooden images of him with erect phallus, both to frighten away thieves and bring fertility, were common features of the Roman orchard. "You'd like to know why the girl kisses this spear of mine, even though I'm made of wood? You don't need to be clairvoyant to work that one out. 'Let's hope,' she's thinking, 'that men will use this spear on me—and brutally.'"

in the same way before Heliogabalus—and no doubt before Agamemnon as well; and is done today in countless Soho dives. What particularly pleases *me* about the unchangingness of this ancient and time-honored form of entertainment is that it allows one to borrow from someone else's imagination. I was nosing recently round the best kind of secondhand bookseller's—a careless one. Set quietly under "Medicine," between an *Introduction to Hepatology* and a *Diseases of the Bronchial System*, was the even duller title *The History of the Human Heart*. It is in fact the very far from dull history of a lively human penis. It was originally published in 1749, the same year as Cleland's masterpiece in the genre, *Fanny Hill*. The author lacks his skill, but he will do.

The first House they entered was a noted Bagnio, where they met with a Covey of Town Partridges, which Camillo liked better than all he had ever drawn a Net over in the Country, and amongst them Miss M., the famous Posture Girl, whose Presence put our Company of Ramblers upon the Crochet of shewing their new Associate a Scene, of which he had never so much as dreamed before.

They were showed a large Room, Wine was brought in, the Drawer dismissed, and after a Bumper the Ladies were ordered to prepare. They immediately stripped stark naked, and mounted themselves on the middle of the Table. Camillo was greatly surprised at this Apparatus, and not less puzzled in guessing for what Purpose the Girls had posted themselves on that Eminence. They were clean limbed, fresh complectioned, and had Skins as white as the driven Snow, which was heightened by the jet-black Color of their Hair. They had very good Faces, and the natural Blush which glowed on their Cheeks rendered them in Camillo's Mind, finished Beauties, and fit to rival Venus herself. From viewing their Faces, he bashfully cast his Eyes on the Altar of Love, which he had never had so fair a View of as this present Time . . .

The Parts of the celebrated Posture Girl had something about them which attracted his Attention more than any things he had either felt or seen. The Throne of Love was thickly covered with jet-black Hair, at least a quarter of a Yard long, which she artfully spread asunder, to display the Entrance into the Magic Grotto. The uncommon Figure of this bushy spot afforded a very odd sort of Amusement to Camillo, which was more heightened by the Rest of the Ceremony which these Wantons went through. They each filled a Glass of Wine, and laying themselves in an extended Posture placed their Glasses on the Mount of Venus, every Man in the Company drinking off the Bumper, as it stood on that tempting Protuberance, while the Wenches were not wanting in their lascivious Motions to heighten the Diversion. Then they went thro' the several Postures and Tricks made use of to raise debilitated Lust when cloyed with natural Enjoyment, and afterwards obliged poor Camillo to shoot the Bridge, and pass under the warm Cataracts, which discomposed him more than if he had been overset in a Gravesend Wherry. However, tho' it raised the Laugh of the whole Company, he bore this Frolick with a good deal of patience, as he was told it was necessary for all new Members to be thus initiated into the Mysteries of their Society. Camillo began now to be disgusted at the prodigious Impudence of the Women; he found in himself no more of that uneasy Emotion he felt at their first setting out, and was desirous of the Company's dismissing them; but his Companions would not part with them, till they had gone through with the whole of their Exercise; the Nymphs, who raised a fresh Contribution on every new Discovery of their impudent Inventions, required no Entreaties to gratify the young Rakes, but proceeded, without the least Sense of Shame, to shew them how far Human Nature could debase itself.

Their last Exploit inflamed these Sons of Debauchery so far that they proposed, as a Conclusion of the Scene, that each Man should chuse his Posture, and go through what they had only seen imitated before. But this was a Step the Nymphs would not comply with, it being the Maxim of these Damsels, never to admit of the Embraces of the Men, for fear of spoiling their Trade. This very much surprised Camillo, who from their former Behavior, persuaded himself there could not be invented any Species of Wickedness with which they would not comply for the Sake of Money; and though before this Refusal, their abandoned Obscenity had quite stifled all thoughts of lying with them, yet now his Desires were as strong as if they had been modest Virgins, and he had seen nothing of their Wantonness; so that he became as earnest to oblige them to comply as any Man in the Company.

This gives the general idea of what went on at Ma Terpsichore's, though it omits a particular of difference: the girls of 1867, not so squeamish as those of 1749, were willingly auctioned off in a final tableau.

However, Charles was not there to make a bid. The less obscene preambles he had quite enjoyed. He put on his much-traveled face, he had seen better things in Paris (or so he whispered to Sir Tom), he played the blasé young know-all. But as the clothes fell, so did his drunkenness; he

241

glanced at the lecherously parted mouths of the shadowed men beside him, he heard Sir Tom already indicating his pick to the bishop's son. The white bodies embraced, contorted, mimicked; but it seemed to Charles that there was a despair behind the fixed suggestive smiles of the performers. One was a child who could only just have reached puberty; and there seemed in her assumption of demure innocence something genuinely virginal, still agonized, not fully hardened by her profession.

Yet as he was revolted, so was he sexually irritated. He loathed the public circumstance of this exhibition; but he was enough of an animal to be privately disturbed and excited. Some time before the end he rose and quietly left the room, as if it were to relieve himself. In the anteroom outside the little *danseuse* who had served the champagne sat by a table with the gentlemen's cloaks and canes. An artificial smile creased her painted face as she rose. Charles stared a moment at her elaborately disordered ringlets, her bare arms and almost bare bosom. He seemed about to speak, but then changed his mind and brusquely gestured for his things. He threw a half sovereign on the table beside the girl and blundered out.

In the street at the alley's end he found several expectant cabs waiting. He took the first, shouted up (such was the cautious Victorian convention) the name of a Kensington street near to the one where he lived, and then threw himself into the seat. He did not feel nobly decent; but as if he had swallowed an insult or funked a duel. His father had lived a life in which such evenings were a commonplace; that he could not stomach them proved he was unnatural. Where now was the traveled man of the world? Shrunk into a miserable coward. And Ernestina, his engagement vows? But to recall them was to be a prisoner waking from a dream that he was free and trying to stand, only to be jerked down by his chains back into the black reality of his cell.

The hansom threaded its way slowly down a narrow street. It was crowded with other hansoms and carriages, for this was still very much in the area of sin. Under each light, in every doorway, stood prostitutes. From the darkness Charles watched them. He felt himself boiling, intolerable. If there had been a sharp spike in front of him he would, echoing Sarah before the thorn tree, have run his hand through it, so strong was his feeling for maceration, punishment, some action that would lance his bile.

A quieter street. And they passed a gaslight under which stood a solitary girl. Perhaps because of the flagrant frequency of the women in the street they had left she seemed

242

forlorn, too inexperienced to venture closer. Yet her profession was unmistakable. She wore a dingy pink cotton dress with imitation roses at the breast; a white shawl round her shoulders. A black hat in the new style, small and masculine, perched over a large netted chignon of auburn hair. She stared at the passing hansom; and something about the shade of the hair, the alert dark-shadowed eyes, the vaguely wistful stance, made Charles crane forward and keep her in view through the oval side-window as the hansom passed. He had an intolerable moment, then he seized his stick and knocked hard with it on the roof above him. The driver stopped at once. There were hurried footsteps; and then the face appeared, slightly below him, beside the open front of the hansom.

She was not really like Sarah. He saw the hair was too red to be natural; and there was a commonness about her, an artificial boldness in her steady eyes and red-lipped smile; too red, like a gash of blood. But just a tinge—something in the firm eyebrows, perhaps, or the mouth.

"You have a room?"

"Yes, sir."

"Tell him where to go."

She disappeared from his sight a moment and said something to the driver behind. Then she stepped up, making the hansom rock, and got in beside him, filling the narrow space with cheap perfume. He felt the light cloth of her sleeve and skirt brush him, but they did not touch. The hansom moved on. There was a silence for a hundred yards or more.

"Is it for all night, sir?"

"Yes."

"I asks 'cause I adds the price of the fare back if it ain't."

He nodded, and stared into the darkness ahead of him. They passed another clopping hundred yards in silence. He felt her relax a little, the smallest pressure against his arm.

"Terrible cold for the time of year."

"Yes." He glanced at her. "You must notice such things."

"I don't do no work when it snows. Some does. But I don't."

More silence. This time Charles spoke.

"You have been long. . . ?"

"Since I was eighteen, sir. Two years come May."

"Ah."

He stole another look at her during the next silence. A horrid mathematics gnawed at Charles's mind: three hundred and sixty-five, say three hundred "working," multiply by two . . . it was six hundred to one that she did not have some disease. Was there some delicate way he could ask? There

243

was not. He glanced at her again in an advantageous moment of outside light. Her complexion seemed unblemished. But he was a fool; as regards syphilis he knew he would have been ten times safer at a luxury establishment like the one he had left. To pick up a mere Cockney streetwalker ... but his fate was sealed. He wished it so. They were heading north, towards the Tottenham Court Road.

"Do you wish me to pay you now?"

"I ain't partickler, sir. Just as you fancy."

"Very well. How much?"

She hesitated. Then: "Normal, sir?"

He flashed a look at her; nodded.

"All night I usual charges ..." and her tiny hesitation was pathetically dishonest, " ... a sovereign."

He felt inside his frock coat and passed her the coin.

"Thank you, sir." She put it discreetly away in her reticule. And then she managed an oblique answer to his secret fear. "I only go with gentlemen, sir. You don't need no worries like that."

In his turn he said, "Thank you."

40

To the lips, ah, of others,
  Those lips have been prest,
And others, ere I was,
  Were clasped to that breast ...
MATTHEW ARNOLD, "Parting" (1853)

The hansom drew up at a house in a narrow side street east of the Tottenham Court Road. Stepping quickly out of the vehicle, the girl went straight up some steps to a door and let herself in. The hansom driver was an old, old man, so long encased in his many-caped driving coat and his deep-banded top hat that it was hard to imagine they had not grown onto his body. Setting his whip in the stand beside his seat and taking his cutty out of his mouth, he held his grimed hand down, cupped, for the money. Meanwhile he stared straight

244

ahead to the end of the dark street, as if he could not bear to set eyes on Charles again. Charles was glad not to be looked at; and yet felt quite as unspeakable as this ancient cab driver seemed determined to make him feel. He had a moment of doubt. He could spring back in, for the girl had disappeared ... but then a black obstinacy made him pay.

Charles found the prostitute waiting in a poorly lit hallway, her back to him. She did not look round, but moved up the stairs as soon as she heard him close the door. There was a smell of cooking, obscure voices from the back of the house.

They went up two stale flights of stairs. She opened a door and held it for him to pass through; and when he had done so, slid a bolt across. Then she went and turned up the gaslights over the fire. She poked that to life and put some more coal on it. Charles looked round. Everything in the room except the bed was shabby, but spotlessly clean. The bed was of iron and brass, the latter so well polished it seemed like gold. In the corner facing it there was a screen behind which he glimpsed a washstand. A few cheap ornaments, some cheap prints on the walls. The frayed moreen curtains were drawn. Nothing in the room suggested the luxurious purpose for which it was used.

"Pardon me, sir. If you'd make yourself at 'ome. I shan't be a minute."

She went through another door into a room at the back of the house. It was in darkness, and he noticed that she closed the door after her very gently. He went and stood with his back to the fire. Through the closed door he heard the faint mutter of an awakened child, a shushing, a few low words. The door opened again and the prostitute reappeared. She had taken off her shawl and her hat. She smiled nervously at him.

"It's my little gel, sir. She won't make no noise. She's good as gold." Sensing his disapproval, she hurried on. "There's a chophouse just a step away, sir, if you're 'ungry."

Charles was not; but nor did he now feel sexually hungry, either. He found it hard to look at her.

"Pray order for yourself what you want. I don't ... that is ... some wine, perhaps, if it can be got."

"French or German, sir?"

"A glass of hock—you like that?"

"Thank you, sir. I'll send the lad out."

And again she disappeared. He heard her call sharply, much less genteel, down the hall.

" 'Arry!"

The murmur of voices, the front door slammed. When she

245

came back he asked if he should not have given her some money. But it seemed this service was included.

"Won't you take the chair, sir?"

And she held out her hands for his hat and stick, which he still held. He handed them over, then parted the tails of his frock coat and sat by the fire. The coal she had put on seemed slow to burn. She knelt before it, and before him, and busied herself again with the poker.

"They're best quality, they didn't ought to be so slow catchin'. It's the cellar. Damp as old 'ouses."

He watched her profile in the red light from the fire. It was not a pretty face, but sturdy, placid, unthinking. Her bust was well developed; her wrists and hands surprisingly delicate, almost fragile. They, and her abundant hair, momentarily sparked off his desire. He almost put out his hand to touch her, but changed his mind. He would feel better when he had more wine. They remained so for a minute or more. At last she looked at him, and he smiled. For the first time that day he had a fleeting sense of peace.

She turned her eyes back to the fire then and murmured, " 'E won't be more'n a minute. It's only two steps."

And so they stayed in silence again. But such moments as these were very strange to a Victorian man; even between husband and wife the intimacy was largely governed by the iron laws of convention. Yet here Charles was, sitting at the fire of this woman he had not known existed an hour before, like . . .

"The father of your little girl. . . ?"

" 'E's a sojjer, sir."

"A soldier?"

She stared at the fire: memories.

" 'E's out in Hindia now."

"Would he not marry you?"

She smiled at his innocence, then shook her head. " 'E gave me money for when I was brought to bed." By which she seemed to suggest that he had done all one could decently expect.

"And could you not find any other means of livelihood?"

"There's work. But it's all day work. And then when I paid to look after little Mary . . ." she shrugged. "Once you been done wrong to, you been done wrong to. Can't be mended, so you 'ave to make out as best you can."

"And you believe this the best way?"

"I don't know no other no more, sir."

But she spoke without much sign of shame or regret. Her fate was determined, and she lacked the imagination to see it.

246

There were feet on the stairs. She rose and went to the door and opened it before the knock. Charles glimpsed a boy of thirteen or so outside, who had evidently been trained not to stare, since his eyes remained down while she herself carried the tray to a table by the window and then returned to the door with her purse. There was the chink of small coins, and the door softly closed. She poured him a glass of wine and brought it to him, setting the half-bottle on a trivet in the hearth beside him, as if all wine should be warmed. Then she sat and removed the cloth from the plate on the tray. Out of the corner of his eye Charles saw a small pie, potatoes, a tumbler of what was evidently gin and water, for she would hardly have had water alone brought up. His hock tasted acid, but he drank it in the hope that his senses would be dulled.

The small crackle from the now burning fire, the quiet hiss of the gas jets, the chink of cutlery: he could not see how they should ever pass to the real purpose of his presence. He drank another glass of the vinegary wine.

But she soon finished her repast. The tray was taken outside. Then she went back into the darkened bedroom where the little girl slept. A minute passed. She reappeared. Now she wore a white *peignoir*, which she held closed. Her hair was loosened and fell down her back; and her hand held the edges of the robe together sufficiently tightly to show she was naked beneath it. Charles rose.

"No 'aste, sir. Finish your wine."

He stared down at the bottle beside him, as if he had not noticed it before; then nodded and sat down again, and poured himself another glass. She moved in front of him and reached, her other hand still holding the *peignoir* together, to turn down the gas to two small green points. Firelight bathed her, softened her young features; and then again she knelt at his feet facing the fire. After a moment she reached out both hands to it and the robe fell a little open. He saw a white breast, shadowed, and not fully bared.

She spoke into the fire. "Would you like me to sit on your knees, sir?"

"Yes . . . please do."

He tossed off his wine. Clutching her robe together again she stood, then sat easily back across his braced legs, her right arm round his shoulders. His left arm he put round her waist, while his right lay, with an absurd unnaturalness, along the low arm of the chair. For a moment her left hand clasped the fabric of her gown, but then she reached it out and caressed his cheek. A moment; she kissed his other cheek. Their eyes met. She glanced down at his mouth, as if

247

shyly, but she went about her business without shyness.

"You're a very 'andsome gentleman."

"You're a pretty girl."

"You like us wicked girls?"

He noted she had dropped the "sir." He tightened his left arm a little.

She reached then and took his recalcitrant right hand and led it under her robe to her bare breast. He felt the stiff point of flesh in the center of his palm. Her hand drew his head to hers, and they kissed, as his hand, now recalling forbidden female flesh, silken and swollen contours, a poem forgotten, sized and approved the breast then slid deeper and lower inside her robe to the incurve of her waist. She was naked, and her mouth tasted faintly of onions.

Perhaps it was that which gave him his first wave of nausea. He concealed it, becoming two people: one who had drunk too much and one who was now sexually excited. The robe fell shamelessly open over the girl's slight belly, the dark well of pubic hair, the white thighs that seduced him both by sight and pressure. His hand did not wander lower than her waist; but it wandered above, touching those open breasts, the neck, the shoulders. She made no advances after that first leading of his hand; she was his passive victim, her head resting on his shoulder, marble made warmth, an Etty nude, the Pygmalion myth brought to a happy end. Another wave of nausea came over him. She sensed it, but misinterpreted.

"I'm too 'eavy for you?"

"No . . . that is . . ."

"It's a nice bed. Soft."

She stood away from him, went to it and folded back the bedclothes carefully, then turned to look at him. She let the robe slip from her shoulders. She was well-formed, with shapely buttocks. A moment, then she sat and swung her legs under the bedclothes and lay back with her eyes closed, in what she transparently thought was a position both discreet and abandoned. A coal began to flicker brightly, casting intense but quavering shadows; a cage, the end-rails of the bed, danced on the wall behind her. Charles stood, fighting the battle in his stomach. It was the hock—he had been insane to drink it. He saw her eyes open and look at him. She hesitated, then reached out those delicate white arms. He made a gesture towards his frock coat.

After a few moments he felt a little better and began seriously to undress; he laid his clothes neatly, much more neatly than he ever did in his own room, over the back of the chair. He had to sit to unbutton his boots. He stared into the fire as he took off his trousers and the undergarment,

248

which reached, in the fashion of those days, somewhat below
his knees. But his shirt he could not bring himself to remove.
The nausea returned. He gripped the lace-fringed mantelpiece, his eyes closed, fighting for control.

This time she took his delay for shyness and threw back
the bedclothes as if to come and lead him to bed. He forced
himself to walk towards her. She sank back again, but without covering her body. He stood by the bed and stared down
at her. She reached out her arms. He still stared, conscious
only of the swimming sensation in his head, the now totally
rebellious fumes of the milk punch, champagne, claret, port,
that damnable hock . . .

"I don't know your name."

She smiled up at him, then reached for his hands and
pulled him down towards her.

"Sarah, sir."

He was racked by an intolerable spasm. Twisting sideways
he began to vomit into the pillow beside her shocked,
flungback head.

41

> . . . Arise and fly
> The reeling faun, the sensual feast;
> Move upward, working out the beast,
> And let the ape and tiger die.
>
> TENNYSON, *In Memoriam* (1850)

For the twenty-ninth time that morning Sam caught the
cook's eye, directed his own to a row of bells over the
kitchen door and then eloquently swept them up to the
ceiling. It was noon. One might have thought Sam glad to
have a morning off; but the only mornings off he coveted
were with more attractive female company than that of the
portly Mrs. Rogers.

" 'E's not 'imself," said the dowager, also for the twenty-
ninth time. If she felt irritated, however, it was with Sam,
not the young lord upstairs. Ever since their return from
Lyme two days before, the valet had managed to hint at dark
goings-on. It is true he had graciously communicated the

news about Winsyatt; but he had regularly added "And that ain't 'alf of what's a-foot." He refused to be drawn. "There's sartin confidences" (a word he pronounced with a long *i*) "as can't be yet spoken of, Mrs. R. But things 'as 'appened my heyes couldn't 'ardly believe they was seein'."

Sam had certainly one immediate subject for bitterness. Charles had omitted to dismiss him for the evening when he went out to see Mr. Freeman. Thus Sam had waited in and up until after midnight, only to be greeted, when he heard the front door open, by a black look from a white face.

"Why the devil aren't you in bed?"

" 'Cos you didn't say you was dinin' out, Mr. Charles."

"I've been at my club."

"Yes, sir."

"And take that insolent look off your damned face."

"Yes, sir."

Sam held out his hands and took—or caught—the various objects, beginning with sundry bits of outdoor apparel and terminating in a sulphurous glare, that Charles threw at him. Then the master marched majestically upstairs. His mind was now very sober, but his body was still a little drunk, a fact Sam's bitter but unseen smirk had only too plainly reflected.

"You're right, Mrs. R. 'E's not 'imself. 'E was blind drunk last night."

"I wouldn't 'ave believed it possible."

"There's lots o' things yours truly wouldn't 'ave believed possible, Mrs. R. As 'as 'appened hall the same."

" 'E never wants to cry off!"

"Wild 'osses wouldn't part my lips, Mrs. R." The cook took a deep-bosomed breath. Her clock ticked beside her range. Sam smiled at her. "But you're sharp, Mrs. R. Very sharp."

Clearly Sam's own feeling of resentment would very soon have accomplished what the wild horses were powerless to effect. But he was saved, and the buxom Mrs. Rogers thwarted, by the bell. Sam went and lifted the two-gallon can of hot water that had been patiently waiting all morning at the back of the range, winked at his colleague, and disappeared.

There are two kinds of hangover: in one you feel ill and incapable, in the other you feel ill and lucid. Charles had in fact been awake, indeed out of bed, some time before he rang. He had the second sort of hangover. He remembered only too clearly the events of the previous night.

His vomiting had driven the already precarious sexual element in that bedroom completely out of sight and mind. His unhappily named choice had hastily risen, pulled on her gown, and then proved herself to be as calm a nurse as she

250

had promised to be a prostitute. She got Charles to his chair by the fire, where he caught sight of the hock bottle, and was promptly sick again. But this time she had ready a basin from the washstand. Charles kept groaning his apologies between his retches.

"Most sorry . . . most unfortunate . . . something disagreed . . ."

"It's all right, sir, it's all right. You just let it come."

And let it come he had had to. She went and got her shawl and threw it round his shoulders. He sat for some time ludicrously like an old granny, crouched over the basin on his knees, his head bowed. After a while he began to feel a little better. Would he like to sleep? He would, but in his own bed. She went and looked down into the street, then left the room while he shakily got dressed. When she came back she herself had put on her clothes. He looked at her aghast.

"You are surely not. . . ?"

"Get you a cab, sir. If you just wait . . ."

"Ah yes . . . thank you."

And he sat down again, while she went downstairs and out of the house. Though he was by no means sure that his nausea was past, he felt in some psychological way profoundly relieved. Never mind what his intention had been; he had not committed the fatal deed. He stared into the glowing fire; and strange as it may seem, smiled wanly.

Then there came a low cry from the next room. A silence, then the sound came again, louder this time and more prolonged. The little girl had evidently wakened. Her crying—silence, wailing, choking, silence, wailing—became intolerable. Charles went to the window and opened the curtains. The mist prevented him seeing very far. There was not a soul to be seen. He realized how infrequent the sound of horses' hooves had become; and guessed that the girl might have to go some way to find his hansom. As he stood undecided, there was a heavy thumping on the wall from the next house. A vindictive male voice shouted angrily. Charles hesitated, then laying his hat and stick on the table, he opened the door through to that other room. He made out by the reflected light a wardrobe and an old box-trunk. The room was very small. In the far corner, beside a closed commode, was a small truckle bed. The child's cries, suddenly renewed, pierced the small room. Charles stood in the lit doorway, foolishly, a terrifying black giant.

"Hush now, hush. Your mother will soon return."

The strange voice, of course, only made things worse. Charles felt the whole neighborhood must wake, so penetrating were the screams. He struck his head in distress, then

251

stepped forward into the shadow beside the child. Seeing how small she was he realized words were useless. He bent over her and gently patted her head. Hot small fingers seized his, but the crying continued. The minute, contorted face ejected its great store of fear with bewildering force. Some desperate expedient had to be found. Charles found it. He groped for his watch, freed its chain from his waistcoat and dangled it over the child. The effect was immediate. The cries turned to mewling whimpers. Then the small arms reached up to grab the delicious silver toy; and were allowed to do so; then lost it in the bedclothes and struggled to sit and failed. The screams began again.

Charles reached to raise the child a little against her pillow. A temptation seized him. He lifted her out of the bed in her long nightgown, then turned and sat on the commode. Holding the small body on his knees he dandled the watch in front of the now eager small arms. She was one of those pudgy-faced Victorian children with little black beads for eyes; an endearing little turnip with black hair. And her instant change of mood, a gurgle of delight when at last she clasped the coveted watch, amused Charles. She began to lall. Charles muttered answers: yes, yes, very pretty, good little girl, pretty pretty. He had a vision of Sir Tom and the bishop's son coming on him at that moment ... the end of his great debauch. The strange dark labyrinths of life; the mystery of meetings.

He smiled; for it was less a sentimental tenderness that little child brought than a restoration of his sense of irony, which was in turn the equivalent of a kind of faith in himself. Earlier that evening, when he was in Sir Tom's brougham, he had had a false sense of living in the present; his rejection then of his past and future had been a mere vicious plunge into irresponsible oblivion. Now he had a far more profound and genuine intuition of the great human illusion about time, which is that its reality is like that of a road—on which one can constantly see where one was and where one probably will be—instead of the truth: that time is a room, a now so close to us that we regularly fail to see it.

Charles's was the very opposite of the Sartrean experience. The simple furniture around him, the warm light from the next room, the humble shadows, above all that small being he held on his knees, so insubstantial after its mother's weight (but he did not think at all of her), they were not encroaching and hostile objects, but constituting and friendly ones. The ultimate hell was infinite and empty space; and they kept it at bay. He felt suddenly able to face his future, which was only a form of that terrible emptiness. Whatever happened to him such moments would recur; must be found, and could be found.

A door opened. The prostitute stood in the light. Charles could not see her face, but he guessed that she was for a moment alarmed. And then relieved.

"Oh sir. Did she cry?"

"Yes. A little. I think she has gone back to sleep now."

"I 'ad to go down to the Warren Street stand. They was all off 'ere."

"You are very kind."

He passed her child to her, and watched her as she tucked it back into its bed; then abruptly turned and left the room. He felt in his pocket and counted out five sovereigns and left them on the table. The child had reawoken, and its mother was quietening it again. He hesitated, then silently left the room.

He was inside the waiting hansom when she came running down the steps and to the door. She stared up at him. Her look was almost puzzled, almost hurt.

"Oh sir . . . thank you. Thank you."

He realized that she had tears in her eyes; no shock to the poor like unearned money.

"You are a brave, kind girl."

He reached out and touched her hand where it clasped the front sill. Then he tapped with his stick.

42

> History is not like some individual person, which uses men to achieve its ends. History is nothing but the actions of men in pursuit of their ends.
>
> MARX, *Die Heilige Familie* (1845)

Charles, as we have learned, did not return to Kensington in quite so philanthropic a mood as he finally left the prostitute's. He had felt sick again during the hour's journey; and had had time to work up a good deal of self-disgust into the bargain. But he woke in a better frame of mind. As men will, he gave his hangover its due, and stared awfully at his haggard face and peered into his parched and acrid mouth; and then decided he was on the whole rather well able to face the world. He certainly faced Sam when he came in with the hot water, and made some sort of apology for his bad temper of the previous night.

"I didn't notice nuffink, Mr. Charles."

"I had a somewhat tiresome evening, Sam. And now be a good fellow and fetch me up a large pot of tea. I have the devil's own thirst."

Sam left, hiding his private opinion that his master had the devil's own something else as well. Charles washed and shaved, and thought about Charles. He was clearly not cut out to be a rake; but nor had he had much training in remorseful pessimism. Had not Mr. Freeman himself said that two years might pass before any decision as to his future need to be taken? Much could happen in two years. Charles did not actually say to himself, "My uncle may die"; but the idea hovered on the fringes of his mind. And then the carnal aspect of the previous night's experience reminded him that legitimate pleasures in that direction would soon be his to enjoy. For now he must abstain. And that child—how many of life's shortcomings children must make up for!

Sam returned with the tea—and with two letters. Life became a road again. He saw at once that the top envelope had been double postmarked; posted in Exeter and forwarded to Kensington from the White Lion in Lyme Regis. The other came direct from Lyme. He hesitated, then to allay suspicion picked up a paperknife and went to the window. He opened the letter from Grogan first; but before we read it, we must read the note Charles had sent on his return to Lyme that morning of his dawn walk to Carslake's Barn. It had said the following:

My dear Doctor Grogan,

I write in great haste to thank you for your invaluable advice and assistance last night, and to assure you once again that I shall be most happy to pay for any care or attentions your colleague and yourself may deem necessary. You will, I trust, and in full understanding that I have seen the folly of my misguided interest, let me know what transpires concerning the meeting that will have taken place when you read this.

Alas, I could not bring myself to broach the subject in Broad Street this morning. My somewhat sudden departure, and various other circumstances with which I will not now bother you, made the moment most conspicuously inopportune. The matter shall be dealt with as soon as I return. I must ask you meanwhile to keep it to yourself.

I leave immediately. My London address is below. With profound gratitude,

C.S.

It had not been an honest letter. But it had had to be
written. Now Charles nervously unfolded the reply to it.

My dear Smithson,

I have delayed writing to you in the hope of obtaining some
éclaircissement of our little Dorset mystery. I regret to say that
the only female I encountered on the morning of my expedition
was Mother Nature—a lady whose conversation I began, after
some three hours' waiting, to find a trifle tedious. In short, the
person did not appear. On my return to Lyme I sent out a sharp
lad to do duty for me. But he too sat *sub tegmine fagi* in pleasant
solitude. I pen these words lightly, yet I confess that when the lad
returned that nightfall I began to fear the worst.

However, it came to my ears the next morning that instructions
had been left at the White Lion for the girl's box to be forwarded
to Exeter. The author of the instructions I cannot discover. No
doubt she sent the message herself. I think we may take it she has
decamped.

My one remaining fear, my dear Smithson, is that she may follow you to London and attempt to thrust her woes upon you there.
I beg you not to dismiss this contingency with a smile. If I had
time I could cite you other cases where just such a course has been
followed. I enclose an address. He is an excellent man, with whom
I have long been in correspondence, and I advise you most strongly
to put the business in his hands should further embarrassment
come *à la lettre* knocking on your door.

Rest assured that no word has passed or shall pass my lips. I
shall not repeat my advice regarding the *charming creature*—
whom I had the pleasure of meeting in the street just now, by the
bye—but I recommend a confession at the earliest opportunity. I
don't fancy the *Absolvitur* will require too harsh or long a penance.

Yr very sincere
MICHAEL GROGAN

Charles had drawn a breath of guilty relief long before he
finished that letter. He was not discovered. He stared a long
moment out of his bedroom window, then opened the second
letter.

He expected pages, but there was only one.

He expected a flood of words, but there were only three.

An address.

He crumpled the sheet of paper in his hand, then returned
to the fire that had been lit by the upstairs maid, to the
accompaniment of his snores, at eight o'clock that morning,
and threw it into the flames. In five seconds it was ashes. He

took the cup of tea that Sam stood waiting to hand to him. Charles drained it at one gulp, and passed the cup and saucer for more.

"I have done my business, Sam. We return to Lyme tomorrow. The ten o'clock train. You will see to the tickets. And take those two messages on my desk to the telegraph office. And then you may have the afternoon off to choose some ribbons for the fair Mary—that is, if you haven't disposed of your heart elsewhere since our return."

Sam had been waiting for that cue. He flicked a glance at his master's back as he refilled the gilt breakfast cup; and made his announcement as he extended the cup on a small silver tray to Charles's reaching fingers.

"Mr. Charles, I'm a-goin' to hask for 'er 'and."

"Are you indeed!"

"Or I would, Mr. Charles, if it weren't I didn't 'ave such hexcellent prospecks under your hemploy."

Charles supped his tea.

"Out with it, Sam. Stop talking riddles."

"If I was merrid I'd 'ave to live out, sir."

Charles's sharp look of instinctive objection showed how little he had thought about the matter. He turned and sat by his fire.

"Now, Sam, heaven forbid that I should be an impediment to your marriage—but surely you're not going to forsake me so soon before mine?"

"You mistake my hintention, Mr. Charles. I was a-thinkin' of harterwards."

"We shall be in a much larger establishment. I'm sure my wife would be happy to have Mary there with her . . . so what is the trouble?"

Sam took a deep breath.

"I've been thinkin' of goin' into business, Mr. Charles. When you're settled, that is, Mr. Charles. I 'ope you know I should never leave you in the hower of need."

"Business! What business?"

"I've set my 'eart on 'aving a little shop, Mr. Charles."

Charles placed the cup back on the speedily proffered salver.

"But don't you . . . I mean, you know, some of the ready?"

"I 'ave made heekomonies, Mr. Charles. And so's my Mary."

"Yes, yes, but there is rent to pay and heavens above, man, goods to buy . . . What sort of business?"

"Draper's and 'aberdasher's, Mr. Charles."

Charles stared at Sam rather as if the Cockney had decided to turn Buddhist. But he recalled one or two little past

incidents; that *penchant* for the genteelism; and the one
aspect of his present profession where Sam had never given
cause for complaint was in his care of clothes. Charles had
indeed more than once (about ten thousand times, to be
exact) made fun of him for his personal vanity in that
direction.

"And you've put by enough to—"

"Halas no, Mr. Charles. We'd 'ave to save very 'ard."

There was a pregnant silence. Sam was busy with milk and
sugar. Charles rubbed the side of his nose in a rather Sam-
like manner. He twigged. He took the third cup of tea.

"How much?"

"I know a shop as I'd like, Mr. Charles. 'E wants an
'undred an' fifty pound for the goodwill and an 'undred for
the stock. An' there's thirty pound rent to be found." He
sized Charles up, then went on, "It ain't I'm not very 'appy
with you, Mr. Charles. On'y a shop's what I halways fancied."

"And how much have you put by?"

Sam hesitated.

"Thirty pound, sir."

Charles did not smile, but went and stood at his bedroom
window.

"How long has it taken you to save that?"

"Three years, sir."

Ten pounds a year may not seem much; but it was a third
of three years' wages, as Charles rapidly calculated; and
made proportionally a much better showing in the thrift line
than Charles himself could have offered. He glanced back at
Sam, who stood meekly waiting—but waiting for what?—by
the side table with the tea things. In the silence that followed
Charles entered upon his first fatal mistake, which was to
give Sam his sincere opinion of the project. Perhaps it was in
a very small way a bluff, a pretending not even faintly to
suspect the whiff of for-services-rendered in Sam's approach;
but it was far more an assumption of the ancient responsibility—and not quite synonymous with sublime arrogance—of
the infallible master for the fallible underling.

"I warn you, Sam, once you take ideas above your station
you will have nothing but unhappiness. You'll be miserable
without a shop. And doubly miserable with it." Sam's head
sunk a fraction lower. "And besides, Sam, I'm used to you
... fond of you. I'm damned if I want to lose you."

"I know, Mr. Charles. Your feelings is 'ighly reproskitated.
With respeck, sir."

"Well then. We're happy with each other. Let us continue
that way."

257

Sam bowed his head and turned to pick up the tea things. His disappointment was flagrant; he was Hope Abandoned, Life Cut Short, Virtue Unrewarded, and a dozen other moping statues.

"Now, Sam spare me the whipped dog. If you marry this girl then of course you must have a married man's wages. And something to set you up. I shall do handsomely by you, rest assured of that."

"That's very kind hindeed of you, Mr. Charles." But the voice was sepulchral, those statues in no way demolished. Charles saw himself a moment from Sam's eyes. He had been seen in their years together to spend a great deal of money; Sam must know he had a great deal more money coming to him on his marriage; and he might not unnaturally—that is, with innocent motive—have come to believe that two or three hundred pounds was not much to ask for.

"Sam, you must not think me ungenerous. The fact is ... well, the reason I went to Winsyatt is that ... well, Sir Robert is going to get married."

"No, sir! Sir Robert! Never!"

Sam's surprise makes one suspect that his real ambition should have been in the theater. He did everything but drop the tray that he was carrying; but this was of course *ante* Stanislavski. Charles faced the window and went on.

"Which means, Sam, that at a time when I have already considerable expense to meet I haven't much to spare."

"I 'ad no idea, Mr. Charles. Why ... I can't 'ardly believe— at 'is hage!"

Charles hastily stopped the impending commiseration. "We must wish Sir Robert every happiness. But there it is. It will soon all be public knowledge. However, Sam—you will say nothing of this."

"Oh Mr. Charles—you knows I knows 'ow to keep a secret."

Charles did give a sharp look round at Sam then, but his servant's eyes were modestly down again. Charles wished desperately that he could see them. But they remained averted from his keen gaze; and drove him into his second fatal mistake—for Sam's despair had come far less from being rebuffed than from suspecting his master had no guilty secret upon which he could be levered.

"Sam, I ... that is, when I'm married, circumstances will be easier ... I don't wish to dash your hopes completely—let me think on it."

In Sam's heart a little flame of exultation leaped into life. He had done it; a lever existed.

"Mr. Charles, sir, I wish I 'adn't spoke. I 'ad no idea."

258

"No, no. I am glad you brought this up. I will perhaps ask Mr. Freeman's advice if I find an opportunity. No doubt he knows what is to be said for such a venture."

"Pure gold, Mr. Charles, pure gold—that's 'ow I'd treat any words of hadvice from that gentleman's mouth."

With this hyperbole Sam left. Charles stared at the closed door. He began to wonder if there wasn't something of a Uriah Heep beginning to erupt on the surface of Sam's personality; a certain duplicity. He had always aped the gentleman in his clothes and manners; and now there was vaguely something else about the spurious gentleman he was aping. It was such an age of change! So many orders beginning to melt and dissolve.

He remained staring for several moments—but then bah! What would granting Sam his wish matter with Ernestina's money in the bank? He turned to his escritoire and unlocked a drawer. From it he drew a pocketbook and scribbled something: no doubt a reminder to speak to Mr. Freeman.

Meanwhile, downstairs, Sam was reading the contents of the two telegrams. One was to the White Lion, informing the landlord of their return. The other read:

> MISS FREEMAN AT MRS. TRANTER'S, BROAD
> STREET, LYME REGIS. MY IMMEDIATE RETURN
> HAS BEEN COMMANDED AND WILL BE MOST
> HAPPILY OBEYED BY YOUR MOST AFFECTIONATE
> CHARLES SMITHSON.

In those days only the uncouth Yankees descended to telegraphese.

This was not the first private correspondence that had been under Sam's eyes that morning. The envelope of the second letter he had brought to Charles had been gummed but not sealed. A little steam does wonders; and Sam had had a whole morning in which to find himself alone for a minute in that kitchen.

Perhaps you have begun to agree with Charles about Sam. He is not revealing himself the most honest of men, that must be said. But the thought of marriage does strange things. It makes the intending partners suspect an inequality in things; it makes them wish they had more to give to each other; it kills the insouciance of youth; its responsibilities isolate, and the more altruistic aspects of the social contract are dimmed. It is easier, in short, to be dishonest for two than for one. Sam did not think of his procedure as dishonest; he called it "playing your cards right." In simple terms it meant now that the marriage with Ernestina must go through; only from her dowry could he hope for his two hundred and fifty pounds; if more spooning between the master and the wicked woman of Lyme were to take place, it must take place under the cardplayer's sharp nose—and might not be altogether a bad thing, since the more guilt Charles had the surer touch he became; but if it went too far ... Sam sucked his lower lip and frowned. It was no wonder he was beginning to feel rather above his station; matchmakers always have.

43

Yet I thought I saw her stand,
A shadow there at my feet,
High over the shadowy land.
TENNYSON, *Maud* (1855)

Perhaps one can find more color for the myth of a rational human behavior in an iron age like the Victorian than in most others. Charles had certainly decided, after his night of rebellion, to go through with his marriage to Ernestina. It had never seriously entered his mind that he would not; Ma Terpsichore's and the prostitute had but been, unlikely though it may seem, confirmations of that intention—last petulant doubts of a thing concluded, last questionings of the unquestionable. He had said as much to himself on his queasy return home, which may explain the rough treatment Sam received. As for Sarah ... the other Sarah had been her surrogate, her sad and sordid end, and his awakening.

For all that, he could have wished her letter had shown a clearer guilt—that she had asked for money (but she could hardly have spent ten pounds in so short a time), or poured out her illicit feelings for him. But it is difficult to read either passion or despair into the three words. "Endicott's Family Hotel"; and not even a date, an initial! It was certainly an act of disobedience, a by-passing of Aunt Tranter; but she could hardly be arraigned for knocking on his door.

It was easy to decide that the implicit invitation must be ignored: he must never see her again. But perhaps Sarah the prostitute had reminded Charles of the uniqueness of Sarah the outcast: that total absence of finer feeling in the one only affirmed its astonishing survival in the other. How shrewd and sensitive she was, in her strange way . . . some of those things she had said after her confession—they haunted one.

He thought a great deal—if recollection is thought—about Sarah on the long journey down to the West. He could not but feel that to have committed her to an institution, however enlightened, would have been a betrayal. I say "her," but the pronoun is one of the most terrifying masks man has invented; what came to Charles was not a pronoun, but eyes, looks, the line of the hair over a temple, a nimble step, a sleeping face. All this was not daydreaming, of course; but earnest consideration of a moral problem and caused by an augustly pure solicitude for the unfortunate woman's future welfare.

The train drew into Exeter. Sam appeared, within a brief pause of its final stopping whistle, at the window of the compartment; he of course had traveled in the third class.

"Are we stayin' the night, Mr. Charles?"

"No. A carriage. A four-wheeler. It looks like rain."

Sam had bet himself a thousand pounds that they would stay in Exeter. But he obeyed without hesitation, just as his master had, at the sight of Sam's face, decided—and somewhere deep in him a decision had remained to take—without hesitation on his course of action. It was really Sam that had determined it: Charles could not face any more prevarication.

It was only when they were already drawing through the eastern outskirts of the city that Charles felt a sense of sadness and of loss, of having now cast the fatal die. It seemed to him astounding that one simple decision, one answer to a trivial question, should determine so much. Until that moment, all had been potential; now all was inexorably fixed. He had done the moral, the decent, the correct thing; and yet it seemed to betray in him some inherent weakness, some willingness to accept his fate, which he knew, by one of those premonitions that are as certain as facts, would one day lead him into the world of commerce; into pleasing Ernestina because she would want to please her father, to whom he owed so much . . . he stared at the countryside they had now entered and felt himself sucked slowly through it as if down some monstrous pipe.

The carriage rolled on, a loosened spring creaking a little at each jolt, as mournfully as a tumbril. The evening sky was overcast and it had begun to drizzle. In such circumstances, traveling on his own, Charles would usually have called Sam down and let him sit inside. But he could not face Sam (not that Sam, who saw nothing but gold on the wet road to Lyme, minded the ostracism). It was as if he would never have solitude again. What little was left, he must enjoy. He thought again of the woman he had left in the city behind them. He thought of her not, of course, as an alternative to Ernestina; nor as someone he might, had he chosen, have married instead. That would never have been possible. Indeed it was hardly Sarah he now thought of—she was merely the symbol around which had accreted all his lost possibilities, his extinct freedoms, his never-to-be-taken journeys. He had to say farewell to something; she was merely and conveniently both close and receding.

There was no doubt. He was one of life's victims, one more ammonite caught in the vast movements of history, stranded now for eternity, a potential turned to a fossil.

After a while he committed the ultimate weakness: he fell asleep.

44

> Duty—that's to say complying
>   With whate'er's expected here . . .
> With the form conforming duly,
> Senseless what it meaneth truly . . .
> 'Tis the stern and prompt suppressing,
>   As an obvious deadly sin,
> All the questing and the guessing
>   Of the soul's own soul within:
> 'Tis the coward acquiescence
>   In a destiny's behest . . .
>
> A. H. CLOUGH, "Duty" (1841)

They arrived at the White Lion just before ten that night. The lights were still on in Aunt Tranter's house; a curtain moved as they passed. Charles performed a quick toilet and leaving Sam to unpack, strode manfully up the hill. Mary was overjoyed to see him; Aunt Tranter, just behind her, was pinkly wreathed in welcoming smiles. She had had strict orders to remove herself as soon as she had greeted the traveler: there was to be no duenna nonsense that evening. Ernestina, with her customary estimation of her own dignity, had remained in the back sitting room.

She did not rise when Charles entered, but gave him a long reproachful look from under her eyelashes. He smiled.

"I forgot to buy flowers in Exeter."

"So I see, sir."

"I was in such haste to be here before you went to bed."

She cast down her eyes and watched her hands, which were engaged in embroidery. Charles moved closer, and the hands rather abruptly stopped work and turned over the small article at which they were working.

"I see I have a rival."

"You deserve to have many."

He knelt beside her and gently raised one of her hands and kissed it. She slipped a little look at him.

"I haven't slept a minute since you went away."

"I can see that by your pallid cheeks and swollen eyes."

She would not smile. "Now you make fun of me."

"If this is what insomnia does to you I shall arrange to have an alarm bell ringing perpetually in our bedroom."

She blushed. Charles rose and sat beside her and drew her head round and kissed her mouth and then her closed eyes, which after being thus touched opened and stared into his, every atom of dryness gone.

He smiled. "Now let me see what you are embroidering for your secret admirer."

She held up her work. It was a watch pocket, in blue velvet—one of those little pouches Victorian gentlemen hung by their dressing tables and put their watches in at night. On the hanging flap there was embroidered a white heart with the initials C and E on either side; on the face of the pouch was begun, but not finished, a couplet in gold thread. Charles read it out loud.

" 'Each time thy watch thou wind' . . . and how the deuce is that to finish?"

"You must guess."

Charles stared at the blue velvet.

" 'Thy wife her teeth will grind'?"

She snatched it out of sight.

"Now I shan't tell. You are no better than a cad." A "cad" in those days meant an omnibus conductor, famous for their gift of low repartee.

"Who would never ask a fare of one so fair."

"False flattery and feeble puns are equally detestable."

"And you, my dearest, are adorable when you are angry."

"Then I shall forgive you—just to be horrid."

She turned a little away from him then, though his arm remained around her waist and the pressure of his hand on

263

hers was returned. They remained in silence a few moments. He kissed her hand once more.

"I may walk with you tomorrow morning? And we'll show the world what fashionable lovers we are, and look bored, and quite unmistakably a marriage of convenience?"

She smiled; then impulsively disclosed the watch pocket.

" 'Each time thy watch thou wind, Of love may I thee remind.' "

"My sweetest."

He gazed into her eyes a moment longer, then felt in his pocket and placed on her lap a small hinged box in dark-red morocco.

"Flowers of a kind."

Shyly she pressed the little clasp back and opened the box; on a bed of crimson velvet lay an elegant Swiss brooch: a tiny oval mosaic of a spray of flowers, bordered by alternate pearls and fragments of coral set in gold. She looked dewily at Charles. He helpfully closed his eyes. She turned and leaned and planted a chaste kiss softly on his lips; then lay with her head on his shoulder, and looked again at the brooch, and kissed that.

Charles remembered the lines of that priapic song. He whispered in her ear. "I wish tomorrow were our wedding day."

It was simple: one lived by irony and sentiment, one observed convention. What might have been was one more subject for detached and ironic observation; as was what might be. One surrendered, in other words; one learned to be what one was.

Charles pressed the girl's arm. "Dearest, I have a small confession to make. It concerns that miserable female at Marlborough House."

She sat up a little, pertly surprised, already amused. "Not poor Tragedy?"

He smiled. "I fear the more vulgar appellation is better suited." He pressed her hand. "It is really most stupid and trivial. What happened was merely this. During one of my little pursuits of the elusive echinoderm . . ."

And so ends the story. What happened to Sarah, I do not know—whatever it was, she never troubled Charles again in person, however long she may have lingered in his memory. This is what most often happens. People sink out of sight, drown in the shadows of closer things.

Charles and Ernestina did not live happily ever after; but they lived together, though Charles finally survived her by a decade (and earnestly mourned her throughout it). They begat what shall it be—let us say seven children. Sir Robert added injury to insult by siring, and within ten months of his alliance to Mrs. Bella Tomkins, not one heir, but two. This fatal pair of twins were what finally drove Charles into business. He was bored to begin with; and then got a taste for the thing. His own sons were given no choice; and their sons today still control the great shop and all its ramifications.

Sam and Mary—but who can be bothered with the biography of servants? They married, and bred, and died, in the monotonous fashion of their kind.

Now who else? Dr. Grogan? He died in his ninety-first year. Since Aunt Tranter also lived into her nineties, we have clear proof of the amiability of the fresh Lyme air.

It cannot be all-effective, though, since Mrs. Poulteney died within two months of Charles's last return to Lyme. Here, I am happy to say, I can summon up enough interest to look into the future—that is, into her after-life. Suitably dressed in black, she arrived in her barouche at the Heavenly Gates. Her footman—for naturally, as in ancient Egypt, her whole household had died with her—descended and gravely opened the carriage door. Mrs. Poulteney mounted the steps and after making a mental note to inform the Creator (when she knew Him better) that His domestics should be more on the alert for important callers, pulled the bellring. The butler at last appeared.

"Ma'am?"

"I am Mrs. Poulteney. I have come to take up residence. Kindly inform your Master."

"His Infinitude has been informed of your decease, ma'm. His angels have already sung a Jubilate in celebration of the event."

"That is most proper and kind of Him." And the worthy lady, pluming and swelling, made to sweep into the imposing white hall she saw beyond the butler's head. But the man did not move aside. Instead he rather impertinently jangled some keys he chanced to have in his hand.

"My man! Make way. I am she. Mrs. Poulteney of Lyme Regis."

"Formerly of Lyme Regis, ma'm. And now of a much more tropical abode."

With that, the brutal flunkey slammed the door in her face. Mrs. Poulteney's immediate reaction was to look round, for fear her domestics might have overheard this scene. But her carriage, which she had thought to hear draw away to the servants' quarters, had mysteriously disappeared. In fact everything had disappeared, road and landscape (rather resembling the Great Drive up to Windsor Castle, for some peculiar reason), all, all had vanished. There was nothing but space—and horror of horrors, a devouring space. One by one, the steps up which Mrs. Poulteney had so imperially mounted began also to disappear. Only three were left; and then only two; then one. Mrs. Poulteney stood on nothing. She was most distinctly heard to say "Lady Cotton is behind this"; and then she fell, flouncing and bannering and ballooning, like a shot crow, down to where her real master waited.

45

And ah for a man to arise in me,
That the man I am may cease to be!
TENNYSON, *Maud* (1855)

And now, having brought this fiction to a thoroughly traditional ending, I had better explain that although all I have described in the last two chapters happened, it did not happen quite in the way you may have been led to believe.

I said earlier that we are all poets, though not many of us write poetry; and so are we all novelists, that is, we have a habit of writing fictional futures for ourselves, although perhaps today we incline more to put ourselves into a film. We screen in our minds hypotheses about how we might behave, about what might happen to us; and these novelistic or cinematic hypotheses often have very much more effect on how we actually do behave, when the real future becomes the present, than we generally allow.

Charles was no exception; and the last few pages you have read are not what happened, but what he spent the hours between London and Exeter imagining might happen. To be sure he did not think in quite the detailed and coherent narrative manner I have employed; nor would I swear that he followed Mrs. Poulteney's postmortal career in quite such interesting detail. But he certainly wished her to the Devil, so it comes to almost the same thing.

Above all he felt himself coming to the end of a story; and to an end he did not like. If you noticed in those last two chapters an abruptness, a lack of consonance, a betrayal of

266

Charles's deeper potentiality and a small matter of his being given a life span of very nearly a century and a quarter; if you entertained a suspicion, not uncommon in literature, that the writer's breath has given out and he has rather arbitrarily ended the race while he feels he's still winning, then do not blame me; because all these feelings, or reflections of them, were very present in Charles's own mind. The book of his existence, so it seemed to him, was about to come to a distinctly shabby close.

And the "I," that entity who found such slickly specious reasons for consigning Sarah to the shadows of oblivion, was not myself; it was merely the personification of a certain massive indifference in things—too hostile for Charles to think of as "God"—that had set its malevolent inertia on the Ernestina side of the scales; that seemed an inexorable onward direction as fixed as that of the train which drew Charles along.

I was not cheating when I said that Charles had decided, in London that day after his escapade, to go through with his marriage; that was his official decision, just as it had once been his official decision (reaction might be a more accurate word) to go into Holy Orders. Where I have cheated was in analyzing the effect that three-word letter continued to have on him. It tormented him, it obsessed him, it confused him. The more he thought about it the more Sarah-like that sending of the address—and nothing more—appeared. It was perfectly in key with all her other behavior, and to be described only by oxy-moron; luring-receding, subtle-simple, proud-begging, defending-accusing. The Victorian was a pro-ix age; and unaccustomed to the Delphic.

But above all it seemed to set Charles a choice; and while one part of him hated having to choose, we come near the secret of his state on that journey west when we know that another part of him felt intolerably excited by the proximity of the moment of choice. He had not the benefit of existentialist terminology; but what he felt was really a very clear case of the anxiety of freedom—that is, the realization that one *is* free and the realization that being free is a situation of terror.

So let us kick Sam out of his hypothetical future and back into his Exeter present. He goes to his master's compartment when the train stops.

"Are we stayin' the night, sir?"

Charles stares at him a moment, a decision still to make, and looks over his head at the overcast sky.

"I fancy it will rain. We'll put up at the Ship."

And so Sam, a thousand unpossessed pounds richer, stood

a few minutes later with his master outside the station, watching the loading of Charles's impedimenta on to the roof of a tired fly. Charles showed a decided restlessness. The portmanteau was at last tied down, and all waited on him.

"I think, Sam, after that confounded train journey, I will stretch my legs. Do you go on with the baggage."

Sam's heart sank.

"With respeck, Mr. Charles, I wouldn't. Not with them rainclouds up there about to break."

"A little rain won't hurt me."

Sam swallowed, bowed.

"Yes, Mr. Charles. Shall I give horders for dinner?"

"Yes . . . that is . . . I'll see when I come in. I may attend Evensong at the Cathedral."

Charles set off up the hill towards the city. Sam watched him gloomily on his way for a little while, then turned to the cabby.

"Eh—'eard of Hendicott's Family 'Otel?"

"Aye."

"Know where it is?"

"Aye."

"Well, you dolly me up to the Ship double quick and you may 'ear somethink to your hadvantage, my man."

And with a suitable aplomb Sam got into the carriage. It very soon overtook Charles, who walked with a flagrant slowness, as if taking the air. But as soon as it had gone out of sight he quickened his pace.

Sam had plenty of experience of dealing with sleepy provincial inns. The luggage was unloaded, the best available rooms chosen, a fire lit, nightwear laid out with other necessities—and all in seven minutes. Then he strode sharply out into the street, where the cabby still waited. A short further journey took place. From inside Sam looked cautiously round, then descended and paid off his driver.

"First left you'll find 'un, sir."

"Thank you, my man. 'Ere's a couple o' browns for you." And with this disgracefully mean tip (even for Exeter) Sam tipped his bowler over his eyes and melted away into the dusk. Halfway down the street he was in, and facing the one the cabby had indicated, stood a Methodist Chapel, with imposing columns under its pediment. Behind one of these the embryo detective installed himself. It was now nearly night, come early under a gray-black sky.

Sam did not have to wait long. His heart leaped as a tall figure came into sight. Evidently at a loss the figure addressed himself to a small boy. The boy promptly led the way to the corner below Sam's viewpoint, and pointed, a gesture that

268

arned him, to judge by his grin, rather more than twopence.

Charles's back receded. Then he stopped and looked up. He retraced a few steps back towards Sam. Then as if impatient with himself he turned again and entered one of the houses. Sam slipped from behind his pillar and ran down the steps and across to the street in which Endicott's Family stood. He waited a while on the corner. But Charles did not reappear. Sam became bolder and lounged casually along the warehouse wall that faced the row of houses. He came to where he could see the hallway of the hotel. It was empty. Several rooms had lights. Some fifteen minutes passed and it began to rain.

Sam bit his nails for a while, in furious thought. Then he began to walk quickly away.

46

As yet, when all is thought and said,
The heart still overrules the head;
Still what we hope we must believe,
And what is given us receive;

Must still believe, for still we hope
That in a world of larger scope,
What here is faithfully begun
Will be completed, not undone.

My child, we still must think, when we
That ampler life together see,
Some true results will yet appear
Of what we are, together, here.

                              A. H. CLOUGH, Poem (1849)

Charles hesitated in the shabby hall, then knocked on the door of a room that was ajar and from which light came. He was bade enter, and so found himself face to face with the proprietress. Much quicker than he summed her up, she summed him: a fifteen-shillinger beyond mistake. Therefore she smiled gratefully.

"A room, sir?"

"No. I . . . that is, I wish to speak with one of your . . . a Miss Woodruff?" Mrs. Endicott's smile abruptly gave way to a long face. Charles's heart dropped. "She is not. . . ?"

"Oh the poor young lady, sir, she was a-coming downstairs the day before yesterday morning and she slipped, sir. She' turned her ankle something horrible. Swole up big as a marrow. I wanted to ask the doctor, sir, but she won't hear of it 'Tis true a turned ankle mends itself. And physicians come very expensive."

Charles looked at the end of his cane. "Then I cannot see her."

"Oh bless me, you can go up, sir. 'Twill raise her spirits You'll be some relative, I daresay?"

"I have to see her . . . on a business matter."

Mrs. Endicott's respect deepened. "Ah . . . a gentleman o the law?"

Charles hesitated, then said, "Yes."

"Then you must go up, sir."

"I think . . . would you please send to ask if my visit were not better put off till she is recovered?"

He felt very much at a loss. He remembered Varguennes sin was to meet in privacy. He had come merely to inquire had hoped for a downstairs sitting room—somewhere both intimate and public. The old woman hesitated, then cast a quick eye at a certain open box beside her rolltop desk and apparently decided that even lawyers can be thieves—a possibility few who have had to meet their fees would dispute Without moving and with a surprising violence she called for one Betty Anne.

Betty Anne appeared and was sent off with a visiting card She seemed gone some time, during which Charles had to repel a number of inquisitive attempts to discover his errand At last Betty Anne came back: he was prayed to go up. He followed the plump maid's back to the top floor and was shown the scene of the accident. The stairs were certainly steep; and in those days, when they could rarely see their own feet, women were always falling: it was a commonplace of domestic life.

They came to a door at the end of a mournful corridor Charles, his heart beating far faster than even the three flights of steep stairs had warranted, was brusquely announced.

"The gennelmun, miss."

He stepped into the room. Sarah was seated by the fire in

chair facing the door, her feet on a stool, with both them
nd her legs covered by a red Welsh blanket. The green
erino shawl was round her shoulders, but could not quite
de the fact that she was in a long-sleeved nightgown. Her
air was loose and fell over her green shoulders. She seemed
› him much smaller—and agonizingly shy. She did not
nile, but looked down at her hands—only, as he first came
, one swift look up, like a frightened penitent, sure of his
nger, before she bowed her head again. He stood with his
at in one hand, his stick and gloves in the other.

"I was passing through Exeter."

Her head bowed a fraction deeper in a mingled under-
anding and shame.

"Had I not better go at once and fetch a doctor?"

She spoke into her lap. "Please not. He would only advise
1e to do what I am already doing."

He could not take his eyes from her—to see her so
inioned, so invalid (though her cheeks were a deep pink),
elpless. And after that eternal indigo dress—the green
1awl, the never before fully revealed richness of that hair. A
1int cedary smell of liniment crept into Charles's nostrils.

"You are not in pain?"

She shook her head. "To do such a thing . . . I cannot
nderstand how I should be so foolish."

"At any rate be thankful that it did not happen in the
'ndercliff."

"Yes."

She seemed hopelessly abashed by his presence. He glanced
ound the small room. A newly made-up fire burned in the
rate. There were some tired stems of narcissus in a Toby jug
n the mantelpiece. But the meanness of the furnishing was
ainfully obvious, and an added embarrassment. On the ceil-
1g were blackened patches—fumes from the oil lamp; like
› many spectral relics of countless drab past occupants of
1e room.

"Perhaps I should . . ."

"No. Please. Sit down. Forgive me. I . . . I did not expect
. ."

He placed his things on the chest of drawers, then sat at
he only other, a wooden chair by the table, across the room
rom her. How should she expect, in spite of her letter, what
.e had himself so firmly ruled out of the question? He sought
or some excuse.

"You have communicated your address to Mrs. Tranter?"

She shook her head. Silence. Charles stared at the carpet.

"Only to myself?"

Again her head bowed. He nodded gravely, as if he had

guessed as much. And then there was more silence. An angry flurry of rain spattered against the panes of the window behind her.

Charles said, "That is what I have come to discuss."

She waited, but he did not go on. Again his eyes were fixed on her. The nightgown buttoned high at the neck and at her wrists. Its whiteness shimmered rose in the firelight, for the lamp on the table beside him was not turned up very high. And her hair, already enhanced by the green shawl, was ravishingly alive where the firelight touched it; as if all her mystery, this most intimate self, was exposed before him proud and submissive, bound and unbound, his slave and his equal. He knew why he had come: it was to see her again. Seeing her was the need; like an intolerable thirst that had to be assuaged.

He forced himself to look away. But his eyes lighted on the two naked marble nymphs above the fireplace: they too took rose in the warm light reflected from the red blanket. They did not help. And Sarah made a little movement. He had to look back to her.

She had raised her hand quickly to her bowed head. Her fingers brushed something away from her cheek, then came to rest on her throat.

"My dear Miss Woodruff, pray don't cry . . . I should not have not come . . . I meant not to . . ."

But she shook her head with a sudden vehemence. He gave her time to recover. And it was while she made little dabbing motions with a handkerchief that he was overcome with a violent sexual desire; a lust a thousand times greater than anything he had felt in the prostitute's room. Her defenseless weeping was perhaps the breach through which the knowledge sprang—but suddenly he comprehended why her face haunted him, why he felt this terrible need to see her again: it was to possess her, to burn into her, to burn, to burn to ashes on that body and in those eyes. To postpone such desire for a week, a month, a year, several years even, that can be done. But for eternity is when the iron bites.

Her next words, to explain her tears, were barely audible.

"I thought never to see you again."

He could not tell her how close she had come to his own truth. She looked up at him and he as quickly looked down. Those same mysterious syncopal symptoms as in the barn swept over him. His heart raced, his hand trembled. He knew if he looked into those eyes he was lost. As if to ban them he shut his own.

The silence was terrible then, as tense as a bridge about to break, a tower to fall; unendurable in its emotion, its truth.

272

bursting to be spoken. Then suddenly there was a little cascade of coals from the fire. Most fell inside the low guard, but one or two bounced off and onto the edge of the blanket that covered Sarah's legs. She jerked it hastily away as Charles knelt quickly and seized the small shovel from the brass bucket. The coals on the carpet were quickly replaced. But the blanket smoldered. He snatched it away from her and throwing it on the ground hastily stamped out the sparks. A smell of singed wool filled the room. One of Sarah's legs still rested on the stool, but she had put the other to the ground. Both feet were bare. He looked down at the blanket, made sure with one or two slaps of his hand that it no longer smoldered, then turned and placed it across her legs once more. He was bent close, his eyes on the arranging. And then, as if by an instinctive gesture, yet one she half dared to calculate, her hand reached shyly out and rested on his. He knew she was looking up at him. He could not move his hand, and suddenly he could not keep his eyes from hers.

There was gratitude in them, and all the old sadness, and a strange concern, as if she knew she was hurting him; but above all she was waiting. Infinitely timid, yet waiting. If there had been the faintest smile on her lips, perhaps he would have remembered Dr. Grogan's theory; but this was a face that seemed almost self-surprised, as lost as himself. How long they looked into each other's eyes he did not know. It seemed an eternity, though in reality it was no more than three or four seconds. Their hands acted first. By some mysterious communion, the fingers interlaced. Then Charles fell on one knee and strained her passionately to him. Their mouths met with a wild violence that shocked both; made her avert her lips. He covered her cheeks, her eyes, with kisses. His hand at last touched that hair, caressed it, felt the small head through its softness, as the thin-clad body was felt against his arms and breast. Suddenly he buried his face in her neck.

"We must not . . . we must not . . . this is madness."

But her arms came round him and pressed his head closer. He did not move. He felt borne on wings of fire, hurtling, but in such tender air, like a child at last let free from school, a prisoner in a green field, a hawk rising. He raised his head and looked at her: an almost savage fierceness. Then they kissed again. But he pressed against her with such force that the chair rolled back a little. He felt her flinch with pain as the bandaged foot fell from the stool. He looked back to it, then at her face, her closed eyes. She turned her head away against the back of the chair, almost as if he repelled her; but her bosom seemed to arch imperceptibly towards him

273

and her hands gripped his convulsively. He glanced at the door behind her; then stood and in two strides was at it.

The bedroom was not lit except by the dusk light and the faint street lamps opposite. But he saw the gray bed, the washstand. Sarah stood awkwardly from the chair, supporting herself against its back, the injured foot lifted from the ground, one end of the shawl fallen from her shoulders. Each reflected the intensity in each other's eyes, the flood, the being swept before it. She seemed to half step, half fall towards him. He sprang forward and caught her in his arms and embraced her. The shawl fell. No more than a layer of flannel lay between him and her nakedness. He strained that body into his, straining his mouth upon hers, with all the hunger of a long frustration—not merely sexual, for a whole ungovernable torrent of things banned, romance, adventure, sin, madness, animality, all these coursed wildly through him.

Her head lay back in his arms, as if she had fainted, when he finally raised his lips from her mouth. He swept her up and carried her through to the bedroom. She lay where he threw her across the bed, half swooned, one arm flung back. He seized her other hand and kissed it feverishly; it caressed his face. He pulled himself away and ran back into the other room. He began to undress wildly, tearing off his clothes as if someone was drowning and he was on the bank. A button from his frock coat flew off and rolled into a corner, but he did not even look to see where it went. His waistcoat was torn off, his boots, his socks, his trousers and undertrousers . . . his pearl tie pin, his cravat. He cast a glance at the outer door, and went to twist the key in its lock. Then, wearing only his long-tailed shirt, he went barelegged into the bedroom.

She had moved a little, since she now lay with her head on the pillow, though still on top of the bed, her face twisted sideways and hidden from his sight by a dark fan of hair. He stood over her a moment, his member erect and thrusting out his shirt. Then he raised his left knee onto the narrow bed and fell on her, raining burning kisses on her mouth, her eyes, her throat. But the passive yet acquiescent body pressed beneath him, the naked feet that touched his own . . . he could not wait. Raising himself a little, he drew up her nightgown. Her legs parted. With a frantic brutality, as he felt his ejaculation about to burst, he found the place and thrust. Her body flinched again, as it had when her foot fell from the stool. He conquered that instinctive constriction, and her arms flung round him as if she would bind him to her for that eternity he could not dream without her. He began to ejaculate at once.

274

"Oh my dearest. My dearest. My sweetest angel . . . Sarah, Sarah . . . oh Sarah."

A few moments later he lay still. Precisely ninety seconds had passed since he had left her to look into the bedroom.

47

Averse, as Dido did with gesture stern
From her false friend's approach in Hades turn,
Wave us away, and keep thy solitude.
MATTHEW ARNOLD, "The Scholar-Gipsy" (1853)

Silence.

They lay as if paralyzed by what they had done. Congealed in sin, frozen with delight. Charles—no gentle postcoital sadness for him, but an immediate and universal horror—was like a city struck out of a quiet sky by an atom bomb. All lay razed; all principle, all future, all faith, all honorable intent. Yet he survived, he lay in the sweetest possession of his life, the last man alive, infinitely isolated . . . but already the radioactivity of guilt crept, crept through his nerves and veins. In the distant shadows Ernestina stood and stared mournfully at him. Mr. Freeman struck him across the face . . . how stone they were, rightly implacable, immovably waiting.

He shifted a little to relieve Sarah of his weight, then turned on his back so that she could lie against him, her head on his shoulder. He stared up at the ceiling. What a mess, what an inutterable mess!

And he held her a little closer. Her hand reached timidly and embraced his. The rain stopped. Heavy footsteps, slow, measured, passed somewhere beneath the window. A police officer, perhaps. The Law.

Charles said, "I am worse than Varguennes." Her only

275

answer was to press his hand, as if to deny and hush him. But he was a man.

"What is to become of us?"

"I cannot think beyond this hour."

Again he pressed her shoulders, kissed her forehead; then stared again at the ceiling. She was so young now, so overwhelmed.

"I must break my engagement."

"I ask nothing of you. I cannot. I am to blame."

"You warned me, you warned me. I am wholly to blame. I knew when I came here . . . I chose to be blind. I put all my obligations behind me."

She murmured, "I wished it so." She said it again, sadly. "I wished it so."

For a while he stroked her hair. It fell over her shoulder, her face, veiling her.

"Sarah . . . it is the sweetest name."

She did not answer. A minute passed, his hand smoothing her hair, as if she were a child. But his mind was elsewhere. As if she sensed it, she at last spoke.

"I know you cannot marry me."

"I must. I wish to. I could never look myself in the face again if I did not."

"I have been wicked. I have long imagined such a day as this. I am not fit to be your wife."

"My dearest—"

"Your position in the world, your friends, your . . . and she—I know she must love you. How should I not know what she feels?"

"But I no longer love her!"

She let his vehemence drain into the silence.

"She is worthy of you. I am not."

At last he began to take her at her word. He made her turn her head and they looked, in the dim outside light, into each other's penumbral eyes. His were full of a kind of horror; and hers were calm, faintly smiling.

"You cannot mean I should go away—as if nothing had happened between us?"

She said nothing; yet in her eyes he read her meaning. He raised himself on one elbow.

"You cannot forgive me so much. Or ask so little."

She sank her head against the pillow, her eyes on some dark future. "Why not, if I love you?"

He strained her to him. The thought of such sacrifice made his eyes smart with tears. The injustice Grogan and he had done her! She was a nobler being than either of them.

276

Charles was flooded with contempt for his sex: their triviality, their credulity, their selfishness. But he was of that sex, and there came to him some of its old devious cowardice: Could not this perhaps be no more than his last fling, the sowing of the last wild oats? But he no sooner thought that than he felt like a murderer acquitted on some technical flaw in the prosecution case. He might stand a free man outside the court; but eternally guilty in his heart.

"I am infinitely strange to myself."

"I have felt that too. It is because we have sinned. And we cannot believe we have sinned." She spoke as if she was staring into an endless night. "All I wish for is your happiness. Now I know there was truly a day upon which you loved me, I can bear ... I can bear any thought ... except that you should die."

He raised himself again then, and looked down at her. She had still a faint smile in her eyes, a deep knowing—a spiritual or psychological answer to his physical knowing of her. He had never felt so close, so one with a woman. He bent and kissed her, and out of a much purer love than that which began to reannounce itself, at the passionate contact of her lips, in his loins. Charles was like many Victorian men. He could not really believe that any woman of refined sensibilities could enjoy being a receptacle for male lust. He had already abused her love for him intolerably; it must not happen again. And the time—he could not stay longer! He sat up.

"The person downstairs ... and my man is waiting for me at my hotel. I beg you to give me a day or two's grace. I cannot think what to do now."

Her eyes were closed. She said, "I am not worthy of you."

He stared at her a moment, then got off the bed and went into the other room.

And there! A thunderbolt struck him.

In looking down as he dressed he perceived a red stain on the front tails of his shirt. For a moment he thought he must have cut himself; but he had felt no pain. He furtively examined himself. Then he gripped the top of the armchair, staring back at the bedroom door—for he had suddenly realized what a more experienced, or less feverish, lover would have suspected much sooner.

He had forced a virgin.

There was a movement in the room behind him. His head whirling, stunned, yet now in a desperate haste, he pulled on his clothes. There was the sound of water being poured into a basin, a chink of china as a soapdish scraped. She had not given herself to Varguennes. She had lied. All her conduct, all her motives in Lyme Regis had been based on a lie. But for what purpose. Why? Why? Why?

Blackmail!

To put him totally in her power!

And all those loathsome succubi of the male mind, their fat fears of a great feminine conspiracy to suck the virility from their veins, to prey upon their idealism, melt them into wax and mold them to their evil fancies . . . these, and a surging back to credibility of the hideous evidence adduced in the La Roncière appeal, filled Charles's mind with an apocalyptic horror.

The discreet sounds of washing ceased. There were various small rustlings—he supposed she was getting into the bed. Dressed, he stood staring at the fire. She was mad, evil, enlacing him in the strangest of nets . . . but *why?*

There was a sound. He turned, his thoughts only too evident on his face. She stood in the doorway, now in her old indigo dress, her hair still loose, yet with something of that old defiance: he remembered for an instant that time he had first come upon her, when she had stood on the ledge over the sea and stared up at him. She must have seen that he had discovered the truth; and once more she forestalled, castrated the accusation in his mind.

She repeated her previous words.

"I am not worthy of you."

And now, he believed her. He whispered, "Varguennes?"

"When I went to where I told in Weymouth . . . I was still some way from the door . . . I saw him come out. With a woman. The kind of woman one cannot mistake." She avoided his fierce eyes. "I drew into a doorway. When they had gone, I walked away."

"But why did you tell—"

She moved abruptly to the window; and he was silenced. She had no limp. There was no strained ankle. She glanced at his freshly accusing look, then turned her back.

"Yes. I have deceived you. But I shall not trouble you again."

"But what have I . . . why should you . . ."

A swarm of mysteries.

She faced him. It had begun to rain heavily again. Her eyes were unflinching, her old defiance returned; and yet now it lay behind something gentler, a reminder to him that he had just possessed her. The old distance, but a softer distance.

"You have given me the consolation of believing that in another world, another age, another life, I might have been your wife. You have given me the strength to go on living . . . in the here and now." Less than ten feet lay between them; and yet it seemed like ten miles. "There is one thing in which I have not deceived you. I loved you . . . I think from the moment I saw you. In that, you were never deceived. What duped you was my loneliness. A resentment, an envy, I don't know. I don't know." She turned again to the window and the rain. "Do not ask me to explain what I have done. I cannot explain it. It is not to be explained."

Charles stared in the fraught silence at her back. As he had so shortly before felt swept towards her, now he felt swept away—and in both cases, she was to blame.

"I cannot accept that. It must be explained."

But she shook her head. "Please go now. I pray for your happiness. I shall never disturb it again."

He did not move. After a moment or two she looked round at him, and evidently read, as she had once before, his secret thought. Her expression was calm, almost fatalistic.

"It is as I told you before. I am far stronger than any man may easily imagine. My life will end when nature ends it."

He bore the sight of her a few seconds more, then turned towards his hat and stick.

"This is my reward. To succor you. To risk a great deal to . . . and now to know I was no more than the dupe of your imaginings."

"Today I have thought of my own happiness. If we were to meet again I could think only of yours. There can be no happiness for you with me. You cannot marry me, Mr. Smithson."

That resumption of formality cut deep. He threw her a hurt look; but she had her back to him, as if in anticipation of it. He took a step towards her.

"How can you address me thus?" She said nothing. "All I ask is to be allowed to understand—"

"I beseech you. Leave!"

She had turned on him. They looked for a moment like two mad people. Charles seemed about to speak, to spring forward, to explode; but then without warning he spun on his heel and left the room.

48

> It is immoral in a man to believe more than he can
> spontaneously receive as being congenial to his mental
> and moral nature.
>
> NEWMAN, *Eighteen Propositions of Liberalism* (1828)

> I hold it truth, with him who sings
>   To one clear harp in divers tones,
>   That men may rise on stepping-stones
> Of their dead selves to higher things.
>
> TENNYSON, *In Memoriam* (1850)

He put on his most formal self as he came down to the hall.
Mrs. Endicott stood at the door to her office, her mouth
already open to speak. But Charles, with a briskly polite "I
thank you, ma'm" was past her and into the night before she
could complete her question; or notice his frock coat lacked
a button.

He walked blindly away through a new downpour of rain.
He noticed it no more than where he was going. His greatest
desire was darkness, invisibility, oblivion in which to regain
calm. But he plunged, without realizing it, into that morally
dark quarter of Exeter I described earlier. Like most morally
dark places it was full of light and life: of shops and taverns,
of people sheltering from the rain in doorways. He took an
abrupt downhill street towards the river Exe. Rows of scum-
bered steps passed either side of a choked central gutter. But
it was quiet. At the bottom a small redstone church, built on
the corner, came into sight; and Charles suddenly felt the
need for sanctuary. He pushed on a small door, so low that

280

he had to stoop to enter. Steps rose to the level of the church floor, which was above the street entrance. A young curate stood at the top of these steps, turning down a last lamp and surprised at this late visit.

"I was about to lock up, sir."

"May I ask to be allowed to pray for a few minutes?"

The curate reversed the extinguishing process and scrutinized the late customer for a long moment. A gentleman.

"My house is just across the way. I am awaited. If you would be so kind as to lock up for me and bring me the key." Charles bowed, and the curate came down beside him. "It is the bishop. In my opinion the house of God should always be open. But our plate is so valuable. Such times we live in."

Thus Charles found himself alone in the church. He heard the curate's footsteps cross the street; and then he locked the old door from the inside and mounted the steps to the church. It smelled of new paint. The one gaslight dimly illumined fresh gilding; but massive Gothic arches of a somber red showed that the church was very old. Charles seated himself halfway down the main aisle and stared through the roodscreen at the crucifix over the altar. Then he got to his knees and whispered the Lord's Prayer, his rigid hands clenched over the prayer-ledge in front of him.

The dark silence and emptiness welled back once the ritual words were said. He began to compose a special prayer for his circumstances: "Forgive me, O Lord, for my selfishness. Forgive me for breaking Thy laws. Forgive me my dishonor, forgive me my unchastity. Forgive me my dissatisfaction with myself, forgive me my lack of faith in Thy wisdom and charity. Forgive and advise me, O Lord in my travail . . ." but then, by means of one of those miserable puns made by a distracted subconscious, Sarah's face rose before him, tear-stained, agonized, with all the features of a Mater Dolorosa by Grünewald he had seen in Colmar, Coblenz, Cologne . . . he could not remember. For a few absurd seconds his mind ran after the forgotten town, it began with a C . . . he got off his knees and sat back in his pew. How empty the church was, how silent. He stared at the crucifix; but instead of Christ's face, he saw only Sarah's. He tried to recommence his prayer. But it was hopeless. He knew it was not heard. He began abruptly to cry.

In all but a very few Victorian atheists (that militant élite led by Bradlaugh) and agnostics there was a profound sense of exclusion, of a gift withdrawn. Among friends of like persuasion they might make fun of the follies of the Church, of its sectarian squabbles, its luxurious bishops and intriguing canons, its absentee rectors* and underpaid curates, its anti-quated theology and all the rest; but Christ remained, a terrible anomaly in reason. He could not be for them what he is to so many of us today, a completely secularized figure, a *man* called Jesus of Nazareth with a brilliant gift for metaphor, for creating a personal mythology, for acting on his beliefs. All the rest of the world believed in his divinity; and thus his reproach came stronger to the unbeliever. Between the cruelties of our own age and our guilt we have erected a vast edifice of government-administered welfare and aid; charity is fully organized. But the Victorians lived much closer to that cruelty; the intelligent and sensitive felt far more personally responsible; and it was thus all the harder, in hard times, to reject the universal symbol of compassion.

Deep in his heart Charles did not wish to be an agnostic. Because he had never needed faith, he had quite happily learned to do without it; and his reason, his knowledge of Lyell and Darwin, had told him he was right to do without its dogma. Yet here he was, not weeping for Sarah, but for his own inability to speak to God. He knew, in that dark church, that the wires were down. No communication was possible.

There was a loud clack in the silence. He turned round, hastily touching his eyes with his sleeve. But whoever had tried to enter apparently accepted that the church was now closed; it was as if a rejected part of Charles himself had walked away. He stood up and began to pace up and down the aisle between the pews, his hands behind his back. Worn names and dates, last fossil remains of other lives, stared illegibly at him from the gravestones embedded in the floor. Perhaps the pacing up and down those stones, the slight sense of blasphemy he had in doing it, perhaps his previous moments of despair, but something did finally bring calm and a kind of clarity back to him. A dialogue began to form, between his better and his worse self—or perhaps between him and that spreadeagled figure in the shadows at the church's end.

* But who can blame them when their superiors set such an example? The curate referred a moment ago to "the bishop"—and this particular bishop, the famous Dr. Phillpotts of Exeter (then with all of Devon and Cornwall under his care), is a case in point. He spent the last ten years of his life in "a comfortable accommodation" at Torquay and was said not to have darkened his cathedral's doors once during that final decade. He was a superb prince of the Anglican Church—every inch a pugnacious reactionary; and did not die till two years after the year we are in.

Where shall I begin?

Begin with what you have done, my friend. And stop wishing you had not done it.

I did not do it. I was led to do it.

What led you to do it?

I was deceived.

What intent lay behind the deception?

I do not know.

But you must judge.

If she had truly loved me she could not have let me go.

If she had truly loved you, could she have continued to deceive?

She gave me no choice. She said herself that marriage between us was impossible.

What reason did she give?

Our difference in social position.

A noble cause.

Then Ernestina. I have given her my solemn promise.

It is already broken.

I will mend it.

With love? Or with guilt?

It does not matter which. A vow is sacred.

If it does not matter which, a vow cannot be sacred.

My duty is clear.

Charles, Charles, I have read that thought in the cruelest eyes. Duty is but a pot. It holds whatever is put in it, from the greatest evil to the greatest good.

She wished me to go. I could see it in her eyes—a contempt.

Shall I tell you what Contempt is doing at this moment? She is weeping her heart out.

I cannot go back.

Do you think water can wash that blood from your loins?

I cannot go back.

Did you have to meet her again in the Undercliff? Did you have to stop this night in Exeter? Did you have to go to her room? Let her hand rest on yours? Did you—

I admit these things! I have sinned. But I was fallen into her snare.

Then why are you now free of her?

There was no answer from Charles. He sat again in his pew. He locked his fingers with a white violence, as if he would break his knuckles, staring, staring into the darkness. But the other voice would not let him be.

My friend, perhaps there is one thing she loves more than

283

you. And what you do not understand is that because she truly loves you she must give you the thing she loves more. I will tell you why she weeps: because you lack the courage to give her back her gift.

What right had she to set me on the rack?

What right had you to be born? To breathe? To be rich?

I do but render unto Caesar—

Or unto Mr. Freeman?

That is a base accusation.

And unto me? Is this your tribute? These nails you hammer through my palms?

With the greatest respect—Ernestina also has palms.

Then let us take one and read it. I see no happiness. She knows she is not truly loved. She is deceived. Not once, but again and again, each day of marriage.

Charles put his arms on the ledge in front of him and buried his head in them. He felt caught in a dilemma that was also a current of indecision: it was almost palpable, not passive but active, driving him forwards into a future it, not he, would choose.

My poor Charles, search your heart—you thought when you came to this city, did you not, to prove to yourself you were not yet in the prison of your future. But escape is not one act, my friend. It is no more achieved by that than you could reach Jerusalem from here by one small step. Each day, Charles, each hour, it has to be taken again. Each minute the nail waits to be hammered in. You know your choice. You stay in prison, what your time calls duty, honor, self-respect, and you are comfortably safe. Or you are free and crucified. Your only companions the stones, the thorns, the turning backs; the silence of cities, and their hate.

I am weak.

But ashamed of your weakness.

What good could my strength bring to the world?

No answer came. But something made Charles rise from his pew and go to the roodscreen. He looked through one of its wooden windows at the Cross above the altar; and then, after a hesitation, stepped through the central door and past the choir stalls to the steps to the altar table. The light at the other end of the church penetrated but feebly there. He could barely make out the features of the Christ, yet a mysterious empathy invaded him. He saw himself hanging there . . . not, to be sure, with any of the nobility and universality of Jesus, but crucified.

284

And yet not on the Cross—on something else. He had thought sometimes of Sarah in a way that might suggest he saw himself crucified on *her;* but such blasphemy, both religious and real, was not in his mind. Rather she seemed there beside him, as it were awaiting the marriage service; yet with another end in view. For a moment he could not seize it—and then it came.

To uncrucify!

In a sudden flash of illumination Charles saw the right purpose of Christianity; it was not to celebrate this barbarous image, not to maintain it on high because there was a useful profit—the redemption of sins—to be derived from so doing, but to bring about a world in which the hanging man could be descended, could be seen not with the rictus of agony on his face, but the smiling peace of a victory brought about by, and in, living men and women.

He seemed as he stood there to see all his age, its tumultuous life, its iron certainties and rigid conventions, its repressed emotion and facetious humor, its cautious science and incautious religion, its corrupt politics and immutable castes, as the great hidden enemy of all his deepest yearnings. That was what had deceived him; and it was totally without love or freedom . . . but also without thought, without intention, without malice, because the deception was in its very nature; and it was not human, but a machine. That was the vicious circle that haunted him; that was the failure, the weakness, the cancer, the vital flaw that had brought him to what he was: more an indecision than a reality, more a dream than a man, more a silence than a word, a bone than an action. And fossils!

He had become, while still alive, as if dead.

It was like coming to a bottomless brink.

And something else: a strange sense he had had, ever since entering that church—and not particular to it, but a presentiment he always had upon entering empty churches—that he was not alone. A whole dense congregation of others stood behind him. He turned and looked back into the nave.

Silent, empty pews.

And Charles thought: if they were truly dead, if there were no afterlife, what should I care of their view of me? They would not know, they could not judge.

Then he made the great leap: *They do not know, they cannot judge.*

Now what he was throwing off haunted, and profoundly damaged, his age. It is stated very clearly by Tennyson in the fiftieth poem of *In Memoriam.* Listen:

Do we indeed desire the dead
    Should still be near us at our side?
    Is there no baseness we would hide?
No inner vileness that we dread?

Shall he for whose applause I strove,
    I had such reverence for his blame,
    See with clear eye some hidden shame
And I be lessen'd in his love?

I wrong the grave with fears untrue:
    Shall love be blamed for want of faith?
    There must be wisdom with great Death;
The dead shall look me thro' and thro'.

Be near us when we climb or fall:
    Ye watch, like God, the rolling hours
    With larger other eyes than ours,
To make allowance for us all.

There must be wisdom with great Death; the dead shall look me thro' and thro'. Charles's whole being rose up against those two foul propositions; against this macabre desire to go backwards into the future, mesmerized eyes on one's dead fathers instead of on one's unborn sons. It was as if his previous belief in the ghostly presence of the past had condemned him, without his ever realizing it, to a life in the grave.

Though this may seem like a leap into atheism, it was not so; it did not diminish Christ in Charles's eyes. Rather it made Him come alive, it uncrucified Him, if not completely, then at least partially. Charles walked slowly back into the nave, turning his back on the indifferent wooden carving. But not on Jesus. He began again to pace up and down, his eyes on the paving stones. What he saw now was like a glimpse of another world: a new reality, a new causality, a new creation. A cascade of concrete visions—if you like, another chapter from his hypothetical autobiography—poured through his mind. At a similar high-flying moment you may recall that Mrs. Poulteney had descended, in three ticks of her marble and ormolu drawing-room clock, from eternal salvation to Lady Cotton. And I would be hiding the truth if I did not reveal that at this moment Charles thought of his uncle. *He* would not blame on Sir Robert a broken marriage and an alliance unworthy of the family; but his uncle would blame himself. Another scene leaped unbidden into his mind: Lady Bella faced with Sarah. Miraculous to relate, he saw

286

who would come out with more dignity; for Ernestina would fight with Lady Bella's weapons, and Sarah ... those eyes—how they would swallow snubs and insults! Comprehend them in silence! Make them dwindle into mere specks of smut in an azure sky!

And dressing Sarah! Taking her to Paris, to Florence, to Rome!

This is clearly not the moment to bring in a comparison with St. Paul on the road to Damascus. But Charles was stopped—alas, with his back to the altar once more—and there was a kind of radiance in his face. It may simply have been that from the gaslight by the steps; he has not translated the nobler but abstract reasons that had coursed through his mind very attractively. But I hope you will believe that Sarah on his arm in the Uffizi did stand, however banally, for the pure essence of cruel but necessary (if we are to survive—and yes, still today) freedom.

He turned then and went back to his pew; and did something very irrational, since he knelt and prayed, though very briefly. Then he went down the aisle, pulled down the wire till the gaslight was a pale will-o'-the-wisp, and left the church.

49

I keep but a man and a maid, ever ready to slander and steal . . .

TENNYSON, *Maud* (1855)

Charles found the curate's house and rang the bell. A maid answered, but the bewhiskered young man himself hovered in the hallway behind her. The maid retreated, as her master came forward to take the heavy old key.

"Thank you, sir. I celebrate Holy Communion at eight every morning. You stay long in Exeter?"

"Alas, no. I am simply *en passage.*"

"I had hoped to see you again. I can be of no further assistance?"

And he gestured, the poor young shrimp, towards a door behind which no doubt lay his study. Charles had already noted a certain ostentation about the church furnishings; and he knew he was being invited to Confession. It did not need magical powers to see through the wall and discern a prie-dieu and a discreet statue of the Virgin; for this was one of the young men born too late for the Tractarian schism and who now dallied naughtily but safely—since Dr. Phillpotts was High Church—with rituals and vestments, a very prevalent form of ecclesiastical dandyism. Charles measured him a moment and took heart in his own new vision: it could not be more foolish than this. So he bowed and refused, and went on his way. He was shriven of established religion for the rest of his life.

His way ... you think, perhaps, that that must lead straight back to Endicott's Family Hotel. A modern man would no doubt have gone straight back there. But Charles's accursed sense of Duty and Propriety stood like castle walls against that. His first task was to cleanse himself of past obligations; only then could he present himself to offer his hand.

He began to understand Sarah's deceit. She knew he loved her; and she knew he had been blind to the true depth of that love. The false version of her betrayal by Varguennes, her other devices, were but stratagems to unblind him; all she had said after she had brought him to the realization was but a test of his new vision. He had failed miserably; and she had then used the same stratagems as a proof of her worthlessness. Out of what nobility must such self-sacrifice spring! If he had but sprung forward and taken her into his arms again, told her she was his, ungainsayably!

And if only—he might have added, but didn't—there were not that fatal dichotomy (perhaps the most dreadful result of their mania for categorization) in the Victorians, which led them to see the "soul" as more real than the body, far more real, their only real self; indeed hardly connected with the body at all, but floating high over the beast; and yet, by some inexplicable flaw in the nature of things, reluctantly dragged along in the wake of the beast's movements, like a white captive balloon behind a disgraceful and disobedient child.

This—the fact that every Victorian had two minds—is the one piece of equipment we must always take with us on our travels back to the nineteenth century. It is a schizophrenia seen at its clearest, its most notorious, in the poets I have quoted from so often—in Tennyson, Clough, Arnold, Hardy; but scarcely less clearly in the extraordinary political veerings from Right to Left and back again of men like the younger Mill and Gladstone; in the ubiquitous neuroses and psychosomatic illnesses of intellectuals otherwise as different as Charles Kingsley and Darwin; in the execration at first poured on the Pre-Raphaelites, who tried—or seemed to be trying—to be one-minded about both art and life; in the endless tug-of-war between Liberty and Restraint, Excess and Moderation, Propriety and Conviction, between the principled man's cry for Universal Education and his terror of Universal Suffrage; transparent also in the mania for editing and revising, so that if we want to know the real Mill or the real Hardy we can learn far more from the deletions and alterations of their autobiographies than from the published versions . . . more from correspondence that somehow escaped burning, from private diaries, from the petty detritus of the concealment operation. Never was the record so completely confused, never a public façade so successfully passed off as the truth on a gullible posterity; and this, I think, makes the best guidebook to the age very possibly *Dr. Jekyll and Mr. Hyde*. Behind its latterday Gothick lies a very profound and epoch-revealing truth.

Every Victorian had two minds; and Charles had at least that. Already, as he walked up Fore Street towards the Ship, he was rehearsing the words his white balloon would utter when the wicked child saw Sarah again; the passionate yet honorable arguments that would reduce her to a tearful gratitude and the confession that she could not live without him. He saw it all, so vividly I feel tempted to set it down. But here is reality, in the form of Sam, standing at the doors of the ancient inn.

"The service was hagreeable, Mr. Charles?"

"I . . . I lost my way, Sam. And I've got damnably wet." Which was not at all the adjective to apply to Sam's eyes. "Fill a tub for me, there's a good fellow. I'll sup in my rooms."

"Yes, Mr. Charles."

Some fifteen minutes later you might have seen Charles stark naked and engaged in an unaccustomed occupation: that of laundering. He had his bloodstained garments pressed against the side of the vast hip bath that had been filled for him and was assiduously rubbing them with a piece of soap. He felt foolish, and did not make a very good job of it. When Sam came, some time later, with the supper tray, the garments lay as if thrown negligently half in and half out of the bath. Sam collected them up without remark; and for once Charles was grateful for his notorious carelessness in such matters.

Having eaten his supper, he opened his writing case.

My dearest,

One half of me is inexpressibly glad to address you thus, while the other wonders how he can so speak of a being he yet but scarcely understands. Something in you I would fain say I know profoundly: and something else I am as ignorant of as when I first saw you. I say this not to excuse, but to explain my behavior this evening. I cannot excuse it; yet I must believe that there was one way in which it may be termed fortunate, since it prompted a searching of my conscience that was long overdue. I shall not go into all the circumstance. But I am resolved, my sweet and mysterious Sarah, that what now binds us shall bind us forevermore. I am but too well aware that I have no right to see you again, let alone to ask to know you fully, in my present situation. My first necessity is therefore to terminate my engagement.

A premonition that it was folly to enter into that arrangement has long been with me—before ever you came into my life. I implore you, therefore, not to feel guilt in that respect. What is to blame is a blindness in myself as to my own real nature. Had I been ten years younger, had I not seen so much in my age and my society with which I am not in sympathy, I have no doubt I could have been happy with Miss Freeman. My mistake was to forget that I am thirty-two, not twenty-two.

I therefore go early tomorrow on the most painful journey to Lyme. You will appreciate that to conclude its purpose is the predominant thought in my mind at this moment. But my duty in that respect done, my thoughts shall be only of you—nay, of *our* future. What strange fate brought me to you I do not know, but, God willing, nothing shall take you from me unless it be yourself that wishes it so. Let me say no more now, my sweet enigma, than that you will have to provide far stronger proofs and arguments than you have hitherto adduced. I cannot believe you will attempt to do so. Your heart knows I am yours and that I would call you mine.

Need I assure you, my dearest Sarah, that my intentions are henceforth of the most honorable? There are a thousand things I wish to ask you, a thousand attentions to pay you, a thousand pleasures to give you. But always with every regard to whatever propriety your delicacy insists on.

I am he who will know no peace, no happiness until he holds you in his arms again.

C.S.

P.S. On re-reading what I have written I perceive a formality my heart does not intend. Forgive it. You are both so close and yet a stranger—I know not how to phrase what I really feel.

Your fondest C.

This anabatic epistle was not arrived at until after several drafts. It had by then grown late, and Charles changed his mind about its immediate dispatch. She, by now, would have wept herself to sleep; he would let her suffer one more black night; but she should wake to joy. He re-read the letter several times; it had a little aftermath of the tone he had used, only a day or two before, in letters from London to Ernestina; but those letters had been agony to write, mere concessions to convention, which is why he had added that postscript. He still felt, as he had told Sarah, a stranger to himself; but now it was with a kind of awed pleasure that he stared at his face in the mirror. He felt a great courage in himself, both present and future—and a uniqueness, a having done something unparalleled. And he had his wish: he was off on a journey again, a journey made doubly delicious by its promised companion. He tried to imagine unknown Sarahs— a Sarah laughing, Sarah singing, Sarah dancing. They were hard to imagine, and yet not impossible . . . he remembered that smile when they had been so nearly discovered by Sam and Mary. It had been a clairvoyant smile, a seeing into the future. And that time he had raised her from her knees— with what infinite and long pleasure he would now do that in their life together!

If these were the thorns and the stones that threatened about him, he could bear them. He did think a moment of one small thorn: Sam. But Sam was like all servants, dismissable.

And summonable. Summoned he was, at a surprisingly early hour that next morning. He found Charles in his dressing gown, with a sealed letter and packet in his hands.

"Sam, I wish you to take these to the address on the envelope. You will wait ten minutes to see if there is an answer. If there is none—I expect none, but wait just in case—if there is none, you are to come straight back here. And hire a fast carriage. We go to Lyme." He added, "But no baggage. We return here tonight."

"Tonight, Mr. Charles! But I thought we was—"

"Never mind what you thought. Just do as I say."

Sam put on his footman face, and withdrew. As he went slowly downstairs it became clear to him that his position was intolerable. How could he fight a battle without information? With so many conflicting rumors as to the disposition of the enemy forces? He stared at the envelope in his hand. Its destination was flagrant: *Miss Woodruff, at Endicott's Family Hotel.* And only one day in Lyme? With portmanteaux to wait here! He turned the small packet over, pressed the envelope.

It seemed fat, three pages at least. He glanced round surreptitiously, then examined the seal. Sam cursed the man who invented wax.

And now he stands again before Charles, who has dressed.
"Well?"
"No answer, Mr. Charles."
Charles could not quite control his face. He turned away.
"And the carriage?"
"Ready and waitin', sir."
"Very well. I shall be down shortly."
Sam withdrew. The door had no sooner closed when Charles raised his hands to his head, then threw them apart, as if to an audience, an actor accepting applause, a smile of gratitude on his lips. For he had, upon his ninety-ninth re-reading of his letter that previous night, added a second postscript. It concerned that brooch we have already seen in Ernestina's hands. Charles begged Sarah to accept it; and by way of a sign, to allow that her acceptance of it meant that she accepted his apologies for his conduct. This second postscript had ended: "The bearer will wait till you have read this. If he should bring the contents of the packet back ... but I know you cannot be so cruel."

Yet the poor man had been in agony during Sam's absence.

And here Sam is again, volubly talking in a low voice, with frequent agonized looks. The scene is in the shadow of a lilac bush, which grows outside the kitchen door in Aunt Tranter's garden and provides a kind of screen from the garden proper. The afternoon sun slants through the branches and first white buds. The listener is Mary, with her cheeks flushed and her hand almost constantly covering her mouth.

" 'Tisn't possible, 'tisn't possible."
"It's 'is uncle. It's turned 'is 'ead."
"But young mistress—oh, what'll 'er do now, Sam?"
And both their eyes traveled up with dread, as if they thought to hear a scream or see a falling body, to the windows through the branches above.
"And hus, Mary. What'll us do?"
"Oh Sam—'tisn't fair ..."
"I love yer, Mary."
"Oh Sam ..."
" 'Tweren't just bein' wicked. I'd as soon die as lose yer now."
"Oh what'll us do?"
"Don't cry, my darling, don't cry. I've 'ad enough of

hupstairs. They're no better'n us." He gripped her by the arms. "If 'is lordship thinks like master, like servant, 'e's mistook, Mary. If it's you or 'im, it's you." He stiffened, like a soldier about to charge. "I'll leave 'is hemploy."

"Sam!"

"I will. I'll 'aul coals. Hanything!"

"But your money—'e woan' give'ee that no more now!"

" 'E ain't got it to give." His bitterness looked at her dismay. But then he smiled and reached out his hands. "But shall I tell yer someone who 'as? If you and me play our cards right?"

50

> I think it inevitably follows, that as new species in the course of time are formed through natural selection, others will become rarer and rarer, and finally extinct. The forms which stand in closest competition with those undergoing modification and improvement will naturally suffer most.
>
> DARWIN, *The Origin of Species* (1859)

They had arrived in Lyme just before two. For a few minutes Charles took possession of the room he had reserved. Again he paced up and down, but now in a nervous agony, steeling himself for the interview ahead. The existentialist terror invaded him again; perhaps he had known it would and so burned his boats by sending that letter to Sarah. He rehearsed again the thousand phrases he had invented on the journey from Exeter; but they fled through his mind like October leaves. He took a deep breath, then his hat, and went out.

Mary, with a broad grin as soon as she saw him, opened the door. He practiced his gravity on her.

"Good afternoon. Is Miss Ernestina at home?"

But before she could answer Ernestina herself appeared at the end of the hall. She had a little smile.

293

"No. My duenna is out to lunch. But you may come in."

She disappeared back into the sitting room. Charles gave his hat to Mary, set his lapels, wished he were dead, then went down the hall and into his ordeal. Ernestina, in sunlight, by a window overlooking the garden, turned gaily.

"I received a letter from Papa this . . . Charles! Charles? Is something wrong?"

And she came towards him. He could not look at her, but stared at the carpet. She stopped. Her frightened and his grave, embarrassed eyes met.

"Charles?"

"I beg you to sit down."

"But what has happened?"

"That is . . . why I have come."

"But why do you look at me like that?"

"Because I do not know how to begin to say what I must."

Still looking at him, she felt behind her and sat on a chair by the window. Still he was silent. She touched a letter on the table beside her.

"Papa . . ." but his quick look made her give up her sentence.

"He was kindness itself . . . but I did not tell him the truth."

"The truth—what truth?"

"That I have, after many hours of the deepest, the most painful consideration, come to the conclusion that I am not worthy of you."

Her face went white. He thought for a moment she would faint and stepped forward to catch her, but she slowly reached a hand to her left arm, as if to feel she was awake.

"Charles . . . you are joking."

"To my eternal shame . . . I am not joking."

"You are not *worthy* of me?"

"Totally unworthy."

"And you . . . oh, but this is some nightmare." She looked up at him with incredulous eyes, then smiled timidly. "You forget your telegram. You are joking."

"How little you know me if you think I could ever joke on such a matter."

"But . . . but . . . your telegram!"

"Was sent before my decision."

Only then, as he lowered his eyes, did she begin to accept the truth. He had already foreseen that it must be the crucial moment. If she fainted, became hysterical . . . he did not know; but he abhorred pain and it would not be too late to recant, to tell all, to throw himself on her mercy. But though Ernestina's eyes closed a long moment, and a kind of shiver

294

seemed to pass through her, she did not faint. She was her father's daughter; she may have wished she might faint; but such a gross betrayal of . . .

"Then kindly explain what you mean."

A momentary relief came to him. She was hurt, but not mortally.

"That I cannot do in one sentence."

She stared with a kind of bitter primness at her hands. "Then use several. I shall not interrupt."

"I have always had, and I continue to have, the greatest respect and affection for you. I have never doubted for a moment that you would make an admirable wife to any man fortunate enough to gain your love. But I have also always been shamefully aware that a part of my regard for you was ignoble. I refer to the fortune that you bring—and the fact that you are an only child. Deep in myself, Ernestina, I have always felt that my life has been without purpose, without achievement. No, pray hear me out. When I realized last winter that an offer of marriage might be favorably entertained by you, I was tempted by Satan. I saw an opportunity, by a brilliant marriage, to reestablish my faith in myself. I beg you not to think that I proceeded only by a cold-blooded calculation. I liked you very much. I sincerely believed that that liking would grow into love."

Slowly her head had risen. She stared at him, but seemed hardly to see him.

"I cannot believe it is you I hear speaking. It is some impostor, some cruel, some heartless . . ."

"I know this must come as a most grievous shock."

"Shock!" Her expression was outraged. "When you can stand so cold and collected—and tell me you have never loved me!"

She had raised her voice and he went to one of the windows that was opened and closed it. Standing closer to her bowed head, he spoke as gently as he could without losing his distance.

"I am not seeking for excuses. I am seeking simply to explain that my crime was not a calculated one. If it were, how could I do what I am doing now? My one desire is to make you understand that I am not a deceiver of anyone but myself. Call me what else you will—weak, selfish . . . what you will—but not callous."

She drew in a little shuddery breath.

"And what brought about this great discovery?"

"My realization, whose heinousness I cannot shirk, that I was disappointed when your father did not end our engagement for me." She gave him a terrible look. "I am trying to

295

be honest. He was not only most generous in the matter of my changed circumstances. He proposed that I should one day become his partner in business."

Her face flashed up again. "I knew it, I knew it. It is because you are marrying into trade. Am I not right?"

He turned to the window. "I had fully accepted that. In any case—to feel ashamed of your father would be the grossest snobbery."

"Saying things doesn't make one any the less guilty of them."

"If you think I viewed his new proposal with horror, you are quite right. But the horror was at my own ineligibility for what was intended—certainly not at the proposal itself. Now please let me finish my . . . explanation."

"It is making my heart break."

He turned away to the window.

"Let us try to cling to that respect we have always had for one another. You must not think I have considered only myself in all this. What haunts me is the injustice I should be doing you—and to your father—by marrying you without that love you deserve. If you and I were different people—but we are not, we know by a look, a word, whether our love is returned—"

She hissed. "We thought we knew."

"My dear Ernestina, it is like faith in Christianity. One can pretend to have it. But the pretense will finally out. I am convinced, if you search your heart, that faint doubts must have already crossed it. No doubt you stifled them, you said, he is—"

She covered her ears, then slowly drew her fingers down over her face. There was a silence. Then she said, "May I speak now?"

"Of course."

"I know to you I have never been anything more than a pretty little . . . article of drawing-room furniture. I know I am innocent. I know I am spoiled. I know I am not unusual. I am not a Helen of Troy or a Cleopatra. I know I say things that sometimes grate on your ears, I bore you about domestic arrangements, I hurt you when I make fun of your fossils. Perhaps I am just a child. But under your love and protection . . . and your education . . . I believed I should become better. I should learn to please you, I should learn to make you love me for what I had become. You may not know it, you cannot know it, but that is why I was first attracted to you. You do know that I had been . . . dangled before a hundred other men. They were not all fortune hunters and nonentities. I did not choose you because I was so innocent I

296

could not make comparisons. But because you seemed more generous, wiser, more experienced. I remember—I will fetch down my diary if you do not believe me—that I wrote, soon after we became engaged, that you have little faith in yourself. I have felt that. You believe yourself a failure, you think yourself despised, I know not what ... but that is what I wished to make my real bridal present to you. Faith in yourself."

There was a long silence. She stayed with lowered head.

He spoke in a low voice. "You remind me of how much I lose. Alas, I know myself too well. One can't resurrect what was never there."

"And that is all what I say means to you?"

"It means a great, a very great deal to me."

He was silent, though she plainly expected him to say more. He had not expected this containment. He was touched, and ashamed, by what she had said; and that he could not show either sentiment was what made him silent. Her voice was very soft and downward.

"In view of what I have said can you not at least ..." but she could not find the words.

"Reconsider my decision?"

She must have heard something in his tone that he had not meant to be there, for she suddenly looked at him with a passionate appeal. Her eyes were wet with suppressed tears, her small face white and pitifully struggling to keep some semblance of calm. He felt it like a knife: how deeply he had wounded.

"Charles, I beg you, I beg you to wait a little. It is true, I am ignorant, I do not know what you want of me ... if you would tell me where I have failed ... how you would wish me to be ... I will do anything, anything, because I would abandon anything to make you happy."

"You must not speak like that."

"I must—I can't help it—only yesterday that telegram, I wept, I have kissed it a hundred times, you must not think that because I tease I do not have deeper feelings. I would ..." but her voice trailed away, as an acrid intuition burst upon her. She threw him a fierce little look. "You are lying. Something has happened since you sent it."

He moved to the fireplace, and stood with his back to her. She began to sob. And that he found unendurable. He at last looked round at her, expecting to see her with her head bowed; but she was weeping openly, with her eyes on him; and as she saw him look, she made a motion, like some terrified, lost child, with her hands towards him, half rose, took a single step, and then fell to her knees. There came to

297

Charles then a sharp revulsion—not against her, but against the situation: his half-truths, his hiding of the essential. Perhaps the closest analogy is to what a surgeon sometimes feels before a particularly terrible battle or accident casualty; a savage determination—for what else can be done?—to get on with the operation. To tell the truth. He waited until a moment came without sobs.

"I wished to spare you. But yes—something has happened."

Very slowly she got to her feet and raised her hands to her cheeks, never for a moment quitting him with her eyes.

"Who?"

"You do not know her. Her name is unimportant."

"And she ... you ..."

He looked away.

"I have known her many years. I thought the attachment was broken. I discovered in London ... that it is not."

"You love her?"

"Love? I don't know . . . whatever it is that makes it impossible to offer one's heart freely to another."

"Why did you not tell me this at the beginning?"

There was a long pause. He could not bear her eyes, which seemed to penetrate every lie he told.

He muttered, "I hoped to spare you the pain of it."

"Or yourself the shame of it? You . . . you are a monster!"

She fell back into her chair, staring at him with dilated eyes. Then she flung her face into her hands. He let her weep, and stared fiercely at a china sheep on the mantelpiece; and never till the day he died saw a china sheep again without a hot flush of self-disgust. When at last she spoke, it was with such force that he flinched.

"If I do not kill myself, shame will!"

"I am not worth a moment's regret. You will meet other men . . . not broken by life. Honorable men, who will . . ." he halted, then burst out, "By all you hold sacred, promise never to say that again!"

She stared fiercely at him. "Did you think I should pardon you?" He mutely shook his head. "My parents, my friends—what am I to tell them? That Mr. Charles Smithson has decided after all that his mistress is more important than his honor, his promise, his . . ."

There was the sound of torn paper. Without looking round he knew that she had vented her anger on her father's letter.

"I believed her gone forever from my life. Extraordinary circumstances . . ."

A silence: as if she considered whether she could throw vitriol at him. Her voice was suddenly cold and venomous.

"You have broken your promise. There is a remedy for members of my sex."

"You have every right to bring such an action. I could only plead guilty."

"The world shall know you for what you are. That is all I care about."

"The world will know, whatever happens."

The enormity of what he had done flooded back through her. She kept shaking her head. He went and took a chair and sat facing her, too far to touch, but close enough to appeal to her better self.

"Can you suppose for one serious moment that I am unpunished? That this has not been the most terrible decision of my life? This hour the most dreaded? The one I shall remember with the deepest remorse till the day I die? I may be—very well, I *am* a deceiver. But you know I am not heartless. I should not be here now if I were. I should have written a letter, fled abroad—"

"I wish you had."

He gave the crown of her head a long look, then stood. He caught sight of himself in a mirror; and the man in the mirror, Charles in another world, seemed the true self. The one in the room was what she said, an impostor; had always been, in his relations with Ernestina, an impostor, an observed other. He went at last into one of his prepared speeches.

"I cannot expect you to feel anything but anger and resentment. All I ask is that when these . . . natural feelings have diminished you will recall that no condemnation of my conduct can approach the severity of my own . . . and that my one excuse is my incapacity longer to deceive a person whom I have learned to respect and admire."

It sounded false; it was false; and Charles was uncomfortably aware of her unpent contempt for him.

"I am trying to picture *her.* I suppose she is titled—has pretensions to birth. Oh . . . if I had only listened to my poor, dear father!"

"What does that mean?"

"He knows the nobility. He has a phrase for them—Fine manners and unpaid bills."

"I am not a member of the nobility."

"You are like your uncle. You behave as if your rank excuses you all concern with what we ordinary creatures of the world believe in. And so does she. What woman could be so vile as to make a man break his vows? I can guess." She spat the guess out. "She is married."

"I will not discuss this."

"Where is she now? In London?"

He stared at Ernestina a moment, then turned on his heel and walked towards the door. She stood.

"My father will drag your name, both your names, through the mire. You will be spurned and detested by all who know you. You will be hounded out of England, you will be—"

He had halted at the door. Now he opened it. And that—or the impossibility of thinking of a sufficient infamy for him—made her stop. Her face was working, as if she wanted to say so much more, but could not. She swayed; and then some contradictory self in her said his name; as if it had been a nightmare, and now she wished to be told she was waking from it.

He did not move. She faltered and then abruptly slumped to the floor by her chair. His first instinctive move was to go to her. But something in the way she had fallen, the rather too careful way her knees had crumpled and her body slipped sideways onto the carpet, stopped him.

He stared a moment down at that collapsed figure, and recognized the catatonia of convention.

He said, "I shall write at once to your father."

She made no sign, but lay with her eyes closed, her hand pathetically extended on the carpet. He strode to the bellrope beside the mantelpiece and pulled it sharply, then strode back to the open door. As soon as he heard Mary's footsteps, he left the room. The maid came running up the stairs from the kitchen. Charles indicated the sitting room.

"She has had a shock. You must on no account leave her. I go to fetch Doctor Grogan." Mary herself looked for a moment as if she might faint. She put her hand on the banister rail and stared at Charles with stricken eyes. "You understand. On no account leave her." She nodded and bobbed, but did not move. "She has merely fainted. Loosen her dress."

With one more terrified look at him, the maid went into the room. Charles waited a few seconds more. He heard a faint moan, then Mary's voice.

"Oh miss, miss, 'tis Mary. The doctor's comin', miss. 'Tis all right, miss, I woan' leave ee."

And Charles for a brief moment stepped back into the room. He saw Mary on her knees, cradling Ernestina up. The mistress's face was turned against the maid's breast. Mary looked up at Charles: those vivid eyes seemed to forbid him to watch or remain. He accepted their candid judgment.

51

> For a long time, as I have said, the strong feudal habits of subordination and deference continued to tell upon the working class. The modern spirit has now almost entirely dissolved those habits . . . More and more this and that man, and this and that body of men, all over the country, are beginning to assert and put in practice an Englishman's right to do what he likes: his right to march where he likes, meet where he likes, enter where he likes, hoot as he likes, threaten as he likes, smash as he likes. All this, I say, tends to anarchy.
>
> MATTHEW ARNOLD, *Culture and Anarchy* (1869)

Dr. Grogan was mercifully not on his rounds. Charles refused the housekeeper's invitation to go in, but waited on the doorstep until the little doctor came hurriedly down to meet him—and stepped, at a gesture from Charles, outside the door so that their words could not be heard.

"I have just broken off my engagement. She is very distressed. I beg you not to ask for explanation—and to go to Broad Street without delay."

Grogan threw Charles an astounded look over his spectacles, then without a word went back indoors. A few seconds later he reappeared with his hat and medical bag. They began walking at once.

"Not . . . ?"

Charles nodded; and for once the little doctor seemed too shocked to say any more. They walked some twenty or thirty steps.

"She is not what you think, Grogan. I am certain of that."

301

"I am without words, Smithson."

"I seek no excuse."

"She knows?"

"That there is another. No more." They turned the corner and began to mount Broad Street. "I must ask you not to reveal her name." The doctor gave him a fierce little side-look. "For Miss Woodruff's sake. Not mine."

The doctor stopped abruptly. "That morning—am I to understand . . . ?"

"I beg you. Go now. I will wait at the inn."

But Grogan remained staring, as if he too could not believe he was not in some nightmare. Charles stood it a moment, then, gesturing the doctor on up the hill, began to cross the street towards the White Lion.

"By heavens, Smithson . . ."

Charles turned a moment, bore the Irishman's angry look, then continued without word on his way. As did the doctor, though he did not quit Charles with his eyes till he had disappeared under the rain-porch.

Charles regained his rooms, in time to see the doctor admitted into Aunt Tranter's house. He entered with him in spirit; he felt like a Judah, an Ephialtes, like every traitor since time began. But he was saved from further self-maceration by a knock on the door. Sam appeared.

"What the devil do you want? I didn't ring." Sam opened his mouth, but no sound emerged. Charles could not bear the shock of that look. "But now you've come—fetch me a glass of brandy."

But that was mere playing for time. The brandy was brought, and Charles sipped it; and then once more had to face his servant's stare.

"It's never true, Mr. Charles?"

"Were you at the house?"

"Yes, Mr. Charles."

Charles went to the bay window overlooking Broad Street. "Yes, it is true. Miss Freeman and I are no longer to marry. Now go. And keep your mouth shut."

"But . . . Mr. Charles, me and my Mary?"

"Later, later. I can't think of such matters now."

He tossed off the last of his brandy and then went to the writing desk and drew out a sheet of notepaper. Some seconds passed. Sam did not move. Or his feet did not move. His gorge was visibly swelling.

"Did you hear what I said?"

Sam had a strange glistening look. "Yes, sir. Honly with respeck I 'ave to consider my hown sitwation."

Charles swung round from his desk.

"And what may that mean?"

"Will you be residin' in London from 'enceforward, sir?"

Charles picked up the pen from the standish.

"I shall very probably go abroad."

"Then I 'ave to beg to hadvise you, sir, that I won't be haccompanin' you."

Charles jumped up. "How dare you address me in that damned impertinent manner! Take yourself off!"

Sam was now the enraged bantam.

"Not 'fore you've 'eard me out. I'm not comin' back to Hexeter. I'm leavin' your hemploy!"

"Sam!" It was a shout of rage.

"As I hought to 'ave done——"

"Go to the devil!"

Sam drew himself up then. For two pins he would have given his master a never-say-die* (as he told Mary later) but he controlled his Cockney fire and remembered that a gentleman's gentleman uses finer weapons. So he went to the door and opened it, then threw a freezingly dignified look back at Charles.

"I don't fancy nowhere, *sir,* as where I might meet a friend o' yours."

The door was closed none too gently. Charles strode to it and ripped it open. Sam was retreating down the corridor.

"How dare you! Come here!"

Sam turned with a grave calm. "If you wishes for hattention, pray ring for one of the 'otel domestics."

And with that parting shot, which left Charles speechless, he disappeared round a corner and downstairs. His grin when he heard the door above violently slammed again did not last long. He had gone and done it. And in truth he felt like a marooned sailor seeing his ship sail away; worse, he had a secret knowledge that he deserved his punishment. Mutiny, I am afraid, was not his only crime.

Charles spent his rage on the empty brandy glass, which he hurled into the fireplace. This was his first taste of the real thorn-and-stone treatment, and he did not like it one bit. For a wild moment he almost rushed out of the White Lion—he would throw himself on his knees at Ernestina's feet, he would plead insanity, inner torment, a testing of her love . . . he kept striking his fist in his open palm. What had he done? What was he doing? What would he do? If even his servants despised and rejected him!

He stood holding his head in his hands. Then he looked at his watch. He should still see Sarah tonight; and a vision of

* A black eye.

303

her face, gentle, acquiescent, soft tears of joy as he held her ... it was enough. He went back to his desk and started to draft the letter to Ernestina's father. He was still engaged on it when Dr. Grogan was announced.

52

Oh, make my love a coffin
Of the gold that shines yellow,
And she shall be buried
By the banks of green willow.

SOMERSET FOLKSONG: "By the Banks of Green Willow"

The sad figure in all this is poor Aunt Tranter. She came back from her lunch expecting to meet Charles. Instead she met her house in universal catastrophe. Mary first greeted her in the hall, white and distraught.

"Child, child, what has happened!"

Mary could only shake her head in agony. A door opened upstairs and the good lady raised her skirt and began to trot up them like a woman half her age. On the landing she met Dr. Grogan, who urgently raised his finger to his lips. It was not until they were in the fateful sitting room, and he had seen Mrs. Tranter seated, that he broke the reality to her.

"It cannot be. It cannot be."

"Dear woman, a thousand times alas ... but it can—and is."

"But Charles ... so affectionate, so loving ... why, only yesterday a telegram ..." and she looked as if she no longer knew her room, or the doctor's quiet, downlooking face.

"His conduct is atrocious. I cannot understand it."

"But what reasons has he given?"

"She would not speak. Now don't alarm yourself. She needs sleep. What I have given her will ensure that. Tomorrow all will be explained."

"Not all the explanations in the world ..."

She began to cry. "There, there, my dear lady. Cry. Nothing relieves the feelings better."

"Poor darling. She will die of a broken heart."

"I think not. I have never yet had to give that as a cause of death."

"You do not know her as I do . . . and oh, what will Emily say? It will all be my fault." Emily was her sister, Mrs. Freeman.

"I think she must be telegraphed at once. Allow me to see to that."

"Oh heavens—and where shall she sleep?"

The doctor smiled, but very gently, at this *non sequitur*. He had had to deal with such cases before; and he knew the best prescription was an endless female fuss.

"Now, my dear Mrs. Tranter, I wish you to listen to me. For a few days you must see to it that your niece is watched day and night. If she wishes to be treated as an invalid, then treat her so. If she wishes tomorrow to get up and leave Lyme, then let her do so. Humor her, you understand. She is young, in excellent health. I guarantee that in six months she will be as gay as a linnet."

"How can you be so cruel! She will never get over it. That wicked . . . but how . . ." A thought struck her and she reached out and touched the doctor's sleeve. "There is another woman!"

Dr. Grogan pinched his nose. "That, I cannot say."

"He is a monster."

"But not so much of a monster that he has not declared himself one. And lost a party a good many monsters would have greedily devoured."

"Yes. Yes. There is that to be thankful for." But her mind was boxed by contradictions. "I shall never forgive him." Another idea struck her. "He is still in the town? I shall go tell him my mind."

He took her arm. "That I must forbid. He himself called me here. He waits now to hear that the poor girl is not in danger. I shall see him. Rest assured that I shall not mince matters. I'll have his hide for this."

"He should be whipped and put in the stocks. When we were young that would have been done. It ought to be done. The poor, poor angel." She stood. "I must go to her."

"And I must see him."

"You will tell him from me that he has ruined the happiness of the sweetest, most trusting—"

"Yes yes yes . . . now calm yourself. And do find out why that serving-lass of yours is taking on so. Anyone would think her heart *had* been broken."

Mrs. Tranter saw the doctor out, then drying her tears, climbed the stairs to Ernestina's room. The curtains were drawn, but daylight filtered round the edges. Mary sat beside the victim. She rose as her mistress entered. Ernestina lay deep in sleep, on her back, but with her head turned to one side. The face was strangely calm and composed, the breathing quiet. There was even the faintest suggestion of a smile on those lips. The irony of that calm smote Mrs. Tranter again; the poor dear child, when she awoke . . . tears sprang again. She raised herself and dabbed her eyes, then looked at Mary for the first time. Now Mary really did look like a soul in the bottom-most pit of misery, in fact everything that Tina ought to have looked, but didn't; and Mrs. Tranter remembered the doctor's somewhat querulous parting words. She beckoned to the maid to follow her and they went out on the landing. With the door ajar, they spoke there in whispers.

"Now tell me what happened, child."

"Mr. Charles 'e called down, m'm, and Miss Tina was a-lying in faints an' 'e run out fer the doctor 'n Miss Tina 'er opens 'er eyes on'y 'er doan' say nothin' so's I 'elps 'er up yere, I didden know 'ow to do, for soon's 'er's on 'er bed, m'm, 'er's tooken by the istricks 'n oh m'm I was so frighted 'twas like 'er was laffin' and screamin' and 'er woulden stop. An' then Doctor Grogan 'e come 'n 'e calm 'er down. Oh m'm."

"There, there, Mary, you were a good girl. And did she say nothing?"

"On'y when us was a-comin' up the stairs, m'm, an' 'er asked where Mr. Charles was to, m'm. I tol'er 'e'd agone to the doctor. 'Twas what started the istricks, m'm."

"Sh. Sh."

For Mary's voice had begun to rise and there were strong symptoms in her as well of the hysterics. Mrs. Tranter had, in any case, a strong urge to console something, so she took Mary into her arms and patted her head. Although she thereby broke all decent laws on the matter of the mistress-servant relationship, I rather think that that heavenly butler did not close his doors in *her* face. The girl's body was racked with pent-up sobs, which she tried to control for the other sufferer's sake. At last she quietened.

"Now what is it?"

"It's Sam, m'm. 'E's downstairs. 'E's 'ad bad words with Mr. Charles, m'm, an' given in 'is notice 'n Mr. Charles woan' giv'un no reffrums now." She stifled a late sob. "Us doan' know what's to become of us."

"Bad words? When was this, child?"

"Jus' afore 'ee come in, m'm. On account o' Miss Tina, m'm."

"But how was that?"

"Sam 'e knew 'twas goin' to 'appen. That Mr. Charles—'e's a wicked wicked man, m'm. Oh m'm, us wanted to tell 'ee but us didden dare."

There was a low sound from the room. Mrs. Tranter went swiftly and looked in; but the face remained calm and deeply asleep. She came out again to the girl with the sunken head.

"I shall watch now, Mary. Let us talk later." The girl bent her head even lower. "This Sam, do you truly love him?"

"Yes, m'm."

"And does he love you?"

" 'Tis why 'e woulden go with 'is master, m'm."

"Tell him to wait. I should like to speak to him. And we'll find him a post."

Mary's tear-stained face rose then.

"I doan' ever want to leav'ee, m'm."

"And you never shall, child—till your wedding day."

Then Mrs. Tranter bent forward and kissed her forehead. She went and sat by Ernestina, while Mary went downstairs. Once in the kitchen she ran, to the cook's disgust, outside and into the lilac shadows and Sam's anxious but eager arms.

53

For we see whither it has brought us . . . the insisting on perfection in one part of our nature and not in all; the singling out of the moral side, the side of obedience and action, for such intent regard; making strictness of the moral conscience so far the principal thing, and putting off for hereafter and for another world the care of being complete at all points, the full and harmonious development of our humanity.

MATTHEW ARNOLD, *Culture and Anarchy* (1869)

"She is . . . recovered?"

"I have put her to sleep."

The doctor walked across the room and stood with his hands behind his back, staring down Broad Street to the sea.

"She . . . she said nothing?"

The doctor shook his head without turning; was silent a moment; then he burst round on Charles.

"I await your explanation, sir!"

And Charles gave it, baldly, without self-extenuation. Of Sarah he said very little. His sole attempt at an excuse was over his deception of Grogan himself; and that he blamed on his conviction that to have committed Sarah to any asylum would have been a gross injustice. The doctor listened with a fierce, intent silence. When Charles had finished he turned again to the window.

"I wish I could remember what particular punishments Dante prescribed for the Antinomians. Then I could prescribe them for you."

"I think I shall have punishment enough."

"That is not possible. Not by my tally."

Charles left a pause.

"I did not reject your advice without much heart-searching."

"Smithson, a gentleman remains a gentleman when he rejects advice. He does not do so when he tells lies."

"I believed them necessary."

"As you believed the satisfaction of your lust necessary."

"I cannot accept that word."

"You had better learn to. It is the one the world will attach to your conduct."

Charles moved to the central table, and stood with one hand resting on it. "Grogan, would you have had me live a lifetime of pretense? Is our age not full enough as it is of a mealy-mouthed hypocrisy, an adulation of all that is false in our natures? Would you have had me add to that?"

"I would have had you think twice before you embroiled that innocent girl in your pursuit of self-knowledge."

"But once that knowledge is granted us, can we escape its dictates? However repugnant their consequences?"

The doctor looked away with a steely little grimace. Charles saw that he was huffed and nervous; and really at a loss, after the first commination, how to deal with this monstrous affront to provincial convention. There was indeed a struggle in progress between the Grogan who had lived now for a quarter of a century in Lyme and the Grogan who had seen the world. There were other things: his liking for Charles, his private opinion—not very far removed from Sir Robert's—that Ernestina was a pretty little thing, but a shallow little thing; there was even an event long buried in his own past whose exact nature need not be revealed beyond that it made his reference to lust a good deal less impersonal than he had made it seem. His tone remained reproving; but he sidestepped the moral question he had been asked.

"I am a doctor, Smithson. I know only one overriding law. All suffering is evil. It may also be necessary. That does not alter its fundamental nature."

"I don't see where good is to spring from, if it is not out of that evil. How can one build a better self unless on the ruins of the old?"

"And the ruins of that poor young creature across the way?"

"It is better she suffers once, to be free of me, than . . ." he fell silent.

"Ah. You are sure of that, are you?" Charles said nothing. The doctor stared down at the street. "You have committed a crime. Your punishment will be to remember it all your life. So don't give yourself absolution yet. Only death will give you that." He took off his glasses, and polished them on a green silk handkerchief. There was a long pause, a very long pause; and at the end of it his voice, though still reproving, was milder.

"You will marry the other?"

Charles breathed a metaphorical sigh of relief. As soon as Grogan had come into the room he had known that his previous self-assertions—that he was indifferent to the opinion of a mere bathing-place doctor—were hollow. There was a humanity in the Irishman Charles greatly respected; in a way Grogan stood for *all* he respected. He knew he could not expect a full remission of sins; but it was enough to sense that total excommunication was not to be his lot.

"That is my most sincere intent."

"She knows? You have told her?"

"Yes."

"And she has accepted your offer, of course?"

"I have every reason to believe so." He explained the circumstances of Sam's errand that morning.

The little doctor turned to face him.

"Smithson, I know you are not vicious. I know you would not have done what you have unless you believed the girl's own account of her extraordinary behavior. But I warn you that a doubt must remain. And such a doubt as must cast a shadow over any future protection you extend to her."

"I have taken that into consideration." Charles risked a thin smile. "As I have the cloud of obfuscating cant our sex talks about women. They are to sit, are they not, like so many articles in a shop and to let us men walk in and turn them over and point at this one or that one—*she* takes my fancy. If they allow this, we call them decent, respectable, modest. But when one of these articles has the impertinence to speak up for herself—"

"She has done rather more than that, I gather."

Charles rode the rebuke. "She has done what is almost a commonplace in high society. I do not know why the countless wives in that *milieu* who dishonor their marriage vows are to be granted exculpation, while . . . besides, I am far more to blame. She merely sent me her address. I was perfectly free to avoid the consequences of going to it."

The doctor threw him a mute little glance. Honesty, now, he had to admit. He resumed his stare down at the street. After a few moments he spoke, much more in his old manner and voice.

"Perhaps I am growing old. I know such breaches of trust as yours are becoming so commonplace that to be shocked by them is to pronounce oneself an old fogey. But I will tell you what bothers me. I share your distaste for cant, whether

310

it be of the religious or the legal variety. The law has always seemed to me an ass, and a great part of religion very little better. I do not attack you on those grounds, I will not attack you on any grounds. I will merely give you my opinion. It is this. You believe yourself to belong to a rational and scientific elect. No, no, I know what you would say, you are not so vain. So be it. Nonetheless, you *wish* to belong to that elect. I do not blame you for that. I have held the same wish myself all my life. But I beg you to remember one thing, Smithson. All through human history the elect have made their cases for election. But Time allows only one plea." The doctor replaced his glasses and turned on Charles. "It is this. That the elect, whatever the particular grounds they advance for their cause, have introduced a finer and fairer morality into this dark world. If they fail that test, then they become no more than despots, sultans, mere seekers after their own pleasure and power. In short, mere victims of their own baser desires. I think you understand what I am driving at—and its especial relevance to yourself from this unhappy day on. If you become a better and a more generous human being, you may be forgiven. But if you become more selfish ... you are doubly damned."

Charles looked down from those exacting eyes. "Though far less cogently, my own conscience had already said as much."

"Then amen. *Jacta alea est.*" He picked up his hat and bag from the table and went to the door. But there he hesitated—then held out his hand. "I wish you well on your march away from the Rubicon."

Charles grasped the proffered hand, almost as if he were drowning. He tried to say something, but failed. There was a moment of stronger pressure from Grogan's fingers, then he turned and opened the door. He looked back, a glint in his eyes.

"And if you do not leave here within the hour I shall be back with the largest horsewhip I can find."

Charles stiffened at that. But the glint remained. Charles swallowed a painful smile and bowed his head in assent. The door closed.

He was left alone with his medicine.

54

My wind is turned to bitter north
That was so soft a south before . . .
A. H. CLOUGH, Poem (1841)

In fairness to Charles it must be said that he sent to find Sam before he left the White Lion. But the servant was not in the taproom or the stables. Charles guessed indeed where he was. He could not send there; and thus he left Lyme without seeing him again. He got into his four-wheeler in the yard, and promptly drew down the blinds. Two hearse-like miles passed before he opened them again, and let the slanting evening sunlight, for it was now five o'clock, brighten the dingy paintwork and upholstery of the carriage.

It did not immediately brighten Charles's spirits. Yet gradually, as he continued to draw away from Lyme, he felt as if a burden had been lifted off his shoulders; a defeat suffered, and yet he had survived it. Grogan's solemn warning—that the rest of his life must be lived in proof of the justice of what he had done—he accepted. But among the rich green fields and May hedgerows of the Devon countryside it was difficult not to see the future as fertile—a new life lay ahead of him, great challenges, but he would rise to them. His guilt seemed almost beneficial: its expiation gave his life its hitherto lacking purpose.

An image from ancient Egypt entered his mind—a sculpture in the British Museum, showing a pharaoh standing beside his wife, who had her arm round his waist, with her other hand on his forearm. It had always seemed to Charles a perfect emblem of conjugal harmony, not least since the figures were carved from the same block of stone. He and Sarah were not yet carved into that harmony; but they were of the same stone.

He gave himself then to thoughts of the future, to practical arrangements. Sarah must be suitably installed in London. They should go abroad as soon as his affairs could be settled, the Kensington house got rid of, his things stored ... perhaps Germany first, then south in winter to Florence or Rome (if the civil conditions allowed) or perhaps Spain. Granada! The Alhambra! Moonlight, the distant sound below of singing gypsies, such grateful, tender eyes ... and in some jasmine-scented room they would lie awake, in each other's arms, infinitely alone, exiled, yet fused in that loneliness, inseparable in that exile.

Night had fallen. Charles craned out and saw the distant lights of Exeter. He called out to the driver to take him first to Endicott's Family Hotel. Then he leaned back and reveled in the scene that was to come. Nothing carnal should disfigure it, of course; that at least he owed to Ernestina as much as to Sarah. But he once again saw an exquisite tableau of tender silence, her hands in his ...

They arrived. Telling the man to wait Charles entered the hotel and knocked on Mrs. Endicott's door.

"Oh it's you, sir."

"Miss Woodruff expects me. I will find my own way."

Already he was turning away towards the stairs.

"The young lady's left, sir!"

"Left! You mean gone out?"

"No, sir. I mean left." He stared weakly at her. "She took the London train this morning, sir."

"But I ... are you sure?"

"Sure as I'm standing here, sir. I distinctly heard her say the railway station to the cabman, sir. And he asked what train, and she said, plain as I'm speaking to you now, the London." The plump old lady came forward. "Well I was surprised myself, sir. Her with three days still paid on her room."

"But did she leave no address?"

"Not a line, sir. Not a word to me where she was going." That black mark very evidently cancelled the good one merited by not asking for three days' money back.

"No message was left for me?"

"I thought it might very likely be you she was a-going off with, sir. That's what I took the liberty to presume."

To stand longer there became an impossibility. "Here is

313

my card. If you hear from her—if you would let me know. Without fail. Here. Something for the service and postage."

Mrs. Endicott smiled ingratiatingly. "Oh thank you, sir. Without fail."

He went out; and as soon came back.

"This morning—a manservant, did he not come with a letter and packet for Miss Woodruff?" Mrs. Endicott looked blank. "Shortly after eight o'clock?" Still the proprietress looked blank. Then she called for Betsy Anne, who appeared and was severely cross-examined by her mistress ... that is, until Charles abruptly left.

He sank back into his carriage and closed his eyes. He felt without volition, plunged into a state of abulia. If only he had not been so scrupulous, if only he had come straight back after ... but Sam. Sam! A thief! A spy! Had he been tempted into Mr. Freeman's pay? Or was his crime explicable as resentment over those wretched three hundred pounds? How well did Charles now understand the scene in Lyme—Sam must have realized he would be discovered as soon as they returned to Exeter; must therefore have read his letter ... Charles flushed a deep red in the darkness. He would break the man's neck if he ever saw him again. For a moment he even contemplated going to a police station office and charging him with ... well, theft at any rate. But at once he saw the futility of that. And what good would it do in the essential: the discovery of Sarah?

He saw only one light in the gloom that descended on him. She had gone to London; she knew he lived in London. But if her motive was to come, as Grogan had once suggested, knocking on his door, would not that motive rather have driven her back to Lyme, where she supposed him to be? And had he not decided that all her intentions were honorable? Must it not seem to her that he was renounced, and lost, forever? The one light flickered, and went out.

He did something that night he had not done for many years. He knelt by his bed and prayed; and the substance of his prayer was that he would find her; if he searched for the rest of his life, he would find her.

55

"Why, about *you!*" Tweedledee exclaimed, clapping his hands triumphantly. "And if he left off dreaming about you, where do you suppose you'd be?"

"Where I am now, of course," said Alice.

"Not you!" Tweedledee retorted contemptuously. "You'd be nowhere. Why, you're only a sort of thing in his dream!"

"If that there King was to wake," added Tweedledum, "you'd go out—bang!—just like a candle!"

"I shouldn't!" Alice exclaimed indignantly.

LEWIS CARROLL, *Through the Looking-Glass* (1872)

Charles arrived at the station in ridiculously good time the next morning; and having gone through the ungentlemanly business of seeing his things loaded into the baggage van and then selected an empty first-class compartment, he sat impatiently waiting for the train to start. Other passengers looked in from time to time, and were rebuffed by that Gorgon stare (this compartment is reserved for non-lepers) the English have so easily at command. A whistle sounded, and Charles thought he had won the solitude he craved. But then, at the very last moment, a massively bearded face appeared at his window. The cold stare was met by the even colder stare of a man in a hurry to get aboard.

The latecomer muttered a "Pardon me, sir" and made his way to the far end of the compartment. He sat, a man of forty or so, his top hat firmly square, his hands on his knees, regaining his breath. There was something rather aggressively secure about him; he was perhaps not quite a gentleman ... an ambitious butler (but butlers did not travel first class) or a successful lay preacher—one of the bullying tabernacle kind, a would-be Spurgeon, converting souls by scorching them with the cheap rhetoric of eternal damnation. A decidedly unpleasant man, thought Charles, and so typical of the age—and therefore emphatically to be snubbed if he tried to enter into conversation.

As sometimes happens when one stares covertly at people and speculates about them, Charles was caught in the act; and reproved for it. There was a very clear suggestion in the sharp look sideways that Charles should keep his eyes to himself. He hastily directed his gaze outside his window and consoled himself that at least the person shunned intimacy as much as he did.

Very soon the even movement lulled Charles into a douce daydream. London was a large city; but she must soon look for work. He had the time, the resources, the will; a week might pass, two, but then she would stand before him; perhaps yet another address would slip through his letter box. The wheels said it: she-could-not-be-so-cruel, she-could-not-be-so-cruel, she-could-not-be-so-cruel ... the train passed through the red and green valleys towards Cullompton. Charles saw its church, without knowing where the place was, and soon afterwards closed his eyes. He had slept poorly that previous night.

For a while his traveling companion took no notice of the sleeping Charles. But as the chin sank deeper and deeper—Charles had taken the precaution of removing his hat—the prophet-bearded man began to stare at him, safe in the knowledge that *his* curiosity would *not* be surprised.

His look was peculiar: sizing, ruminative, more than a shade disapproving, as if he knew very well what sort of man this was (as Charles had believed to see very well what sort of man *he* was) and did not much like the knowledge or the species. It was true that, unobserved, he looked a little less frigid and authoritarian a person; but there remained about his features an unpleasant aura of self-confidence—or if not quite confidence in self, at least a confidence in his judgment of others, of how much he could get out of them, expect from them, tax them.

A stare of a minute or so's duration, of this kind, might have been explicable. Train journeys are boring; it is amusing to spy on strangers; and so on. But this stare, which became positively cannibalistic in its intensity, lasted far longer than a minute. It lasted beyond Taunton, though it was briefly interrupted there when the noise on the platform made Charles wake for a few moments. But when he sank back into his slumbers, the eyes fastened on him again in the same leech-like manner.

You may one day come under a similar gaze. And you may—in the less reserved context of our own century—be aware of it. The intent watcher will not wait till you are asleep. It will no doubt suggest something unpleasant, some kind of devious sexual approach . . . a desire to know you in a way you do not want to be known by a stranger. In my experience there is only one profession that gives that particular look, with its bizarre blend of the inquisitive and the magistral; of the ironic and the soliciting.

Now could I use you?

Now what could I do with you?

It is precisely, it has always seemed to me, the look an omnipotent god—if there were such an absurd thing—should be shown to have. Not at all what we think of as a divine look; but one of a distinctly mean and dubious (as the theoreticians of the *nouveau roman* have pointed out) moral quality. I see this with particular clarity on the face, only too familiar to me, of the bearded man who stares at Charles. And I will keep up the pretense no longer.

Now the question I am asking, as I stare at Charles, is not quite the same as the two above. But rather, what the devil am I going to do with you? I have already thought of ending Charles's career here and now; of leaving him for eternity on his way to London. But the conventions of Victorian fiction allow, allowed no place for the open, the inconclusive ending; and I preached earlier of the freedom characters must be given. My problem is simple—what Charles wants is clear? It is indeed. But what the protagonist wants is not so clear; and I am not at all sure where she is at the moment. Of course if these two were two fragments of real life, instead of two figments of my imagination, the issue of the dilemma is obvious: the one want combats the other want, and fails or succeeds, as the actuality may be. Fiction usually pretends to conform to the reality: the writer puts the conflicting wants in the ring and then describes the fight—but in fact fixes the fight, letting that want he himself favors win. And we judge writers of fiction both by the skill they show in fixing the fights (in other words, in persuading us that they were not fixed) and by the kind of fighter they fix in favor of: the good one, the tragic one, the evil one, the funny one, and so on.

But the chief argument for fight-fixing is to show one's readers what one thinks of the world around one—whether one is a pessimist, an optimist, what you will. I have pretended to slip back into 1867; but of course that year is in reality a century past. It is futile to show optimism or pessimism, or anything else about it, because we know what has happened since.

So I continue to stare at Charles and see no reason this time for fixing the fight upon which he is about to engage. That leaves me with two alternatives. I let the fight proceed and take no more than a recording part in it; or I take both sides in it. I stare at that vaguely effete but not completely futile face. And as we near London, I think I see a solution; that is, I see the dilemma is false. The only way I can take no part in the fight is to show two versions of it. That leaves me with only one problem: I cannot give both versions at once, yet whichever is the second will seem, so strong is the tyranny of the last chapter, the final, the "real" version.

I take my purse from the pocket of my frock coat, extract a florin, I rest it on my right thumbnail, I flick it spinning, two feet into the air and catch it in my left hand.

So be it. And I am suddenly aware that Charles has opened his eyes and is looking at me. There is something more than disapproval in his eyes now; he perceives I am either a gambler or mentally deranged. I return his disapproval, and my florin to my purse. He picks up his hat, brushes some invisible speck of dirt (a surrogate for myself) from its nap, and places it on his head.

We draw under one of the great cast-iron beams that support the roof of Paddington station. We arrive, he steps down to the platform, beckoning to a porter. In a few moments, having given his instructions, he turns. The bearded man has disappeared in the throng.

56

Ah Christ, that it were possible
For one short hour to see
The souls we loved, that they might tell us
What and where they be.

TENNYSON, *Maud* (1855)

Private Inquiry Office, Patronized by the Aristocracy, and
under the sole direction of Mr. Pollaky himself. Relations
with both the British and the Foreign Detective Police.
DELICATE AND CONFIDENTIAL INQUIRIES INSTITUTED WITH
SECRECY AND DISPATCH IN ENGLAND, THE CONTINENT AND THE
COLONIES. EVIDENCE COLLECTED FOR CASES IN THE DIVORCE
COURT, &C.

MID-VICTORIAN ADVERTISEMENT

---

*A week might pass, two, but then she would stand before
him ...* The third week begins, and she has not stood before
him. Charles cannot be faulted; he has been here, there,
everywhere.

He had achieved this ubiquity by hiring four detectives—
whether they were under the sole direction of Mr. Pollaky, I
am not sure, but they worked hard. They had to, for they
were a very new profession, a mere eleven years old, and
held in general contempt. A gentleman in 1866 who stabbed
one to death was considered to have done a very proper
thing. "If people go about got up as garrotters," warned
Punch, "they must take the consequences."

Charles's men had first tried the governess agencies, without success; they had tried the Educational Boards of all the denominations that ran Church schools. Hiring a carriage, he had himself spent fruitless hours patrolling, a pair of intent eyes that scanned each younger female face that passed, the genteel-poor districts of London. In one such Sarah must be lodging: in Peckham, in Pentonville, in Putney; in a dozen similar districts of neat new roads and one-domestic houses he searched. He also helped his men to investigate the booming new female clerical agencies. A generalized hostility to Adam was already evident in them, since they had to bear the full brunt of masculine prejudice and were to become among the most important seedbeds of the emancipation movement. I think these experiences, though fruitless in the one matter he cared about, were not all wasted on Charles. Slowly he began to understand one aspect of Sarah better: her feeling of resentment, of an unfair because remediable bias in society.

One morning he had woken to find himself very depressed. The dreadful possibility of prostitution, that fate she had once hinted at, became a certainty. That evening he went in a state of panic to the same Haymarket area he visited earlier. What the driver imagined, I cannot suppose; but he must certainly have thought his fare the most fastidious man who ever existed. They drove up and down those streets for two hours. Only once did they stop; the driver saw a red-haired prostitute under a gaslight. But almost at once two taps bade him drive on again.

Other consequences of his choice of freedom had meanwhile not waited to exact their toll. To his finally achieved letter to Mr. Freeman he received no answer for ten days. But then he had to sign for one, delivered ominously by hand, from Mr. Freeman's solicitors.

Sir,
In re Miss Ernestina Freeman
We are instructed by Mr. Ernest Freeman, father of the above-mentioned Miss Ernestina Freeman, to request you to attend at these chambers at 3 o'clock this coming Friday. Your failure to attend will be regarded as an acknowledgment of our client's right to proceed.

AUBREY & BAGGOTT

Charles took the letter to his own solicitors. They had handled the Smithson family affairs since the eighteenth century. And the present younger Montague, facing whose desk the confessed sinner now shamefacedly sat, was only a little older than Charles himself. The two men had been at Winchester together; and without being close friends, knew and liked each other well enough.

"Well, what does it mean, Harry?"

"It means, my dear boy, that you have the devil's own luck. They have cold feet."

"Then why should they want to see me?"

"They won't let you off altogether, Charles. That is asking too much. My guess is that you will be asked to make a *confessio delicti*."

"A statement of guilt?"

"Just so. I am afraid you must anticipate an ugly document. But I can only advise you to sign it. You have no case."

On that Friday afternoon Charles and Montague were ushered into a funereal waiting room in one of the Inns of Court. Charles felt it was something like a duel; Montague was his second. They were made to cool their heels until a quarter past three. But since this preliminary penance had been predicted by Montague, they bore it with a certain nervous amusement.

At last they were summoned. A short and choleric old man rose from behind a large desk. A little behind him stood Mr. Freeman. He had no eyes but for Charles, and they were very cold eyes indeed; all amusement vanished. Charles bowed to him, but no acknowledgment was made. The two solicitors shook hands curtly. There was a fifth person present: a tall, thin, balding man with penetrating dark eyes, at the sight of whom Montague imperceptibly flinched.

"You know Mr. Serjeant Murphy?"

"By reputation only."

A serjeant-at-law was in Victorian times a top counsel; and Serjeant Murphy was a killer, the most feared man of his day.

Mr. Aubrey peremptorily indicated the chairs the two visitors were to take, then sat down himself again. Mr. Freeman remained implacably standing. Mr. Aubrey shuffled papers, which gave Charles time he did not want to absorb the usual intimidating atmosphere of such places: the learned volumes, the rolls of sheepskin bound in green ferret, the mournful box-files of dead cases ranged high around the room like the urns of an overpopulated *columbarium*.

The old solicitor looked severely up.

"I think, Mr. Montague, that the facts of this abominable breach of engagement are not in dispute. I do not know what construction your client has put upon his conduct to you. But he has himself provided abundant evidence of his own guilt in this letter to Mr. Freeman, though I note that with the usual impudence of his kind he has sought to—"

"Mr. Aubrey, such language in these circumstances—"

Serjeant Murphy pounced. "Would you prefer to hear the language *I* should use, Mr. Montague—and in open court?"

Montague took a breath and looked down. Old Aubrey stared at him with a massive disapproval. "Montague, I knew your late grandfather well. I fancy he would have thought twice before acting for such a client as yours—but let that pass for the nonce. I consider this letter . . ." and he held it up, as if with tongs ". . . I consider this disgraceful letter adds most impertinent insult to an already gross injury, both by its shameless attempt at self-exoneration and the complete absence from it of any reference to the criminal and sordid liaison that the writer well knows is the blackest aspect of his crime." He glowered at Charles. "You may, sir, have thought Mr. Freeman not to be fully cognizant of your amours. You are wrong. We know the name of the female with whom you have entered into such base conversation. We have a witness to circumstances I find too disgusting to name."

Charles flushed red. Mr. Freeman's eyes bored into him. He could only lower his head; and curse Sam. Montague spoke.

"My client did not come here to defend his conduct."

"Then you would not defend an action?"

"A person of your eminence in our profession must know that I cannot answer that question."

Serjeant Murphy intervened again. "You would not defend an action if one were brought?"

"With respect, sir, I must reserve judgment on that matter."

A vulpine smile distorted the serjeant-at-law's lips.

"The judgment is not at issue, Mr. Montague."

"May we proceed, Mr. Aubrey?"

Mr. Aubrey glanced at the serjeant, who nodded grim assent.

"This is not an occasion, Mr. Montague, when I should advise too much standing upon plea." He shuffled papers again. "I will be brief. My advice to Mr. Freeman has been clear. In my long experience, my very long experience, this is the vilest example of dishonorable behavior I have ever had under my survey. Even did not your client merit the harsh judgment he would inevitably receive, I believe firmly that such vicious conduct should be exhibited as a warning to others." He left a long silence, then, for the words to sink deep. Charles wished he could control the blood in his cheeks. Mr. Freeman at least was now looking down; but Serjeant Murphy knew very well how to use a flushing witness. He put on what admiring junior counsel called his basilisk quiz, in which irony and sadism were nicely prominent.

Mr. Aubrey, in a somber new key, went on. "However, for reasons I shall not go into, Mr. Freeman has elected to show a mercy the case in no way warrants. He does not, upon conditions, immediately have it in mind to proceed."

Charles swallowed, and glanced at Montague.

"I am sure my client is grateful to yours."

"I have, with esteemed advice . . ." Mr. Aubrey bowed briefly towards the serjeant, who bobbed his head without taking his eyes off the wretched Charles ". . . prepared an admission of guilt. I should instruct you that Mr. Freeman's decision not to proceed immediately is most strictly contingent upon your client's signing, on this occasion and in our presence, and witnessed by all present, this document."

And he handed it to Montague, who glanced at it, then looked up.

"May I request five minutes' discussion in private with my client?"

"I am most surprised you should find discussion necessary." He puffed up a little, but Montague stood firm. "Then very well, very well. If you must."

So Harry Montague and Charles found themselves back in the funereal waiting room. Montague read the document, then handed it drily to Charles.

"Well, here's your medicine. You've got to take it, dear boy."

And while Montague stared out at the window, Charles read the admission of guilt.

I, Charles Algernon Henry Smithson, do fully, freely and not upon any consideration but my desire to declare the truth, admit that:

1. I contracted to marry Miss Ernestina Freeman;

2. I was given no cause whatsoever by the innocent party (the said Miss Ernestina Freeman) to break my solemn contract with her;

3. I was fully and exactly apprised of her rank in society, her character, her marriage portion and future prospects before my engagement to her hand and that nothing I learned subsequently of the aforesaid Miss Ernestina Freeman in any way contradicted or denied what I had been told;

4. I did break that contract without just cause or any justification whatsoever beyond my own criminal selfishness and faithlessness;

5. I entered upon a clandestine liaison with a person named Sarah Emily Woodruff, resident at Lyme Regis and Exeter, and I did attempt to conceal this liaison;

6. My conduct throughout this matter has been dishonorable, and by it I have forever forfeited the right to be considered a gentleman.

Furthermore, I acknowledge the right of the injured party to proceed against me *sine die* and without term or condition.

Furthermore, I acknowledge that the injured party may make whatsoever use she desires of this document.

Furthermore, my signature hereto appended is given of my own free will, in full understanding of the conditions herein, in full confession of my conduct, and under no duress whatsoever, upon no prior or posterior consideration whatsoever and no right of redress, rebuttal, demurral or denial in any particular, now and henceforth under all the abovementioned terms.

"Have you no comment on it?"

"I fancy that there must have been a dispute over the drafting. No lawyer would happily put in that sixth clause. If it came to court, one might well argue that no gentleman, however foolish he had been, would make such an admission except under duress. A counsel could make quite a lot of that. It is really in our favor. I'm surprised Aubrey and Murphy have allowed it. My guess is that it is Papa's clause. He wants you to eat humble pie."

"It is vile."

He looked for a moment as if he would tear it to pieces.

Montague gently took it from him. "The law is not concerned with truth, Charles. You should know that by now."

"And that 'may make whatsoever use she desires'—what in heaven's name does that mean?"

"It could mean that the document is inserted in *The Times*. I seem to recall something similar was done some years ago. But I have a feeling old Freeman wants to keep this matter quiet. He would have had you in court if he wanted to put you in the stocks."

"So I must sign."

"If you like I can go back and argue for different phrases—some form that would reserve to you the right to plead extenuating circumstances if it came to trial. But I strongly advise against. The very harshness of this as it stands would argue far better for you. It pays us best to pay their price. Then if needs be we can argue the bill was a deuced sight too stiff."

Charles nodded, and they stood.

"There's one thing, Harry. I wish I knew how Ernestina is. I cannot ask him."

"I'll see if I can have a word with old Aubrey afterwards.

He's not such a bad old stick. He has to play it up for Papa."

So they returned; and the admission was signed, first by Charles, then by each of the others in turn. All remained standing. There was a moment's awkward silence. Then at last Mr. Freeman spoke.

"And now, you blackguard, never darken my life again. I wish I were a younger man. If—"

"My dear Mr. Freeman!"

Old Aubrey's sharp voice silenced his client. Charles hesitated, bowed to the two lawyers, then left followed by Montague.

But outside Montague said, "Wait in the carriage for me." A minute or two later he climbed in beside Charles.

"She is as well as can be expected. Those are his words. He also gave me to understand what Freeman intends to do if you go in for the marriage game again. Charles, he will show what you have just signed to the next father-in-law to be. He means you to remain a bachelor all your life."

"I had guessed as much."

"Old Aubrey also told me, by the way, to whom you owe your release on parole."

"To her? That too I had guessed."

"He would have had his pound of flesh. But the young lady evidently rules that household."

The carriage rolled on for a hundred yards before Charles spoke.

"I am defiled to the end of my life."

"My dear Charles, if you play the Muslim in a world of Puritans, you can expect no other treatment. I am as fond as the next man of a pretty ankle. I don't blame you. But don't tell me that the price is not fairly marked."

The carriage rolled on. Charles stared gloomily out at the sunny street.

"I wish I were dead."

"Then let us go to Verrey's and demolish a lobster or two. And you shall tell me about the mysterious Miss Woodruff before you die."

That humiliating interview depressed Charles for days. He wanted desperately to go abroad, never to see England again. His club, his acquaintances, he could not face them; he gave strict instructions—he was at home to no one. He threw himself into the search for Sarah. One day the detective office turned up a Miss Woodbury, newly employed at a girls' academy in Stoke Newington. She had auburn hair, she seemed to fit the description he had supplied. He spent an agonizing hour one afternoon outside the school. Miss Woodbury came out, at the head of a crocodile of young ladies. She bore only the faintest resemblance to Sarah.

June came, an exceptionally fine one. Charles saw it out, but towards the end of it he stopped searching. The detective office remained optimistic, but they had their fees to consider. Exeter was searched as London had been; a man was even sent to make discreet inquiries at Lyme and Charmouth; and all in vain. One evening Charles asked Montague to have dinner with him at the Kensington house, and frankly, miserably, placed himself in his hands. What should he do? Montague did not hesitate to tell him. He should go abroad.

"But what can her purpose have been? To give herself to me—and then to dismiss me as if I were nothing to her."

"The strong presumption—forgive me—is that that latter possibility is the truth. Could not that doctor have been right? Are you sure her motive was not one of vindictive destruction? To ruin your prospects . . . to reduce you to what you are, Charles?"

"I cannot believe it."

"But *prima facie* you *must* believe it."

"Beneath all her stories and deceptions she had a candor . . . an honesty. Perhaps she has died. She has no money. No family."

"Then let me send a clerk to look at the Register of Death."

Charles took this sensible advice almost as if it were an insult. But the next day he followed it; and no Sarah Woodruff's death was recorded.

He dallied another week. Then abruptly, one evening, he decided to go abroad.

57

Each for himself is still the rule:
We learn it when we go to school—
The devil take the hindmost, O!

A. H. CLOUGH, Poem (1849)

And now let us jump twenty months. It is a brisk early February day in the year 1869. Gladstone has in the interval at last reached No. 10 Downing Street; the last public execution in England has taken place; Mill's *Subjection of Women* and Girton College are about to appear. The Thames is its usual infamous mud-gray. But the sky above is derisively blue; and looking up, one might be in Florence.

Looking down, along the new embankment in Chelsea, there are traces of snow on the ground. Yet there is also, if only in the sunlight, the first faint ghost of spring. *I am ver* . . . I am sure the young woman whom I should have liked to show pushing a perambulator (but can't, since they do not come into use for another decade) had never heard of Catullus, nor would have thought much of all that going on about unhappy love even if she had. But she knew the sentiment about spring. After all, she had just left the result of an earlier spring at home (a mile away to the west) and so blanketed and swaddled and swathed that it might just as well have been a bulb beneath the ground. It is also clear, trimly though she contrives to dress, that like all good gardeners she prefers her bulbs planted *en masse*. There is something in that idle slow walk of expectant mothers; the least offensive arrogance in the world, though still an arrogance.

This idle and subtly proud young woman leans for a mo-

327

ment over the parapet and stares at the gray ebb. Pink cheeks, and superb wheaten-lashed eyes, eyes that concede a little in blueness to the sky over her, but nothing in brilliance; London could never have bred a thing so pure. Yet when she turns and surveys the handsome row of brick houses, some new, some old, that front the river across the road it is very evident that she holds nothing against London. And it is a face without envy, as it takes in the well-to-do houses; but full of a naive happiness that such fine things exist.

A hansom approaches, from the direction of central London. The blue-gray eyes watch it, in a way that suggests the watcher still finds such banal elements of the London scene fascinating and strange. It draws to a stop outside a large house opposite. A woman emerges, steps down to the pavement, takes a coin from her purse.

The mouth of the girl on the embankment falls open. A moment's pallor attacks the pink, and then she flushes. The cabby touches the brim of his hat with two fingers. His fare walks quickly towards the front door of the house behind her. The girl moves forward to the curb, half hiding behind a tree trunk. The woman opens the front door, disappears inside.

" 'Twas 'er, Sam. I saw 'er clear as—"

"I can't hardly believe it."

But he could; indeed, some sixth or seventh sense in him had almost expected it. He had looked up the old cook, Mrs. Rogers, on his return to London; and received from her a detailed account of Charles's final black weeks in Kensington. That was a long time ago now. Outwardly he had shared her disapproval of their former master. But inwardly something had stirred; being a matchmaker is one thing. A match-breaker is something other.

Sam and Mary were staring at each other—a dark wonderment in her eyes matching a dark doubt in his—in a front parlor that was minuscule, yet not too badly furnished. A bright fire burned in the grate. And as they questioned each other the door opened and a tiny maid, an unprepossessing girl of fourteen, came in carrying the now partly unswaddled infant—the last good crop, I believe, ever to come out of Carslake's Barn. Sam immediately took the bundle in his arms and dandled it and caused screams, a fairly invariable procedure when he returned from work. Mary hastily took the precious burden and grinned at the foolish father, while the little waif by the door grinned in sympathy at both. And now we can see distinctly that Mary is many months gone with another child.

"Well, my love, I'm hoff to partake of refreshment. You put the supper on, 'Arriet?"

"Yes, sir. Read'in narf-n-nour, sir."

"There's a good girl. My love." And as if nothing was on his mind, he kissed Mary on the cheek, then tickled the baby's ribs.

He did not look quite so happy a man five minutes later, when he sat in the sawdusted corner of a nearby public house, with a gin and hot water in front of him. He certainly had every outward reason to be happy. He did not own his own shop, but he had something nearly as good. The first baby had been a girl, but that was a small disappointment he felt confident would soon be remedied.

Sam had played his cards very right in Lyme. Aunt Tranter had been a soft touch from the start. He had thrown himself, with Mary's aid, on her mercy. Had he not lost all his prospects by his brave giving in of notice? Was it not gospel that Mr. Charles had promised him a loan of four hundred (always ask a higher price than you dare) to set him up in business? What business?

"Same as Mr. Freeman's, m'm, honly in a very, very 'umble way."

And he had played the Sarah card very well. For the first few days nothing would make him betray his late master's guilty secrets; his lips were sealed. But Mrs. Tranter was so kind—Colonel Locke at Jericho House was looking for a manservant, and Sam's unemployment was of a very short duration. So was his remaining bachelorhood; and the ceremony that concluded it was at the bride's mistress's expense. Clearly he had to make some return.

Like all lonely old ladies Aunt Tranter was forever in search of someone to adopt and help; and she was not allowed to forget that Sam wanted to go into the haberdashery line. Thus it was that one day, when staying in London with her sister, Mrs. Tranter ventured to broach the matter to her brother-in-law. At first he was inclined to shake his head. But then he was gently reminded how honorably the young servant had behaved; and he knew better than Mrs. Tranter to what good use Sam's information had been and might still be put.

"Very well, Ann. I will see what there is. There may be a vacancy."

Thus Sam gained a footing, a very lowly one, in the great store. But it was enough. What deficiencies he had in education he supplied with his natural sharpness. His training as a

329

servant stood him in good stead in dealing with customers. He dressed excellently. And one day he did something better.

It was a splendid April morning some six months after his married return to London, and just nine before the evening that saw him so unchipper in his place of refreshment. Mr. Freeman had elected to walk to his store from the Hyde Park house. He passed at last along its serried windows and entered the store, the sign for a great springing, scraping and bowing on the part of his ground-floor staff. Customers were few at that early hour. He raised his hat in his customary seigneurial way, but then to everyone's astonishment promptly turned and went out again. The nervous superintendent of the floor stepped outside as well. He saw the tycoon standing in front of a window and staring at it. The superintendent's heart fell, but he sidled up discreetly behind Mr. Freeman.

"An experiment, Mr. Freeman. I will have it removed at once."

Three other men stopped beside them. Mr. Freeman cast them a quick look, then took the superintendent by the arm and led him a few steps away.

"Now watch, Mr. Simpson."

They stood there for some five minutes. Again and again people passed the other windows and stopped at that one. Some, as Mr. Freeman himself had done, took it in without noticing, then retraced their steps to look at it.

I am afraid it will be an anticlimax to describe it. But you would have had to see those other windows, monotonously cluttered and monotonously ticketed, to appreciate its distinction; and you have to remember that unlike our age, when the finest flower of mankind devote their lives to the great god Publicity, the Victorians believed in the absurd notion that good wine needs no bush. The back of the display was a simple draped cloth of dark purple. Floating in front was a striking array, suspended on thin wires, of gentlemen's collars of every conceivable shape, size and style. But the cunning in the thing was that they were arranged to form words. And they cried, they positively bellowed: FREEMAN'S FOR CHOICE.

"That, Mr. Simpson, is the best window dressing we have done this year."

"Exactly, Mr. Freeman. Very bold. Very eye-catching."

" 'Freeman's for Choice.' That is precisely what we offer—why else do we carry such a large stock? 'Freeman's for Choice'—excellent! I want that phrase in all our circulars and advertisements from now on."

He marched back towards the entrance. The superintendent smiled.

"We owe this to you in great part, Mr. Freeman, sir. That young man—Mr. Farrow?—you remember you took a personal interest in his coming to us?"

Mr. Freeman stopped. "Farrow—his first name is Sam?"

"I believe so, sir."

"Bring him to me."

"He came in at five o'clock, sir, especially to do it."

Thus Sam was at last brought bashfully face to face with the great man.

"Excellent work, Farrow."

Sam bowed deep. "It was my hutmost pleasure to do it, sir."

"How much are we paying Farrow, Mr. Simpson?"

"Twenty-five shillings, sir."

"Twenty-seven and sixpence."

And he walked on before Sam could express his gratitude. Better was to come, for an envelope was handed to him when he went to collect his money at the end of the week. In it were three sovereigns and a card saying, "Bonus for zeal and invention."

Now, only nine months later, his salary had risen to the giddy heights of thirty-two and sixpence; and he had a strong suspicion, since he had become an indispensable member of the window-dressing staff, that any time he asked for a rise he would get it.

Sam bought himself another and extraordinary supplement of gin and returned to his seat. The unhappy thing about him—a defect that his modern descendants in the publicity game have managed to get free of—was that he had a conscience . . . or perhaps he had simply a feeling of unjustified happiness and good luck. The Faust myth is archetypal in civilized man; never mind that Sam's civilization had not taught him enough even to know who Faust was, he was sufficiently sophisticated to have heard of pacts with the Devil and of the course they took. One did very well for a while, but one day the Devil would claim his own. Fortune is a hard taskmaster; it stimulates the imagination into foreseeing its loss, and in strict relation, very often, to its kindness.

And it worried him, too, that he had never told Mary of what he had done. There were no other secrets between them; and he trusted her judgment. Every now and again his old longing to be his own master in his own shop would come back to him; was there not now proof of his natural aptitude? But it was Mary, with her sound rural sense of the best field to play, who gently—and once or twice, not so gently—sent him back to his Oxford Street grindstone.

Even if it was hardly yet reflected in their accents and use of the language, these two were rising in the world; and knew it. To Mary, it was all like a dream. To be married to a man earning over thirty shillings a week! When her own father, the carter, had never risen above ten! To live in a house that cost £19 a year to rent!

And, most marvelous of all, to have recently been able to interview eleven lesser mortals for a post one had, only two years before, occupied oneself! Why eleven? Mary, I am afraid, thought a large part of playing the mistress was being hard to please—a fallacy in which she copied the niece rather than the aunt. But then she also followed a procedure not unknown among young wives with good-looking young husbands. Her selection of a skivvy had been based very little on intelligence and efficiency; and very much on total unattractiveness. She told Sam she finally offered Harriet the six pounds a year because she felt sorry for her; it was not quite a lie.

When he returned home to his mutton stew, that evening of the double ration of gin, he put his arm round the swollen waist and kissed its owner; then looked down at the flower mosaic brooch she wore between her breasts—always wore at home and always took off when she went out, in case some thief garrotted her for it.

" 'Ow's the old pearl and coral then?"

She smiled and held it up a little.

"Happy to know 'ee, Sam."

And they stayed there, staring down at the emblem of their good fortune; always deserved, in her case; and now finally to be paid for, in his.

58

> I sought and sought. But O her soul
> Has not since thrown
> Upon my own
> One beam! Yes, she is gone, is gone.
> HARDY, "At a Seaside Town in 1869"

And what of Charles? I pity any detective who would have
had to dog him through those twenty months. Almost every
city in Europe saw him, but rarely for long. The pyramids
had seen him; and so had the Holy Land. He saw a thousand
sights, and sites, for he spent time also in Greece and Sicily,
but unseeingly; they were no more than the thin wall that
stood between him and nothingness, an ultimate vacuity, a
total purposelessness. Wherever he stopped more than a few
days, an intolerable lethargy and melancholia came upon
him. He became as dependent on traveling as an addict on
his opium. Usually he traveled alone, at most with some
dragoman or courier-valet of the country he was in. Very
occasionally he took up with other travelers and endured
their company for a few days; but they were almost always
French or German gentlemen. The English he avoided like
the plague; a whole host of friendly fellow countrymen received a drench of the same freezing reserve when they
approached him.

Paleontology, now too emotionally connected with the
events of that fatal spring, no longer interested him. When he
had closed down the Kensington house, he had allowed the
Geological Museum to take the pick of his collection; the
rest he had given to students. His furniture had been stored;

333

Montague was told to offer the lease of the Belgravia house anew when it fell in. Charles would never live in it.

He read much, and kept a journal of his travels; but it was an exterior thing, about places and incidents, not about his own mind—a mere way of filling time in the long evenings in deserted khans and *alberghi*. His only attempt to express his deeper self was in the way of verse, for he discovered in Tennyson a greatness comparable with that of Darwin in his field. The greatness he found was, to be sure, not the greatness the age saw in the Poet Laureate. *Maud*, a poem then almost universally despised—considered quite unworthy of the master—became Charles's favorite; he must have read it a dozen times, and parts of it a hundred. It was the one book he carried constantly with him. His own verse was feeble in comparison; he would rather have died than show it to anyone else. But here is one brief specimen just to show how he saw himself during his exile.

> Oh cruel seas I cross, and mountains harsh,
> O hundred cities of an alien tongue,
> To me no more than some accursed marsh
> Are all your happy scenes I pass among.
>
> Where e'er I go I ask of life the same;
> What drove me here? And now what drives me
>   hence?
> No more is it at best than flight from shame,
> At worst an iron law's mere consequence?

And to get the taste of that from your mouth, let me quote a far greater poem—one he committed to heart, and one thing he and I *could* have agreed on: perhaps the noblest short poem of the whole Victorian era.

> Yes; in the sea of life enisl'd,
> With echoing straits between us thrown,
> Dotting the shoreless watery wild,
> We mortal millions live *alone*.
>   The islands feel the enclasping flow,
> And then their endless bounds they know.
>
> But when the moon their hollows lights
> And they are swept by balms of spring,
> And in their glens, on starry nights.
> The nightingales divinely sing;
> And lovely notes, from shore to shore,
> Across the sounds and channels pour,

334

Oh then a longing like despair
Is to their farthest caverns sent;
For surely once, they feel, we were
Parts of a single continent.
Now round us spreads the watery plain—
Oh might our marges meet again!

Who order'd, that their longing's fire
Should be, as soon as kindled, cool'd?
Who renders vain their deep desire?—
    A God, a God their severance ruled;
And bade betwixt their shores to be
The unplumb'd, salt, estranging sea.*

Yet through all this self-riddling gloom Charles somehow
never entertained thoughts of suicide. When he had had his
great vision of himself freed from his age, his ancestry and
class and country, he had not realized how much the freedom
was embodied in Sarah; in the assumption of a shared exile.
He no longer much believed in that freedom; he felt he had
merely changed traps, or prisons. But yet there was something in his isolation that he could cling to; he was the
outcast, the not like other men, the result of a decision few
could have taken, no matter whether it was ultimately foolish
or wise. From time to time the sight of some newly wed
couple would remind him of Ernestina. He would search his
soul then. Did he envy them or pity them? He found that
there at least he had few regrets. However bitter his destiny,
it was nobler than that one he had rejected.

These European and Mediterranean travels lasted some
fifteen months, during which he not once returned to England. He corresponded intimately with no one; most of his
few letters were addressed to Montague, and dealt with
business, instructions where next to send money and the rest.
Montague had been empowered to place from time to time
advertisements in the London newspapers: "Would Sarah
Emily Woodruff or anyone knowing her present domicile
. . ." but there was never an answer.

Sir Robert had taken the news of the broken engagement
badly when it first came to him, by letter; but then, under the
honeyed influence of his own imminent happiness, he had
shrugged it off. Charles was young, damn it, he would find as
good, a great deal better, a girl somewhere else; and he had

*Matthew Arnold, "To Marguerite" (1853).

at least spared Sir Robert the embarrassment of the Freeman connection. The nephew went once, before he left England, to pay his respects to Mrs. Bella Tomkins; he did not like the lady, and felt sorry for his uncle. He then declined the renewed offer of the Little House; and did not speak of Sarah. He had promised to return to attend the wedding; but that promise was easily broken by the invention of a dose of malaria. Twins did not come, as he had imagined, but a son and heir duly made his appearance in the thirteenth month of his exile. By that time he was too well inured to his fatality to feel much more, after the letter of congratulation was sent, than a determination never to set foot in Winsyatt again.

If he did not remain quite celibate technically—it was well known among the better hotels of Europe that English gentlemen went abroad to misbehave themselves, and opportunities were frequent—he remained so emotionally. He performed (or deformed) the act with a kind of mute cynicism, rather as he stared at ancient Greek temples or ate his meals. It was mere hygiene. Love had left the world. Sometimes, in some cathedral or art gallery, he would for a moment dream Sarah beside him. After such moments he might have been seen to draw himself up and take a deep breath. It was not only that he forbade himself the luxury of a vain nostalgia; he became increasingly unsure of the frontier between the real Sarah and the Sarah he had created in so many such dreams: the one Eve personified, all mystery and love and profundity, and the other a half-scheming, half-crazed governess from an obscure seaside town. He even saw himself coming upon her again—and seeing nothing in her but his own folly and delusion. He did not cancel the insertion of the advertisements; but he began to think it as well that they might never be answered.

His greatest enemy was boredom; and it was boredom, to be precise an evening in Paris when he realized that he neither wanted to be in Paris nor to travel again to Italy, or Spain, or anywhere else in Europe, that finally drove him home.

You must think I mean England; but I don't: that could never become home for Charles again, though that is where he went for a week, when he left Paris. It had so happened that on his way from Leghorn to Paris he had traveled in the company of two Americans, an elderly gentleman and his nephew. They hailed from Philadelphia. Perhaps it was the pleasure of conversing with someone in a not too alien tongue, but Charles rather fell for them; their unsophisticated pleasure in their sightseeing—he guided them himself round Avignon and took them to admire Vézelay—was absurd, to be sure. Yet it was accompanied by a lack of cant. They were not at all the stupid Yankees the Victorian British liked to suppose were universal in the States. Their inferiority was strictly limited to their innocence of Europe.

The elder Philadelphian was indeed a well-read man, and a shrewd judge of life. One evening after dinner he and Charles had engaged, with the nephew as audience, on a lengthy discussion as to the respective merits of the mother country and the rebellious colony; and the American's criticisms, though politely phrased, of England awoke a very responsive chord in Charles. He detected, under the American accent, very similar views to his own; and he even glimpsed, though very dimly and only by virtue of a Darwinian analogy, that one day America might supersede the older species. I do not mean, of course, that he thought of emigrating there, though thousands of a poorer English class were doing that every year. The Canaan they saw across the Atlantic (encouraged by some of the most disgraceful lies in the history of advertising) was not the Canaan he dreamed: a land inhabited by a soberer, simpler kind of gentleman—just like this Philadelphian and his pleasantly attentive nephew—living in a simpler society. It had been put very concisely to him by the uncle: "In general back home we say what we think. My impression of London was—forgive me, Mr. Smithson—heaven help you if you *don't* say what you *don't* think."

Nor was that all. Charles put the idea up to Montague over a dinner in London. As to America, Montague was lukewarm.

"I can't imagine that there are many speakables per acre there, Charles. You can't offer yourself as the repository of the riffraff of Europe and conduct a civilized society, all at the same time. Though I daresay some of the older cities are agreeable enough, in their way." He sipped his port. "Yet there, by the bye, is where *she* may be. I suppose that must have occurred to you. I hear these cheap-passage packets are full of young women in pursuit of a husband." He added hastily, "Not that that would be *her* reason, of course."

"I had not thought of it. To tell you the truth, I haven't thought very much of her at all, these last months. I have given up hope."

"Then go to America, and drown your sorrows on the bosom of some charming Pocahontas. I hear a well-born English gentleman can have his pick of some very beautiful young women—*pour la dot comme pour la figure*—if he so inclines."

Charles smiled: whether at the idea of the doubly beautiful young women or at the knowledge, not yet imparted to Montague, that his passage was already booked, must be left to the imagination.

59

Weary of myself, and sick of asking
What I am, and what I ought to be,
At the vessel's prow I stand, which bears me
Forwards, forwards, o'er the starlit sea.
MATTHEW ARNOLD, "Self-Dependence" (1854)

He did not have a happy passage from Liverpool. He spoke frequently to the storm-basin; and when he was not being sick, spent most of his time wondering why he had ever embarked for the primitive other side of the world. Perhaps it was just as well. He had begun to envisage Boston as a miserable assembly of log cabins—and the reality, one sunlit morning, of a city of mellow brick and white wooden spires, with that one opulently gold dome, came as a pleasant reassurance. Nor did Boston belie its first appearance. Just as he had fallen for his Philadelphians, he fell for the mixed graciousness and candor of Boston society. He was not exactly fêted; but within a week of his arrival the two or three introductions he had brought with him had multiplied into open invitations to several houses. He was invited to use the Athenaeum, he had shaken hands with a senator, no less; and with the wrinkled claw of one even greater, if less hectoringly loquacious—the elder Dana, a Founding Father of American letters, and then in his eightieth year. A far more famous writer still, whom one might have not very interestedly chatted to if one had chanced to gain entry to the Lowell circle in Cambridge, and who was himself on the early threshold of a decision precisely the opposite in its motives and predispositions, a ship, as it were, straining at its moorings in a contrary current and arming for its sinuous and loxodromic voyage to the richer though silted harbor of Rye (but I must not ape the master), Charles did not meet.

Even though he dutifully paid his respects to the Cradle of Liberty in Faneuil Hall, he encountered also a certain amount of hostility, for Britain was not forgiven its recent devious part in the Civil War, and there existed a stereotype of John Bull just as grossly oversimplified as that of Uncle Sam. But Charles quite plainly did not fit that stereotype; he proclaimed that he saw very well the justice of the War of Independence, he admired Boston as the center of American learning, of the Anti-Slavery Movement, and countless other things. He let himself be ribbed about tea parties and redcoats with a smiling sang-froid, and took very great care not to condescend. I think two things pleased him best—the delicious newness of the nature: new plants, new trees, new birds—and, as he discovered when he crossed the river of his name and visited Harvard, some entrancing new fossils. And the other pleasure lay in the Americans themselves. At first, perhaps, he noticed a certain lack of the finer shades of irony; and he had to surmount one or two embarrassing *contretemps* when humorously intended remarks were taken at face value. But there were such compensations . . . a frankness, a directness of approach, a charming curiosity that accompanied the open hospitality: a naïvety, perhaps, yet with a face that seemed delightfully fresh-complexioned after the farded culture of Europe. This face took, very soon, a distinctly female cast. Young American women were far more freely spoken than their European contemporaries; the transatlantic emancipation movement was already twenty years old. Charles found their forwardness very attractive.

The attraction was reciprocated, since in Boston at any rate a superiority in the more feminine aspects of social taste was still readily conceded to London. He might, perhaps, very soon have lost his heart; but there traveled with him always the memory of that dreadful document Mr. Freeman had extorted. It stood between him and every innocent girl's face he saw; only one face could forgive and exorcize it.

Besides, in so many of these American faces he saw a shadow of Sarah: they had something of her challenge, her directness. In a way they revived his old image of her: she had been a remarkable woman, and she would have been at home here. In fact, he thought more and more of Montague's suggestion: perhaps she *was* at home here. He had spent the previous fifteen months in countries where the national differences in look and costume very seldom revived memory of her. Here he was among a womanhood of largely

Anglo-Saxon and Irish stock. A dozen times, in his first days, he was brought to a stop by a certain shade of auburn hair, a free way of walking, a figure.

Once, as he made his way to the Athenaeum across the Common, he saw a girl ahead of him on an oblique path. He strode across the grass, he was so sure. But she was not Sarah. And he had to stammer an apology. He went on his way shaken, so intense in those few moments had been his excitement. The next day he advertised in a Boston newspaper. Wherever he went after that he advertised.

The first snow fell, and Charles moved south. He visited Manhattan, and liked it less than Boston. Then spent a very agreeable fortnight with his France-met friends in their city; the famous later joke ("First prize, one week in Philadelphia; second prize, two weeks") he would not have found just. From there he drifted south; so Baltimore saw him, and Washington, Richmond and Raleigh, and a constant delight of new nature, new climate: new meteorological climate, that is, for the political climate—we are now in the December of 1868—was the very reverse of delightful. Charles found himself in devastated towns and among very bitter men, the victims of Reconstruction; with a disastrous president, Andrew Johnson, about to give way to a catastrophic one, Ulysses S. Grant. He found he had to grow British again in Virginia, though by an irony he did not appreciate, the ancestors of the gentlemen he conversed with there and in the Carolinas were almost alone in the colonial upper classes of 1775 in supporting the Revolution; he even heard wild talk of a new secession and reunification with Britain. But he passed diplomatically and unscathed through all these troubles, not fully understanding what was going on, but sensing the strange vastness and frustrated energy of this split nation.

His feelings were perhaps not very different from an Englishman in the United States of today: so much that repelled, so much that was good; so much chicanery, so much honesty; so much brutality and violence, so much concern and striving for a better society. He passed the month of January in battered Charleston; and now for the first time he began to wonder whether he was traveling or emigrating. He noticed that certain American turns of phrase and inflections were creeping into his speech; he found himself taking sides—or more precisely, being split rather like America itself, since he both thought it right to abolish slavery and sympathized with the anger of the Southerners who knew only too well what the carpetbaggers' solicitude for Negro emancipation was really about. He found himself at home among the sweet

340

belles and rancorous captains and colonels, but then remembered Boston—pinker cheeks and whiter souls ... more Puritan souls, anyway. He saw himself happier there, in the final analysis; and as if to prove it by paradox set off to go farther south.

He was no longer bored. What the experience of America, perhaps in particular the America of that time, had given him—or given him back—was a kind of faith in freedom; the determination he saw around him, however unhappy its immediate consequences, to master a national destiny had a liberating rather than a depressing effect. He began to see the often risible provinciality of his hosts as a condition of their lack of hypocrisy. Even the only too abundant evidence of a restless dissatisfaction, a tendency to take the law into one's own hands—a process which always turns the judge into the executioner—in short, the endemic violence caused by a *Liberté*-besotted constitution, found some justification in Charles's eyes. A spirit of anarchy was all over the South; and yet even that seemed to him preferable to the rigid iron rule of his own country.

But he said all this for himself. One calm evening, while still at Charleston, he chanced to find himself on a promontory facing towards Europe three thousand miles away. He wrote a poem there; a better, a little better than the last of his you read.

> Came they to seek some greater truth
> Than Albion's hoary locks allow?
> Lies there a question in their youth
> We have not dared to ask ere now?
>
> I stand, a stranger in their clime,
> Yet common to their minds and ends;
> Methinks in them I see a time
> To which a happier man ascends
>
> And there shall all his brothers be—
> A Paradise wrought upon these rocks
> Of hate and vile inequity.
> What matter if the mother mocks
>
> The infant child's first feeble hands?
> What matter if today he fail
> Provided that at last he stands
> And breaks the blind maternal pale?

For he shall one day walk in pride
The vast calm indigoes of this land
And eastward turn, and bless the tide
That brought him to the saving strand.

And there, amid the iambic slog-and-smog and rhetorical question marks, and the really not too bad "vast calm indigoes," let us leave Charles for a paragraph.

It was nearly three months after Mary had told her news—the very end of April. But in that interval Fortune had put Sam further in her debt by giving him the male second edition he so much wanted. It was a Sunday, an evening full of green-gold buds and church bells, with little chinkings and clatterings downstairs that showed his newly risen young wife and her help were preparing his supper; and with one child struggling to stand at the knees on which the three-weeks-old brother lay, dark little screwed-up eyes that already delighted Sam ("Sharp as razors, the little monkey"), it happened: something in those eyes did cut Sam's not absolutely Bostonian soul.

Two days later Charles, by then peregrinated to New Orleans, came from a promenade in the Vieux Carré into his hotel. The clerk handed him a cable.

It said: SHE IS FOUND. LONDON. MONTAGUE.

Charles read the words and turned away. After so long, so much between . . . he stared without seeing out into the busy street. From nowhere, no emotional correlative, he felt his eyes smart with tears. He moved outside, onto the porch of the hotel, and there lit himself a stogie. A minute or two later he returned to the desk.

"The next ship to Europe—can you tell me when she sails?"

60

Lalage's come; aye
Come is she now, O!
HARDY, "Timing Her"

He dismissed the cab at the bridge. It was the very last day
of May, warm, affluent, the fronts of houses embowered in
trees, the sky half blue, half fleeced with white clouds. The
shadow of one fell for a minute across Chelsea, though the
warehouses across the river still stood in sunlight.

Montague had known nothing. The information had come
through the post; a sheet of paper containing nothing beyond
the name and address. Standing by the solicitor's desk,
Charles recalled the previous address he had received from
Sarah; but this was in a stiff copperplate. Only in the brevity
could he see her.

Montague had, at Charles's cabled command, acted with
great care. No approach was to be made to her, no alarm—
no opportunity for further flight—given. A clerk played detective, with the same description given to the real detectives
in his pocket. He reported that a young lady conforming to
the particulars was indeed apparently residing at the address;
that the person in question went under the name of Mrs.
Roughwood. The ingenuous transposition of syllables removed any lingering doubt as to the accuracy of the information; and removed, after the first momentary shock, the
implications of the married title. Such stratagems were quite
common with single women in London; and proved the
opposite of what was implied. Sarah had not married.

"I see it was posted in London. You have no idea . . ."

"It was sent here, so plainly it comes from someone who knows of our advertisements. It was addressed personally to you, so the someone knows whom we were acting for, yet appears uninterested in the reward we offered. That seems to suggest the young lady herself."

"But why should she delay so long to reveal herself? And besides, this is not her hand." Montague silently confessed himself at a loss. "Your clerk obtained no further information?"

"He followed instructions, Charles. I forbade him to make inquiries. By chance he was within hearing in the street when a neighbor wished her good morning. That is how we have the name."

"And the house?"

"A respectable family residence. They are his very words."

"She is presumably governess there."

"That seems very likely."

Charles had turned then to the window, which was just as well; for the way Montague had looked at his back suggested a certain lack of frankness. He had forbidden the clerk to ask questions; but he had not forbidden himself to question the clerk.

"You intend to see her?"

"My dear Harry, I have not crossed the Atlantic . . ." Charles smiled in apology for his exasperated tone. "I know what you would ask. I can't answer. Forgive me, this matter is too personal. And the truth is, I don't know what I feel. I think I shall not know till I see her again. All I do know is that . . . she continues to haunt me. That I *must* speak to her, I must . . . you understand."

"You must question the Sphinx."

"If you care to put it so."

"As long as you bear in mind what happened to those who failed to solve the enigma."

Charles made a rueful grimace. "If silence or death is the alternative—then you had better prepare the funeral oration."

"I somehow suspect that that will not be needed."

They had smiled.

But he was not smiling now, as he approached the Sphinx's house. He knew nothing of the area; he had a notion that it was a kind of inferior substitute for Greenwich—a place where retired naval officers finished their days. The Victorian Thames was a far fouler river than today's, every one of its tides hideously awash with sewage. On one occasion the stench was so insupportable that it drove the House of Lords out of their chamber; the cholera was blamed on it; and a riverside house was far from having the social cachet it has in our own deodorized century. For all that, Charles could see that the houses were quite handsome; perverse though their inhabitants must be in their choice of environment, they were plainly not driven there by poverty.

At last, and with an inner trembling, a sense of pallor, a sense too of indignity—his new American self had been swept away before the massive, ingrained past and he was embarrassedly conscious of being a gentleman about to call on a superior form of servant—he came to the fatal gate. It was of wrought iron, and opened onto a path that led briefly to a tall house of brick—though most of that was hidden to the roof by a luxuriant blanket of wisteria, just now beginning to open its first pale-blue pendants of bloom.

He raised the brass knocker and tapped it twice; waited some twenty seconds, and knocked again. This time the door was opened. A maid stood before him. He glimpsed a wide hall behind her—many paintings, so many the place seemed more an art gallery.

"I wish to speak to a Mrs. . . . Roughwood. I believe she resides here."

The maid was a slim young creature, wide-eyed, and without the customary lace cap. In fact, had she not worn an apron, he would not have known how to address her.

"Your name, if you please?"

He noted the absence of the "sir"; perhaps she was not a maid; her accent was far superior to a maid's. He handed her his card.

"Pray tell her I have come a long way to see her."

She unashamedly read the card. She was not a maid. She seemed to hesitate. But then there was a sound at the dark far end of the hall. A man some six or seven years older than Charles stood in a doorway. The girl turned gratefully to him.

"This gentleman wishes to see Sarah."

"Yes?"

He held a pen in his hand. Charles removed his hat and spoke from the threshold.

"If you would be so good . . . a private matter . . . I knew her well before she came to London."

There was something slightly distasteful in the man's intent though very brief appraisal of Charles; a faintly Jewish air about him, a certain careless ostentation in the clothes; a touch of the young Disraeli. The man glanced at the girl.

"She is . . . ?"

"I think they talk. That is all."

"They" were apparently her charges: the children.

"Then take him up, my dear. Sir."

With a little bow he disappeared as abruptly as he had appeared. The girl indicated that Charles should follow her. He was left to close the door for himself. As she began to mount the stairs he had time to glance at the crowded paintings and drawings. He was sufficiently knowledgeable about modern art to recognize the school to which most of them belonged; and indeed, the celebrated, the notorious artist whose monogram was to be seen on several of them. The furore he had caused some twenty years before had now died down; what had then been seen as fit only for burning now commanded a price. The gentleman with the pen was a collector of art; of somewhat suspect art; but he was no less evidently a man of some wealth.

Charles followed the girl's slender back up a flight of stairs; still more paintings, and still with a predominance of the suspect school. But he was by now too anxious to give them any attention. As they embarked on a second flight of stairs he ventured a question.

"Mrs. Roughwood is employed here as governess?"

The girl stopped in midstair and looked back: an amused surprise. Then her eyes fell.

"She is no longer a governess."

Her eyes came up to his for a moment. Then she moved on her way.

They came to a second landing. His sibylline guide turned at a door.

"Kindly wait here."

She entered the room, leaving the door ajar. From outside Charles had a glimpse of an open window, a lace curtain blowing back lightly in the summer air, a shimmer, through intervening leaves, of the river beyond. There was a low murmur of voices. He shifted his position, to see better into the room. Now he saw two men, two gentlemen. They were standing before a painting on an easel, which was set obliquely to the window, to benefit from its light. The taller of the two bent to examine some detail, thereby revealing the other who stood behind him. By chance he looked straight through the door and into Charles's eyes. He made the faintest inclination, then glanced at someone on the hidden other side of the room.

Charles stood stunned.

For this was a face he knew; a face he had even once listened to for an hour or more, with Ernestina beside him. It was impossible, yet ... and the man downstairs! Those paintings and drawings! He turned hastily away and looked, a man

346

woken into, not out of, a nightmare, through a tall window at the rear end of the landing to a green back-garden below. He saw nothing; but only the folly of his own assumption that fallen women must continue falling—for had he not come to arrest the law of gravity? He was as shaken as a man who suddenly finds the world around him standing on its head.

A sound.

He flashed a look round. She stood there against the door she had just closed, her hand on its brass knob, in the abrupt loss of sunlight, difficult to see clearly.

And her dress! It was so different that he thought for a moment she was someone else. He had always seen her in his mind in the former clothes, a haunted face rising from a widowed darkness. But this was someone in the full uniform of the New Woman, flagrantly rejecting all formal contemporary notions of female fashion. Her skirt was of a rich dark blue and held at the waist by a crimson belt with a gilt star clasp; which also enclosed the pink-and white striped silk blouse, long-sleeved, flowing, with a delicate small collar of white lace, to which a small cameo acted as tie. The hair was bound loosely back by a red ribbon.

This electric and bohemian apparition evoked two immediate responses in Charles; one was that instead of looking two years older, she looked two years younger; and the other, that in some incomprehensible way he had not returned to England but done a round voyage back to America. For just so did many of the smart young women over there dress during the day. They saw the sense of such clothes—their simplicity and attractiveness after the wretched bustles, stays and crinolines. In the United States Charles had found the style, with its sly and paradoxically coquettish hints at emancipation in other ways, very charming; now, and under so many other new suspicions, his cheeks took a color not far removed from the dianthus pink of the stripes on her shirt.

But against this shock—what was she now, what had she become!—there rushed a surge of relief. Those eyes, that mouth, that always implicit air of defiance ... it was all still there. She *was* the remarkable creature of his happier memories—but blossomed, realized, winged from the black pupa.

For ten long moments nothing was spoken. Then she clutched her hands nervously in front of the gilt clasp and looked down.

"How came you here, Mr. Smithson?"

She had not sent the address. She was not grateful. He did not remember that her inquiry was identical to one he had once asked her when she came on *him* unexpectedly; but he

347

sensed that now their positions were strangely reversed. He was now the suppliant, she the reluctant listener.

"My solicitor was told you live here. I do not know by whom."

"Your solicitor?"

"Did you not know I broke my engagement to Miss Freeman?"

Now she was the one who was shocked. Her eyes probed his a long moment, then looked down. She had not known. He drew a step closer and spoke in a low voice.

"I have searched every corner of this city. Every month I have advertised in the hope of . . ."

Now they both stared at the ground between them; at the handsome Turkey carpet that ran the length of the landing. He tried to normalize his voice.

"I see you are . . ." he lacked words; but he meant, altogether changed.

She said, "Life has been kind to me."

"That gentleman in there—is he not . . . ?"

She nodded in answer to the name in his still incredulous eyes.

"And this house belongs to . . ."

She took a small breath then, so accusing had become his tone. There lurked in his mind idly heard gossip. Not of the man he had seen in the room; but of the one he had seen downstairs. Without warning Sarah moved to the stairs that went yet higher in the house. Charles stood rooted. She gave him a hesitant glance down.

"Please come."

He followed her up the stairs, to find she had entered a room that faced north, over the large gardens below. It was an artist's studio. On a table near the door lay a litter of drawings; on an easel a barely begun oil, the mere ground-lines, a hint of a young woman looking sadly down, foliage sketched faint behind her head; other turned canvases by the wall; by another wall, a row of hooks, from which hung a multi-colored array of female dresses, scarves, shawls; a large pottery jar; tables of impedimenta—tubes, brushes, color-pots. A *bas relief*, small sculptures, an urn with bulrushes. There seemed hardly a square foot without its object.

Sarah stood at a window, her back to him.

"I am his amanuensis. His assistant."

"You serve as his model?"

"Sometimes."

"I see."

But he saw nothing; or rather, he saw in the corner of his eye one of the sketches on the table by the door. It was of a

348

female nude, nude that is from the waist up, and holding an amphora at her hip. The face did not seem to be Sarah's; but the angle was such that he could not be sure.

"You have lived here since you left Exeter?"

"I have lived here this last year."

If only he could ask her how; how had they met? On what terms did they live? He hesitated, then laid his hat, stick and gloves on a seat by the door. Her hair was now to be seen in all its richness, reaching almost down to her waist. She seemed smaller than he remembered; more slight. A pigeon fluttered to alight on the sill in front of her; took fright, and slipped away. Downstairs a door opened and closed. There was a faint sound of men's voices as they made their way below. The room divided them. All divided them. The silence became unbearable.

He had come to raise her from penury, from some crabbed post in a crabbed house. In full armor, ready to slay the dragon—and now the damsel had broken all the rules. No chains, no sobs, no beseeching hands. He was the man who appears at a formal *soirée* under the impression it was to be a fancy dress ball.

"He knows you are not married?"

"I pass as a widow."

His next question was clumsy; but he had lost all tact.

"I believe his wife is dead?"

"She is dead. But not in his heart."

"He has not remarried?"

"He shares this house with his brother." Then she added the name of another person who lived there, as if to imply that Charles's scarcely concealed fears were, under this evidence of population, groundless. But the name she added was the one most calculated to make any respectable Victorian of the late 1860s stiffen with disapproval. The horror evoked by his poetry had been publicly expressed by John Morley, one of those worthies born to be spokesmen (i.e., empty façades) for their age. Charles remembered the quintessential phrase of his condemnation: "the libidinous laureate of a pack of satyrs." And the master of the house himself! Had he not heard that he took opium? A vision of some orgiastic *ménage à quatre*—*à cinq* if one counted the girl who had shown him up—rose in his mind. But there was nothing orgiastic about Sarah's appearance; to advance the poet as a reference even argued a certain innocence; and what should the famous lecturer and critic glimpsed through the door, a man of somewhat exaggerated ideas, certainly, but widely respected and admired, be doing in such a den of iniquity?

I am overemphasizing the worse, that is the time-serving,

Morleyish half of Charles's mind; his better self, that self that once before had enabled him to see immediately through the malice of Lyme to her real nature, fought hard to dismiss his suspicions.

He began to explain himself in a quiet voice; with another voice in his mind that cursed his formality, that barrier in him that could not tell of the countless lonely days, lonely nights, her spirit beside him, over him, before him ... tears, and he did not know how to say tears. He told her of what had happened that night in Exeter. Of his decision; of Sam's gross betrayal.

He had hoped she might turn. But she remained staring, her face hidden from him, down into the greenery below. Somewhere there, children played. He fell silent, then moved close behind her.

"What I say means nothing to you?"

"It means very much to me. So much I ..."

He said gently, "I beg you to continue."

"I am at a loss for words."

And she moved away, as if she could not look at him when close. Only when she was beside the easel did she venture to do so.

She murmured, "I do not know what to say."

Yet she said it without emotion, without any of the dawning gratitude he so desperately sought; with no more, in cruel truth, than a baffled simplicity.

"You told me you loved me. You gave me the greatest proof a woman can that ... that what possessed us was no ordinary degree of mutual sympathy and attraction."

"I do not deny that."

There was a flash of hurt resentment in his eyes. She looked down before them. Silence flowed back into the room, and now Charles turned to the window.

"But you have found newer and more pressing affections."

"I did not think ever to see you again."

"That does not answer my question."

"I have forbidden myself to regret the impossible."

"That still does not—"

"Mr. Smithson, I am *not* his mistress. If you knew him, if you knew the tragedy of his private life ... you could not for a moment be so ..." But she fell silent. He had gone too far; and now he stood with rapped knuckles and red cheeks. Silence again; and then she said evenly, "I *have* found new affections. But they are not of the kind you suggest."

"Then I don't know how I am to interpret your very evident embarrassment at seeing you again." She said nothing.

"Though I can readily imagine you now have ... friends who are far more interesting and amusing than I could ever pretend to be." But he added quickly, "You force me to express myself in a way that I abhor." Still she said nothing. He turned on her with a bitter small smile. "I see how it is. It is I who have become the misanthropist."

That honesty did better for him. She gave him a quick look, one not without concern. She hesitated, then came to a decision.

"I did not mean to make you so. I meant to do what was best. I had abused your trust, your generosity, I, yes, I had thrown myself at you, forced myself upon you, knowing very well that you had other obligations. A madness was in me at that time. I did not see it clearly till that day in Exeter. The worst you thought of me then was nothing but the truth." She paused, he waited. "I have since seen artists destroy work that might to the amateur seem perfectly good. I remonstrated once. I was told that if an artist is not his own sternest judge he is not fit to be an artist. I believe that is right. I believe I was right to destroy what had begun between us. There was a falsehood in it, a—"

"I was not to blame for that."

"No, you were not to blame." She paused, then went on in a gentler tone. "Mr. Smithson, I remarked a phrase of Mr. Ruskin's recently. He wrote of an inconsistency of conception. He meant that the natural had been adulterated by the artificial, the pure by the impure. I think that is what happened two years ago." She said in a lower voice, "And I know but too well which part I contributed."

He had a reawoken sense of that strange assumption of intellectual equality in her. He saw, too, what had always been dissonant between them: the formality of his language—seen at its worst in the love letter she had never received—and the directness of hers. Two languages, betraying on the one side a hollowness, a foolish constraint—but she had just said it, an artificiality of conception—and on the other a substance and purity of thought and judgment; the difference between a simple colophon, say, and some page decorated by Noel Humphreys, all scrollwork, elaboration, rococo horror of void. That was the true inconsistency between them, though her kindness—or her anxiety to be rid of him—tried to conceal it.

"May I pursue the metaphor? Cannot what you call the natural and pure part of the conception be redeemed—be taken up again?"

"I fear not."

But she would not look at him as she said that.

351

"I was four thousand miles from here when the news that you had been found came to me. That was a month ago. I have not passed an hour since then without thinking of this conversation. You ... you cannot answer me with observations, however apposite, on art."

"They were intended to apply to life as well."

"Then what you are saying is that you never loved me."

"I could not say that."

She had turned from him. He went behind her again.

"But you must say that! You must say, 'I was totally evil, I never saw in him other than an instrument I could use, a destruction I could encompass. For now I don't care that he still loves me, that in all his travels he has not seen a woman to compare with me, that he is a ghost, a shadow, a half-being for as long as he remains separated from me.'" She had bowed her head. He lowered his voice. "You must say, 'I do not care that his crime was to have shown a few hours' indecision, I don't care that he has expiated it by sacrificing his good name, his ...' not that that matters, I would sacrifice everything I possess a hundred times again if I could but know ... my dearest Sarah, I ...'"

He had brought himself perilously near tears. He reached his hand tentatively towards her shoulder, touched it; but no sooner touched it than some imperceptible stiffening of her stance made him let it fall.

"There *is* another."

"Yes. There is another."

He threw her averted face an outraged look, took a deep breath, then strode towards the door.

"I beg you. There is something else I must say."

"You have said the one thing that matters."

"The other is not what you think!"

Her tone was so new, so intense, that he arrested his movement towards his hat. He glanced back at her. He saw a split being: the old, accusing Sarah and one who begged him to listen. He stared at the ground.

"There *is* another in the sense that you mean. He is ... an artist I have met here. He wishes to marry me. I admire him, I respect him both as man and as artist. But I shall never marry him. If I were forced this moment to choose between Mr. .... between him and yourself, you would not leave this house the unhappier. I beg you to believe that." She had come a little towards him, her eyes on his, at their most direct; and he had to believe her. He looked down again. "The rival you both share is myself. I do not wish to marry. I do not wish to marry because ... first, because of my past, which habituated me to loneliness. I had always thought that

352

I hated it. I now live in a world where loneliness is most easy to avoid. And I have found that I treasure it. I do not want to share my life. I wish to be what I am, not what a husband, however kind, however indulgent, must expect me to become in marriage."

"And your second reason?"

"My second reason is my present. I never expected to be happy in life. Yet I find myself happy where I am situated now. I have varied and congenial work—work so pleasant that I no longer think of it as such. I am admitted to the daily conversation of genius. Such men have their faults. Their vices. But they are not those the world chooses to imagine. The persons I have met here have let me see a community of honorable endeavor, of noble purpose, I had not till now known existed in this world." She turned away towards the easel. "Mr. Smithson, I am happy, I am at last arrived, or so it seems to me, where I belong. I say that most humbly. I have no genius myself, I have no more than the capacity to aid genius in very small and humble ways. You may think I have been very fortunate. No one knows it better than myself. But I believe I owe a debt to my good fortune. I am not to seek it elsewhere. I am to see it as precarious, as a thing of which I must not allow myself to be bereft." She paused again, then faced him. "You may think what you will of me, but I cannot wish my life other than it is at the moment. And not even when I am besought by a man I esteem, who touches me more than I show, from whom I do not deserve such a faithful generosity of affection." She lowered her eyes. "And whom I beg to comprehend me."

There had been several points where Charles would have liked to interrupt this credo. Its contentions seemed all heresy to him; yet deep inside him his admiration for the heretic grew. She was like no other; more than ever like no other. He saw London, her new life, had subtly altered her; had refined her vocabulary and accent, had articulated intuition, had deepened her clarity of insight; had now anchored her, where before had been a far less secure mooring, to her basic conception of life and her role in it. Her bright clothes had misled him at first. But he began to perceive they were no more than a factor of her new self-knowledge and self-possession; she no longer needed an outward uniform. He saw it; yet would not see it. He came back a little way into the center of the room.

"But you cannot reject the purpose for which woman was brought into creation. And for what? I say nothing against Mr. ...." he gestured at the painting on the easel "... and his

353

circle. But you cannot place serving them above the natural law." He pressed his advantage. "I too have changed. I have learned much of myself, of what was previously false in me. I make no conditions. All that Miss Sarah Woodruff is, Mrs. Charles Smithson may continue to be. I would not ban you your new world or your continuing pleasure in it. I offer no more than an enlargement of your present happiness."

She went to the window, and he advanced to the easel, his eyes on her. She half turned.

"You do not understand. It is not your fault. You are very kind. But I am not to be understood."

"You forget you have said that to me before. I think you make it a matter of pride."

"I meant that I am not to be understood even by myself. And I can't tell you why, but I believe my happiness depends on my not understanding."

Charles smiled, in spite of himself. "This is absurdity. You refuse to entertain my proposal because I might bring you to understand yourself."

"I refuse, as I refused the other gentleman, because you cannot understand that to me it is not an absurdity."

She had her back turned again; and he began to see a glimmer of hope, for she seemed to show, as she picked at something on the white transom before her, some of the telltale embarrassment of a willful child.

"You shan't escape there. You may reserve to yourself all the mystery you want. It shall remain sacrosanct to me."

"It is not you I fear. It is your love for me. I know only too well that nothing remains sacrosanct there."

He felt like someone denied a fortune by some trivial phrase in a legal document; the victim of a conquest of irrational law over rational intent. But she would not submit to reason; to sentiment she might lie more open. He hesitated, then went closer.

"Have you thought much of me in my absence?"

She looked at him then; a look that was almost dry, as if she had foreseen this new line of attack, and almost welcomed it. She turned away after a moment, and stared at the roofs of the houses across the gardens.

"I thought much of you to begin with. I thought much of you some six months later, when I first saw one of the notices you had had put in——"

"Then you did know!"

But she went implacably on. "And which obliged me to change my lodgings and my name. I made inquiries. I knew then, but not before, that you had not married Miss Freeman."

354

He stood both frozen and incredulous for five long seconds; and then she threw him a little glance round. He thought he saw a faint exultation in it, a having always had this trump card ready—and worse, of having waited, to produce it, to see the full extent of his own hand. She moved quietly away, and there was more horror in the quietness, the apparent indifference, than in the movement. He followed her with his eyes. And perhaps he did at last begin to grasp her mystery. Some terrible perversion of human sexual destiny had begun; he was no more than a footsoldier, a pawn in a far vaster battle; and like all battles it was not about love, but about possession and territory. He saw deeper: it was not that she hated men, not that she materially despised him more than other men, but that her maneuvers were simply a part of her armory, mere instruments to a greater end. He saw deeper still: that her supposed present happiness was another lie. In her central being she suffered still, in the same old way; and that was the mystery she was truly and finally afraid he might discover.

There was silence. "Then you have not only ruined my life. You have taken pleasure in doing so."

"I knew nothing but unhappiness could come from such a meeting as this."

"I think you lie. I think you reveled in the thought of my misery. And I think it was you who sent that letter to my solicitor." She looked him a sharp denial, but he met her with a cold grimace. "You forget I already know, to my cost, what an accomplished actress you can be when it suits your purpose. I can guess why I am now summoned to be given the *coup de grâce*. You have a new victim. I may slake your insatiable and unwomanly hatred of my sex one last time ... and now I may be dismissed."

"You misjudge me."

But she said it far too calmly, as if she remained proof to all his accusations; even, deep in herself, perversely savored them. He gave a bitter shake of the head.

"No. It is as I say. You have not only planted the dagger in my breast, you have delighted in twisting it." She stood now staring at him, as if against her will, but hypnotized, the defiant criminal awaiting sentence. He pronounced it. "A day will come when you shall be called to account for what you have done to me. And if there is justice in heaven—your punishment shall outlast eternity."

Melodramatic words; yet words sometimes matter less than the depth of feeling behind them—and these came out of Charles's whole being and despair. What cried out behind them was not melodrama, but tragedy. For a long moment she continued to stare at him; something of the terrible outrage in his soul was reflected in her eyes. With an acute abruptness she lowered her head.

He hesitated one last second; his face was like the poised-crumbling wall of a dam, so vast was the weight of anathema pressing to roar down. But as suddenly as she had looked guilty, he ground his jaws shut, turned on his heel and marched towards the door.

Gathering her skirt in one hand, she ran after him. He spun round at the sound, she stood lost a moment. But before he could move on she had stepped swiftly past him to the door. He found his exit blocked.

"I cannot let you go believing that."

Her breast rose, as if she were out of breath; her eyes on his, as if she put all reliance on stopping him in their directness. But when he made an angry gesture of his hand, she spoke.

"There is a lady in this house who knows me, who understands me better than anyone else in the world. She wishes to see you. I beg you to let her do so. She will explain ... my real nature far better than I can myself. She will explain that my conduct towards you is less blameworthy than you suppose."

His eyes blazed upon hers; as if he would now let that dam break. He made a visibly difficult effort to control himself; to lose the flames, regain the ice; and succeeded.

"I am astounded that you should think a stranger to me could extenuate your behavior. And now—"

"She is waiting. She knows you are here."

"I do not care if it is the Queen herself. I will not see her."

"I shall not be present."

Her cheeks had grown very red, almost as red as Charles's. For the first—and last—time in his life he was tempted to use physical force on a member of the weaker sex.

"Stand aside!"

But she shook her head. It was beyond words now; a matter of will. Her demeanor was intense, almost tragic; and yet something strange haunted her eyes—something had happened, some dim air from another world was blowing imperceptibly between them. She watched him as if she knew she had set him at bay; a little frightened, uncertain what he would do; and yet without hostility. Almost as if, behind the surface, there was nothing but a curiosity: a watching for the result of an experiment. Something in Charles faltered. His eyes fell. Behind all his rage stood the knowledge that he loved her still; that this was the one being whose loss he could never forget. He spoke to the gilt clasp.

"What am I to understand by this?"

"What a less honorable gentleman might have guessed some time ago."

He ransacked her eyes. Was there the faintest smile in them? No, there could not be. There was not. She held him in those inscrutable eyes a moment more, than left the door and crossed the room to a bellpull by the fireplace. He was free to go; but he watched her without moving. "What a less honorable gentleman ..." What new enormity was threatened now! Another woman, who knew and understood her better than ... that hatred of man ... this house inhabited by ... he dared not say it to himself. She drew back the brass button and then came towards him again.

"She will come at once." Sarah opened the door; gave him an oblique look. "I beg you to listen to what she has to say ... and to accord her the respect due to her situation and age."

And she was gone. But she had, in those last words, left an essential clue. He divined at once whom he was about to meet. It was her employer's sister, the poetess (I will hide names no more) Miss Christina Rossetti. Of course! Had he not always found in her verse, on the rare occasons he had looked at it, a certain incomprehensible mysticism? A passionate obscurity, the sense of a mind too inward and femininely involute; to be frank, rather absurdly muddled over the frontiers of human and divine love?

He strode to the door and opened it. Sarah was at a door at the far end of the landing, about to enter. She looked round and he opened his mouth to speak. But there was a quiet sound below. Someone was mounting the stairs. Sarah raised a finger to her lips and disappeared inside the room.

Charles hesitated, then went back inside the studio and walked to the window. He saw now who was to blame for Sarah's philosophy of life—she whom *Punch* had once called the sobbing abbess, the hysterical spinster of the Pre-Raphaelite Brotherhood. How desperately he wished he had not returned! If only he had made further inquiries before casting himself into this miserable situation! But here he was; and he suddenly found himself determining, and not without a grim relish, that the lady poetess should not have it all her own way. To her he might be no more than a grain of sand among countless millions, a mere dull weed in this exotic garden of ...

There was a sound. He turned, and with a very set-cold face. But it was not Miss Rossetti, merely the girl who had shown him up, and holding a small child crooked in her arm. It seemed she had seen the door ajar, and simply peeped in

357

on her way to some nursery. She appeared surprised to see him alone.

"Mrs. Roughwood has left?"

"She gave me to understand . . . a lady wishes to have a few words in private with me. She is rung for."

The girl inclined her head. "I see."

But instead of withdrawing, as Charles had expected, she came forward into the room and set the child down on a carpet by the easel. She felt in the pocket of her apron and handed down a rag doll, then knelt a brief moment, as if to make sure the child was perfectly happy. Then without warning she straightened and moved gracefully towards the door. Charles stood meanwhile with an expression somewhere between offense and puzzlement.

"I trust the lady will come very shortly?"

The girl turned. She had a small smile on her lips. Then she glanced down at the child on the carpet.

"She is come."

For at least ten seconds after the door closed Charles stared. It was a little girl, with dark hair and chubby arms; a little more than a baby, yet far less than a child. She seemed suddenly to realize that Charles was animate. The doll was handed up towards him, with a meaningless sound. He had an impression of solemn gray irises in a regular face, a certain timid doubt, a not being quite sure what he was . . . a second later he was kneeling in front of her on the carpet, helping her to stand on her uncertain legs, scanning that small face like some archaeologist who had just unearthed the first example of a lost ancient script. The little girl showed unmistakable signs of not liking this scrutiny. Perhaps he gripped the fragile arms too tightly. He fumbled hastily for his watch, as he had once before in a similar predicament. It had the same good effect; and in a few moments he was able to lift the infant without protest and carry her to a chair by the window. She sat on his knees, intent on the silver toy; and he, he was intent on her face, her hands, her every inch.

And on every word that had been spoken in that room. Language is like shot silk; so much depends on the angle at which it is held.

He heard the quiet opening of the door. But he did not turn. In a moment a hand lay on the high backrail of the wooden chair on which he sat. He did not speak and the owner of the hand did not speak; absorbed by the watch, the child too was silent. In some distant house an amateur, a lady with time on her hands—not in them, for the execution was poor, redeemed only by distance—began to play the piano: a Chopin mazurka, filtered through walls, through leaves and

358

sunlight. Only that jerkily onward sound indicated progression. Otherwise it was the impossible: History reduced to a living stop, a photograph in flesh.

But the little girl grew bored, and reached for her mother's arms. She was lifted, dandled, then carried away a few steps. Charles remained staring out of the window a long moment. Then he stood and faced Sarah and her burden. Her eyes were still grave, but she had a little smile. Now, he *was* being taunted. But he would have traveled four million miles to be taunted so.

The child reached towards the floor, having seen its doll there. Sarah stooped a moment, retrieved it and gave it to her. For a moment she watched the absorption of the child against her shoulder in the toy; then her eyes came to rest on Charles's feet. She could not look him in the eyes.

"What is her name?"

"Lalage." She pronounced it as a dactyl, the *g* hard. Still she could not raise her eyes. "Mr. Rossetti approached me one day in the street. I did not know it, but he had been watching me. He asked to be allowed to draw me. She was not yet born. He was most kind in all ways when he knew of my circumstances. He himself proposed the name. He is her godfather." She murmured, "I know it is strange."

Strange certainly were Charles's feelings; and the ultimate strangeness was only increased by this curious soliciting of his opinion on such, in such circumstances, a trivial matter; as if at the moment his ship had struck a reef his advice was asked on the right material for the cabin upholstery. Yet numbed, he found himself answering.

"It is Greek. From *lalageo*, to babble like a brook."

Sarah bowed her head, as if modestly grateful for this etymological information. Still Charles stared at her, his masts crashing, the cries of the drowning in his mind's ears. He would never forgive her.

He heard her whisper, "You do not like it?"

"I . . ." he swallowed. "Yes. It is a pretty name."

And again her head bowed. But he could not move, could not rid his eyes of their terrible interrogation; as a man stares at the fallen masonry that might, had he passed a moment later, have crushed him to extinction; at hazard, that element the human mentality so habitually disregards, dismisses to the lumber room of myth, made flesh in this figure, this double figure before him. Her eyes stayed down, masked by the dark lashes. But he saw, or sensed, tears upon them. He took two or three involuntary steps towards her. Then again he stopped. He could not, he could not . . . the words, though low, burst from him.

"But why? Why? What if I had never . . ."

Her head sank even lower. He barely caught her answer.

"It had to be so."

And he comprehended: it had been in God's hands, in His forgiveness of their sins. Yet still he stared down at her hidden face.

"And all those cruel words you spoke . . . forced me to speak in answer?"

"Had to be spoken."

At last she looked up at him. Her eyes were full of tears, and her look unbearably naked. Such looks we have all once or twice in our lives received and shared; they are those in which worlds melt, pasts dissolve, moments when we know, in the resolution of profoundest need, that the rock of ages can never be anything else but love, here, now, in these two hands' joining, in this blind silence in which one head comes to rest beneath the other; and which Charles, after a compressed eternity, breaks, though the question is more breathed than spoken.

"Shall I ever understand your parables?"

The head against his breast shakes with a mute vehemence. A long moment. The pressure of lips upon auburn hair. In the distant house the untalented lady, no doubt seized by remorse (or perhaps by poor Chopin's tortured ghost), stops playing. And Lalage, as if brought by the merciful silence to reflect on the aesthetics of music and having reflected, to bang her rag doll against his bent cheek, reminds her father—high time indeed—that a thousand violins cloy very rapidly without percussion.

360

61

Evolution is simply the process by which chance (the
random mutations in the nucleic acid helix caused by
natural radiation) cooperates with natural law to create living forms better and better adapted to survive.

MARTIN GARDNER, *The Ambidextrous Universe* (1967)

True piety is *acting what one knows.*
MATTHEW ARNOLD, *Notebooks* (1868)

It is a time-proven rule of the novelist's craft never to
introduce any but very minor new characters at the end of a
book. I hope Lalage may be forgiven; but the extremely
important-looking person that has, during the last scene, been
leaning against the parapet of the embankment across the
way from 16 Cheyne Walk, the residence of Mr. Dante
Gabriel Rossetti (who took—and died of—chloral, by the
way, not opium) may seem at first sight to represent a gross
breach of the rule. I did not want to introduce him; but since
he is the sort of man who cannot bear to be left out of
the limelight, the kind of man who travels first class or not at
all, for whom the first is the only pronoun, who in short has
first things on the brain, and since I am the kind of man who
refuses to intervene in nature (even the worst), he has got
himself in—or as he would put it, has got himself in *as he
really is.* I shall not labor the implication that he was previously got in as he really wasn't, and is therefore not truly a
new character at all; but rest assured that this personage is,
in spite of appearances, a very minor figure—as minimal, in
fact, as a gamma-ray particle.

As he really is ... and his true colors are not pleasant ones. The once full, patriarchal beard of the railway compartment has been trimmed down to something rather foppish and Frenchified. There is about the clothes, in the lavishly embroidered summer waistcoat, in the three rings on the fingers, the panatella in its amber holder, the malachite-headed cane, a distinct touch of the flashy. He looks very much as if he has given up preaching and gone in for grand opera; and done much better at the latter than the former. There is, in short, more than a touch of the successful impresario about him.

And now, as he negligently supports himself on the parapet, he squeezes the tip of his nose lightly between the knuckles of his beringed first and middle fingers. One has the impression he can hardly contain his amusement. He is staring back towards Mr. Rossetti's house; and with an almost proprietory air, as if it is some new theater he has just bought and is pretty confident he can fill. In this he has not changed: he very evidently regards the world as his to possess and use as he likes.

But now he straightens. This *flânerie* in Chelsea has been a pleasant interlude, but more important business awaits him. He takes out his watch—a Breguet—and selects a small key from a vast number on a second gold chain. He makes a small adjustment to the time. It seems—though unusual in an instrument from the bench of the greatest of watchmakers—that he was running a quarter of an hour fast. It is doubly strange, for there is no visible clock by which he could have discovered the error in his own timepiece. But the reason may be guessed. He is meanly providing himself with an excuse for being late at his next appointment. A certain kind of tycoon cannot bear to seem at fault over even the most trivial matters.

He beckons peremptorily with his cane towards an open landau that waits some hundred yards away. It trots smartly up to the curb beside him. The footman springs down and opens the door. The impresario mounts, sits, leans expansively back against the crimson leather, dismisses the monogramed rug the footman offers towards his legs. The footman catches the door to, bows, then rejoins his fellow servant on the box. An instruction is called out, the coachman touches his cockaded hat with his whip handle.

And the equipage draws briskly away.

"No. It is as I say. You have not only planted the dagger in my breast, you have delighted in twisting it." She stood

362

now staring at Charles, as if against her will, but hypnotized, the defiant criminal awaiting sentence. He pronounced it. "A day will come when you shall be called to account for what you have done to me. And if there is justice in heaven—your punishment shall outlast eternity!"

He hesitated one last second; his face was like the poised-crumbling walls of a dam, so vast was the weight of anathema pressing to roar down. But as suddenly as she had looked guilty, he ground his jaws shut, turned on his heel and marched towards the door.

"Mr. Smithson!"

He took a step or two more; stopped, threw her a look back over his shoulder; and then with the violence of a determined unforgivingness, stared at the foot of the door in front of him. He heard the light rustle of her clothes. She stood just behind him.

"Is this not proof of what I said just now? That we had better never to have set eyes on each other again?"

"Your logic assumes that I knew your real nature. I did not."

"Are you sure?"

"I thought your mistress in Lyme a selfish and bigoted woman. I now perceive she was a saint compared to her companion."

"And I should not be selfish if I said, knowing I cannot love you as a wife must, you may marry me?"

Charles gave her a freezing look. "There was a time when you spoke of me as your last resource. As your one remaining hope in life. Our situations are now reversed. You have no time for me. Very well. But don't try to defend yourself. It can only add malice to an already sufficient injury."

It had been in his mind all through: his most powerful, though also his most despicable, argument. And as he said it, he could not hide his trembling, his being at the end of his tether, at least as regards his feeling of outrage. He threw her one last tortured look, then forced himself onward to open the door.

"Mr. Smithson!"

Again. And now he felt her hand on his arm. A second time he stood arrested, hating that hand, his weakness in letting it paralyze him. It was as if she were trying to tell him something she could not say in words. No more, perhaps, than a gesture of regret, of apology. Yet if it had been that, her hand would surely have fallen as soon as it touched him; and this not only psychologically, but physically detained him. Very slowly he brought his head round and looked at her; and to his shock saw that there was in her eyes, if not about her lips, a suggestion of a smile, a ghost of that one he had received before, so strangely, when they were nearly surprised by Sam and Mary. Was it irony, a telling him not to take life so seriously? A last gloating over his misery? But there again, as he probed her with his own distressed and totally humorless eyes, her hand should surely have dropped. Yet still he felt its pressure on his arm; as if she were saying, look, can you not see, a solution exists?

It came upon him. He looked down to her hand, and then up to the face again. Slowly, as if in answer, her cheeks were suffused with red, and the smile drained from her eyes. Her hand fell to her side. And they remained staring at each other as if their clothes had suddenly dropped away and left them facing each other in nakedness; but to him far less a sexual nakedness than a clinical one, one in which the hidden cancer stood revealed in all its loathsome reality. He sought her eyes for some evidence of her real intentions, and found only a spirit prepared to sacrifice everything but itself— ready to surrender truth, feeling, perhaps even all womanly modesty in order to save its own integrity. And there, in that possible eventual sacrifice, he was for a moment tempted. He could see a fear behind the now clear knowledge that she had made a false move; and that to accept her offer of a Platonic —and even if one day more intimate, never consecrated— friendship would be to hurt her most.

But he no sooner saw that than he saw the reality of such an arrangement—how he would become the secret butt of this corrupt house, the starched *soupirant*, the pet donkey. He saw his own true superiority to her: which was not of birth or education, not of intelligence, not of sex, but of an ability to give that was also an inability to compromise. She could give only to possess; and to possess him—whether because he was what he was, whether because possession was so imperative in her that it had to be constantly renewed, could never be satisfied by one conquest only, whether ... but he could not, and would never, know—to possess him was not enough.

And he saw finally that she knew he would refuse. From the first she had manipulated him. She would do so to the end.

He threw her one last burning look of rejection, then left the room. She made no further attempt to detain him. He stared straight ahead, as if the pictures on the walls down through which he passed were so many silent spectators. He was the last honorable man on the way to the scaffold. He had a great desire to cry; but nothing should wring tears

364

from him in that house. And to cry out. As he came down to the hallway, the girl who had shown him up appeared from a room, holding a small child in her arms. She opened her mouth to speak. Charles's wild yet icy look silenced her. He left the house.

And at the gate, the future made present, found he did not know where to go. It as as if he found himself reborn, though with all his adult faculties and memories. But with the baby's helplessness—all to be recommenced, all to be learned again! He crossed the road obliquely, blindly, never once looking back, to the embankment. It was deserted; only, in the distance, a trotting landau, which had turned out of sight by the time he reached the parapet.

Without knowing why he stared down at the gray river, now close, at high tide. It meant return to America; it meant thirty-four years of struggling upwards—all in vain, in vain, in vain, all height lost; it meant, of this he was sure, a celibacy of the heart as total as hers; it meant—and as all the things that it meant, both prospective and retrospective, began to sweep down over him in a black avalanche, he did at last turn and look back at the house he had left. At an open upstairs window a white net curtain seemed to fall back into place.

But it was indeed only a seeming, a mere idle movement of the May wind. For Sarah has remained in the studio, staring down at the garden below, at a child and a young woman, the child's mother perhaps, who sit on the grass engaged in making a daisy chain. There are tears in her eyes? She is too far away for me to tell; no more now, since the windowpanes catch the luminosity of the summer sky, than a shadow behind a light.

You may think, of course, that not to accept the offer implicit in that detaining hand was Charles's final foolishness; that it betrayed at least a certain weakness of purpose in Sarah's attitude. You may think that she was right: that her battle for territory was a legitimate uprising of the invaded against the perennial invader. But what you must not think is that this is a less plausible ending to their story.

For I have returned, albeit deviously, to my original principle: that there is no intervening god beyond whatever can be seen, in that way, in the first epigraph to this chapter; thus only life as we have, within our hazard-given abilities, made it ourselves, life as Marx defined it—*the actions of men* (and of women) *in pursuit of their ends*. The fundamental principle that should guide these actions, that I believe myself always guided Sarah's, I have set as the second epigraph. A modern existentialist would no doubt substitute "humanity" or "authenticity" for "piety"; but he would recognize Arnold's intent.

The river of life, of mysterious laws and mysterious choice, flows past a deserted embankment; and along that other deserted embankment Charles now begins to pace, a man behind the invisible gun carriage on which rests his own corpse. He walks towards an imminent, self-given death? I think not; for he has at last found an atom of faith in himself, a true uniqueness, on which to build; has already begun, though he would still bitterly deny it, though there are tears in his eyes to support his denial, to realize that life, however advantageously Sarah may in some ways seem to fit the role of Sphinx, is not a symbol, is not one riddle and one failure to guess it, is not to inhabit one face alone or to be given up after one losing throw of the dice; but is to be, however inadequately, emptily, hopelessly into the city's iron heart, endured. And out again, upon the unplumb'd, salt, estranging sea.